THE ETHICAL ASSASSIN

THE
ETHICAL
ASSASSIN

A NOVEL

DAVID LISS

BALLANTINE BOOKS · NEW YORK

This is a work of fiction. Names, characters, places, and incidents
are the products of the author's imagination or are used fictitiously.
Any resemblance to actual events, locales, or persons, living or dead,
is entirely coincidental.

Published in the United States by Ballantine Books, an imprint
of The Random House Publishing Group, a division of
Random House, Inc., New York.

BALLANTINE and colophon are registered trademarks
of Random House, Inc.

LIBRARY OF CONGRESS CATALOGING-IN-PUBLICATION DATA

Liss, David
The ethical assassin: a novel / David Liss.
p.   cm.
ISBN 1-4000-6421-X
1. Encyclopedias and dictionaries—Marketing—Fiction.   2. Sales personnel—
Fiction.   3. Assassination—Fiction.   4. Assassins—Fiction.   I. Title.
PS3562.I7814T48 2006   813'.6—dc22   2005046446

Printed in the United States of America on acid-free paper

www.ballantinebooks.com

987654321

FIRST EDITION

Book design by Carole Lowenstein

THE ETHICAL ASSASSIN

Chapter 1

I T WAS FRIDAY EVENING, just after seven o'clock, and still bright as noon. In Florida, August is perpetual, relentless, refusing to unclench its fist, and despite the looming sunset it was close to a hundred degrees. The heat settled in my body, dull and enervating, and it accentuated the smell that hung in the air—a stink both tangible and elusive, like the skin of grease on a cold bowl of stew. It was more than a smell, but a thing, heavy enough to weigh like cotton balls shoved into the back of your throat. A putrid miasma whirled and eddied through the streets of the trailer park. I don't mean hot-garbage-by-the-curb smells—rotting chicken carcasses and old diapers and potato peelings. No such luck. It smelled like a prison camp outhouse. Worse.

I stood there on the spiderwebbed concrete step leading up to the mobile home, propping open the screen door with my shoulder. Sweat trickled down my side and clung to my overworked undershirt. I'd been at it since a little after lunch, and I was in a haze now, an automaton lost in the blankness of ringing doorbells, delivering my pitch, lurching forward again. I glanced left and right at the faded white mobile homes and thought it both amusing and profoundly sad that I couldn't remember coming down this street.

I wanted nothing more than to make it inside someone's home, to get out of the heat. The trailer's window-unit air conditioner hummed and rattled and almost bucked, trickling condensation into an eroded gully of white sand. I was overdressed for the heat, and every few hours I needed a blast of AC, like an antidote, in order to keep up the fight. I'd chosen my attire not for comfort but to look smart and to do business: tan chinos, wrinkles smoothed out by the humidity, a thickly striped blue-and-white shirt, and a square-cut, knit turquoise tie, maybe three inches wide. It was 1985, and I thought the tie looked pretty cool.

I knocked again and then jammed my thumb into the glowing peach navel of the doorbell. No answer. The muted hum of a television or maybe a stereo barely pierced the door, and I saw a slight rustle of the slatted blinds, but still no answer. Not that I blamed them, whoever they were, squatting behind their sofa, pantomiming *Shhhh* with fingers pressed to lips. I was on their stoop, a teenager in a tie, trying to sell them something, they would think—rightly so—and who needed that? Then again, who needed them? It was a self-selecting system. I'd been doing this for only three months, but I knew that much already. The ones who came to the door were the ones you wanted to come to the door. The ones who let you in were the ones you wanted to let you in.

The heavy brown leather bag, which my stepfather had given me reluctant permission to borrow from its mildewing box in the garage, dug a trench into my shoulder. Touching the thing always made me feel dirty, and it smelled like split-pea soup. He hadn't used the bag in years, but my stepfather had still thought it important to act put-upon before he reluctantly agreed to let me clean out the mouse droppings and polish it with leather restorer.

I adjusted the strap to lessen the pain and plodded down the steps and along the old walkway that bisected the lawn—really just an ocean of sand peppered with a few islands of crabgrass. At the street I looked in both directions, unsure which way to go, which way I'd come from, but down to my left I saw a flyer flapping lazily against the corner mailbox, affixed with a long swath of dull silver duct tape. The missing cat flyer. I'd seen—what?—two or three of those that day? Maybe twice as many missing dog flyers. Not all the same dog or cat, either, and I was sure I'd passed by this one already. It had a photocopied picture of a white or tan tabby with dark splotches across its face, its mouth open, tongue barely visible. Anyone seeing a plump kitty named Francine should call the number below.

I headed away from the flyer. I was sticking to the same side of the street, passing a vacant lot to get to the next trailer. My legs, defying the demand for pep from my brain, moved slowly, shuffling almost. I looked again at my watch, which hadn't much budged since just before I rang the bell. At least four hours to go, and I needed to rest. I needed to be able to sit still for a while, but that wasn't really it. What I needed was relief from thinking about the job, even a good night's sleep, as if such a thing were possible, but I could give up all hope of sleep. It wouldn't happen on the road, when I worked all day and half the night. Not at home, on my one day off, when there were errands to run and friends and family to see before the cycle began again. I'd been operating on less than four hours a night for three months now. How long could I do it? Bobby, my crew boss, said he'd been doing it for years, and he seemed okay.

I had no plans of doing it for years. Just one year, that was all, and that was plenty. I was pretty good at the job—more than pretty good—and I made money, but there I was, seventeen years old, and I could feel myself aging, feel soreness accumulating in my joints, feel a beleaguered rounding in my shoulders. My eyes didn't seem to work as well, my memory had begun to frazzle, my bathroom habits were irregular. It was the lifestyle. I'd gone to sleep at home, just outside Ft. Lauderdale, the night before. The alarm had jerked me out of bed at six so I could get to the local office by eight, where I'd sat in pep meetings until we all hopped in the car and headed out to the Jacksonville area, checked into a motel, and got to work. Another standard weekend gets under way.

Tires rumbled behind me, and I instinctively veered over toward the empty lot, careful to avoid the nests of fire ants and the prickly weeds that would find their way to my dark gray gym socks, which only a seventeen-year-old could convince himself passed for respectable as long as no one saw the sporty stripes.

Keeping over to the side was the smart thing in places like this. Locals wouldn't have to look at me twice to see that I was way out of my element. They would throw mostly empty beer cans or swerve at me, half-playful and half-homicidal. They would shout things, and I thought it a pretty good guess they were withering insults, insults that would sting like salt in my eyes if I could hear them, but they'd be garbled against the *whoosh* of a speeding truck and the crackling speakers blasting 38 Special. I didn't know if the other guys had to put up with the same crap, but I doubted it.

A dark blue Ford pickup rolled to a stop. It looked freshly washed, and its paint glistened like a tar pit in the glare of the almost setting sun. The passenger-side window lurched down, and the driver, a guy in his thirties with a black T-shirt, learned over toward the window. He looked handsome in an odd way, like the debonair guy in a cartoon out to steal the hero's girl, but like a cartoon character, he was oddly distorted. He was puffy. Not fat or heavy or anything. Just puffy, like a corpse beginning decomposition or a man suffering from an allergic reaction.

The puffiness was weird, sure, but what I mostly noticed was his hair. He kept it sheared to almost a military cut, but in the back it came down in a straight fan to his shoulders. Today they call this style a mullet. In 1985 I'd never seen a mullet before, had no idea what a mullet was, what it was called, or why someone might choose to endure such a thing except for the simple thrifty pleasure that comes from having two haircuts on one head. All I knew was that it looked monumentally stupid.

"Where you going?" the guy asked. His voice buckled under the weight of his syrupy accent, uniquely Florida. Half pecan pie, half key lime. We were about thirty miles outside of Jacksonville, and heavy accents were par for the course.

I'd lived in Florida since the third grade and had long been afraid of just about everyone outside a major urban center. In no way did I consider this cowardice, but common sense. Despite the popular belief that big cities like Ft. Lauderdale and Jacksonville and Miami were nothing but suburbs of New York or Boston, they were, in reality, dense with longtime Florida natives, a vocal minority of whom included Confederate flag wavers, "Dixie" hummers, and cross burners. These cities were also full of transplants from all over the country, so things balanced out reasonably well. Step out to the boonies, and the flavor became considerably less cosmopolitan.

I now stood, as far as I was concerned, in the boonies, which meant that the iridescent KICK MY JEW ASS sign on my forehead, visible only to those who preferred Hank Williams Jr. to Sr., began to throb and fire off sparks. I conjured a polite smile for the pickup driver, but the smile turned out badly, crooked and sheepish.

For an instant, I considered giving the guy my line, about how I was in the neighborhood to speak with parents about education, but I knew instantly it was a bad idea. Puffy Guy with his weird hair and his pampered pickup radiated a low tolerance for bullshit. My crew boss, Bobby, could probably get away with the pitch. Hell, Bobby would probably score off the guy, but I was not Bobby. I was good, maybe the best guy in Bobby's crew—maybe the best guy Bobby had found in a long while. But I wasn't Bobby.

"I'm selling," I said with a startling realization, like the flip of a switch, that I wasn't merely uneasy, I was afraid. Even in all that heat, I felt cold, and my muscles had begun to tense. "Door-to-door," I added. I took the bag off my shoulder and set it down between my black dress sneakers.

The man leaned a little farther toward me and grinned a mouth full of haphazardly arranged teeth. The two front ones, in particular, were long like a rabbit's, but widely spaced and moving in opposite directions. Their crookedness stood out all the more for their unusual, even radiant, whiteness. I wished I hadn't seen them, because now I had to try not to stare.

"You got a permit for that?" He yanked at something between his legs and came up with a nearly full bottle of Yoo-hoo, which he put to his lips for a good ten seconds. When he set it down again, the bottle was now more than half-empty. I suppose an optimist would say it was half-full.

A permit. I'd never heard of such a thing. Did I need a permit? Bobby hadn't said anything about it; he'd merely dropped me off and told me to hit the trailer park hard. Bobby loved trailer parks.

I had to stay focused, act confident, presume this guy wouldn't try anything too crazy, not in the middle of the street, albeit a sinisterly deserted street. "My boss told me to sell here," I said, looking at the pavement rather than his teeth.

"I didn't ask who told you to do nothing," the guy said, shaking his head with sadness at the poor state of things. "I asked if you had a permit."

I tried to tell myself I shouldn't be so afraid. Nervous, sure. Anxious, guarded, alert—you bet. But this was like being ten years old again, caught in the nasty neighbor's yard or messing around with your friend's father's power tools. "Do I need one?"

The guy in the pickup fixed his gaze on me. He curled his upper lip into a half pucker, half scowl. "Answer the question, boy. You stupid?"

I shook my head, partly in disbelief and partly in answer to his question. "I don't have a permit," I said. I tried to look away again, but his eyes were bearing down on me.

Then the redneck burst into a huge, crooked-tooth grin. "Well, it's a good thing you don't need one, then, ain't it?"

It took me a minute to understand what had happened, and then I forced a nervous attempt at an I'm-a-good-sport laugh. "Yeah, I guess it is."

"You listen up. You best stay out of trouble. You know what happens to people caught breaking the law round here?"

"They're asked to squeal like pigs?" I tried to keep it from coming out, but despite my fear it slipped through my grasp and got away from me. It could happen to anyone.

The redneck's dark eyes went narrow over his long nose. "You being a smart-ass?"

What the hell kind of question was that? Could there be any explanation for what I'd said other than smart-assedness? I decided not to point that out.

When people say that they had the metallic taste of fear in their mouth, that metal is generally copper. My mouth tasted like copper. "Just keeping things light," I managed, along with a forced expression of calm and affability.

"What's a smart-ass like you doing out here, anyhow? Why ain't you in your college?"

"I'm trying to earn money for college," I told him, hoping my industry would impress him.

It didn't. "Ain't you something, college boy? Am I going to have to come out of here and smack you in the pussy?"

There was, of course, no dignified way to answer that question. Maybe Bobby would be able to shrug it off, crack some self-effacing joke to make the guy in the pickup like him. Next thing you know, they'd be laughing like old friends. Not me. The only thing I could think of was groveling— or to imagine an alternate universe version of me, the Lem who would walk over to the open window and pound the guy in the face until his nose burst and his stupid haircut was matted with blood. The Lem in this universe didn't do that sort of thing, but it always seemed to me that if I could do it once, if I could be the sort of person who might beat the living shit out of a jerk giving me a hard time, then that fact would be written on my body, my face, in my walk, and I wouldn't be, once again, under the thumb of a bully high on his own power over me.

"I don't think so," I said at last. "I don't think a pussy slapping is, in the most technical sense, necessary."

"You're a little doofus, you know that?" the guy said, and he rolled up his window, thick arms rotating as he cranked the handle. He took a clipboard from the passenger seat and began looking over some papers. After licking his thumb and index finger as if they were lollipops, he pushed back a few sheets. His two wild front teeth protruded from his mouth and began to rake in his lower lip.

Doofus. Not the worst thing I'd ever been called, but it stung in its banality. On the positive side, however, the redneck rolled up his window, so my fear began to abate a little until it became a low throb. I had been dismissed, and it was time to get going, though the creepy redneck was still keeping an eye on me.

So I hoisted the bag back onto my shoulder and walked to the next trailer, this one gray with green trim. The lot, like all the others, was a patch of sand and grass, weeds encroaching from the far borders. A sickly-looking palm tree hunched in the front yard with a medicinal cup thrust into the trunk like an old man's corncob pipe. The front windows had pull-down shades, like civilized people put in bedrooms, but they weren't extended all the way down. Even from the street I could see light inside and the flicker of television.

No lawn furniture, no toys, no garish welcome mat. There was nothing moochie. That was the bookman word, the word Bobby had taught us. The bookman loves moochie. Moochie is plastic kiddie crap scattered everywhere. Moochie is garden gnomes, wind chimes, excessive and early—or late—holiday decorations, anything that suggested that here lived people who liked to spend money they didn't have on things they didn't need. Spending money on things their kids didn't need—well, that was about as moochie as it got. Driving his crew around, Bobby would sometimes do a sort of seated jig when he saw a house with an above-ground plastic swimming pool with an attached plastic slide. "A blind monkey could close those guys," he'd announce. His big Moon Pie face, which was always radiant, would light up so you'd need to put on your sunglasses to look at the guy. "Man, that's moochie."

But this trailer before me had been untouched by mooch. If the pickup hadn't still been parked there, I would likely have skipped the house. Bobby said never to skip. Knocking on the door of a loser doesn't take but a minute, and you never know. More than once I'd sold at places without a hint of moochiness, but it was getting late now, and I was tired, and I wanted matching Big Wheels or a naked Barbie or a company of toy soldiers crawling prone through the Quang Tri province of the lawn— anything to make me feel I was on the right track.

In the absence of moochiness, however, I'd take sanctuary, so I propped open the screen door, feeling a few tablespoons of sweat drop from my armpit down to my midtorso. Two small green lizards sat motionless on the other side of the gray mesh; one bobbed up and down, its scarlet throat fan flashing warning or love or something.

I knocked while the lizards stared with their little bullet heads cocked. Then I heard a distant shuffle of movement, the slightest hint of sound to which this job had made me sensitive. It took a moment before a woman came to the door. She propped it open just a little, glanced at me, and then looked to the pickup in the street. "What is it?" she asked in a harsh half whisper that nearly knocked me back in its urgency and desperation.

She was young, but getting old in a hurry. Her face, pretty at least in theory, was splattered with light freckles and punctuated by a pert little nose, but her eyes, the brown of the redneck's Yoo-hoo, were raked with deep crow's-feet and underscored by extraordinarily dark rings. Her fine, beach-sand-colored hair was pulled back in a ponytail that could be either youthful or haggard. There was something about her expression—she reminded me of a balloon from which the air was slowly leaking. Not so that you could see it deflate or hear its flatulence, but you'd leave that balloon looking fine and come back in an hour to find it drooping and slack.

I pretended I didn't notice her misery, and I grinned. The grin hid my hunger, my thirst, my boredom, my fear of the bucktoothed redneck in the Ford pickup, my hopelessness in the absence of visible moochiness, my despair at the thought that Bobby would not come by the Kwick Stop to pick me up for another four hours.

At least I'd already scored that day, getting into a house in my first hour out. I'd made $200 right there, just like that, from those poor assholes. Not poor as in sad-sack, but poor as in ill-fitting clothes, broken furniture, leaking kitchen faucet, and a refrigerator empty but for Wonder bread, off-brand bologna, Miracle Whip, and Coke. Let me be absolutely clear about this. Not once, not one single time, no matter how happy I was to make a sale, did I ever do it without the acid tinge of regret. I felt evil and predatory, and often enough I had to bite back the urge to walk out halfway through the pitch, because I knew the prospects couldn't afford the monthly payments. They would pass the credit app, I was almost sure of it, but when it came to paying the bills, they'd have to trade in the Coke for generic cola.

So why did I keep doing it? In part because I needed the money, but there was something else, something bigger and more seductive than money, drawing me in. I was *good* at sales, good at it in a way I'd never been good at anything in my life. Sure, I'd done well in school, on my SATs, that sort of thing. But those were solitary activities, this was public, communal, social. I, Lem Altick, was getting the best of others in a social situation, and let me tell you, that was new, and it was delicious. I would look at the prospects slouching into their sofa, people who'd never done anything to hurt me, and I had them. I *had* them, and they didn't even know it. They'd hand over the check and shake my hand. They'd invite me back, ask me to stay for dinner, ask me to meet their parents. Half the people I tricked into buying told me if I ever needed anything, if I ever needed a place to stay, I shouldn't hesitate. They lapped up everything I served, and, evil or not, it felt good. It made me ashamed, but it still felt good.

Now I wanted another one. The company offered a $200 bonus for a double, and I wanted to rack up another score before I saw Bobby again. Of course I wanted the money; $600 for the day would be pretty satisfying. And I'd done it before, my very first day on the job, in fact—an act that had all but anointed me the new boy wonder. The truth was, I loved the look on Bobby's face—the happy surprise, the sheer giddiness of his expression. I couldn't have said why Bobby's approval was so important; it even troubled me that I cared so much. But I did care.

"Hi there. I'm Lem Altick," I told the gaunt, sort-of-pretty-sort-of-bitter woman, "and I'm in your neighborhood today talking to parents, trying to get some feedback on how they feel about the local schools and the quality of education. Do you by any chance have children, ma'am?"

She blinked at me a couple of times—appraising sorts of blinks. The lizards were blinking, too, but more slowly, and their eyelids came up from the bottom. "Yeah," she said after a moment to think. Her gaze went right past mine and toward the blue pickup, which was still parked alongside the road. "I got kids. But they ain't here."

"And may I ask how old they are?"

She blinked again, this time more suspiciously. It had been only a couple of years since a boy named Adam Walsh had disappeared from a mall in Hollywood, Florida. His head had been found a couple of weeks later a few hundred miles to the north. Nobody had ever again looked the same way at kids or at strangers who showed an interest in kids.

"Seven and ten." Her hand gripped the side of the door more tightly, and her fingers went white around her chipped fuchsia-polished nails. She was still looking at the Ford.

"Those are great ages, aren't they?" Not that I knew. I'd never spent much time around kids since being one myself, and in my experience, those ages were as unredeemably rotten as the rest. Still, parents liked to hear that sort of thing, or at least I figured they did. "So, if your husband is home, I was hoping I might be able to take just a few minutes to ask you some questions for a survey. Then I'll be out of your hair. You'd like to answer a few questions about your ideas on education, wouldn't you?"

"You with him?" she asked, gesturing toward the pickup with a flick of her first two fingers.

I shook my head. "No, ma'am. I am here in your neighborhood to talk to parents about education."

"What are you selling?"

"Not a thing," I told her. I feigned a slight, almost imperceptible surprise. *Me? Ask you to buy something? How very silly.* "I'm not a salesman, and if I were, I'd have nothing to sell you. I'm just asking some questions about the local educational system and your level of satisfaction. The people I work for would love to hear what you and your husband have to say. Wouldn't you like to tell us what you think of the local schools?"

She pondered this for a moment, clearly unfamiliar with the idea that anyone could possibly care what she had to say. I'd seen the look before. "I don't have the time," she said.

"But that's exactly why you should talk to me," I said, using a technique called "the reverse." You told the prospect that why they couldn't do it or why they couldn't afford it was exactly the reason they could. Then you dug deep and came up with a reason that it was true. "You know, studies show that the more time you dedicate to education, the more free time you have." I made that up, but I thought it sounded reasonable.

I guess she did, too. She glanced again over to the Ford and then back to me. "Fine." She pressed open the screen door. The lizards held their ground.

I followed her inside, the fear of the redneck now almost forgotten in the excitement of a looming commission. I had not been doing this long, not compared with Bobby's five years, but I knew getting inside the house was the hardest part. I might go days without anyone letting me in, but I'd never once made it in without making the sale. Not once. Bobby said that was the sign of a real bookman, and that's what I was turning out to be. A real bookman.

I stood in the trailer. Me, this desiccated woman, and her still unseen husband. Only one of us was going to walk out of there alive.

Chapter 2

INSIDE, THE SMELL OF OLD CIGARETTES replaced the stench of garbage and filth. Everyone in my family smoked cigarettes, every last relative with the exception of my stepfather, who smoked cigars and pipes. I'd always hated the odor, hated the way it seeped into my clothes, my books, my food. When I was young enough to still bring a lunch to school, my turkey sandwich would smell like Lucky Strikes—my mother's improbable brand.

The woman, who also smelled of cigarettes and had nicotine stains on her fingers, told me her name was Karen. The husband looked younger than she did, but also like he was aging faster, and I could see his balloon would be out of air before hers. Like Karen, he was unusually thin, with a hollowed-out look to him. He wore a sleeveless Ronnie James Dio shirt that showed bony arms insulated with layers of wiry muscles. Straight reddish hair fell to his shoulders in a southern-fried rock cut. He was good-looking in the same way as Karen, which was to say he might have been more appealing if he didn't give the impression of someone who hadn't eaten, slept, or washed in the better part of a week.

He came in from the trailer's kitchen, holding a bottle of Killian's Red by its neck as though he were trying to strangle it. "Bastard," he said. Then he switched the bottle to his left hand and held out his right for shaking.

I wasn't sure why he would call me a bastard, so I held back.

"Bastard," he repeated. "It's my name. It's a nickname, really. It ain't my real name, but it's my real nickname."

I shook with what I considered an appropriate amount of skepticism.

"So, where'd you find this guy?" Bastard asked his wife. It came out just a little too fast, a little too loud, to be good-natured. With a tic of the neck, he flung back his longish hair.

"He wants to ask us some questions about the girls." Karen had wandered into the kitchen, separated from the living room by a short bar. She gestured with her head toward me, or maybe toward the door. The two of them were jerking their heads around as if they were in a Devo video.

Bastard stared. "The girls, huh? You look too young to be a lawyer. Or a cop."

I attempted a smile to mask the kudzu creep of alarm working over me. "It's nothing like that. I'm here to talk about education."

Bastard put his arm around my shoulder. "Education, huh?"

"That's right."

The arm came off almost right away, but the inside of the trailer was beginning to feel more dangerous than outside. I'd seen some weird stuff inside people's homes—*Faces of Death* videocassettes mixed in with the Mickey Mouse cartoons, a jar of used condoms on a coffee table, even a collection of shrunken heads once—but this weirdly intimate moment put me on my guard. I didn't leave, though, because the redneck was surely still out there, and that made it a lose-lose deal. Might as well stay where there was a chance of closing a deal.

Not much of a chance, though. I took a guarded look at the trailer; it was the kind of place that warded off salesmen the way garlic warded off vampires. They had no toys scattered around, no empty cases from kids' videos or coloring books or haphazard Lego towers. They had no toys of any kind. And there wasn't much in the way of adult crap, either. There were no plastic hanging plants or not-available-in-stores garish cuckoo clocks or oil paintings of clowns.

Instead, they had a beige couch and a phenomenally not matching blue easy chair and a cracked glass coffee table full of beer bottles and beer bottle rings and coffee cup stains. A single coffee mug—white with OLDHAM HEALTH SERVICES printed in bold black letters—rested against the glass in such a way that I felt sure it would take both hands to pry it off. The coffee inside had condensed into tar.

In the kitchen, the linoleum floor, the kind of tan that looked dirty when clean and extra dirty when dirty, was chipped and peeling and in places curling up. In one spot it had rolled up over a white towel and looked like a Yodels.

Yet despite it all, there was some small reason to hope. Yes, their stuff was absolutely awful, and yes, they clearly had no money, except— Except. A chipped Lladró, a ballerina in midtwirl, sat on top of the television. Maybe it had been a gift or inherited from a grandparent or found by the trash. It didn't matter. It was a Lladró, and Lladrós were gold. Lladrós were moochie. The spirit of mooch, no matter how diminished and repressed, dwelled within.

Bastard now put a hand on my back. "So, you're like, asking parents questions about their thoughts on education? Something like that?"

Had he heard me at the door? "That's right. About education and your kids." The kids who, I noticed, left no hint that they'd ever passed through their own home.

"So, what you selling?" A spark of amusement flashed in his dull eyes.

"I'm just here to ask questions about education. I'm not here to sell."

"Okay, see you later, jerk-off. There's the door. Get out."

I was about to open my mouth, to observe politely that his wife had said she wanted to take the survey, and after all, it would only be a few minutes. But I didn't get that far. Karen pulled him aside to the bedroom, where they exchanged some heated and hushed words. In a minute or two they came out, and Bastard had a plastic grin on his face.

"Sorry about that," he told me. "I guess I didn't realize how much Karen wanted to talk about, you know, education." He slapped my back. "You want a beer?"

"Just water or soda or something, if you don't mind."

"No problem, buddy," Bastard said with an enthusiasm that frightened me more than the shoulder squeezing.

Karen led me to the kitchen card table, where she directed me to sit with my back to the door in a metal folding chair, the kind they brought out for ad hoc municipal gatherings in school gymnasiums. She made some uneasy small talk and handed me lemonade in another OLDHAM HEALTH SERVICES coffee cup. I still felt a phantom tingling on my shoulder where Bastard had grabbed me, but the anxiety was beginning to dissipate. They were strange—strange and unhappy—but almost certainly harmless.

I tried not to drink the lemonade in a single gulp. "This who you work for?" I asked, gesturing toward the coffee cup. I didn't direct the question toward either of them in particular.

Bastard shook his head, let out a little noise, something short of a laugh. "Nah. We just have them."

"They're nice," I said. "Nice and thick. Keep the coffee warm." I waited a moment to let the idiocy of my words dissipate. "What do you folks do?"

"Karen used to waitress some," Bastard told me, "till her back started to bother her. I'm the site manager for a hog farm."

Site manager sounded impressive enough, as though they'd be able to make the payments, at least, which was all I needed. I unfastened the strap of my bag, and took out one of the photocopied survey sheets.

I set my papers on the kitchen table next to the basket of plastic fruit—another faint hint of moochiness there—and asked Bastard and Karen the questions. When I'd been in training, I'd balked at first seeing them, sure anyone with a pulse would smell the bullshit a mile off. But Bobby had laughed, assured me that this sales pitch had been designed by experts. It was one of the most successful pitches ever devised. Having sold for three months now, I had no problem believing it.

Would your child benefit from greater access to knowledge? Would you be happier if your child was learning more? Do your children have questions left unanswered by their education? The last one was my personal favorite: *Do you believe that people continue to learn even after they complete their schooling?*

"They say you learn something new every day," Bastard announced cheerfully. "Isn't that right? Hell, just last week I learned I was even stupider than I thought." He let out a big laugh and then slapped his leg. Then he slapped my leg. Not hard, but even so.

Karen watched Bastard. There was a kind of suspicion there, even a wariness. If I had not known they were married, I might have thought they'd never met before. As it was, I figured they were well on their way to petty claims divorce court. Not the best environment in which to sell, but pickings were, at the moment, slim.

I dutifully wrote down their answers and took a moment to review the responses, to study them. I put on a serious face, knit my brow, contemplated the gravity of their answers.

"All right," I said. "I just want to be sure I understand you now. So you think that education for children is important?"

"Sure," Bastard said.

"Karen?" I asked.

"Yeah." She nodded.

This was all part of the pitch—make them agree as much and as often as possible. Get them in the habit of saying yes, and they'll forget how to say no.

"And you think that items, products, or services that aid in a child's education are good ideas? Bastard? Karen?"

They both agreed.

"You know," I said with an expression of puzzled amazement—I hoped it looked spontaneous, but I'd practiced it in the mirror—"looking over all of this, it seems like you two are just the sort of parents my employers would love to have me talk to. You obviously care a great deal about your children's education, and you have a deep commitment to seeing that their educational needs are met. My company has sent us out here to try to measure the level of interest for a product they intend to introduce in this area. Now—Karen, Bastard—since you two are obviously such education-oriented parents, it occurs to me that you're exactly the sort of people I've been authorized to show a preview of these products, assuming, of course, you're interested. Do you think you'd like to look at something that is beautiful, affordable, and, best of all, will significantly increase the education and, ultimately, income potential of your children?"

"Okay," Bastard said.

Karen said nothing. The lines around her eyes deepened, her cheeks collapsed, and her thin lips parted as she began to speak.

I would not let her. I'd never been asked to leave at this point, but I knew perfectly well that it could happen, that it would happen here if I let it. Outside, the redneck in the pickup might still be waiting, and I didn't want to find out one way or the other.

"Let me tell you up front," I said, barely managing to beat her to the punch, "that I've got a lot of people I need to see in this area. I'm happy to take the time out to show you this stuff, but first we need to make a contract, the three of us. If at any point you lose interest or you think that it's not the sort of educational tool you'd like to provide for your children, just let me know. I'll get up and leave. I don't want to waste your time, and I'm sure you understand that I don't want to waste my time, either. So can you promise me that? The minute you don't want to see any more, you'll speak up? That's fair, isn't it?"

"Fair." Bastard let out a loud, phlegmy snort. "Congress never passed a law saying life had to be fair. Not unless you're a Spanish, a black, a woman, or a congressman."

I smiled politely, doing my best to appear nonjudgmental, another skill I'd honed over the past three months. "C'mon, Bastard. Let's be serious. It's fair, isn't it."

"Sure. Fair," he agreed. He looked up at the ceiling and let out a long sigh.

"How about you, Karen? Do you think you would be able to tell me if you lose interest in these valuable educational tools that will improve the quality of your children's lives?"

She exchanged a look with her husband and then reached over to the counter for a pack of Virginia Slims and a cherry red Bic. "Yeah, sure."

"Okay, then. You guys ready?" Just another gratuitous yes question.

"We said we're ready," Bastard grumbled toward the ceiling.

I nodded in the kindly but authoritative way Bobby had taught me and reached into my bag for the first brochure, a glossy, colorful little booklet with a couple of well-groomed, successful-looking kids spread out on a carpeted floor with their books. These were kids like they would never raise, in all likelihood never know. These were the kids they wanted instead of the ones they had. And that made Bastard and Karen the perfect candidates for me.

Bobby had taught us that there was pretty much no way to sell books to comfortable suburbanites. It had taken me a while to understand, but I understood now. Karen and Bastard looked at their first pamphlet and soaked in their first glimpse of the future of their children, and they saw what they were supposed to see—a different life. The kids in the pamphlets weren't the ignorant, ill-behaved, destructive children of ignorant, ill-behaved, destructive adults. They weren't living in trailer park squalor, but lounging in affluent suburban bliss. They laughed and played and learned, their inner potential and outer grooming nurtured by unceasing exposure to wonderful tomes of secret knowledge. The ability to discover the five principal exports of Greece or the social structure of bonobo groups or the mysterious history of the Mayan Empire would make everything different. The mere proximity to books that contained these glorious facts and more meant the difference between success and failure.

I managed a quick peek at my watch. Almost seven-thirty now. I was confident that by ten o'clock these people would be financing a $1,200 set of encyclopedias.

The resistance, not surprisingly, came from the aptly named Bastard. I made it through the bonus books—the handbook of emergency health care, the field guide to local wildlife, the compendium of educational games for kids—but hadn't yet reached the presentation of the sample volume of *Champion Encyclopedias* when I'd had about all I could take of Bastard. He interrupted me, made fun of the books, imitated my voice, tickled his wife, tried to tickle me once, got up to make a sandwich.

"Now," I said, holding up the children's history of the United States, "you can see how this is the sort of book your children would find educational and would improve their understanding of American history, can't you?"

"Yeah," said Karen.

Somewhere along the way, consumer longing had taken the place of blank apathy. The rugged skepticism on her face had smoothed away, and her lips had parted not in preparation to object, but in slack acquisitive desire.

"You think they'll ever have a woman president?" Bastard asked. "I bet she'll be a real honey. With big knockers. Great big knockers, man. Bigger than Karen's, anyhow."

"And you understand, don't you, that an improved understanding of American history will be of use to your children?" I asked.

"Yeah," Karen said, jamming a cigarette, smoked down to the scorched filter, into the makeshift ashtray—the bottom third of a torn-open Pepsi can, whose jagged edges she avoided with grace. "There's all kinds of tests in school where they have to know those things, and that book would help them get better grades." She'd learned along the way that I liked to hear concrete examples of how the books would help, and she was now working hard to come up with good ones.

"But will it get them dates? That's what I want to know," Bastard said.

"Maybe if I'd known all about Ben Franklin and Betsy Ross, I'd have gotten laid more in school."

I'd been working against it since I'd started the pitch, but there was only so much cheer I could maintain. It was just common sense that I wasn't going to make the sale without Bastard, and I wasn't going to get Bastard without breaking him. I had to do something, so I reached for a move Bobby had told me about. It had sounded so brilliant when he'd explained it, I'd been looking for an opportunity to try it.

I let out a sigh. "You know what," I said. "Clearly these materials are not for you. Bastard, I asked you to let me know if you weren't interested, but it seems like you haven't been honest with me. It's *okay* that you're not interested. These materials won't appeal to every parent—some are just more education oriented than others—and that's fine. I only wish you hadn't let me sit here for so long, wasting all of our time." Then I began to gather my things. Not slowly so as to seem like I wanted to be pulled back, but with the wooden determination of a lawyer who'd just lost a trial and wanted to get the hell out of the courtroom.

"Wait," said Karen. "*I'm* interested."

"What the fuck," Bastard said. "Let the little shit go."

"Bastard, apologize," the wife ordered. "I want them."

"What the fuck for? The *girls*?" he sneered.

"We'll send them." Her voice sounded small, pathetic. Then something shifted, and she sounded hard. "Apologize, or I swear to Christ, I'll tell him everything."

I didn't know who the "him" might be, but I knew it wasn't me. And I was beginning to get the sense I'd walked into the middle of something and my best bet was to cut my losses and get the hell out. With stoic calm, I placed the last book into my bag and stood.

"*Bastard, do it!*"

He let out a sigh. "I'm sorry, Lem. Okay? It's not that I'm not interested. I just don't like to sit still for so long. Go easy on me, buddy. Show us the rest."

"Please stay," said Karen. Her voice had become small, the voice of a child begging for education. Please, sir, may I learn some more?

I nodded slowly, a sage weighing his options. I'd been willing to bail, but now I saw this was a clear victory. The real trick was to keep from grinning. They'd begged me to stay. They might as well just take out the checkbook now and save everyone the time.

By a quarter to ten, I'd spread everything out on the table right next to the wrecked soda can crammed full of lipstick-ringed cigarette butts. It was all there—the books and brochures, the pricing sheet, the payment schedule, and, of course, the credit application, the all-important app. Karen had taken out the checkbook for the down payment: $125. Like my own mother, fastidious before the tranquilizers, she filled out the receipt portion prior to writing the check, and she did it with torturous slowness. I wanted it in my possession. I wanted it done. Until they handed over the check, there was always the chance they'd back out.

I didn't want to let it get to where the check might break the deal. I'd closed this deal before even mentioning the check. I had Karen hungry, starving for these books. I'd broken Bastard, who now sat without making a sound other than a strangely wheezy breathing, as though he were winded from the act of respiration itself. He looked at me with big, moist eyes, hoping for approval. And I shoveled the approval out in spades.

Karen pressed down one pink-tipped finger and tore the check along the perforated edge, then held it out to me. She might have set it on the table, but she wanted me to take it from her hand. I'd seen it before; it always happened late in the sale. Encyclopedia sales had allowed me to shed my high school skin, my loser skin, and turn into something else, something that some women found even a little sexy—because I had power. The bookman has power the way a teacher or a political candidate or the lead in a production of *Our Town* has power. It's the power of the spotlight. I was young and had energy and enthusiasm, and I had come into her home and given her reason to hope. She didn't exactly want to sleep with me and didn't exactly not want to. I understood it with absolute clarity.

I had just about put my fingers on the check when I heard the front door open. I didn't turn around, in part because I wanted that check and in part because I'd trained myself not to look at visitors, not to listen to phone calls. This wasn't my house, and it wasn't my business.

I didn't stray from the check grab. At least not until I saw Karen's eyes go wide and her face go pale and her mouth form into the comical surprise of an O. At the same moment, Bastard toppled over along with his chair, felled by an invisible punch, a punch that left a gaping hole, a dark and bloody hole, in the middle of his forehead.

Now I heard it. A puffy squeak of air, and Karen fell over, too. Not the whole chair, just Karen, out of her seat and onto the floor. The second shot hadn't been as neat as the first, and above her eyes it looked as though someone had smashed her with the claw end of a hammer. Blood began to pool around hair on the beige linoleum floor. The air was full of something sharp and nasty. Cordite. I didn't know what cordite was, I couldn't even remember how I knew the word, but I knew that's what I was smelling. The stink assaulted me, along with the horrible understanding. Two shots had been fired, two people hit in the head. Two people had been murdered.

I wasn't supposed to be here. I'd been accepted into Columbia University, but my parents had refused to pay. I was raising money, that's all. I just wanted money for college. None of this had anything to do with me, and I squeezed my eyes shut, wishing it away. But it wasn't going anywhere.

I turned around.

Chapter 3

ONLY A FEW DAYS before I came to town with the bookmen, Jim
Doe had been getting restless. He'd told himself to lay off; the risks
just weren't worth it. But then he'd be in his prowl car, watching the drivers go by, sometimes too lazy to stop an asshole going ten or even fifteen
miles over the limit. Doing that, he'd get horny as hell. Just something
about sitting there, the radio on low volume with the Oak Ridge Boys or
Alabama warbling out their bullshit, the smell of Burger King French fries
congealing, the sharp tang of chocolate and Rebel Yell coming from his
spiked bottle of Yoo-hoo. It reminded him of exactly what he knew he
oughtn't do. It was instinct, after all. You couldn't ask a wolf to stop being
a wolf. He saw a sex-red sports car that looked damn near perfect, and Doe
set those lights flashing and the siren wailing. The sound alone gave him
a monster stiffy, and he felt like he was seventeen again.

I can sense the grumbling. How, you are wondering, do I know all this? Am
I secretly Jim Doe in addition to being Lem Altick? Is this a multiple-
personality story?

It's not. But the events of this weekend were significant in my life, just
about as significant as it gets, and I've invested massive quantities of time
in talking to the survivors, the people who escaped, the people who evaded
the cops, the cops they evaded, those who went to jail, and those who
avoided jail. I've talked to them all. I've synthesized it. So I feel I have a
reasonably good idea what was going on in Jim Doe's head.

Besides, you've read those memoirs; you know the ones I mean. The poor Irish childhood ones where the writer recalls with preternatural clarity which hat his aunt Siobhan wore to his seventh birthday party and what the cake tasted like and which relative gave him the orange for a present and which the hard-boiled egg. I'm not buying it. No one remembers that kind of detail. It's all creative license to flesh out a true story. So that's what I'm doing. It's my story, and I'm going to tell it the way I want to tell it.

So back to Jim Doe and the red sports car.

The driver wasn't as good-looking as Doe had been hoping, but she was in her twenties. Early thirties at the most. She had big, curly blond hair, which he liked, and she was dressed kind of sexy in one of those collarless T-shirts that the women had all been wearing since *Flashdance*. None of that compensated for her big nose and fat lips, all smashed against her face, and her eyes, which were too small for her head. Still, he'd stopped her. Might as well see what was what.

It was already getting dark. He ought to be over at Pam's place by now. It was Jenny's birthday, and he guessed he should go by and bring her something. She was four now, and she'd known what a birthday was for a couple of years, and it would probably be a big deal if her father didn't get her a present. He'd hear about it from Pam if he didn't show. Not only that, he'd have to hear it from that fucking bitch Aimee Toms.

Sooner or later he'd see Aimee out at the Thirsty Bass or the Sports Hut or the Denny's, and she'd come sit down and look oh-so-sad and smile a little and tell him how disappointed Jenny had been on her birthday that her daddy didn't get her nothing. She had that attitude. All the assholes at the sheriff's department had it, but Aimee had it most of all. She turned up her nose at him. Aimee—turning up her nose at him. Unbelievable. If she knew so much, how come she looked like a dyke? Answer that one.

So she'd come over, her linebacker shoulders all squared off, and she'd shake her head or maybe his hand. She wasn't trying to tell Jim what to do. Of course it was awkward, but she was Pam's friend *and* a cop, and she knew how it was for both of them. Lots of cops got divorced, but the children—the children were the important thing.

Maybe if someone ever got drunk enough to get her pregnant, she'd know if children were important or not. Of course, Doe didn't much like to think about that time he had been drunk enough to go after her, when

he'd grabbed her ass and started singing, "Amy, what you gonna do?"—
that god-awful Pure Prairie League song. She had just wiggled out of his
grasp like she was the queen of England. Or because she liked women, he
supposed. Like Pam. Aimee was probably getting it on with his ex-wife.
What kind of a crazy world was this, anyhow?

So if she tried any of that, Jim knew how he'd handle himself. Pretty
simple, really. He'd take out his gun and blow the back of Aimee's head
right off. Bam! Just like that. Oh shit, Aimee. Where's the back of your
head? Let's you and me try to find it together. You know, as Pam's friend
and as a cop.

Getting sneered at by Aimee Toms—nothing but a county cop who
thought she could push him around. Doe was chief of fucking police here.
And mayor. How much money was she taking in? Maybe thirty a year if
she was lucky—if she took a little on the side, which she would never do,
of course, because that would be wrong. Let Pam be her little dyke friend.
She could be Jenny's father and save him the trouble.

When he got done with the driver, Doe figured he'd go by the drug-
store and get Jenny something. A doll or some Play-Doh. Really, he just
wanted to keep Pam from snapping her turtle mouth at him and Aimee
from giving him that pitying look that was going to lose her the back of her
head one of these days. Truth was, he couldn't much stand Jenny, with her
hugging his leg and clinging and her "Daddy Daddy Daddy." Pam was getting older, but she still had a decent face, okay tits, and an acceptable if
ever-spreading ass, and the kid had Chief Jim Doe for a daddy, so why was
his own daughter so damn repulsive? And they needed to stop feeding her
whatever it was they fed her, because it was chock-full of ugly and she was
turning into a pig. A man who'd been around could tell it like it was, and
Doe knew that fat and ugly was an evil combination for a girl.

Doe climbed out of the cruiser and stood there for a moment, peering
over at the driver behind his mirrored sunglasses. He wanted to get a better look and let her take in the sight of the big, bad cop who had her in his
crosshairs. He knew what he looked like. He never missed the surprised little smiles. *Well, hello, Officer.* Like one of those male strippers they had for
bachelorette parties. So what if he had a little gut now? Women didn't care
about things like that. They cared about power and swagger, and he had
plenty of those.

When Doe walked over to the window of her Jap sports car, she pressed her lips together in a smashed, fat little smile. *Hello there, good-looking.* "Is there a problem, Officer?"

Doe hitched up his belt, which he liked to do so they could see all the stuff—the gun and the cuffs and nightstick—it was like Spanish fly. He took off his wide-brimmed brown hat and wiped his forehead with his sleeve. He put the hat back on and shot her a smile. He knew his teeth were perfectly white, despite the fact that he didn't brush as often as he ought to. And maybe they were a little crooked, but it was the sort of thing only he would notice because he was so hard on himself.

"License and registration, ma'am?"

She had them ready and handed them over. "Can you tell me what this is about? I'm sort of in a hurry."

"I sure got that impression, way you was driving," Doe said. "Lisa Roland from Miami, huh? Miami's pretty far away."

"I was visiting a co-worker who moved up here. I was just heading over to the highway."

They always wanted to tell their life story, like they wanted his approval or something. "Why're you in such a big hurry to get home, Lisa? You don't like this part of the state?"

"I just wanted to get home, is all."

"You like all them hotels and tourists in Miami?"

"It's where I live."

"You got a boyfriend back there waiting on you? Is that it?"

"Look, what is this about?"

"What is it about? Lisa, you know you was speeding?"

"I don't think I was."

"You don't, huh? Well, it so happens I got you on the radar gun going a pretty good amount above the speed limit."

"You must be mistaken." She bit her lip, looked to her side, behind her. She must have been nervous about something. If she hadn't been speeding, then why was she so nervous?

"Must I, now? Well, if I am, I don't know about it."

"Come on, Officer. It just so happens that I'd been looking at my speedometer, and I was sticking very closely to the fifty-five mark."

"I got you at fifty-seven, Lisa."

"Fifty-seven. Christ. I mean, come on. I can't believe you would even stop me for going two miles above the limit."

"Well," he said, taking off his hat again and giving his forehead a wiping, "way I see it, the speed limit is the *limit*. That don't mean it's the speed you want to be sort of near. It means that's the fastest you can go. The *limit*. Now, if you have a water heater and it says that you can't put your water over two hundred degrees or it will explode . . . what you gonna do? Let it get to two hundred and two and then say you were only two degrees over? I think if it gets to one ninety-five, you're going to do everything you can to put things right. Speed limit's the same, in my view."

"Don't those radar detectors have a margin of error to within a few miles per hour?"

"I guess they might," Doe told her, "but it happens that within the limits of Meadowbrook Grove, the speed limit is forty-five miles per hour. It's clearly posted on the roads, ma'am. So you were not just over the limit, you were well over."

"Christ," she said. "Meadowbrook Grove. What the hell is that?"

"It's this municipality, Lisa. You're about half a mile into it, and it runs about another mile and a half east."

"It's a speed trap," she said. It came out in a jolt of understanding, and she made no effort to hide her contempt. "Your trailer park is a speed trap."

Doe shook his head. "It's sad when people who are looking to keep folks safe are called all sorts of names. You want to get into an accident? Is that it? Take a couple of other people with you?"

The woman sighed. "Fine. Whatever. Just give me the ticket."

Doe leaned forward, elbows on her rolled-down windows. "What did you say?"

"I said to just go ahead and give me the ticket."

"You oughtn't to tell an officer of the law what to do."

Something crossed her face, some sort of recognition, like when you're poking a stick at a king snake, teasing it and jabbing at it, and you suddenly realize it's not a king, but a coral, that it could kill you anytime it damn well wants. Lisa saw what she should have seen earlier. "Officer, I didn't mean anything disrespectful. I just wanted to—"

Had she been flirting? Probably, the whore. She put out her hand and gently, really with just the nails, scraped along the skin of his forearm, barely even disturbing the tightly coiled black hairs.

It was all the excuse Doe needed. Technically, he didn't need any excuse at all, but he liked to have one. Let them think it was something they did. Let them think later on, If only I hadn't touched him. Better they should blame themselves.

The touch was all he was looking for. Doe took a step back and pulled his gun from his holster and pointed it at the woman, not two feet from her head. He knew what it must look like to her—this big, dark, hot, throbbing thing shoved right in her face. "Never touch a police officer!" he shouted. "You are committing assault, a felony. Put your hands on the wheel."

She shrieked. They did that sometimes.

"Hands on the wheel!" He sounded very much like a man who believed his own life to be in danger, like he needed her to do this to keep from shooting her. "Hands on the wheel! Now! Eyes straight ahead! Do it, or I *will* shoot!"

She continued to shriek. Her little eyes became wide as tiny saucers, and her curly blond hair went fright wig. Somehow despite her screaming she managed to move her hands halfway up her body, where they did a little spaz shake, and then she got them up to the wheel.

"All right, now. Lisa, you do what I say and no one needs to get hurt, right? You're under arrest for assault on a police officer." He grabbed the door handle, pulled it open, and took a quick step back, as though he expected molten rock to come pouring out.

It was better to play it like it was real. If you did the cocky cop thing, they might despair or they might get full of righteous anger, and then you could really have a problem on your hands. If, on the other hand, you acted like you were afraid of them, it gave them a strange sort of hope, like the whole misunderstanding could still get straightened out.

With the gun still extended, he reached out and pulled one hand behind her back, then the other. Holding them firmly in place, he put the gun back in the holster and placed the cuffs on her wrists. Too tight, he knew. They would hurt like hell.

Her ugly face got uglier as he shoved her toward his cruiser. Cars slowed down along the road—practically a highway at this stretch, with more than five miles between lights—to watch, figuring her for a drug dealer or who knows what. But they weren't thinking that all she'd done was speed and then whine about it. They saw her in cuffs and they saw his uniform and they knew who was right and who was wrong.

Doe shoved her into the back of the cruiser, behind the passenger seat, and then went around to the driver's side. He waited for a break in the traffic and then pulled out onto the road.

They had gone less than a quarter of a mile before she managed to get any words past her sobbing. "What's going to happen to me?"

"I guess you'll find out," he told her.

"I didn't do anything wrong."

"Then you don't have to worry. Isn't that the way the law works?"

"Yes," she managed. No more than a whisper.

"There you go, then."

Doe turned off the road just before they got near the hog complex. It smelled something terrible from the waste lagoon, which was what they called it. A fucking shithole for a bunch of pigs that needed to be killed before they could die on their own, was what he called it. Smelled like shit, too. Worse than shit. Like the worst shit you could ever imagine. Rancid rotting shit. It smelled like the shit that shit shits out its asshole. Some days you couldn't hardly smell it at all unless you got close, but when it was humid, which was a lot of the time, and when there was a good easterly wind, all of Meadowbrook Grove stank like frothing, wormy, bubbling, fermented shit. But that's what the hog complex was there to do. To smell bad. So no one could smell that other smell, that moneymaking smell.

And that pig shit smell had some other useful features, which was why Doe liked to bring his girls there. Not just because it was isolated and no one ever came down this road, but also because he knew what that smell did. They'd get the feeling even before they realized they were smelling it. It crept up on them, like their terror.

Doe pulled the car a good quarter mile up the dirt road through the haphazard pines to just around a bend. He had to get out to unlock the flimsy metal gate, there as a line pissed in the sand rather than as real security. Then he went back in to pull the car through, out again to lock up, and back behind the wheel one last time. But safety first was his motto. They were pretty well shaded by the cluttered growth of trees, and he'd be able to see someone coming, in the unlikely event that some lost driver decided to head that way.

In the clearing, the hog lot stood like a massive metal shack, and behind that was the waste lagoon. Doe turned off the motor, and as he did so he realized he was grinning; he'd been grinning for so long that his cheeks ached. Christ, he must look like a jack-o'-lantern from hell.

"So, Lisa. You got a job?" He leaned back in his seat, settling into that familiar good sensation—hard and light at the same time. He finished off his bottle of Yoo-hoo. The bourbon had kicked in strong, and he felt just about right. Nothing but bourbon, either. He knew that people, people in the know, figured he was doing crank, but he didn't touch the stuff. He knew what it did. Shit, just look at Karen. Turned her all skank. Look at Bastard. Turned him half-incompetent.

The woman in the back pivoted her head, checking out her surroundings for the first time, perhaps, noticing that they were in a clearing in the middle of nowhere. Her nose wrinkled, and then her whole face creased as she got a whiff of the waste lagoon. "Where are we?"

"Things are kind of busy down at the station. I thought we'd do our interrogation right here. More comfortable, don't you think?"

She struggled a bit, as though that would get her anything but more metal slicing into her skin. "I want to get out of here. I want to call a lawyer."

"A lawyer? What for, honey? You said before you didn't do nothing wrong. Lawyers are for criminals, ain't they?"

"I want to see a lawyer. Or a judge."

"Judge is just a fancy lawyer, in my book."

Doe got out of the car, taking his time, taking a minute to admire the blue of the sky, the long wisps of clouds like the strings of cotton that come out of an aspirin bottle. Then, acting as if he'd suddenly remembered where he was, he opened the back door and climbed in. He was careful to leave the door nice and open, since there was no inside handle, and if it closed, they'd both be trapped back there. The last thing he wanted was to be trapped with an ugly horse like Lisa. He sat next to her and traded the evil grin for a smile he knew to be charming. "What'd you say you do, now?"

"I work for Channel Eight in Miami," she said after a moment of sobbing.

Channel Eight? She sure as hell wasn't on the TV, not with her mushy face. "That right? What you do there? Some kind of a fancy secretary? Is that it? You sit on the boss's lap and take dictation? I could use me some dick-tation."

She looked down and didn't answer, which struck Doe as rude. Someone was talking to her, and she didn't answer. What, did she think she was Miss Universe or something? She needed to look in a mirror sometime, see what she really was. And now that he was close, he could see things were worse than he'd realized—acne scars covered with makeup, a pale but discernible mustache. Lisa had no business taking an attitude with him. To make this point clear, he put his hand flat against her forehead, very gently, really, and then gave it a little shove.

She didn't make a noise this time, but the waterworks were going, streaming down her face. "Please let me go," she said.

"Let you go? Hell, this ain't Russia. We have laws here. Procedures that have to be followed. You think you can just talk your way out of paying your debt to society?" He bobbed his head for a moment, like he was agreeing with someone somewhere, some words the woman couldn't hear. Then he turned to her. "So," he said, "a dog-face like you would probably be pretty grateful for a chance to suck cock, don't you think?"

"Oh God," she murmured. She tried to squeeze herself away from him, which was what they did, but there was nowhere to go. This was the backseat of a Ford LTD, for Christ's sake. But that's what they did. They tried to get away.

Doe loved this part. They were so scared, and they'd do whatever he said. And they loved it, too. That was the crazy thing. He knew they'd be getting off on remembering it. Sometimes he got phone calls late at night—hang-ups—and he knew what was going on. It was women he'd had in the back of the cruiser. They wanted some more, they wanted to see him again, but they were also embarrassed. They knew they weren't supposed to want it. But they did. All this *Oh God, no*-ing was just part of a script.

The truth was that it also made him a little bit sad on Jenny's account, because she was probably going to end up a dog-faced whore like this one. His own daughter, a dog-faced whore. In high school she'd be sucking dick in the bathroom because that would be the only way she'd get boys to like her, which they wouldn't, but it would take her a couple of years of getting smacked around to figure that out. He knew a couple of high school girls like that right now. He felt bad for them and all, but there wasn't much to be done about it, so there was no point in avoiding their company, now, was there?

And here was Lisa, squirming, crying, wiggling like a toad under a shovel. Meanwhile, he had a telephone pole in his pants. He unzipped himself and pulled it out. "Look at that, Lisa. You look at that. Now, you be a good girl and do your job, and we'll see what we can do about dropping the charges. Be a good girl, we'll have you back in your car in fifteen minutes. Quarter hour from now, you'll be cruising down the highway, heading back to Miami."

That always helped. You give them something real to hold on to, put them in the future. Just get it over with, and they could go. Which they could. He wasn't a monster or anything.

He saw that he had her. She turned to him slowly. Her little piggy eyes were red and narrow and pinched with fear, but he saw something like hope there, too. That grim determination to suck and bear it. And the twinkle in her eye, like she knew she was lucky to have a man like Jim Doe force himself on her. Maybe this wasn't how she'd always dreamed of it, but she'd dreamed of it just the same.

"Okay," she whispered. Softly. To herself, mostly, he guessed. She had to get herself together. Why, he didn't know. She'd sucked cock before. And if some pretty little thing locked him in a backseat and told him to eat her pussy, you wouldn't see Doe having to talk himself into it. But he supposed everyone was different.

"Okay," she said again, this time more to him. "You'll let me go?"

"I told you I would," Doe said urgently. With all this talk he was losing his momentum, starting to get soft. "Now get to sucking, girl."

"Okay," she said again. "But you have to take off my cuffs, first."

"Nice try, Lisa."

"Please," she said. "They hurt. I'll be good."

I'll be good. Like she was a little kid. Well, why not? He'd done it before. Sometimes they just needed to feel a little easy, and he knew this girl wasn't going to get all funny on him. She was broken.

"All right, sugar," he said. "But nothing tricky. Keep your hands where I can see them."

He reached around and unlocked her cuffs, wincing at the sound of the click and then the girl's sigh of relief.

"Thank you." She sniffed in a big honking snort of boogers, which he didn't much like, since who wanted to get head mixed with a mess of snot? But fuck it, he reasoned.

"Now I done something for you," he said. "I think you owe me a little favor."

His first thought was that she was coming in a little fast. His second was, *Holy Christ!* The fringes of his vision went red with agony, the unbearably sharp, but also dull, thud of pain in his balls that spread like an electric alien fungus to his hips and down his thighs and up his spine. And then again. It hurt so much that he couldn't even make sense of it. Somewhere in the back of his mind he understood. She was punching him in the balls. Not just punching him, pummeling him. Wind up and release like a rocket.

He tried to back away from her, out the door, but his back was to the car seat, and in the *thud, thud, thud* of her fist against his 'nads, he was in a free fall of pain, up became down, left became right. He couldn't figure out which way to go. Instead, he started to reach for his gun.

On some level he knew that shooting her in the back of his LTD with his dick out, on his own property, when who knew how many people had seen him stop her, and with her car still sitting by the side of the road, was a bad idea. On the other hand, he had this vague notion that if he could put a bullet in her stupid ugly face, she would stop and the pain would be gone. The pain was somehow linked to her being alive. It didn't make sense, and he even knew it didn't make sense, but he didn't care.

The problem was that he didn't have the gun. Everything was hazy and distorted, and he was feeling around for his belt, but he couldn't find it. The other thing was that while the pain was still there, the thudding had stopped. That was an improvement.

But not much. Lisa had managed to get his belt off him, the tricky fucking whore, so she had his keys, his nightstick. And she had his gun. The pain heaved back and forth below his waist, and he hoped to Christ she hadn't crushed his balls. The horizon shifted, and he understood that he was on his side in the back of the seat. She was standing in front of him, the car door open, her T-shirt disheveled and wet from tears or perspiration, her hair all wild like some crazed fuck bunny in a porn movie.

"You goddamn prick," she said.

The gun was pointed at him, which he didn't like, but even in his agony he could see that she didn't know how to hold a gun—she had it in both hands like a cop on some dumb-ass show. If he had to guess, he'd say she'd never fired one, probably hadn't taken the safety off. Not that he wanted to take the chance she'd figure it out if she needed to, since she'd already proved herself clever. Still, she might be the cleverest ugly bitch in the world, but if he'd been able to move his body below his waist, he would have gotten up, taken that thing away from her, and broken her potato of a nose with it. That's what he would have done.

"You wanted to know what I do for Channel Eight. I'm a reporter, you asshole. Get ready for camera crews."

She kicked the door shut, trapping him into the back of his car.

The smell of pig shit from the waste lagoon washed over him like an insult, like a big ugly laugh, like a tax audit, like a dose of VD. Doe was trapped. He was in pain. His balls were smashed. The Yoo-hoo and bourbon churned menacingly in his stomach and then came up onto the seat, onto his chest, his face, his arms. He felt himself passing out, and he stayed passed out until the next morning when his deputy finally found him and woke him with a series of delicate and mocking taps of his nightstick against the window.

Chapter 4

M Y HEART POUNDED, and a clenched coil of fear hardened in my chest. I had witnessed the death of two people. I would be next. I was going to die. Everything was cold and icy and slow, unreal and so achingly, physically, undeniably real as to be a new state of consciousness.

I never decided to turn and face the killer, but it happened. I pivoted my neck and saw an unusually tall man standing behind me, holding a gun pointed in my general direction, if not exactly at me. The lunar eclipse of his head blocked the overhead naked bulb, and for an instant he was a dark, wild-haired silhouette. The gun, which I could see clearly, had a longish black cylinder at the tip, which I recognized from TV shows as a silencer.

"Crap!" the man said. He moved and came into view, looking not raging or murderous, but puzzled. "Who are *you*?"

I opened my mouth but said nothing. It wasn't that in my terror I'd forgotten my name or how to make the sounds come out; it was more that I knew my name would mean nothing to him. He wanted some sort of description that would place me in context, something that would help him decide if he should let me live or not, and I wasn't up to the task.

With the gun still pointed toward me, the man gazed at my confused face with an expression of patience both coolly reptilian and strangely warm. He had blond hair, white really, that spiked out Warholishly, and he was unusually thin, like Karen and Bastard, but he didn't look sickly and drawn the way they had. In fact, he seemed sort of fit and stylish in his black Chuck Taylors, black jeans, white dress shirt buttoned all the way up, and black gloves. A collegiate-looking backpack dangled insouciantly over his right shoulder. Even in the smoky light of the trailer, his emerald eyes stood out against the whiteness of his skin.

"Stay calm," he said. He had the demeanor of a man totally in control, but in the tiniest fraction of a second, his composure appeared to crack and then reassemble itself, going from statue to rubble to statue again.

He took a step to his left and then to his right, a truncated sort of pacing. "You might have noticed that I haven't killed you, and I can pretty much tell you that I'm not planning on killing you. I'm not a murderer. I'm an assassin. Worst that will happen, if you do something stupid and piss me off, I'll shoot you in the knee. It will hurt like hell, might leave you crippled, so I don't want to do it. Just be cool, and do what I say, and I promise you're going to be just fine." He looked around and then let out a breath of air so that his lips vibrated. "Crap. I was so hopped up on adrenaline, I didn't even see you until I took them down."

I continued to stare, in something like shock, I suppose. The terror swelled in my head like a dull roar against my ears, and my heart pounded, but the thud of it felt distant and detached, the tinny echo of someone banging on something far away. My neck ached from craning, but I didn't want to look away. Too much shifting might make him nervous.

"What are you doing here?" the assassin asked. "You don't look like a friend of theirs."

I knew I'd better answer a direct question, but something in the pulley-and-wheel mechanism of my vocal cords wouldn't move. I swallowed hard, painfully, forcing something down, and tried again. "Selling encyclopedias."

The green eyes went wide. "To those assholes? Jesus. You should have done it a few years ago. Maybe a little knowledge would have saved them. But you know what? I doubt it."

Don't ask him, I warned myself. Just shut up, play it cool, see what he wants. He hasn't killed you yet, so maybe he won't. He says he won't. Don't ask him anything. "Why did you kill them?" I asked anyway.

"You don't need to know that. You just need to know that they deserved it." He grabbed the chair next to mine and sat down, moving in deliberate and authoritative movements, as if he were about to deliver an older brother's kindly lecture on saying no to drugs. I could now see that the assassin was younger than I had first realized, maybe twenty-four or twenty-five. He looked cheerful, as though he had a good sense of humor, almost certainly dry humor—the kind of guy you might want at your party or to live on the same floor of your dorm. Even as I thought it I knew it sounded idiotic, but there it was.

"I'd like you to pack up your stuff," the assassin said. "Don't leave any evidence of being here."

I couldn't make myself move. It seemed like the stench from the trailer park had begun to seep inside, to beat down the smell of tobacco and gunpowder and sweat, but then I realized it was the smell of the bodies—shit and piss and blood. And there were those dead faces with their empty eyes. My gaze kept drifting over to their ruined heads, frozen in terminal surprise.

"This is important," the killer said, not unkindly. "I need you to clean up your stuff."

I rose in hypnotic compliance, expecting to discover his promise not to hurt me to be a lie. The instant I turned my back, I'd hear the squeak of the silencer and the burning rupture of metal in my back. I knew he was going to kill me. Yet at the same time, I didn't quite believe it. Maybe it was intuition or wishful thinking, but when he said he didn't want to kill me, part of me believed he meant it—and not desperate, pathetic belief, either. It didn't seem to me like the desperate hope of the blindfolded condemned, feeling the roughness of the noose as it slipped over his neck while certain the reprieve would come. For whatever reason, the idea that I could get out of this alive struck me as entirely plausible.

I looked at my stuff. All of the book materials were on the table, and miraculously, none had been splattered with blood. My hands, big surprise, trembled like an outboard motor, but I began to pick up the brochures and samples and pricing sheets, holding each gingerly as though I were a cop collecting evidence, and I dropped them into my stepfather's moldy bag. I took the check Karen had written and shoved it in my pocket. Meanwhile, the assassin began to organize Karen and Bastard's stuff. He placed the checkbook next to a pile of bills by the phone, returned the pens to a cup on the counter separating the kitchen from the living room. Careful not to step in any blood, he brought my cup over to the sink and washed it methodically with a sponge, somehow keeping his gloves reasonably dry.

He was so cool about it, so damn cool, moving around the room with unflappable focus, the sort of person who acted as though everything had gone according to plan, even when it hadn't. My being in the trailer hadn't thrown him off for more than an instant. He'd changed the plan, was all. I flipped out when I overslept by five minutes, but this guy was centered.

He stepped back over the bodies, over the blood, and sat next to me. I ought to have cringed at his proximity, but I don't think I did. Under the heat of his gaze, my mind emptied of everything except a loose, preverbal fear and an irrational hope.

The assassin pointed the gun toward the ceiling, unscrewed the silencer, and then ejected the clip and removed a bullet from the firing chamber. Keeping his eye on me, he placed these accessories in his backpack and then set the gun on the table. I stared at it. We didn't have guns in my family. We didn't have firearms or knives or even baseball bats under the bed. We didn't handle weapons. If there were mice in the house, we called an exterminator and let him touch the traps and the poison. I came from a background of squeamishness, and I'd been raised to believe as a matter of faith that if I handled anything with the capacity to do harm, it would turn on me like a mutinous robot and destroy its master.

Now, there it was, right in front of me: the gun. Just like in the movies. I understood the pistol wasn't loaded, but for a moment I thought I should grab it, do something heroic. Maybe I could smack the assassin with the gun. Pistol-whip him or something tough guy-ish like that. While I pondered my options, however, the assassin took another gun out of his backpack, so pistol-whipping became less of an option.

Once again, he sort of aimed his firearm at me, less at me than in my direction, not to terrify me, but to make sure I kept my head, remembered who stood where in the hierarchy. "Give me your wallet."

I didn't want to give up my wallet. It had my money, my driver's license, the credit card my stepfather had reluctantly handed over, which I was allowed to use only in absolute emergencies, and even then I could expect to get yelled at. On the other hand, if the assassin wanted my wallet, I told myself, maybe he really wouldn't kill me. It would be easy to take a wallet off my dead body. So I reached into my back pocket, maneuvered it out—not so easy since it and my pants were moist with sweat—and handed it over. The assassin deftly thumbed through it, unimpeded by his black gloves, and then removed my driver's license, in which I looked unspeakably dorky and was wearing a velour shirt, which surely must have seemed like a good idea at the time, though now the decision mystified me.

The assassin studied it briefly. "I'll keep this, if you don't mind, Lemuel."

He wanted to take my license. That meant something significant; it portended of terrible things to come, though I couldn't quite shape the ideas in my mind.

"Now, pick up the other gun. Come on. I promise if you cooperate, you're not going to get hurt."

I didn't want to touch it. I didn't want to go anywhere near it. And what would happen if I did? Would he shoot me, claim self-defense, claim I'd shot Bastard and Karen? Picking up the gun was insanity, but so was not picking it up, so I slowly wrapped my fingers around the handle and lifted. It was both heavier and lighter than I imagined, and it trembled in my hand.

"Aim it at the refrigerator," the assassin said.

Beyond the point of making trouble or arguing, I did as I was told.

"Squeeze the trigger."

Though I knew he'd taken out the clip, which I understood meant the gun was unloaded, I still winced as I followed the order. I pressed down hard, expecting the rich boom of a TV shot report, but I got nothing except a hollow click. I kept my arm out. The gun continued to shake.

"Good job, Lemuel. Now put the gun down on the table."

I did.

"So, here's the deal," the assassin said. "Your fingerprints are now on the murder weapon. Bad for you, good for me, but let me be clear about this. You leave here, you keep quiet about what you saw, and no one will ever find this gun, no one will know you were here, and there will be no problem for either of us. I'm not looking to frame you, just to keep you from reporting to anyone what you saw. So if you decide you want to go to the police, they'll get an anonymous tip about you, Lemuel Altick, and discover the hidden location of this gun, which will mark you as the killer. On the other hand, if you accept that there are bigger things at play here than you can understand—and accordingly keep quiet—the police will never link you to what happened here today. Now, you can see I'm being fair about this, so keep that in mind if you have any moral qualms. Believe me, these were bad, bad people, and they had it coming. So, are we cool here?"

I nodded slowly, thinking for the first time that the assassin was probably gay. He wasn't effeminate or anything like that, but there was something about him, about the way he moved and spoke, that seemed full of unarticulated significance. Then a little voice inside me said that it didn't matter if he was gay. It didn't matter if he liked to do three-ways with proboscis monkeys. I had to stay focused if I was going to avoid getting killed. And now I had a new problem: Maybe he really would let me live, but only so he could frame me for murder.

I looked up, and he was shaking his head. "I really wish you hadn't stumbled into this. What's a clean-cut kid like you doing selling encyclopedias? You going to college?"

I swallowed hard. "I'm raising money. I got in, but I can't afford it, so I deferred."

He pointed at me. "Quick! What's your favorite Shakespeare play?"

I couldn't believe I was even having this conversation. "I'm not sure. *Twelfth Night*, maybe."

He raised an eyebrow. "Yeah? Why?"

"I don't know. It's supposed to be a comedy, but it's really kind of cruel and creepy. The play's villain is the guy who's actually just trying to restore order."

"Interesting." He nodded thoughtfully. Then he waved a hand in the air. "Who cares, anyway, right? Shakespeare's overrated. Now Milton. There's a poet."

The fear, which I had done a reasonable job of pushing back for a while, was now so intense that it flashed around me like electricity in a Tesla ball. Crazy people ranted like this before they killed you, didn't they? That's what I'd learned from the movies. Even if I was misreading those signals, I had just seen two people killed. Every time my attention shifted to something else, every time I tried to comfort myself with the realization that the assassin probably wouldn't strike again, that knowledge came back with a gruesome thump. Two people were dead. Forever. Whatever Bastard and Karen had done, they didn't deserve to be gunned down like animals.

Even so, with the sadness that crept over me at the thought of the indelible cruelty of murder, I felt the beginnings of something—admiration, maybe, though that wasn't quite right—for the man who had done the killing. The assassin terrified me, but I also wanted his approval. I knew it made no sense, but I felt I had to earn his trust, which was why I spoke out.

"There's something else," I said with deliberate slowness, a hopeless effort to control the trembling in my voice. "Besides Shakespeare, I mean. A guy saw me go in here."

He arched an eyebrow. "What sort of guy?"

"Just a guy. A creepy redneck."

"When?"

"Three hours ago, I guess."

The assassin waved his hand dismissively. "Forget it. He won't remember who you are, what you were doing here, any of that. He's not going to give you trouble. And if he does bring in the cops, tell them that you tried to sell them some books, it didn't fly, and you took off. There's nothing to link you to these guys, to suggest you had a motive. Nothing like that."

"I don't know."

"If the cops come to see you, say you were in and out without luck, saw nothing unusual—except maybe this creepy redneck—and that's all you have to say. They'll be off your case in no time and on that redneck's. Can you trust me on that?"

Could I trust him? He'd barged into my life, murdered a pair of prospects in front of my eyes, and then set me up to take the blame. I nodded.

"Fab," the assassin said. "Now, I'd say it was time for you to be getting out of here."

Leaving seemed to be a pretty good idea. More than I could have hoped for. I stood on wobbling legs, held on to the table until I could support myself properly, and began a sideways shuffle toward the front door, careful to keep an eye on the killer at all times.

"Lemuel," the assassin said, "I hope you'll consider the back way. Secrecy and all."

Vaguely humiliated, I went into the living room and unlocked the back door. I stepped out into the yard, where the heat and the dank, outhouse-stench humidity startled me out of my fear for a moment. I had seen people killed just feet away from me, I had sat at the table with their killer, and I had made it out alive. I was not going to be killed.

Now I just had to get away from there before the cops showed up.

It would be easy to cut over to the neighbor's property, so I closed the door behind me and stepped out into the dank darkness. The ghost of the moon was glowing behind a heavy blanket of clouds. The crickets chirped their near screeching chorus, and nearby, an unfathomable tropical frog bellowed its equatorial song. A mosquito dive-bombed my ear, but I ignored the explosive buzz. Instead I trudged forward, vaguely aware as I walked that the lights in Bastard and Karen's trailer went metaphorically out.

Bastard and Karen. He irritating and vaguely sinister. She jagged and beaten down. Dead. The two of them dead. Their kids, off somewhere, were now orphans and had no idea. Their young lives, as they had lived them, were finished. And I had been a party to it. I had witnessed the unspeakable horror of their deaths and then sat with their killer and, I realized, found him strangely charming. It wasn't as though I could have saved Bastard and Karen, but I told myself I could do something now. I could go to the police, and go fast, maybe in time for them to catch the assassin while he was still in the trailer. And even if they didn't get there in time, no one would believe that I had killed them.

Then again, they might.

The assassin, when not assassinating, acted like a reasonable guy. It could be that he believed, really believed, that Bastard and Karen deserved it. But did anyone deserve it? Did I live in a world in which bad people were killed by righteous assassins? Nothing in my life told me it was so, but then again, this night had been in my life.

The first two trailers I passed were dark, though I heard an angry dog's sonorous barking in the middle distance. I came out onto a street, though not the one on which Bastard and Karen lived, which somehow made me feel better. It was a little less than a mile to the Kwick Stop, and only a couple of cars passed me, speeding by in automotive oblivion. I told myself over and over again that I just might get away with this, I just might get my life back.

Chapter 5

THE CUTTING BOARD lacked music. It was a large restaurant, with a moderately unfortunate name, composed of a series of interlinked wood-paneled rooms filled out with white-clothed tables and heavy wooden chairs. Yet it lacked music, and that disappointed B.B. He liked music, soft music, trickling in so quietly that he could hardly hear it. Ambient as a distant highway, but still evanescently there, adding texture to the meal, a little heft if the conversation lagged, a touch of the cinematic sound track. Classical was fine, the soft sort of classical, not the loud stuff with horns and kettledrums, but the truth was that B.B. liked elevator music. He knew everyone got a kick out of trashing elevator music, and let them have their laugh, but in the end they had to agree there was something reassuring about these songs everyone already knew, maybe in a more raucous form, handed back all soft and powdery, prechewed, going down so smooth that you didn't even know there was something in your throat.

This restaurant skipped the music. And no fish tank. He liked a fish tank. B.B. wasn't one of those guys who took cruel pleasure picking which fish gets to die—he had to make cruel decisions enough for work—but he liked to look at fish. He liked to watch them swim, especially the big goldfish with the bulging eyes, and he liked the bubbling in the tank.

The Cutting Board had palm trees, though—a few small groves of plastic palms stuck here and there to give the place a touch of class. Palm trees were important for obscuring views. He didn't want to be seen, and he didn't want to see. The glory of a fine restaurant was its semiprivacy. Pillars could work, too, but he liked the palm trees since the fronds added extra cover. The restaurant was also into low, ambient lighting, so in the end, the dark and the plastic trees made it acceptable despite its other drawbacks. B.B. would return at some point. It would never be on his A-list, but he would put it on rotation. In any case, he didn't like to visit a place more than once every six months. The last thing you want is for the waiters to start to recognize you, recognizing that the last time you were in it was a different boy, and the time before that, too.

It was a little steak-and-seafood place near the Ft. Lauderdale airport, far enough away from Miami that he wouldn't just happen to bump into anyone he knew, and catering largely to the old and retired set, so that his sort of people—the nonwithered, the surgically nonwithered, the power-golf players, the Rolex wearers, and the convertible drivers—would never be caught dead in a place like this. B.B. believed firmly in picking places that drew the old and the retired. A man could be a prince in the eyes of a waiter simply by not sending back the drinking water for being the wrong temperature.

On the other side of B.B.'s candlelit table, Chuck Finn sat in concentration as he worked a breadstick with a waxy slab of butter. He'd have it under control for a second or two before it slipped out from under his knife, and Chuck would lurch in sudden and astonishingly ungraceful motions to regain his grip on it. And each time he would smile at B.B., flash those slightly crooked teeth in sophisticated self-deprecation, and then go back to his business. The third time, B.B. had been forced to reach across the table to keep the boy from knocking his goblet of Saint-Estèphe onto the tablecloth. At $45 a bottle, he wasn't about to let any of it tip over, particularly when the boy had taken his first sip, probably his first sip of wine ever, and nodded with knowing appreciation. At a steakhouse, a man drinks a nice Bordeaux. It doesn't get much more complicated than that. Most of the other boys, maybe all of the other boys, had taken a sip, grimaced, and asked for a Coke. Chuck had half closed his eyes in pleasure and let the tip of his very pink tongue tickle his upper lip. Chuck got it, and B.B. began to suspect that he had on his hands not only a boy willing to be mentored, but one ready to be mentored.

He'd taken only one sip, and then somehow the glass was covered with greasy boy-fingerprints. B.B. understood that's what it was to be a boy. Boys made messes. They almost knocked over wine. Sometimes they did knock over wine, and unless you were eager to keep from drawing attention to yourself, you didn't much care because you didn't keep boys from being boys. That wasn't a mentor's job. A mentor turned a boy in the right direction so that at some future date, when the time was right, he'd become a man. That's how you mentored.

"Be graceful, Chuck," B.B. said in what he hoped was his most mentorly tone. "Grace is poise, and poise is power. Look at me. You want to be like me when you grow up."

B.B. pointed at himself when he spoke, as if he were exhibit A. If you pointed at yourself, people looked, and he had no reason to mind that. He had turned fifty-five this year—a bit on the mature side, though still in his prime—but people mistook him for forty, forty-five max. Partly it was the Grecian Formula, the use of which he had elevated to an art, and partly it was the lifestyle. An hour with the Nautilus machines three times a week wasn't much of an investment for youth. Then there were the clothes.

He dressed, and there was no other term for it, *Miami Vice*. He'd been considering linen suits and T-shirts before the show came on the air, but once he saw those guys strutting around in those clothes, B.B. knew it was the look for him. It was the right look for a man of hidden but smoldering power. And that show—God bless it—was single-handedly transforming Miami from a necropolis of retirees, marbled with pockets of black or Cuban poverty, into someplace almost hip, almost fabulous, almost glamorous. The smell of mothballs and Ben-Gay drifted off, replaced by the scent of suntan lotion and titillating aftershave.

B.B. watched as Chuck continued to work the butter, and the breadstick was now glossy and slick and, though it might have been a trick of the light, even starting to sag a little.

"I think that's enough butter." He said it in a mentorly tone—sympathetic but firm.

"I like a lot of butter," Chuck said with naïve cheer.

"I understand you want it, but there's such a thing as discipline, Chuck. Discipline will make you a man."

"Can't argue with that." Chuck set the butter knife, with its half-used pat still clinging, onto the tablecloth.

"Place the butter knife on the bread plate, where it belongs, young man."

"Good point," Chuck observed. He set the breadstick on the bread plate as well, wiped his hands on the heavy linen napkin on his lap, and then took another sip of the Saint-Estèphe. "That's really good. How did you get to know so much about wine?"

Working as a waiter in Las Vegas, trying to make it through my shift so I could go lose even more money I didn't have, get into it even deeper with a bodybuilding, shirtless Greek loan shark would not have suited as an answer, so B.B. offered a knowing shrug, hoping it would impress.

He had selected boys before, boys from his charity, the Young Men's Foundation. These were special boys he thought would be able to dine with him, spend a few hours alone in his company, and mature from the experience. He looked for calm and steadiness in the boys, but he also looked for the ability to keep a secret. These dinners were special, and because they were special, they weren't any of the world's business. The dinners were only for those very exceptional boys worthy of extra mentoring, but in the three years he had been taking boys out to eat, a thought had always nagged at him—that he selected his dining companions for their ability to keep a secret rather than for their readiness to be mentored.

Now, here was Chuck—quiet, slightly introverted if not antisocial, trashy-novel-reading, journal-writing, obliviously-badly-haircutted Chuck—who knew how to keep a secret but had a sense of humor, had an intuitive appreciation for complex wines, obedient and pliable, but with an impish resistance. B.B. felt an excited tingle shoot out from the center of his body like a miniature supernova. Here, he dared to speculate, might well be the boy he'd been looking for, the special mentee, the reason he had wanted to help boys in the first place.

What if Chuck was everything he appeared? Smart, interested, full of soft-clay potential? Could B.B. arrange to spend more time with him? What would the boy's worthless mother say? What would Desiree say? Nothing could work without Desiree, and he knew, without quite admitting it to himself, that Desiree would not be happy.

Chuck now turned his attention to the breadstick. He picked it up and was readying himself to take a bite when B.B. reached out with one hand and gently encircled Chuck's wrist. Normally he didn't like to touch the boys. He didn't want them or anyone else to think that there was something not right about his mentoring. Nevertheless, sometimes when two people were together there was going to be a certain amount of touching. Life worked that way. They might accidentally brush up against each other. B.B. might put an affectionate hand on a boy's shoulder or tousle his hair, press a hand to his back, give him a pat on the butt to hurry him along. Or it might be something like this.

Chuck had been an instant away from putting the breadstick in his mouth when B.B. saw the fingernails. Black dirt, packed into discrete geologic chunks, hibernating under the shelter of nails weeks overdue for trimming. Some things you could dismiss, put in the boys-will-be-boys category, look the other way. Some things, however, you could not. Some things were too much to ignore. If B.B. was a mentor, then he had to mentor.

He kept his grip gentle but the hand motionless. "I want you to put the breadstick down," B.B. said, "and go wash your hands before you eat. Scrub those fingernails good. I don't want to see any dirt under them when you get back."

Chuck looked at his nails and then at B.B. He had no father, an impatient gnome of a mother, an older brother in a wheelchair as the result of a car accident—the impatient gnome of a mother had slammed her Chevy Nova into a sable palm a few years back, and B.B. suspected to the point of deep certainty that there'd been heavy drinking involved. Chuck slept on a tattered foldout couch with springs, he felt sure, as pliant and welcoming as upturned dinner forks. He did miserably in school because he tuned out his teachers and read whatever he felt like during class. He wasn't the weakest kid around, but he got his share of ass kicking, and he gave his share, too.

Chuck had plenty of pride, and it was the frail and bitter pride of a desperate boy. B.B. had seen it often enough—these powerless boys growing red in the face, flashing their teeth like cornered lemurs, lashing out at their mentor because their pride demanded they lash out at someone, even if it was the only person in the world who truly wanted to help. B.B. understood it, anticipated it, knew how to defuse it.

This time, however, he did not get it.

Chuck studied his fingernails and then turned to B.B. with another of those self-deprecating smiles that made B.B. feel as though something in his body had just melted.

"They are pretty dirty," he agreed. "I'll go wash up."

B.B. let go of the wrist. "You're a fine young man," he said. And then he watched Chuck walk away. The kid looked good, there was no denying that. He'd made an effort to clean his best clothes—a pair of green chinos and a button-down white shirt. He wore a cloth belt, his socks matched his brown shoes, and his brown shoes had been polished. It all meant one thing: The boy was letting himself be mentored.

He was back in under two minutes. He'd just scrubbed and returned. Hadn't even taken the time to piss. Now he sat, took another drink of the wine, and nodded at B.B. as though they'd just entered into a contract. "Thanks for taking me out like this, Mr. Gunn. I really appreciate it."

"It's my pleasure, Chuck. You are an exceptional young man, and I'm happy to help you in any way I can."

"That's really nice of you." Chuck held B.B.'s gaze with mature confidence.

The astronomical tingling was back, turning into B.B.'s own private cosmic event. It was almost as though Chuck were trying to tell him something, trying to let B.B. know that he was comfortable with the friendship between a young man and his mentor. B.B. looked at the boy with his thin frame, his face a little too round for his body, his tousled brown hair and strangely brilliant brown eyes. The boy *was* trying to tell him something, that he was ready for mentoring, whatever mentoring B.B. might wish to pursue, and the air at the table was electric.

Chuck finished his glass of wine, and B.B. poured him another. Then the boy bit into the breadstick with a ferocious clamp of his jaws. Crumbs sprayed out across the table, and the sound of it echoed halfway across the restaurant. Chuck looked up at his mentor, alarm preparing to settle on his face, but he saw B.B.'s amused smile, and he let out a little laugh. They both laughed. Several of the retirement zombies looked over with disapproving scowls. B.B. made eye contact with all of them, dared them to say anything.

When the black man approached their table, at first B.B. thought it might be the manager there to complain. Maybe one of the retirees had convinced them to initiate an effective-immediately no children policy. But the black man didn't work for the restaurant. It was the darkness that kept B.B. from recognizing him right away. Otto Rose.

He wore a blue suit, and even in the dark B.B. could tell it was just a nudge short of electric blue, but the rest of the outfit was conservative and businesslike: richly polished oxfords, a white shirt, a rep tie crafted into a massive and artful four-in-hand. Otto hovered over the table with that imperial grace he loved to exude. He looked something like a cross between an actor and a third world dictator. Though barely thirty, which was irritating enough, he appeared hardly more than twenty, even with his head shaved. B.B. had been watching his hair thin with each year, maybe even each month, but Otto shaved his head and looked good doing it. The slick of his skin glowed from the candles of the surrounding tables.

The sudden and inexplicable appearance of Otto Rose was, by any standards B.B. could think of, bad news. Bad news because no one but Desiree was supposed to know where B.B. was. Bad news because Otto Rose was standing there, watching him mentor, watching him dine with an eleven-year-old boy in an expensive steakhouse, a bottle of Saint-Estèphe opened and two glasses, one for an underage boy. Bad news because Otto might be a business friend, but he was the kind of friend B.B. would love to shed. Bad news because there was no reason in the world why Rose should want to find him unless it was bad news.

"Hello, young man," Rose said to Chuck. His West Indian accent came out thick and chunky, full of island hospitality and humor, the way it always did when he cranked up the charm. He set his hand on the bottle of Bordeaux. "Can I pour you some more wine, or has Mr. Gunn been taking care of you?"

Chuck held on to his breadstick and looked up at Rose, not quite making eye contact, but he didn't say anything. B.B. expected as much. South Florida might be diverse—there were Cubans and Jews and regular white people and Haitians and West Indians and regular black people and all sorts of South Americans and Orientals and who the hell knew what else—but the fact was none of them wanted anything to do with any of the others. White kids clammed up around black people. Black kids clammed up around white people. B.B. had seen it a million times when mentoring, and if you were going to mentor, you had to understand these things.

Rose, however, was undeterred. "I am Otto Rose. What is your name, young sir?" He stuck out his hand for shaking.

Chuck appeared to know he was trapped, and being trapped, he chose to forge ahead. "I'm Chuck," he said in a steady voice. The handshake looked firm and unafraid.

"And Mr. Gunn is your friend? He is a fine man to have for a friend."

"He's my mentor," Chuck said. "He's been very nice to me."

"And this is a fine restaurant for mentoring," Rose said, the humor percolating just under the surface of his voice. "And nothing goes with mentoring like a glass of wine." He picked up Chuck's glass and gave it a good sniff with his eyes closed. "A Saint-Estèphe?" he asked as he put down the glass.

"Wow." Chuck's eyes went wide. "You can tell that from the smell?"

"I read it on the bottle."

B.B. saw that the retirees in the restaurant were looking over at them. They didn't like the big, bald black man standing around. The waiters were eyeing them as well, and it would only be a moment until one of them came by to ask if the gentleman wished to join their table. B.B. would be fucked if Rose said he would, so it was time to snip this one in the bud.

B.B. pushed himself out of the chair and away from the table, rising with *Miami Vice* poise. He might be half a foot shorter than Rose, but he held his own next to the guy. B.B. knew who he was, knew what he commanded, knew that there were people all over the state who would shit in their pants if they heard B. B. Gunn was pissed off. It was time to make sure Otto knew enough to shit in his pants.

"Excuse me for a moment," he said to Chuck. "I'll be back as soon as I take care of some grown-up business."

"Okay," Chuck said. There was something forlorn in his voice.

B.B. knew instantly that Chuck might be a mature kid, he might be a spunky kid with a good sense of humor and the will to rise above the misery of his life, but he didn't want to be left alone. He wanted, maybe above all things, companionship, and that was but one more reason to be pissed off at Otto Rose for showing up like this and fucking up his dinner.

"Follow me," B.B. said to Rose. It was time to establish the pecking order in his barnyard. Rose thought he was clever, finding out where B.B. was eating, making sly little insinuations about Chuck. But now it was Rose following while the alpha male led.

They stepped outside, and the temperature rose by nearly thirty degrees in an instant. It was humid and sticky, and the sounds of cars off I-95 hissed past.

Desiree was out there, leaning against B.B.'s convertible Mercedes, arms folded over her breasts. She wore moderately, though not obscenely, tight Guess jeans and a lavender bikini top. The pink of the massive scar along her side glistened in the neon light of the restaurant.

Rose broke out into a gregarious grin. "Desiree, my darling. How are you, lovely?" He leaned over and rested a hand on her scar, as he always did, just to show that it didn't trouble him, and gave her a kiss on the cheek. "I didn't see you on the way in."

Desiree allowed herself to be kissed, but her lips were pressed tight into a cynical little smile. "Sure you did, though you made a pretty good show of acting like you didn't."

He pressed a hand to his heart. "You hurt me when you say such things."

B.B. couldn't be bothered to let this play out. "If you saw him coming in, why the hell didn't you stop him?"

She shrugged. "What for? You'd have come out, and we'd be right where we are now."

What for? Jesus, did he have to spell it out for her? It was mentoring time. She knew perfectly well he didn't want to be bothered while mentoring. She knew, and she'd let Rose in because she was still angry with him. It had been a month, and she was still angry, and it was starting to make B.B. crazy. She was his assistant, and he wasn't sure he even wanted to think about what life would be like without her, but life with her was starting to be a problem.

"Okay," B.B. said. He took an authoritative suck of air. "Let's make this fast."

"Of course. You have that young man in there."

"I'm mentoring him," B.B. said.

"Oh, I am certain of it. I see he likes breadsticks."

Fuck if B.B. was going to take this kind of thing from Otto Rose. "What do you want? How did you know I was here, and what is it that can't wait until morning?"

"You're easier to find than you think," Rose said, "and as to why it can't wait, I think you'll be happy I did. Number one, I've just received a tip. There's a reporter in Jacksonville."

"They've got a newspaper there," B.B. said. "And TV stations, last time I checked. Of course there are reporters."

Rose let out his island laugh. "There's a reporter there out to do a story on your crew."

"Shit. From where?"

"I don't know. I don't know if the reporter plans to observe or if there's someone on the inside already who is a reporter undercover. I don't know what this person thinks he knows, but there's probably more of a story there than he realizes."

B.B. bit his lip. "Okay, we'll take care of it. What's number two?"

"You know the legislature is taking up that bill in the next session to severely limit door-to-door sales. I've just received word that if I go against it, I am going to face severe fund-raising problems. Now, you know I want to help you out, B.B. I've always stood up for you, always valued our relationship. But it's going to cost me to go against this bill, and if it's going to cost me, I'm going to have to make up that cost somewhere."

"He wants another donation," Desiree said. She'd been doing a lot of that sort of thing lately, stating the obvious as though B.B. wouldn't have understood what Rose meant without her help.

"Christ, Otto, can't this wait?"

"I came to see you about the reporter, but since I was here, well, it seemed like as good a time as any. Of course, I know you were busy mentoring. If you would rather mentor than take care of business, that is your own concern. Still, I am not entirely certain you want the business community to learn just how important this mentoring is to you."

Fuck if here wasn't Rose putting on the squeeze, trying to use his charitable nature against him. A man wanted to help out the unfortunate, and he had to answer to one opportunistic cynic after another. And the thing was, Rose put all that work into crime prevention, after-school programs for the kids in Overtown, but no one could say anything about that because he was black and those kids were black, and all of that meant that Rose was a saint. So now he had to stand out here, talking bullshit with a state legislator while Chuck sat by himself at the table, his friendly mood deteriorating with each minute.

"How much are we talking about?" Desiree asked.

"Same as last time, my darling."

Same as last time meant $25,000. These little payouts were adding up to huge money.

"Give us a moment, Otto," Desiree said. She put a hand on B.B.'s arm and led him about twenty feet into the parking lot. "What do you think?"

"I think I don't want to pay him any more money."

"Of course not, but if this bill goes through, you're going to have a lot of problems."

"So you're saying we should pay?"

"Probably, but make it clear that this is the last time. You don't want him to think he can come to you to strap on the feed bag every time he's feeling he needs a few extra dollars. This is starting to feel like a shake-down."

B.B. nodded. "When we get rid of him, get on the phone to the Gambler and make sure he gets the heads-up about the reporter. And his crew should be making a payment after the weekend. Make sure he can get the cash to us."

"Okay."

They walked back over to Rose, who was still grinning as though he were about to deliver a singing telegram.

"I'll have the money by next week," B.B. said, "but this is the last time."

"Come now, my friend. You know I cannot make any guarantees."

"We can't make any guarantees, either. You get me, don't you?"

"Of course, B.B."

"I've got to get back inside."

"Yes. That boy might be tempted to start mentoring himself," Rose said.

With B.B. back inside the restaurant, Desiree remained leaning against the clean car, arms still folded as she looked at Otto. Her shoulder-length dirty-blond hair blew lightly in the wind and lifted her chin, which accentuated the sharpness of her nose. She knew that if she held her head just so, she could make herself look pointier and angrier, and she wanted to look angry now. Desiree wasn't quite ready to confront B.B. She wasn't quite ready to say the things she needed to say. The end had to come, and she knew it, but it didn't need to come tonight.

It wasn't fear. People who had never met B.B., who knew him only by reputation or by the size and ingenuity of his operation, feared him. De-siree, however, knew better. No, it wasn't fear. It was obligation—and it was pity. But she felt no pity for Otto Rose.

"Oh, come, Desiree. Don't give me that look, beautiful. You know it is business. If you work for a man like B.B., you must expect men like me to deal with him as he deserves."

She shook her head. "Don't back me into a corner, Otto, by saying things about B.B."

"You're right. You are nothing if not loyal. I am sorry I spoke so. I won't say another word about B.B., but may I say a word about you?"

"If you must." She let her expression slacken a little, took some of the heat off.

Otto took a step closer. "You are much too—too *good*—to work for a man like B.B. I don't merely mean good at your job, though I do believe that. I mean you are a good person."

"You don't seem to have a problem doing business with B.B."

He laughed. "I'm a politician, my dear. It is too late for me to be good. But it is not too late for you, young and talented and lovely as you are. Why don't you leave him?"

The question needed dodging, and Desiree fought the urge to physically duck. She didn't want to deal with his probing now. "I owe him, okay, Otto? That's all I want to say."

"I know you owe him. But how much can you owe? Do you owe him enough to help him do what he does? Or to help him with those boys?"

"He is just their mentor, Otto. No one can say anything about B.B. and his boys. I live in the same house with him, remember? I'm the live-in help."

"Yes, of course. The better to make the world believe that the two of you are lovers. He may not do anything with those boys, Desiree, you must know that he *wants* to, and how long before he gives in to that?"

"I don't want to hear it. I won't listen."

"I don't mean to push. It is only that I want to help you, and I become eager. Let's then not talk about B.B. Let's talk about you, my dear."

"What, do you want to ask me out on a date?" she asked, but she kept her voice playful, careful to sound anything but bitter or sarcastic.

"I would not dare to hope for such good fortune," Otto said. "I have something a bit more formal in mind. I know you depend on B.B. for protection, so maybe you would feel you had more options if there was someone else offering you protection."

"You?"

"I could offer you a job in my office, Desiree. I know your worth, and I can promise you it would be a high-ranking job. Of course, nothing in politics pays well, but it would be a fine opportunity for a talented young lady like yourself."

"What kind of protection can you offer me when you might be voted out of office every election cycle?"

He laughed. "Who is there to challenge me? You must at least listen to my advice, darling."

She nodded.

"Let's sit in my car for a few minutes."

"You sure you're not asking me out on a date?" she said.

"I am almost sure," Otto said.

He led her to his massive Oldsmobile, painted a shiny sun yellow. He opened the passenger side for her, and she slid onto the leather seats. He went around to the other side, slid the key in the ignition, and got the engine revving. In a moment he had the air-conditioning going and the low murmur of dance music from the radio.

He put a hand on top of hers. Maybe he did plan to offer her a job, but he wasn't sure she wouldn't be willing to give him more. "Shall I tell what I have in mind?" he asked.

"First, I should tell you something," she said. Then she lashed out, cobra fast, and had a hand on his throat. She slid over to his side and straddled him, as if they were having sex. She could feel the bulge in his pants, and she could feel it diminishing. In an instant it was both hands on his throat, and she was leaning forward, putting all of her weight—not ever above 110 pounds—straight down on him.

She liked the heat of his skin, the bulging under her palms, under her thighs. It was sexy, but not exactly sexual. It was powerful, and she liked that.

Desiree knew well that she had small hands, and they weren't strong, even for their size. Surprise and the confines of the car worked in her favor, but Otto could escape her grip almost certainly if he tried, if he really tried; still, she had a few crucial seconds here, the advantage of his disorientation, and she planned to be well away from him before he even thought to struggle.

"Otto, we've done business together for a long time," she said, "and it's been good for everyone, but if you ever pull shit like this again, I'll kill you. You try to humiliate B.B., try to make suggestions about him, use it as leverage, whatever—you're going to disappear. You think you're smarter than he is, and you think I'm cute, and maybe you are and I am. But don't you ever forget what else we are." She let go of his throat. "You don't want to be his enemy."

Otto coughed and put a hand to his Adam's apple but was otherwise quiet and still.

An old couple strolled through the parking lot, staring unabashedly at the small white woman straddling the large black man in the car.

"I've got some phone calls to make," Desiree said. She gave him a quick kiss, just a peck, really, but directly on his dry lips, and then slid off and opened the driver's-side door. The old man had looked away, but the woman continued to stare over at her.

"You want to say something?" Desiree asked, and she turned her empty, judgmental eyes away.

Otto was just now rousing himself from his wounded surprise. He reached out to close his door, but he met her eyes as he did so, and, of all things, he offered her another of his grins. "Does this mean you don't want the job, my darling?"

"Not at this moment." She strolled over to B.B.'s Mercedes and shook her head softly. The thing was, Otto might have been a player and a schemer, and in his own way he might have been every bit as bad as B.B., but he had a sense of humor, and that alone made her hope she wouldn't have to wrap her hands around his throat again.

Chapter 6

THERE I WAS, survivor of a double homicide, in the Kwick Stop's public bathroom. Halfway to the store I realized I needed to piss and piss badly, so badly that I couldn't believe I hadn't pissed myself during the shootings. It was all I could do to keep from ducking behind a tree and taking a whiz under the canopy of stars; but public urination, even obscured public urination, seemed a bad idea. What if I had been caught? What if the cops picked me up and found evidence? Hairs and fibers and that sort of thing? My knowledge of police investigations came from a pastiche of television and movies, so I had no idea how it worked in real life.

When I walked into the store, I spotted the bathrooms in an instant—in the door-to-door book trade, you grow skillful at quickly finding the toilets in convenience stores—and rushed back without even the pretense of calm. In general, I didn't like to act as though I needed the bathroom; it embarrassed me that complete strangers should know about my body functions.

In this case, however, I was in no frame of mind for the casual shop, a pantomime of interest in beef jerky and then a rub of palm against palm, like, Oh, I sure could do with a hand washing, before a calm stroll into the bathroom.

When I looked up from the urinal, I realized I must have already pissed since nothing was coming out and the crampy, stretched feeling had faded into a tranquil fatigue. I zipped up and washed, checking in the mirror for signs of blood. Nothing in my hair or on my hands or clothes. It all looked okay. I splashed some water on my face again because I thought that's what you do in a crisis. You wash your face. Did it really help, or was it a myth circulated by the soap industry? Not that soap stockholders would gain much here; the inverted pear-shaped dispenser contained only encrusted pink dregs of soap gone by. Nothing in the way of towels—only one of those rotating towel machines, where someone else's dirt gets pressed or washed or just permanently affixed before it comes back around again. I grabbed a wad of toilet paper from a loose roll propped above the dispenser and then dabbed it gently against my face.

The bathroom smelled like shit and piss and sickly floral deodorizers struggling to beat down the stench of crap and piss. My hands trembled violently, and I felt the need to puke. The problem with puking was that I would have to get on my hands and knees to do it, and the floor was covered with a deep coat of gummy dried urine, and there was a fuzzy lump of gray shit in the toilet. My reptile brain had no intention of letting me mark territory already well scented up by creatures more powerful and less hygienic than I.

Instead, I reached into my pocket for the check, the check Karen had written so that she could buy books for her now orphaned daughters. "Karen Wane," it said in the top left corner. It seemed odd that she and her husband wouldn't share the same account.

If I were worried about them passing the credit app, it might be worth considering, but under the circumstances it hardly mattered. I tore up the check and dropped the pieces in the horrifically unflushed toilet. One of the shreds fell into a viscous pool by the toilet's side, and I had to pick it up by its tiny dry corner and then daintily drop it in. I flushed, using the toe of my shoe so I wouldn't have to touch anything, and then went to wash my hands again.

Should I have flushed the check in two different toilets? Of course, it wasn't as if cops were going to don hazmat suits and go wading through treatment plants in search of check fragments. Still, I had to pound down that feeling of nausea again, a process that involved closing my eyes and trying hard to think of nothing. In about a minute I felt sure I wouldn't puke, so I pushed open the door and got out of there.

The convenience store was a couple of miles from the motel. I could easily have walked it, would have preferred to, but that wasn't the way it worked. I had to wait for Bobby, so I grabbed a sixteen-ounce ginger ale from one of the wall-length refrigerator displays in the hopes it would set-tle my stomach. Then I stood on line behind a guy wearing jeans and a black T-shirt.

I couldn't see the man's face, and all but a few strands of hair were hid-den under a baseball cap with a glittery Confederate flag emblazoned along the front, but I could tell he was probably in his thirties or forties, and he was chatting with the girl at the counter, a teenager, plenty young but not very pretty. She had a long-faced, horsey look to her, with an up-side-down U-shaped mouth that seemed never to close entirely; the whole package ended up resembling nothing so much as an Easter Island statue. No matter, as the man in the Confederate hat liked her plenty, and his eyes rested with particular interest on her large, squishy-looking breasts, which flashed out of a short-sleeved blouse one or two buttons past mod-esty. The Confederate laughed at something and slapped the counter and peered into the girl's shirt unapologetically.

"Oh shit," he said. "I think I must have dropped my quarter in there. Let me just get it out." He raised his hand like it was getting ready to slide into the cleavage.

"Jim," the girl said through a fan of splayed fingers, "you stop that." She glanced at me as though trying to decide something, then looked back at the Confederate. "You're so bad."

On the radio, an eager voice encouraged everyone to "Wang Chung" tonight, which was one of the many confusing songs I figured I'd under-stand when I knew more of the world. Sort of like the lyrics to "Bohemian Rhapsody," the comprehension of which I assumed required a familiarity with European arts and music. An educated person would know precisely what a scaramouch was and why he ought to do the fandango.

The unnaturally bright fluorescent lighting in the store made me feel as if I were onstage or caught in a police searchlight, which was a particu-larly unhappy metaphor. Getting out of there, escaping the lights, the bad pop, the freakish customer and clerk, took on a kind of urgency. I would gladly have stolen the ginger ale if I'd thought I might get away with it. The Kwick Stop, never the sort of place where I felt comfortable, now seemed too small, and it was getting smaller. I didn't want to leave the ginger ale, and I didn't want to say anything to the counter girl. It also seemed a fore-gone conclusion that the man with the Confederate hat wouldn't much like a kid with a northern accent and a tie telling him he had to hurry it up. But I was thirsty and my stomach lurched violently, so I twisted open the cap and took a drink. It did make me feel a little better. Less like puking, anyway.

"You can't drink that before you pay for it," the Confederate man told me. He grinned broadly, exposing a mouth full of wild and white teeth. "It's called stealing, and we got laws about that here."

Only now did I recognize him. The guy from the Ford pickup outside of Bastard and Karen's trailer. The split-level haircut was tucked under his hat, but it was the same guy. An icy terror burst in my chest and radiated out to my limbs. But what the hell was I going to do? Run? The guy had *seen* me go into a trailer where two people were murdered.

The nausea, I realized, most likely stemmed from my desire to suppress the one obvious fact in all of this—once those bodies were found, the cops were going to come looking for me. No matter what the assassin had told me, no matter what sweet lies he tried to conjure, I knew full well that I would be their prime suspect. It wasn't a matter of maybes or ifs. They would want me. APB on Lem Altick. Take no chances with Lem Altick, boys, he's probably armed and dangerous. The only question was if my being totally innocent would save me.

I walked up to the counter and put down a dollar. The soda was seventy-nine cents.

"Wait your turn," the girl told me. "Can't you see that there's people ahead of you?"

"There aren't people," I said. My voice sounded edgy and nervous, and I wished I would shut up. "There's person, and he's not buying anything."

"You being rude to this little girl?" the Confederate asked.

"Rude as in pushy?" I asked. "Or rude as in trying to stick my hand down her shirt?"

"Boy, you don't know who you're messing with," the Confederate said.

But I did. I knew I was messing with a guy who wouldn't give a second thought about sucker-punching me and kicking my head when I was down. Still, I was apt to run my mouth. The thing I'd learned over the years was that the only power I had against someone like this was in mouthing off. It didn't keep me from getting my ass kicked. It might even promote an ass kicking, but at least I got to perpetuate the stereotype of weak kids being verbally dexterous.

But this wasn't high school, and I'd already learned tonight that the stakes were higher than a few bruises and a dose of humiliation. It was time, I decided, to show some deference.

"I didn't mean to be pushy," I said quietly. "I just want to pay."

"It ain't *time* for you to pay. You think you go walking around here in your tie and your fancy briefcase and you don't have to wait on line? You think you're somehow better than us?"

The math, science, and language arts curricula had been pretty weak, but the one thing I'd learned back in middle school was that accusations of thinking I was better than someone else were a prelude to violence. Some asshole revving his engine, in the process of convincing himself or witnesses or God that the ass kicking he was about to unleash was utterly righteous.

I needed to cool things down, but it was hard to figure out my next move when my brain was spinning with terror. There was a tiny hamster wheel of fear clacking around, and I just couldn't get my thoughts to settle. So I said what was probably the worst thing I could have. I said, " 'We.' "

The Confederate angled his head and stared. "What?"

It was an out-of-body experience. I saw myself speaking, and I had no power to stop.

"You meant, 'You think you're better than *we.*' We is a subject. 'We *are here.*' Who is here? We are. Us, on the other hand, is an object, the recipient of action. '*Bob* gave the ball to *us.*' Who gave the ball? Bob, the subject, did. To whom did he give it? Us, the object."

A stupid smile flattened out across my face.

The Confederate stared as though I were a formaldehyde freak behind Coney Island glass. The girl behind the counter took a step back. Her eyes went wide and she half raised her hands as though to protect her face from the coming blast.

The blast never came. Outside the store, Bobby's Chrysler Cordoba pulled gloriously, miraculously, into the parking lot. The most fortunate timing in the history of the world—far better luck than my nearly eighteen years had led me to expect or even hope for. "That's my ride," I said, as though we'd been hanging out, talking sports.

The Confederate didn't say anything. I looked to the counter girl, but she would not meet my eyes. Nothing to do but forget the soda, so I put it down on a pile of Coors cases and began to head for the door.

"You leave now, and you're stealing." It was the counter girl. Her voice had grown small, and her hands, which now hung limp by her side, trembled just a little.

I stopped. "Then let me pay," I said.

"You gotta wait your turn." Her voice was just above a whisper.

Now the redneck bent toward me. He wasn't unusually tall, just under six feet, and he had maybe an inch or so on me, but he bent forward like a giant stooping to offer advice to a midget. "What do you think you're doing?" he asked. "Correcting me?"

I turned away, hoping to God that Bobby could see me, would come to my rescue if he spotted trouble. Feeling the burn of the redneck's eyes, I picked up the soda and took the dollar out from my pocket. I put it back on the counter. I didn't care that they were assholes, and I didn't care about the change. I cared only about getting out of there.

I turned away and pushed open the door, which chimed merrily along with the sound of my laughter, unhinged with giddy disbelief.

I had survived a double murder, I had survived an interview with the killer, I had survived a sure beating by a redneck whom I had insulted. I ought to have felt some measure of relief, but a churning dread burned away at my stomach. I had survived only that moment, and plenty more moments were coming.

Chapter 7

NO ONE ELSE was in the car yet, which was some small comfort since it was a two-door and I hated being crowded into the backseat. In the months since I'd signed up, I'd become Bobby's biggest earner, and that meant I received certain trivial privileges, like good pickup times and the moochiest neighborhoods.

"You don't look so hot," Bobby said. "You blank?"

I shook my head and then peered into the store to make sure we weren't in any trouble. The Confederate had gone back to flirting with the counter girl, and appearances suggested I'd been more or less forgotten.

"No, I scored." I opened my bag and handed Bobby the paperwork. "I almost got a double, but it didn't pan out."

Bobby smiled. "Hell, my man. You scored two days in a row. You're on fire." Pronounced, for sales motivation effect, "fie-yah." "Just stay pos, keep thinking pos thoughts. It's the pos attitude that will get you the double or triple tomorrow."

Bobby was a big guy, big like a football player or more like an ex–football player. He had meaty arms and thick legs, no neck, but he also had a sizable gut that jutted out over his cloth belt. Bobby's face was wide and boyish and almost preternaturally charismatic. I wanted to be too smart to be drawn in by Bobby's charm, but I was drawn in all the same.

The fact was, I found it impossible not to like Bobby. He enjoyed everyone's company, and he displayed a generosity beyond anything I had ever seen. Part of it was his command of the power of money. Bobby wanted always to demonstrate to his crew that he had cash, that cash was good, and that cash made you happy. He would buy us beer and lunch and, on occasion, a night out. During long drives, when we stopped for fast food, Bobby tipped the counter workers at McDonald's and Burger King. He tipped tollbooth attendants and hotel clerks. He was, to use his word, *pos.*

"You don't have a check here," Bobby said, waving my paperwork at me. He ran a hand through his short, almost military style hair. "You didn't get green on me and forget again?"

I had scored a double my first day on the job. My first day. No one expected people to score their first day, so Bobby hadn't yet talked me through the credit app, and consequently I hadn't asked my buyers to fill one out. Bobby had then taken me over to both houses—and this was now after midnight and all lights were out—getting the people out of bed so they could sit around in their robes and fill out credit apps. I would rather have given up the sales, but Bobby worked himself up into a feverishly rotating tornado of sales energy, and he'd insisted. Then again, he knew he could get away with it. He had that chummy grin and inviting laugh and that way of saying hello that made strangers think they must have met him before and simply forgotten. I would have had the door slammed in my face, but Bobby had the wife at the second house making us all instant hot chocolate, the kind with the little marshmallows that melted into gooey clouds.

And he had motivation. I made $200 off each sale, Bobby made $150 each time I or anyone else in his crew scored. That's why people wanted to be a crew boss. You made money for getting other people to do work.

The paperwork Bobby now held in his big hands belonged to Karen and Bastard. I had handed over the wrong sheets. The momentary relief I'd felt at escaping the redneck was now gone. I was back to the roller-coaster feeling of plummeting straight down.

"Sorry," I said. I was bearing down, clenching my abdominal muscles, to keep the fear from seeping into my voice. It was like trying to stanch a gaping wound. I knew that the more time went by, the more time I could spend living a normal life, the less I would remember Karen lying on the floor, her eyes wide open, a jagged crater in her forehead, blood pooling around her like a halo. I'd forget the acrid and coppery smell in the air. I wanted it gone.

"That was the one I blew." I fished around in my bag and got the paperwork from early that afternoon. The quiet little couple in the run-down green trailer. Their two kids and four dogs. The stench of unpaid bills. That had been a walk in the park.

Bobby looked it over, nodded definitively. "This looks pretty good," he said before filing the papers in his own bag. "Shouldn't be a problem passing." I had missed out on commissions and bonuses because credit apps hadn't passed. I'd even missed out on a big one, a huge one, because of credit apps. My third week on the job, I'd rung a doorbell and a skinny man, pale as cream cheese, wearing a bikini brief swimsuit, bald but for a wedge of hair no thicker than a watchband, had come to the door and grinned at me. "What are you selling?" he'd asked.

Somehow I'd sensed that it wasn't the right time for the usual line, so I'd said, straight out, that I was selling encyclopedias. "Come on back, then," the man had said. "Let's see what you can do."

Galen Edwine, my host, was in the midst of a barbecue with about eight or nine other families. While the kids splashed around in the moochie aboveground pool, I pitched them all—nearly twenty adults. They drank beer, they ate burgers, they laughed at my jokes. I was like the hired entertainment. And when it was all over, I'd sold four of them. Four. A grand slam. Grand slams happened, but rare enough that they were legendary. That day there was a $1,000 bonus for a grand slam, so I racked up $1,800 for a day's work.

Except I didn't because none of the credit apps passed. Not a single one. It had happened to me before and it had happened since, and it never ceased to piss me off, but the tragedy of that day really got to me. I *had* a grand slam, and then it turned to dust. Still, the reputation stuck, and even if I hadn't earned the commissions, I'd earned a certain respect.

"So," Bobby pressed, "what happened here?" He held up Karen and Bastard's app.

I shook my head. "They balked at the check."

"Shit, Lemmy. You got inside and you couldn't close? That's not like you."

I shrugged in the hopes that this conversation might simply go away. "It just sort of worked out that way, you know?"

"When was all this?"

Maybe I should have lied, but it didn't occur to me. I didn't see where he was going with this. "I don't know. Tonight. A few hours ago."

He glanced at the credit app for a minute, as if he were looking for some forgotten detail. "Let's go back there. If this was only a few hours ago, I bet I can work them."

I put a hand on the car for support. I shook my head. There was no way I wanted to return to the scene of the crime. "I don't think it will do any good."

"Come on, Lem. I can work them. What, you don't want the money? You don't want the bonus? Commission and bonus, so we're talking about another four hundred in your pocket."

"I just don't think it will help. I don't want to go."

"Well, I want to try. Where's Highland Road?"

"I don't remember." I looked away.

"Wait here. I'll go in and ask."

Bobby moved to go into the Kwick Stop. I figured asking for directions, especially from a guy who seemed already to want to kick my ass, a guy who had seen me go into Karen and Bastard's house, and *then* going would be worse than just going. I let out a sigh and told Bobby that I now remembered the way, and we drove back to the trailer. It was just a few minutes along the quiet streets, but the ride seemed to go on forever, and it seemed all too short. Bobby parked the car along the curb and got out, slamming the door hard enough to make me wince.

The trailer looked quiet. Freakishly quiet, a beacon of stillness in the ocean of shrill insect sounds. No trailer had ever looked as still as this one. Somewhere, not too far away, a dog barked—an urgent bark that dogs saved for when a murder suspect lurked nearby.

Bobby walked over to the trailer, up the three cracked concrete stairs, and rang the bell.

I looked back and forth compulsively. A beat-up Datsun trawled past on a perpendicular street half a block down. Did it slow down to look at us? Hard to say.

Bobby rang the doorbell again, and this time he pulled back on the screen door and pounded softly, if pounding can ever be soft, just below the eyehole. I caught myself thinking that they were never going to write that check if they were pissed off at being pulled out of bed.

From the steps, Bobby leaned over to peer into the kitchen window. He pressed hard against the thin glass, and I was sure he would go crashing through.

"Christ," he said. "Either they're not home or they're dead."

I laughed and then realized Bobby hadn't said anything funny, so I stopped. Together we walked back to the Cordoba, where I slouched in the front seat, breathing in fear and indescribable relief while we headed out for the next pickup.

The inadequate air-conditioning washed over me, and I tried to recede into the freshly washed leather. I wanted to pass out and I wanted to weep and, on some level, I wanted Bobby to hug me. But Bobby busied himself by fiddling with the radio stations, finally settling on Blue Öyster Cult, but somehow the song's insistence that I refrain from fearing the Reaper didn't make me feel much better.

"A single isn't bad," he said, maybe thinking that I probably needed a good pep talk. "Not bad for a day's work. You're still in the game, but a double's better, right? . . . Huh? But you'll get a double tomorrow. You're a power hitter, Lem. You're doing great."

If I hadn't been numb from having witnessed a double homicide, I felt sure that Bobby's pos comments would have perked me up. I hated the way I lapped up Bobby's praise, as if being a good bookman, selling a set of books to people who would never use them and couldn't afford them, were worth a pat on the head. Good doggie, Lem. But I loved it. Two people dead, holes in their heads, blood and brains on the peeling linoleum, and I still sort of loved it.

The other three guys in the Ft. Lauderdale crew—Ronny Neil, Scott, and Kevin—piled one by one into the backseat, each at his own pickup stop. They all harbored resentment against me, since Scott was both fat and unimpressed by conventional ideas of personal hygiene, and he crammed the rest of them in tight. I, meanwhile, basked in legroom and relatively sweet air.

Kevin was a quiet guy, a bit short and stocky, but affable in a self-contained way. It was easy to forget he was around, even on long road trips. He laughed at other people's jokes but never told his own. He always agreed when someone said he was hungry but probably would have starved to death before suggesting we stop to eat.

Ronny Neil and Scott, on the other hand, were not so retiring. They had joined up together and were like wartime buddies who enlisted from the same town and were assigned to the same platoon. Their friendship consisted, as near as I could tell, of Ronny Neil hitting Scott in the back of the head and calling him a fat asshole.

Ronny Neil thought of himself as being strikingly handsome, and maybe he was. He had a sharply detailed face with big brown eyes of the sort that I thought women were said to like. His straight, straw-colored hair came down to his collar, and he was deeply muscled without being bulky. Not like there was time to lift weights while we sold books, but I did on occasion catch him doing push-ups and sit-ups around the motel room. On those days that I managed to get up early enough to take in a run before the morning meeting, Ronny Neil would earnestly advise me to take up lifting weights instead of doing pussy exercises. But, he would muse, if there was one thing a Jew ought to know how to do, it was run fast.

Each time he picked someone up—at the designated convenience store—Bobby would take the guy around to the back of the car and open the trunk to shield their conversation from the rest of the crew. Once they entered the car, you couldn't ask if they'd scored or blanked. You couldn't ask how they did. You weren't allowed to tell stories about anything that happened to you that day unless the story was in no way related to scoring or blanking. Bobby and the other bosses knew there was no way to keep people from talking about it. If someone hit a triple or a grand slam—sometimes even a double—everyone in all the crews would know by the next morning, but you couldn't say anything in the car.

These rules appeared not to apply to Ronny Neil, who didn't know how to shut up, about scoring or anything else. Ronny Neil was a year older than me and he'd gone to a high school across the county from mine, so I hadn't known him, but the rumor machine had churned out some interesting details. By all accounts, he'd been a serviceable place-kicker for the school's football team, but he'd been convinced of his greatness and convinced that a football scholarship would be his for the taking. As it turned out, the only offer he received was from a historically black college in South Carolina that was interested in diversifying its student population. Ronny Neil had gone off in a huff and come back at the end of his freshman year with his scholarship revoked. Here details get fuzzy. He was kicked out either because he failed to keep his grades up, because he'd been involved in a drunken and sordid sex scandal that the university wanted desperately to keep quiet, or—and this was my personal favorite—he'd never quite gotten the hang of avoiding the word *jigaboo*, even when black students outnumbered him three hundred to one.

On the drives back to the motel, he'd tell us about how he'd scored, and he'd share with us some of the more implausible incidents from his colorful life. He'd tell us about how he'd filled in briefly for the bass player of Molly Hatchet, how he'd been asked to join the navy SEALs, how he'd finger-fucked Adrienne Barbeau after his cousin's wedding—though it was never clear what a movie star was doing at his cousin's wedding. He told these stories with such surety that they left me wondering if my own sense of the universe was hopelessly skewed. Was it possible that I lived in a world in which Adrienne Barbeau might let herself be finger-fucked by a moron like Ronny Neil Cramer? It hardly seemed likely, but how could I really know?

On the other hand, he bragged about things that were true, too. Like about how the last time we were in Jacksonville, when we'd stayed at the same motel, he'd stolen a passkey off the cleaning cart and slipped into half a dozen rooms, lifting cameras and watches and cash out of wallets. He'd laughed himself sick watching Sameen, the Indian man who owned the place, defending his wife—the hotel maid—from accusations of theft. He told us that the previous year, before the election, he'd put on a suit and tie and gone around soliciting donations for the Republican Party. He'd have people make out checks to "RNC," and then he'd just write in the rest of his last name. Seedy check-cashing places on Federal Highway had no problem cashing his checks for R. N. Cramer.

Tonight he was going on about how some hot redhead had been begging for him while her husband watched, helpless to do anything about it.

"You sure it wasn't the husband wanted you?" Scott asked, the words coming out as a high-pitched jumble of spit from his rather serious lisp.

"Yes, I'm thur," Ronny Neil said. He flicked Scott in the ear. "You smell worse than a piece of shit, you tongue-tied dumb-ass."

For someone who'd just been insulted, injured, and mocked for a speech impediment, Scott took it all in stride. I felt a sympathetic knot of outrage on behalf of a guy I couldn't stand.

"How would you know what a piece of shit smells like," he asked sagely, "unless you were going up to them and sniffing at them?"

"I know what a piece of shit thellths like, you fucking pussy, because

I'm thitting next to one." Still, Ronny Neil looked away, embarrassed that Scott had drawn blood with so cutting a zinger.

When we got back to the motel, we walked through its forlorn main parking lot, cradled between two parts of the two-storied L-shape. Here were the cars of the lost, the wandering, the short on gas, the long on fatigue, people who had left their dreams up north or out west and were now willing to let their lives take meaning from nothing more complicated than the absence of snow. In the light of day, the buildings were pale green and bright turquoise, a Florida symphony of color. At night it appeared desolately gray.

We filed into the Gambler's room. His real name was Kenny Rogers, so the nickname had come with depressing inevitability, but we treated it as though it were the height of wit. As I understood it, the Gambler didn't own the company that contracted with *Champion Encyclopedias'* publisher, but he was high up. The chain of command was lost in interlinking strands of haziness, and I suspected intentionally so, but I knew one thing with absolute certainty: Every set of books that got sold meant money in the Gambler's pocket.

He was probably in his fifties, though he looked younger. His slightly long white hair gave him an angelic cast, and he had one of those easy-grinning faces that made him a natural at sales. He looked you right in the eye when he spoke to you, as if you were the only person in the world. He smiled at everyone with fond familiarity, the lines around his eyes crinkling with good humor. "A born fucking salesman," Bobby had called him. He still rang doorbells two or three days a week, to stay fresh, and rumor had it that he hadn't blanked in more than five years.

When I walked in, the Gambler hadn't yet arrived. He was always the last to show, strutting into the room like a rock star coming out onstage. Ronny Neil and Scott were off in the corner, talking loudly about Ronny Neil's truck back home and how big the tires were, about how a cop had stopped him for speeding but let him go because he admired the tires.

The Gambler's Gainesville crew finally came in, strolling with the confident sense of superiority of a king's retinue. The Gambler drove a van, so he had a large crew—nine in all—but only one woman. Encyclopedia sales held particular challenges for women, and even the good ones generally didn't last for more than two or three weeks. Rare was the crew with more than a single woman. Long hours spent walking by deserted roadsides, going alone into strangers' homes, lecherous customers, and lewd insinuations from the other bookmen dwindled their ranks, and I suspected, with great sadness, that this one wouldn't last, either. Nevertheless, I'd been thinking about her since her appearance the previous weekend.

Chitra. Chitra Radhakrishnan. During the past week, I'd caught myself saying her name aloud, just for the pleasure of hearing its music. Her name sounded kind of like her accent. Soft, lilting, lyrical. And she was beautiful. Stunning. Far better looking than any woman I thought myself entitled to like, even from a distance. Tall and graceful, with caramel skin and black hair pulled into a ponytail and big eyes the color of coffee with skim milk. Her fingers were long and tapered, finished off with bright red polish, and she wore tons of silver rings, even on her thumb, which I'd never seen anyone else do.

I hardly knew her, I'd had only a single extended conversation with her, but those words had been electric. For all that, I couldn't say why this woman should be the one to send me into a tumbling vortex of infatuation. There were other women in the group, though not many, and there had been, in a purely objective sense, far prettier ones in the past. I'd never had a crush on any of them.

I had to consider the possibility that it was Chitra's foreignness. Perhaps her being Indian among the otherwise all white population made her a misfit and therefore accessible. Or maybe for all her beauty, and it was considerable, there was something vaguely awkward about her—a slightly ungainly walk, an absent, self-effacing way of holding her head in conversation.

Whatever it was, I wasn't alone in admiring her. Even Ronny Neil, who complained bitterly about his daily interactions with mud people, couldn't take his eyes off her. Now he rose and went over to her, just like that. The words came out of him, easy as anything. I couldn't hear except that Ronny Neil said, "Hi there, baby," and Chitra smiled at him as if he'd said something worth smiling about.

I felt a comforting rage—comforting because of its familiarity and because it had nothing to do with the murder, which for a moment I could tuck into a neat little compartment toward the back of my brain. I could understand why Ronny Neil liked Chitra. She was beautiful. That would be enough for him. But why would Chitra even speak to Ronny Neil? Surely she was the anti–Ronny Neil, with her quiet reserve, her skeptical glances at the Gambler, the kindness she radiated that stood in counter-balance to Ronny Neil's malevolence.

I knew almost nothing about her, but I was already certain that Chitra was smart, and Chitra was discerning, but she was also from India. She had been here since she was eleven—she'd told me that in a brief conversation I had strategized into existence the previous Saturday night—but she was still from a foreign country. She spoke English well, having studied it even before moving here, but she spoke in the formal way many foreigners had, suggesting they're always tripping over something, always making decisions, worried about mistakes.

To me, her foreignness raised the possibility that she might not be able to recognize the furnace of assholery that smoldered inside Ronny Neil. Surely they didn't have rednecks in Uttar Dinajpur, from which she told me her family had emigrated. They had assholes of their own variety, obviously—singularly Uttar Dinajpur–ish assholes, assholes who would send up asshole flags the instant they entered an Uttar Dinajpur bar or restaurant—but it might be hard for an American instantly to see such a person for who he was. Chitra was clever, but Ronny Neil might nevertheless prove illegible to her. So I had my eye on her. To keep her safe.

Ronny Neil sat next to her, and the two of them started talking quietly. The fact that I couldn't hear a word of it made me furious, and for a moment I considered getting up, going over to them, inserting myself into the mix. The problem was, I knew it would make me look foolish and desperate, make my situation immeasurably worse.

My position was just fine for the moment. The previous week, after a couple of rapidly consumed cans of Miller beer, I'd managed to work up the courage to sit next to her and casually introduce myself. She'd listened to my bookman advice, laughed at my bookman war stories—a genuine laugh, too, an infectious, almost convulsive giggle that came with mild torso rocking. She talked about the novels she liked, how after the summer she would be starting at Mount Holyoke, where, she had already decided, she would do a dual major in comp lit and philosophy. She loved living in the United States, she said, but she missed Indian music and street food and the dozens of varieties of mangoes you could buy in the markets. The conversation had been marvelous and full of promise, but I hadn't initiated it until two in the morning, and I had hardly overcome my initial nervousness before she announced she absolutely had to get some sleep.

I saw her the next morning but did nothing more than smile politely and say good morning, lest I betray the fact that I liked her. Now I kept still, averted my eyes for as long as I could before sneaking glances. Then I watched them talk while trying not to think about the dead bodies I'd seen that night. Though "dead bodies" already seemed a bit of sanitizing. I hadn't seen dead bodies, I'd seen bodies becoming dead. That, surely, ought to keep me from dwelling on Chitra, on the graceful length of her neck, on the vaguest hint of cleavage that peeked out from her white blouse. It ought to have, but somehow it didn't.

Meanwhile, the Gambler had started talking. He'd been saying something about how it was all in the attitude, about how the people out there *wanted* what we had to sell.

"Oh yes, my friends," he cried out. His face was darkening, not with the blood red of exertion, but with the vibrant pink of exuberance. "You know, I see them out there every day. They're out in front of their homes with their plastic swimming pools and their Big Wheels and their lawn jockeys. You know what they are, don't you? They're moochie. They want to buy something. They're looking around with their greedy little eyes, and they're thinking, What can I buy? What can I spend my money on that is going to make me feel better about myself?"

The Gambler stopped and unbuttoned the collar of his blue oxford and loosened his tie with one finger like Rodney Dangerfield not getting respect. "See, they don't understand money. You do. They want to get rid of it. They want you to have it. You know why? Because money is a good thing to have. You know those songs? You know the ones—they tell you money isn't important. Only love matters. That's right. Love. You get together with your special love, and as long as you have each other, nothing else counts. You can live in a run-down shack as long as you have love. You can drive a beat-up old car as long as you have love. That's awful pretty."

And then he did that odd thing. His arms were out, flailing wide, as if he were about to hug a bear, and he just paused, held the pose in the air. He didn't do this every session, not even every weekend, but I'd seen him do it three or four times before. It was weird theater, but the crowd loved it. Everyone broke out into applause and cheers while the Gambler held the position for twenty, maybe thirty seconds, and then he went back to his rant.

"Yeah," he said, as though he hadn't been playing statue, "those words are nice, but those songs don't tell you about when the guy from that better neighborhood drives by in his brand-new Cadillac on his way to his beautiful home, and he winks at that in-love woman standing in front of her run-down shack. See, now that beat-up car don't seem like it's enough.

"Those people you sell to, they're looking for something. And so are you. They're looking for what you can give them—a sense of doing the right thing. My Lord, friends, it is so beautiful. You believe in God? You better thank God right now for helping you to find this job, this job that lets you help others while you help yourself."

This went on for another half an hour. The Gambler made those who had scored feel like royalty, and those who had blanked would burn to get back out there and try again. He possessed and harnessed an incredible energy that I saw and understood, even though it left me unmoved. Where everyone else fed off his enthusiasm, I saw a core of meanness, as though it were not money but anger that kept him going. I saw the guy who would happily steal the poor in-love woman from her poor but in-love man just for the pleasure of meanness.

"Now, there's one more thing," the Gambler told the crowd. He was winded, slightly bent, and breathing deeply. "I just learned that there may be a reporter who's interested in us. I don't know the details, but he's gonna be taking a look at what we do. May already be here among us, for all I know. And let me tell you a little something about the news, folks, EN-CYCLOPEDIA SALESMEN BRING KNOWLEDGE AND OPPORTUNITY TO NEEDY FAMILIES doesn't make as good a headline as ENCYCLOPEDIA SALESMEN TRICK CUSTOMERS. Hard as it is to believe, that's how they're going to want to show us. So if a reporter comes up to any of you, I don't want you to say anything. Not a thing other than 'No comment.' You hear? You find out their name, who they work for, get a business card if you can, and bring it to me. Are we all on the same page?"

"Yes!" the room roared.

"These people want to stop you from making money and our customers from learning. I don't know what the hell their problem is, but as long as I'm head of this crew, we're going to keep on making the world a better place, and we're gonna make money while we do it."

After the meeting, everyone began to file out by the pool, the way we did every night. I moved through the crowd, trying to keep an eye on Chitra. I heard her say something to Ronny Neil and walk off. He hesitated and followed, but I got the sense they weren't going together.

By the pool, the crew bosses would be grabbing cases of tall boys, Bud or Miller or Coors or whatever was cheapest, and shoving them in coolers. Someone would bring out a radio or a tape player. If people in the rooms above them minded the noise, we never heard about it.

I always joined them, at least for a while, but that night I wasn't up to it. I needed to be alone. The after-sales meeting had been a torture, but at least it had distracted me for a few minutes; now, alone again, I felt like I had to get away. I wasn't able to make idle conversation, to laugh at stupid jokes. I was afraid that if I had a beer or two, I'd start to cry.

I went back to the motel room. It had two beds shared by four guys— Ronny Neil demanded his own bed, and Scott and Kevin were willing to share, which meant I ended up on the floor. We didn't pay for the motel ourselves, so I couldn't complain. It was hard to tell how much was the room and how much the roommates, but when I walked in, the scents of mold and sweat and cigarettes and something stale and crusty slapped my senses. Even so, the feeling of solitude and privacy comforted me.

I sat by myself for a moment, staring at the blank, gray face of the TV. Maybe there was something about the murders. Maybe I should be watching. I continued to stare, afraid of what I might see or not see, until, in a surge of bravery, I lunged forward and turned it on.

The late news would be long over by now, but I figured if there was a murder, the local news stations would jump at the chance to use their generally useless live broadcast equipment. Nothing. No police cars or helicopters hovering over the mobile home. I sat at the edge of the bed, hands pressed against the tattered bedspread that smelled like a mix of ashtray and aftershave, and stared with unfocused eyes at Johnny Carson, who was laughing hysterically at Eddie Murphy. I didn't really know who or what Eddie Murphy was imitating, but I took comfort in Johnny Carson's appreciation. Could I really have witnessed a murder in a world full of Carson's belly laughs?

I wanted to embrace the doubt, but there were too many questions. So I opened the night table drawer and took out the phone book to look up Oldham Health Services. Nothing in the yellow pages or the business white pages. It didn't prove anything. It could be reasonably close by without being in the same county, but unless I knew where it was, I didn't see how I could get a number to call them and ask them who they were and—and what? If they knew a guy named Bastard? That wasn't exactly a conversation I wanted to have.

I stood up and looked out the window, pressing the thick brownish curtain to one side and trying not to cough from the storm of dust I'd unleashed. About thirty book people were out now. The tinkle of music and laughter filtered through the window. I'd flipped off the gurgling air conditioner for a moment so I could hear what there was to hear. Through the glass I could just discern the furiously optimistic jangle of "Walking on Sunshine." That song was everywhere that summer, and as much as I hated it, its rhythms pumped with an undeniable pull. It announced cheerfully that people were having fun somewhere else. Quite possibly everywhere else. And sure, it was stupid, mind-numbing fun, but it was still fun, and sitting in a tobacco-saturated motel room with globs of ancient semen encrusted into the carpet, trying to decide if I'd really seen two people gunned down that night, was a hell of a lot less fun than walking on sunshine down to the pool, drinking watery beer, and possibly even flirting with Chitra.

I looked out the window again and there was Chitra, sitting on the edge of a slatted reclining chair, the sort sunbathers across the country—the world, for all I knew—endured in order to tan themselves. A tall boy was wrapped around those long, silver-ringed, red-tipped fingers. Like everyone else, she still wore her selling clothes—in her case, black slacks and white blouse, so she looked like a waitress. A beautiful waitress.

The fact was, I was going to be eighteen in January, and this virginity business was beginning to get me down. Not in a frenetic, must-visit-the-whorehouse, *Porky's* sort of way, but more in a life-is-passing-me-by way. It felt as though everyone I knew had been invited to a party from which I was barred. I could hear the music and the peals of laughter and the clinking of crystal champagne flutes, but I couldn't get in.

From my room, I could make out Chitra's distant smiling face. It was a big, easy, open, and unself-conscious grin. She was one of those pretty girls who didn't fully appreciate or factor in the effect pretty girls had on men, so she believed the world to be a much nicer place than it was. The brutality of people like Ronny Neil remained invisible to her not only because she wouldn't know a redneck if he did doughnuts on her lawn in his four-by-four, but also because they weren't assholes around her, were they? They didn't insult her, crowd her space, make her feel that only the thinnest gossamer thread kept her safe from a monumental ass kicking. No, they tripped over themselves, they told her how nice she looked, they gave up their seats for her, they offered her a piece of Kit Kat. And for a moment, I felt an incredible jolt of envy—envy not of those who were close to Chitra, but of Chitra herself and that beautiful, protected, fantastical universe into which she'd been given a free pass.

Now she threw back her head and let out a full, tinkling laugh, so high-pitched that I could hear it this far away, through the glass, over the music from the boom box. She was surrounded by a group of people. Marie from the Jacksonville office, a couple of people from Tampa, Harold from Gainesville, who I suspected might be a rival.

At first I didn't recognize the guy who was doing such a great job of amusing her. The umbrella at their table was up, and the angle was odd. I could tell from the clothes it wasn't Ronny Neil, and anyway, Ronny Neil wasn't very funny. He might tell some dirty jokes or racist jokes in the car, but they were stupid, and only Scott laughed at them. They sure as hell weren't going to make Chitra throw back her head and let loose.

And then I saw the comedian. Tall, thin, black jeans, white button-down with the collar done up, even whiter hair puffing upward and outward.

It was the assassin. Chitra was talking with the assassin.

Chapter 8

Empty Bud cans already littered the outdoor stairwell. The Gambler and Bobby and the other crew bosses asked us not to litter, but there was no way to get a bunch of exhausted bookmen, thrilled after a long day to be sitting and drinking beer, to pick up after themselves. The bosses didn't really care as long as the books were sold, and Sameen and Lajwati Lal, who owned the motel, were content if not exactly happy as long as the bills were paid. We stayed at this motel every time we came to Jacksonville, and they weren't about to mess with a decent-size account, so in the end nothing got done.

I rounded the stairs, nearly slipping in a puddle of spilled beer but recovering by leaping into the air and landing at the bottom of the first floor.

To get to the pool I had to cross a little courtyard, go past the reception lobby, and come out the other end. I never got that far. When I landed I smelled something sweet and familiar, and it wasn't until I felt a hand on my shoulder that I processed the scent.

It was pot. Not that I found anything especially sinister about pot. Sure, I associated its use with my father, but my father also wore pants, and I wasn't about to eschew them on similar grounds. I'd smoked a few times, and though it always made me headachy and paranoid, I figured that sometimes you had to be a good sport and go along to get along. But here, on the road, with the bookmen, I associated pot with just one thing: rednecks.

"Where's the Hebrew fire?" Scott lisped in his high-pitched voice. It wasn't bad enough the guy had an impediment, he sounded as if he'd just sucked in helium as well. He had one of his dinner-plate hands on my shoulder, and there was nothing friendly about it. He pressed hard, but even so I could have gotten away if that's what I'd wanted; however, doing so would have involved some squirming, which struck me as humiliating. Better, I thought, to act as though I didn't care. This strategy was one I'd turned to again and again in middle school and high school. It never worked, but I clung to the routine as desperately as a sailor clung to prayer in the face of a storm.

"Yeah, where ith it?" Ronny Neil said. Harassing me didn't mean that Scott was above contempt.

I looked at Scott's hand. "I've got somewhere to go," I said. The sour odor of his unwashed body began to pierce the shell of the pot.

"Where would you have to go?" Scott asked. His eyes were already red and half-closed, and he teetered a little uncomfortably on his feet. I tried not to stare at a cluster of pimples on his chin, big and foamy white at the top.

"Yeah," Ronny Neil repeated, tossing his hair back like an actor in a shampoo commercial. He took a big suck from the pipe, held it for a moment, and blew the smoke in my face.

I understood the gravity of smoke blowing. A man blew smoke in your face, you beat the shit out of him if you had the chance. It was a hanging offense, a reason to go nuclear.

"Bobby wants to see me," I said in a scratchy voice. It seemed like a good lie. No one wanted to get on Bobby's bad side. There was no percentage in that.

"Fuck Bobby and fuck you and fuck all your asshole friends," Ronny Neil said.

"That," I observed, "is a lot of fucking."

"You little shit," Scott added. He jabbed his finger in my stomach. Not insanely hard, but hard enough to hurt.

Ronny Neil smacked Scott in the back of the head. "I tell you to hit him, you fat fuck?"

"I just poked him," Scott answered defiantly.

"Well, don't juth pokth himth. Don't juth poke nobody until I tell you to, asshole." He turned to me. "You think Bobby is so great? He ain't shit around here, and he don't know shit about what's going on. The Gambler trusts *us*. You understand? Not you and not Bobby. So stop hiding behind him like he was your mama."

"Bobby's a fucking asshole," Scott said. "He gives all the best areas to a pussy like you."

"A puthy like you," Ronny Neil repeated.

"You know what, I'm starting to feel like a third wheel in this conversation," I said. "I think the polite thing would be for me to excuse myself."

"I think the polite thing would be for you to stick it up your ass."

"It's funny," I said, "how the standards of politeness vary from culture to culture."

"You think you're smart. You blank again tonight?" Ronny Neil handed the pipe over to Scott, who looked at his hand for a moment, trying to figure out how to keep me where he wanted without touching me. Scott then studied the ground and moved around on unsteady feet to block me from getting away.

"I didn't blank," I said. "Not that it's your business."

"When you fall asleep tonight," Scott said, "we're gonna fuck you up."

I had heard this threat before, but it never amounted to anything. They didn't want to get fired, they just wanted to make me afraid. And it worked, because even though they hadn't done anything yet didn't mean they weren't going to. They were certainly capable of it. Guys like Ronny Neil and Scott had no real future, not one they could imagine or look forward to. The end of high school had always meant that I could put the worst behind me; for Ronny Neil and Scott, it meant that the best was over. They were entirely capable of doing something horrible and irreversible, of sending themselves to jail, all on a whim.

My clenched determination not to waver before them was beginning to crumble. I'd seen too much today, and now I could feel the tears welling back somewhere in my throat. I needed to find some way to end this.

"Just what do you boys think you're doing?"

We all turned around. Sameen Lal came storming out of the registration office, a paddle I somehow recognized as a cricket bat in one hand. He was in his forties, slender and tall, and had a thick head of black hair, well-defined cheekbones, and small, intense eyes, a natty little mustache. We stayed in his motel many times, and he recognized some of us and had opinions about the ones he recognized. He and his wife had singled me out for friendly waves, a "Good morning," a sympathetic nod at night. They somehow knew my name. They also appeared to understand that Ronny Neil and Scott were bad news.

"I smell something illegal," Sameen said. "I want you boys to clear out of here."

"How you doing, there, Semen? I smelled it, too," Ronny Neil said. "I think Lem here's been smoking ganja. Best you should call the police and turn him in."

Hardly my idea of a good joke, tonight less so than ever. Fortunately, Sameen understood what he was dealing with.

"I find your story very unlikely. Now, this is my motel, and I'm telling you to clear off, or I'll report this to your boss."

"I wouldn't do that if I were you. I'd hate to see this here motel of yours burn to the ground, if you take my meaning."

"His meaning is arson," I said, working hard to sound dry now that my rescuer was here.

"I never threatened nothing," Ronny Neil said. "You just remember that when this here place burns down that I never threatened nothing."

"I do not want to hear your threats," Sameen said. "You are a pair of very bad boys. Now, clear off, I said."

"Okay, then." Ronny Neil took hold of my arm and began to lead me away. "Let's go."

Sameen raised the cricket bat. Only a few inches, but it was clear he meant business and that he understood a lot more than his retiring demeanor suggested. "Let go of him, and clear off by yourselves."

"I don't like the way you're ordering us around, Semen," Ronny Neil said. "You don't decide who goes where, now, do you?"

The two of them stared at each other, each waiting for something definitive to happen. Over by the pool, above the throb of conversation and music, I heard a few words, unmistakably Chitra's voice, and I wanted to find some way to excuse myself. For her sake, yes, but for my own, too. I didn't want to be there to witness more violence, not even if it meant Ronny Neil having his head bashed in by a vigilante wicket keeper.

"Excuse me, Mr. Lal, you've got a customer waiting for you, sir, so if you don't mind, I'll look out for Lemuel."

The assassin walked toward us with an easy if slightly slouched gait. He had a spirited grin, and one hand was up in a half wave. Ronny Neil, Scott, and Sameen stared. They stared at this crazy-looking guy with his wild white hair and gangling enthusiasm.

"I'm Lemuel's friend," the assassin said to Sameen. "He's okay now."

"How do you know my name?" Sameen asked.

"It's inscribed on your cricket bat."

Sameen squinted with suspicion. "Can I leave you with him?" he asked me.

I nodded. I was afraid to do anything else.

Sameen nodded back. "You come see me if you have any more problems," he said to me, and then went back to his office.

I liked that Sameen had come out to help me. I was grateful, even touched, but I'd never believed that this inoffensive, nearly invisible man, even with his bat, would be a match for Ronny Neil and Scott. The assassin, on the other hand, was another story.

The brief gust of relief I felt was gone in an instant. The assassin might get Ronny Neil and Scott to back off, but I couldn't help feeling I was better off with Ronny Neil and Scott. I wanted to beg them not to leave me alone with him.

"What do you want?" Ronny Neil asked, his voice slow and viscous. He held himself straight, but he was a good three inches shorter than the stranger.

"Just looking for Lemuel," the assassin said. He put a hand on my shoulder and began to lead me toward the pool.

I didn't want to go. I wanted to cling to something, to resist. But there was no resisting him, and I went.

"That your boyfriend?" Ronny Neil called.

I ignored them. But the assassin didn't. He turned and cocked his thumb and index finger into a gun and fired invisible digit bullets at each of them.

How frightened should I be? I wondered. I had already known he was down here. I had been coming to the pool because he was there. And we were in public. For all that, however, I felt the chill of terror simply from his proximity.

As though he belonged, as though he were the host and I the visitor, the assassin led me to the throng of bookmen by the pool. For a criminal, he didn't fear crowds much.

In my haze, I didn't see her come up to us. But then there she was. "I've met your friend," Chitra said, gesturing toward the assassin with her red-tipped fingers. She stood next to me, smiling warmly, even goofily, as if she'd started in on a beer that would be one too many. And talking to me — our first exchange of the weekend. For all my fear, I felt the thrill at hearing her voice, which was soft and high, the accent sort of British and sort of not. "He's quite funny."

I grabbed a tall boy, popped it open, and drank without tasting, trying not to gulp. "Yeah, he's a great guy," I said to Chitra. I then turned to the killer. "What are you doing here?" I tried to keep the trembling out of my voice, tried to hit the tone I would have used with anyone I knew who had turned up unexpectedly. I wildly missed the mark.

"Looking for you, Lemuel. Will you excuse me for a minute?"

"Of course," Chitra said.

The assassin put his hand on my back, pushing me away from the crowd. I didn't much care for him touching me in that way, in part because he was a killer, but also because people already were quick to label me as gay. Not that they really much contemplated my sexual proclivities, but the insult came easily to guys like Ronny Neil and Scott, for whom "faggot" interchanged nicely with "pussy" and "Jew-boy."

The assassin stopped by the candy machine that rested between the two public bathrooms. The nauseatingly sweet scent of deodorizer wafted out.

"Why'd you go back to the trailer, Lemuel?" the assassin asked.

So there it was, the reason he had followed me here. I felt the *whoosh* of panic in my ears. I'd been caught. But caught at what, exactly? Maybe, I tried to tell myself, I should relax. Now that I knew what it was, I could deal with it. Maybe. On the other hand, a guy who resolved his problems by killing now had a bone to pick with me, and that was discouraging.

"I didn't have a choice." The words tumbled out, hasty and hollow. Nothing in the assassin's body language suggested menace, but I had to believe that I was talking to save my life. "I accidentally handed the wrong credit app to my crew boss." I explained the rest, how Bobby wanted to go back, wouldn't take no for an answer.

The assassin considered my explanation for only a matter of seconds. "All right," he said. "But your pit boss didn't see anything strange?"

I shook my head. "He just rang the doorbell and knocked, and then we took off."

"Because it looked kind of funny to me," the assassin said. "From where I was watching, it looked funny."

"Yeah, I know. But I couldn't do anything about it."

"I guess there's no harm done, huh?" He gave me a little pat on the shoulder. "And I got to meet that nice girl." He leaned closer. "I think she likes you," he said in a stage whisper.

"Really? What did she say?" The absurdity of the question, of the conversation, descended on me at once, and I blushed.

"She said she thought you were cute. Which you are, in a timid sort of way."

"Can I get my driver's license back?" I wanted to hear more about what Chitra had said, I wanted to interrogate the assassin, get every detail of what she said, how she said it, how it came up, her body language, her expression. I almost began the interrogation, but I had to remember that this was not a friend, not someone with whom I could talk about a girl. I was also eager to change the subject from the very probably gay assassin's evaluation of my cuteness.

He shrugged. "Okay." He reached into his pocket and pulled it out. "But I've got your name and address memorized, so, you know, I can find you if you decide you want to be a jerk about this. But I don't think that's going to be a problem. And, hell. It's one thing to frame someone for murder, kind of another to make him wait on line at the DMV."

"As long as you have your sense of priorities in order." I put the license back in my pocket, strangely comforted. The assassin was acting reasonable, so maybe I really didn't need to worry. I couldn't believe it, though. The fact that he wasn't always, at every moment, homicidal didn't change what he'd done, and it didn't make me worry about him any less.

I was about to say something that I hoped would encourage his departure when I saw something in my mind, saw it in a cinematic flash. We'd been right there, cleaned up all around it, but there was something we missed. "Fuck," I whispered.

The assassin raised one eyebrow. "Yes?"

"The checkbook." It came out like a croak. "Karen wrote a check for the books, and she wrote a note in her checkbook. The receipt. I was the only one working that area. The cops will be able to figure out it was me."

"Crap." The assassin shook his head. "Why didn't you think of that before?"

"I wasn't exactly prepared for this," I yelped. "I'm not a professional. I didn't have a list of things to tick off."

"Yeah, you're right. You are right." He stood for a moment, still, processing the new information. "Okay, Lemuel. We've got to go back."

"What? We can't."

"Well, we have to. Otherwise you, my friend, are going to jail."

"I don't want to go back there," I said in a quiet voice. "I can't do it."

"You want me to go by myself? To save your butt? That's hardly fair."

I thought to say that I wasn't the one who'd killed Bastard and Karen in the first place, but I knew how the words would sound coming out of my mouth, absurd and petty all at once. And you just didn't get petulant with a killer.

The assassin looked at me, cocked his head like a deer in a petting zoo. "You're not afraid of me, are you, Lemuel?"

It might have sounded odd or creepy, but in fact there was something kind of touching about it. The killer didn't want me to be afraid.

"You know . . . ," I began. I didn't know where to take it.

"I told you. I'm not going to hurt you. You're going to have to trust me, now, because we're in this together."

"Fuck this," I announced. "And fuck you, too." Then, on second thought, I added, "Nothing personal, I mean, but this isn't me. This isn't my life. I'm not involved in killings and assassinations and break-ins. I can't be part of this. First thing in the morning, I'm going to call a cab, go to the bus station, and go home."

"That's a great idea," the assassin said. "Running away is a reasonable strategy sometimes. There are some things that should be run away from. The only problem is, Lemuel, this one is going to come running after you. I understand that you want to be done with it all, and I want you to be done with it, but for that to happen, you're going to have to see it through. You run away now, all eyes are going to be on you."

I didn't want to accept it, but I knew it was true. "I can't believe this."

"I don't blame you," the assassin said, "but denial is not going to get you through this. Lemuel, *I'm* going to get you through this."

He gazed at me, a beatific smile on his pale skin, and I believed it. Inexplicable as it was, I believed it. The rational thing would have been to run screaming, to barricade myself in the room and call the cops. That was the only way I might get out of it, but the assassin was so smooth, so crafty, I couldn't quite believe that I would get the better of him. If I called the cops, I'd end up in jail, and if I rebuffed the assassin, I'd end up in jail. I didn't want to go anywhere with him. He was a killer, and I didn't want to be alone with a killer.

"Okay," I breathed.

"Now, we have to go get that checkbook. The two of us, okay? You can do this."

I nodded, unable to summon any words.

The assassin drove a slightly beat-up Datsun hatchback, charcoal or gray or something. It was hard to tell in the dark. I had vaguely imagined he would drive an Aston Martin or a Jaguar or something James Bond–ish, with ejector seats, retractable machine-gun turrets, a button that would instantly turn it into a speedboat. Mainly it had old magazines and empty orange juice cartons cramping the floor on the passenger side. There was a pile of paperback books on the backseat—books with odd titles like *Animal Liberation* and *The History of Sexuality, Volume One*. How many volumes did a history of sexuality require?

I'd been nervous getting in. We weren't allowed to leave the motel, and we weren't allowed to go anywhere with friends who might live in town. If I had reported Ronny Neil and Scott's harassment, I had no doubt that they would have thrown themselves into paroxysms of outrage at my tattling, acting like a baby. I also knew they would not hesitate to turn me in if they saw me leave. Still, so what if they did? Given the enormity of the crime I was covering up, slipping out at night didn't seem all that terrible.

The assassin kept his eyes straight ahead of him, hands at two and ten o'clock on the wheel. He looked calm and comfortable, just an ordinary evening of an ordinary life. I felt neither calm nor comfortable. My heart pounded, my stomach churned and the nausea returned, this time interlaced with glutinous chunks of fear. Leaving in pursuit of the checkbook had seemed like my only move, but now I had to wonder if I had just signed on to my own death.

"Why are you going to such trouble to help me?" I asked, mostly just to break the horrific silence. The assassin had some kind of strange, hollow, thudding music playing softly from his tape deck. The singer groaned that love would tear him apart again. "You could just fuck me over if you wanted to."

"I could. You're right. But I don't want to."

"Why?"

"To begin with, if the cops get you, there's always a chance that you'll lead them to me. It's unlikely, but it could happen. Better they should get no one than get you. Besides, it would be wrong for you to go to jail for this. Even if you were arrested and acquitted, that would be monumentally unfair if I could prevent it. I did what I did to those people because it was the ethical thing to do. It hardly makes sense to let someone else suffer for my convenience. What's the point of behaving ethically if it's going to have unethical consequences?"

"You want to tell me why it was ethical to kill them?"

"Melford."

"What?"

"Melford Kean. That's my name. I figured, you know, now that we're working together, you ought to know my name. So maybe you'll trust me. And now you don't have to think of me as 'the killer' or something." He thrust out his right hand.

Feeling fully the absurdity of it, I shook. He had a firm shake, but Melford Kean's hand felt thin and precise, like a musical instrument. It wasn't the hand of a killer—more like that of a surgeon or an artist. And the calm confidence of his shake helped to distract me from the notion that his giving me his name didn't make me feel safer, it made me feel less safe. I knew his name. Didn't that make me a danger to him? I didn't point that out, however. Rather, I said, "I've been thinking of you as 'the assassin.'"

"That's sort of cool. The assassin. Mysterious agent of unknown forces." He laughed.

I didn't get why it was funny. I thought it was more or less true.

"Since we're friends and all," I proposed, "maybe you can tell me why you killed them."

"I can't, Lemuel. I'd like to, but I can't because you're not ready to hear it yet. If I tell you, you'll say, 'He's crazy,' and your opinion of me and what I do will be set in stone. But I'm not crazy. I just see things more clearly than most people."

"Isn't that what crazy people say?"

"Point taken. But it's also what people who see more clearly say. The question is when to believe those who say it. You know about ideology?"

"You mean like politics?"

"I mean ideology in the Marxist sense. The way in which culture produces the illusion of normative reality. Social discourse tells us what's real, and our perception of reality depends as much on that discourse as it does on our senses. Sometimes even more. You have to understand that we're all peering at the world through a gauze, a haze, a filter—and that filter is ideology. We see not what's there, but what we're supposed to believe is there. Ideology makes some things invisible and makes some things that aren't there seem like they're visible. It's true not just of political discourse, but of everything. Like stories. Why do stories always have to have a love component? It seems natural, right? But it's only natural because we think it is. Or fashion. Ideology is why people in one era might think their clothes look normal and neutral, but twenty years later they're absurd. One minute striped jeans are cool, the next they're a joke."

"So, you're above all that?" I asked.

"The striped jeans? Yes. But for the most part, I'm bound up in ideology the same as everyone else. Yet knowing that it's there grants us some small power over ideology, and if you squint, you can see a little more clearly than most. That's really the best you can hope for. Because we're all the products of ideology, none of us, even the smartest and the most aware, most revolutionary, can escape it—but we can try. We have to always try. And maybe you can try, too, so when I see you squinting, I'll tell you."

"That sounds like an awful lot of crap to me." I wished I could take it back the minute I said it.

"Look, I know it's bogus to just leave you in the dark, so let me ask you a question. I don't think you'll be able to answer it right now, but when you can, I'll know that you are able to see past our cultural blinders. Then I'll be able to tell you why I did what I did. Okay? . . . Good. Now, prisons have been around for many centuries, right?"

"Is that your question?"

"No, there'll be a whole bunch of little questions. They'll be leading up to the big question. I'll tell you when we get there. So, prisons, right? Why do we send criminals to prisons?"

I peered out the window into the darkness. Dark houses, dark streets rolling by in the middle of the night. People quietly sleeping, watching TV, having sex, eating late night snacks. I sat in a car talking about prisons with a crazy man. "For doing things like killing people in their mobile homes?" I ventured. It was like the grammar lesson in the convenience store. I needed to learn to shut up.

"You're a funny guy, Lemuel. We send them to prisons to punish them, right? But why? Why that punishment?"

"What else do you want to do with them?"

"Hell, you could do lots of stuff. Let's say someone is a housebreaker, slips into homes, takes jewelry, money, whatever. Doesn't hurt anyone, but just takes stuff. There are lots of ways to deal with him. You could kill him, you could cut off his hands, you could make him wear special clothes or give him a special tattoo, you could make him do community service, you could provide him with counseling or religious training. You could look at his background and decide he needs more education. You could exile him. You could send him to study with Tibetan monks. Why do we use prisons?"

"I don't know. That's what we use."

Melford took a hand off the steering wheel for a moment so he could point at me. "Correct. Because that's what we use. Ideology, my friend. From the moment of birth, we are trained to see things a certain way, and that way seems natural and inevitable, not worth questioning. We look at the world and we think we see the truth, but what we see is what we are supposed to see. We turn on the television and happy people are eating at Burger King or drinking Coke, and it makes perfect sense to us that burgers and Coke are the path to happiness."

"That's just advertising," I said.

"But advertising is part of the social discourse, and it shapes our minds, our identities, as much as — if not more so than — anything our parents or schools teach us. Ideology is more than a series of cultural assumptions. It makes us subjects, Lemuel. We are subject to it, so that we serve culture rather than culture serving us. We see ourselves as autonomous and free, but the limits of our freedom have always already been delineated by the ideology that provides the border of our tunnel vision."

"And who controls the ideology? The Freemasons?"

He smirked at me. "I love conspiracy theories. The Freemasons, the Illuminati, the Jesuits, the Jews, the Bilderberg Group, and my personal favorite: the Council on Foreign Relations. Great stuff. But where these conspiracy theorists go wrong is that they see the result as evidence of schemers. To them, because there's a conspiracy, there must be conspirators."

"And that's wrong?"

"Dead wrong. The machinery of cultural ideology is on autopilot, Lemuel. It is a force—like a boulder going down a hill. It is going somewhere, picking up speed, and damn close to unstoppable, but there is no intelligence behind the boulder. It is beholden to physical laws, not its own will."

"What about the rich guys in smoke-filled rooms who plot to make us eat more fast food and drink more sodas?"

"They're not driving the boulder. They're being crushed by it, just like the rest of us."

I took a polite moment to consider this idea, and then I moved on. "This isn't helping me with the prison question."

"It's pretty basic, really. Because of our ideology, sending criminals to prison strikes us as inevitable. Not as a choice, one option of many, but as *the* thing. Now, let's go back to our hypothetical housebreaker. What is supposed to happen to him in prison?"

I shook my head and smiled at the absurdity of it all, playing this peripatetic game with a killer. And it was absurd, but the thing was, I enjoyed it. For the few seconds that I could forget who Melford Kean really was, what I had seen him do earlier that evening, I enjoyed talking to him. Melford held himself as if he were important, as if he knew things, really knew them, and this whole business with prisons might not make sense, but I felt sure it would lead to something, and to something interesting, too.

"I guess he's supposed to consider his crimes and feel miserable about his imprisonment so that when he gets out he won't do it again."

"Okay, sure. Punishment. Go to your room for talking fresh. Next time you want to talk fresh, you won't since you know what'll happen to you. Punishment, yes, but also punishment as rehabilitation. Take a criminal and turn him into a productive citizen. So, when you take a housebreaker and you send him to jail, what do you think happens to him? What does he learn?"

"Well, I guess in reality he doesn't really rehabilitate. I mean, it's pretty common knowledge that if you send a housebreaker to prison, he comes back an armed robber or a murderer or a rapist or something."

Melford nodded. "Okay, so criminals go to prison and learn how to become better criminals. Does that sound about right?"

"Yeah."

"You think President Reagan knows that?"

"Probably."

"What about our senators and representatives and governors? They know?"

"I guess. How could they not?"

"Wardens? Prison guards? Policemen?"

"They probably know better than most."

"Okay, are you ready for the big question? Everybody knows that prisons don't work to rehabilitate. If, in fact, we know they do just the opposite, which is to say they turn minor criminals into major ones, why do we have them? Why do we send our social outcasts to criminal academies? There's your question. When you can answer it, and you know the answer is right, I'll tell you why I had to do what I did."

"What is this? Like a riddle?"

"No, Lemuel. It's not a riddle. It's a test. I want to see what you can see. And if you can't at least try to peer past the gauze, there's no point in knowing what's on the other side, because no matter what I say, you won't be able to hear it."

Melford made a left onto Highland Street, where Bastard and Karen had made their home up until the time of their murder. We cruised about halfway down the block, and I wondered if he was planning on stopping right in front of the trailer. Probably not, I decided. Just casing the neighborhood first.

That turned out to be a smart move, since when we drove past we saw that there was a cop car in the driveway. We almost missed it because the lights were off. No headlights, no blue and red flashes of strobing disaster. In the darkness, with no car lights and no porch lights, a policeman in a brown uniform and a wide hat stood talking to a woman, one hand on her shoulder. And she was crying.

Chapter 9

"COME ON," Melford said once we made it safely past the cop, who didn't hop in his car and come chasing after us. He didn't even notice us. "What did you expect? They had to find the bodies sooner or later. You can't be surprised."

"I was hoping we could get the checkbook," I said, my tone shrill and nearly hysterical.

"Right. The checkbook. Well, the check wasn't written out to you, was it? It was written out to a company?"

"Educational Advantage Media. That's who I work for."

"Holy cow. You've got to love their shamelessness. So, how will they know you were the one providing the educational advantage?"

"I was the only one working that area. Plus my fingerprints are all over the trailer. If they sample everyone's, they'll come up with a match for me. Fuck," I added. I pounded my knee with the palm of my hand.

"Doesn't prove anything. So, you went there, you tried to sell them some books, it didn't work out. You have no motive. If you just sit tight, you'll be fine." Melford placed a hand gently on my shoulder.

Great. Now the gay assassin is going to make a pass at me. "That isn't my idea of a solution. Sitting tight and being acquitted."

The hand, mercifully, went back to the steering wheel. "It won't get past the grand jury."

"Wow, that's comforting. Next you'll cheer me up by promising me a sentence of nothing more than time served. Just a few minutes ago, you were talking about how unfair it would be for me to even be arrested."

"Okay, okay." He held up a hand as if I were his nagging wife. "I'll think of something."

Melford parked the car, and for the first time since we saw the police cruiser outside Karen and Bastard's trailer, I examined my surroundings. We were outside a bar or something like a bar—a run-down-looking shack of a building with peeling white paint and a couple of dozen vehicles, mostly pickups, parked out front. The parking lot was an empty patch of land, pounded down by the weight of tires and drunks.

It wasn't exactly like the music screeched to a halt when we walked in, but it might as well have. Men looked up from their beer. Men looked up from the pool table. The men at the bar craned their necks to look. No women that I could see. Not a single one.

Part of me wanted to believe that Melford knew exactly what he was doing, but the bar seemed to me a very bad idea. The braggadocio of David Allan Coe blasted from the jukebox and did a fair job of drowning out the sound of blood thumping in my ears. The sight of the cop had so terrified me that a cold pain had ripped across my body, as though someone had stabbed me in the heart with an icicle.

The place was a longish room with a concrete floor and cinder-block walls with a "Miller Time" clock, a flashing Budweiser sign, and a giant poster of buxom Coors girls. There were no chairs, just picnic tables and benches, and in the far corner stood a large, old-fashioned jukebox—the kind with the rounded top. Closer to the surprisingly ornate wooden bar were four well-kept pool tables, all of them occupied. As far as I was concerned, it meant that there were, at any given moment, eight rednecks with weapons at the ready.

Melford led the way to the bar, where we took a seat while he waved over the bartender, a burly, ponytailed man who looked a hard-lived fifty—haggard, with multiple burns on his hands that suggested he'd been letting someone jab at him all night with a lit cigarette. Melford ordered two Rolling Rocks, which the bartender set down with a skeptical thud. I eyed the faded blue tattoos that crept up his forearm. He eyed my turquoise knit tie, which I wished I had remembered to take off. Behind us, pool balls cracked with sharp menace.

"Four dollars," the bartender said. "You boys want something to eat before the kitchen closes up? Got good burgers here, but Tommy, the cook, is about fifteen minutes away from being too drunk to man the grill."

"Got that on a timer?" Melford asked.

"Just gotta watch the color of his face. We're about fifteen minutes away now from him passing out or sitting in the corner and crying. We also take bets on which it's going to be."

"I'll have to wait until I know Tommy better."

"Fair enough, but the smart money tonight is on tears. So, you boys want burgers?"

Despite everything that happened, I realized I was hungry, a hollowed-out sort of hunger that left me feeling on the brink of organ failure. "I'll have one," I said. "Medium rare."

"You want fries or onion rings?" he asked.

"Onion rings."

"Just an order of onion rings," Melford asked, picking at the label on his beer bottle.

"You got it. One burger with rings and one order of just rings."

"No burger at all," Melford corrected him. "I'm not having anything, and he'll just have an order of onion rings. Better make it a double. He looks hungry."

The bartender leaned forward. "How is it that you know what your friend wants more than he does?"

"How is it you know your cook's going to be crying and not sleeping?"

The bartender tilted his head in a gesture of concession. "You got a point."

Melford smiled. "Onion rings." He put a five on the bar. "Keep the change."

The bartender gave him a half nod.

"I have to eat onion rings?" I asked. "Is that part of the secret code of ideology, too?"

"Sort of. You want to hang out with me, you have to give up eating meat."

"I don't want to hang out with you. I want you out of my life, and I want this day out of my life. Isn't it enough of a punishment to hang out with you? I have to give up burgers, too?"

"I can understand how you feel," Melford said. "I don't take it personally. It's been a big day for you."

"Thanks for being so freaking understanding." I looked away and took a breath to calm myself. I had to remember that just because Melford said

Karen and Bastard had it coming didn't mean they had. It might be best not to piss him off. So I changed the subject. "No meat? What, are you some kind of a vegetarian?"

"Yes, Lemuel, in observing that I don't eat meat, you have correctly deduced I'm a vegetarian. And you know what? If you knew how animals were tortured, you'd give up eating meat on your own. But you don't know, and you probably don't care, so I'm forcing you to give up meat. We'll backtrack later and you'll learn why. For now, you can follow me and walk the ethical path."

"I'm going to take ethics lessons from you?"

"Funny how that works."

"I've never met a vegetarian before," I said. "No wonder you're so thin."

"Are you my mother? Is my mother wearing a latex mask or something? Holy crap, Lemuel. Just don't eat anything that involves killing or exploiting any animals, and you'll be okay. And I don't want to hear about how I'm a fine one to talk. If we only ate evil animals who'd made bad ethical choices, then that would be good enough for me. I'd sooner eat those two in the trailer park than a hamburger."

"You're not doing a good job of convincing me that you're not crazy."

"Let's talk about something more pleasant. Tell me about that charming lady of yours. What was her name? Chanda?"

"Chitra," I said, in part feeling like an idiot for talking about this while such a horrible crisis was in the hopper and in part wanting to thank Melford for giving me the chance to talk about her.

"She gonna be your girlfriend?" he asked, not a hint of mockery in his voice.

I shrugged, vaguely embarrassed. "I've got some more pressing things to worry about at the moment. Besides, I hardly know her. I only met her last week."

"You only met me today, and look how close we are."

I chose to ignore that. "I don't see how anything could happen. I've got to work all year to save money for college, and she goes to Mount Holyoke in a couple of months."

"There's always the long-distance relationship," he pointed out.

"I guess. It sounds like it would be hard to keep up, with all the distractions and everything. But I suppose it's less frightening when she's going to a girls' school."

"Women's college."

"What?"

He sipped at his beer. "It's not a girls' school. It's a women's college."

"Who, if I may ask, cares?" I was in no mood for stupid nitpicking.

"I care. And you do, too. Words count, Lemuel, they have power and resonance. There will never be true equality without gender-sensitive language."

It was at that moment that something hard smacked me in the back of the head. It came on suddenly, and it startled me more than it hurt. I turned around, and two men with pool cues stood there. Laughing.

They both wore faded jeans and T-shirts—one was tattered and black, the other was pale yellow and said BOB'S OYSTERS across the front. Underneath there was a picture of an oyster with the words *Shuck me* coming out of its—I don't know, mouth, oyster hole, or whatever they call it.

Against the tightening of my throat and the pounding of my heart, I felt a raging anguish building inside. The anguish of *Why me?* There were two of us sitting there. I, as far as I knew, looked like just an ordinary kid. I had a tie, sure, but so what? Melford, on the other hand, with his freaky, post-electrocution bleached hair, would surely be a better target. Instead, they went for me. They always went for me.

The silence lasted less than a couple of seconds. They stared. I looked away.

"You guys are kind of far from the pool table, aren't you?" Melford said.

He's going to kill them, I thought, numb now with powerlessness. There's going to be more killing, right here. I'm going to have to watch more people die, a whole room full of them.

Bob's Oysters grinned, showing a mouth full of nicely browning teeth. "Maybe so," he said. "What you want to do about it?"

"Me?" Melford shrugged. "I don't really want to do anything about it. What do you want to do about it?"

"What?" he asked.

"What?" Melford asked.

"What did you say?"

"What did *you* say?"

"I don't know what in fuck you're up to."

"To be honest, I'm not up to anything."

"I don't like no faggots coming in here," said the one in the black T-shirt.

"I think our foreign policy in El Salvador is misguided," Melford said.

The black T-shirt guy knit his brow. "What the shit are you talking about?"

"I don't know. I thought we were just saying, you know, stuff we think. Your comment seemed pretty random, so I figured I'd come up with one of my own." He lifted his beer and drank down half the bottle, finishing it off with a mighty gulp. He wiggled it at them, documenting its emptiness. "You want another beer?"

"What's it to you?"

"Nothing. I was just going to order up some beer, and since we're having a conversation, it seemed polite to order one for you. You want it?"

The guy paused as his desire for beer clashed with his pointless anger. Maybe if Melford had seemed nervous or twitchy or afraid, it might have gone differently, but I was already beginning to understand the power of Melford's calm.

"Okay, sure," said the black T-shirt guy. He blinked rapidly and bit his lip, as though he had misunderstood something and now didn't want to admit it.

The two pool players exchanged glances. Bob's Oysters shrugged.

Melford signaled the bartender and ordered the beers. The pool players took theirs, the black T-shirt nodded his thanks at Melford, and he and his friend wandered back over to the table. They were dazed, not looking at each other.

"What the hell," I whispered into a basket of steaming onion rings, which had arrived during the confrontation. "I thought we were going to get our asses kicked."

"I didn't. See, that guy figured one of two responses—I'd fight him or I'd turn coward. All I did was take a different angle, and suddenly the threat of violence is gone. Nothing to it."

He made it sound so simple. "Yeah. What happens if he decided to knock you off your stool and go upside your head with the pool cue?"

Melford patted his pocket. "Then I'd have killed him."

I let that hang in the air for a moment, unsure if the answer pleased or terrified me.

"Why didn't you just kill them anyway?"

"I'm willing to defend myself, and I'm willing to fight for what's right, but I'm not indiscriminate. All I wanted was to get out of the situation without you getting hurt, and I took care of it in the way I thought would cause the least harm."

I stared at him, feeling not only relief and gratitude, but a strange sort of admiration. It was then that I first realized that, in the same way I liked it when Bobby praised me for books well sold, I liked Melford's attention, too. I liked that Melford seemed to like me, wanted to spend time with me. Melford was *somebody*—a crazy, violent, and inexplicable somebody, but a somebody all the same and, as I'd just seen, an occasionally heroic somebody.

"What are we going to do about the checkbook?" I asked.

"We're going to wait."

"For what?"

"Well, you know where that mobile home is located? What the jurisdiction is?"

I shook my head.

"The city of Meadowbrook Grove, a remarkably unpleasant little slice of land carved out of the county, that consists of a very large trailer park and a small farm with a hog lot. The cop you saw outside the trailer is the chief of police. Also the mayor—a monumental creep named Jim Doe. And he doesn't much like the county cops. Chances are he's going to hold off on calling the real cops until the morning. Otherwise he'll have to be up all night. So we're going to wait. We're going to wait until it gets good and late, and then we're going into the trailer, sliding under some yellow crime scene tape, and getting the checkbook." He looked over at my basket. "Can I have an onion ring?"

I didn't know when, if ever, bars around here closed, but this one showed no sign of slowing down at a quarter of three, when Melford tapped me on the arm and said it was time to go. I followed dutifully.

In the car, Melford was playing another tape now, a sad and jangling something that I liked, mostly despite myself. Maybe it was the four beers. "What is this?"

"The Smiths," Melford said. "The album's called *Meat Is Murder*."

I laughed.

"Something's funny?"

"It just seems a little strong," I said. "I mean, if you want to be a vegetarian, that's fine. But meat isn't murder. It's meat."

Melford shook his head. "Why? Why is it okay to expose creatures who have feelings and wants and desires to any pain we choose so we can have unnecessary food? We can get all the nutrients we need from vegetables and fruits and beans and nuts. This society has made the tacit decision that animals aren't really living things, just products in a factory, due no more consideration than automobile parts. So the Smiths are right, Lemuel. Meat is murder."

I probably wouldn't have said it without the beer, but I'd had the beer. "Okay, fine. Meat is murder. But you know what else is murder? Wait, let me think. Oh, yeah. I remember now: murder. Murder is murder. That's right. Killing a couple of people who are minding their own business. Breaking into their home and shooting them in the head. That's murder, too, I think. The Smiths have an album about that?"

Melford shook his head as if I were a kid who couldn't grasp some simple idea. "I told you. They were assassinated."

"But I'm not ready to know why."

"That's right."

"And I'm a bad person for eating meat."

"No, you're a normal person for eating meat, because the unchecked torment and painful slaughter of animals has become the norm in our culture. You can't be judged for eating meat. Up to this point, anyhow. On the other hand, if you listen to what I tell you, if you think about it even a little, and then you go back to eating meat—then, yes, you're a bad person."

"Torment my eye," I said. "It's not like they drag the cows off to dark cells and wake them up for mock executions. The animals stand around, they moo, they eat grass, and when the time comes, they get killed. Their lives are a little shorter than they would be otherwise, but they don't have to worry about starvation or predators and disease. Maybe it's a decent trade-off."

"Sure, that sounds great. Farmer Brown comes out once in a while to pat their rumps or maybe pick a little on his banjo while he chews on a stalk of hay. Wake up, friend. That idyllic farm doesn't exist anymore, if it ever did. Small farms are being absorbed by giant corporations. They're building what are called factory farms, in which the maximum possible number of animals are warehoused in dark buildings, pumped full of drugs to make it possible for them to survive in these unnatural conditions. They're given growth hormones so they'll get big and meaty, even though they don't want to eat. They're given antibiotics so they won't get sick, even though they're spending their whole lives on top of each other. And then you, my friend, nibble on your big, juicy porterhouse, and you know what? You're eating antibiotics and bovine growth hormone. Eat enough beef, and who knows what's going to happen to you. If a woman eats beef and pork and chicken when she's pregnant, what is she passing along to her baby? Besides being unspeakably cruel, this is a public health disaster waiting to happen."

"Yeah, if the public is so threatened, then how come the public doesn't care?"

"The public." He let out a dismissive sigh. "Remember ideology. The public is told meat is safe and good and healthful, and so the public complies."

"So, what do you live on—eggs and cheese?" I asked.

He laughed. "No way. I'm a vegan, man. I don't eat any animal products. None."

"Oh, come on. You can't stand to exploit the labor of a chicken?"

"If you could prove to me the chickens didn't suffer, I'd eat their eggs," he told me. "But you have no idea. Those chickens are packed into cages so tight, they can't even turn around. Their beaks and feet get infected, and they're in agony. Maybe even more than cows and pigs, chickens suffer unspeakable torments, probably because they're birds and we care even less what happens to them. We are talking about animals that never experience a single moment of life without pain, fear, or discomfort. And those are the females. The males born to egg-laying populations are just tossed into sacks until they're ground up alive and fed to the females. You want me to tell you about how dairy cows live?"

"Not especially. I want you to tell me how you live. What is there to eat?"

"At home, my kitchen is very well stocked, and I eat fine. But the truth is, if you're going to be vegan, and you will be, you can't eat out a whole lot unless you're willing to be creative. But you can look at yourself in the mirror and know you've been doing the right thing. Plus, you get the added bonus of feeling more righteous than others. And it makes a great conversation at parties." He gave me a knowing nod. "Women love vegetarians,

Lemuel. They'll think you're deep. You get to college, start fussing about what you can and can't eat, believe me, the women will start conversations about it and they'll swoon over your sensitive soul."

We took another pass by the trailer and saw it was now abandoned. No sign of cops or crime scene, so Melford turned down the stereo and parked at a strip mall lot with a closed convenience store, a dry cleaner, and something that called itself a jewelry store but looked, through the lattice of metal grating, more like a pawnshop. Taped to a phone booth next to the car was another missing pet flyer, this one for a brown Scottish terrier called Nestle.

It was only three blocks, cut mostly through the backs of other mobile homes, to Bastard and Karen's house. The temperature had dropped to the mid-eighties, but the air was still thick with humidity, and the trailer park smelled like a backed-up toilet. None of this seemed to bother Melford, who knew where to find breaks in fences, where to cross over to avoid barking dogs—all of which told me that he had spent a fair amount of time casing this route. So maybe killing Bastard and Karen hadn't been just some random act of violence.

We reached the back of the trailer—which, in fact, had no yellow crime scene tape—and Melford pulled out something that looked like a cheap ray gun from a *Dr. Who* episode—some kind of a handle with multiple wires of a variety of thicknesses protruding. "Pick gun," he explained. "Very handy thing to keep around." Eyes narrowed in concentration, he went at the back door of the trailer for just a moment before we heard a click. Melford pushed the door open while he slid the pick gun back into his pocket.

Now he took out a pen flashlight, which he flipped around the kitchen for a moment. "Huh," he said. "That's funny. Check it out."

I hadn't wanted to look at them again; in fact, I'd taken comfort in the blackness of the room, which allowed me to shield myself from the sight of the no doubt stiff bodies, but I glanced over anyhow, knowing that it was what Melford expected of me. I stared, thinking that Melford's deployment of the word *funny* didn't quite cut it.

Bastard and Karen still lay there, eyes open, stiff as bloody and bloodless mannequins.

By their side was a third body.

Chapter 10

MAYBE IT WASN'T FAIR, but I blamed my stepfather for everything bad that happened that weekend. And sure, it was at least partly Andy's fault, but the odd thing was, it all played out the way it did because of the only two good ideas Andy had ever had, the two ideas that changed my life for the better.

He'd had countless bad ideas—that I should get new clothes no more than every two years, that I should wait until I turned sixteen before getting a learner's permit, that I should clean out the barbecue each time he used it so the best pieces of charcoal could be salvaged for reuse. This one filled me with the most resentment, because when I came in from the garage, covered with sweat and soot, nostrils caked with black powder, coughing up gray phlegm, I found it impossible to deny the Dickensian bleakness of my life.

The first good idea came the summer after my freshman year in high school. Andy Roman had married my mother six years earlier, and I had been gaining weight steadily ever since. My mother said nothing while her son went from skinny to husky to fat, said nothing while I carted away bags of Oreos and boxes of doughnuts to my room to eat during solitary marathon sessions of *Happy Days* and *Good Times* reruns. The apathy, I later learned, originated from the heroic quantities of Valium she took. I thought she was simply inclined to sleepiness and partial to naps. I accepted that some people napped between breakfast and lunch and then after lunch until it was time to start making dinner.

If Andy knew about her little pill fixation—and he must have—he didn't show much concern. Despite her fogginess, in which my mother sometimes wandered from room to room, clutching a plastic soup ladle or pot holder while searching for something she couldn't quite recall, she managed to clean the house and make his meals—and that was all Andy required.

On occasion he'd try to interest her in his obsession with my increasing weight, but my mother just shrugged and muttered observations about growing boys. He wasn't having it, and one day he announced that he would take care of it if she wouldn't. Taking care of it marked the beginning of a disciplined regimen of derision to help slim me down. But six months of calling me Big Booty and helpful suggestions that I get off my fat butt and go outside and play in the fresh air and sunshine failed to achieve significant results, so in a rare moment of intellectual retrenching, he took on a new approach.

"Time for a serious talk," he said to me over breakfast one morning. My mother, staring at us through the slits of her eyes, had already announced that she was going to lie down, so it was just me and Andy.

He was then in his mid-fifties, fifteen years older than my mother and looking like a man taking a nosedive into senior citizenship. He was jowly and liver spotted and had heavy bags under his cloudy green eyes. Despite his harsh assessment of me, he was himself a good thirty pounds overweight. Most of his head still had decent coverage, but what he had was gray and thinning and too long for a man of his age. He played golf with the ceaseless intensity of a Florida lawyer, which he was, and constant exposure to the sun gave his skin the look of an overbaked apple. However, he came from a generation that believed you could never be too tan, and pachyderm skin was far preferable to the shame of pallor.

Andy pushed up his black-rimmed bifocals over his nose, which had become noticeably bulbous in the last two years. "I know you want to go away to college when you graduate high school," he said. "But let's face it. Everyone wants to go away, and what's so great about you that anyplace decent should let you in? Am I right?"

Less than a year earlier, I had realized, in a kind of aesthetic epiphany, that I hated Florida. I hated the heat, I hated the white shoes and white belts, I hated the golf and the tennis and the beaches and the run-down art deco buildings that smelled of old people and the palm trees and the rednecks and the loud transplanted northerners and the clueless Canadians who visited during the winter and the unremarkable sadness of the poor, mostly black, people who fished for their dinner in the stagnant canals. I hated the crabgrass and the sandy vacant lots and poisonous snakes and deadly walking catfish and dog-eating alligators, the unavoidable sharp-spored plants and gargantuan palmetto bugs and fist-size spiders and swarming fire ants and the rest of the tropical mutants that daily reminded us that human beings had no business living here. All of which I knew, on some fundamental but unarticulated level, meant that I hated my life and I wanted a new one. I'd been talking ever since about going away to college, going far away, as though the intervening three years were only a mild obstacle.

"You need to think about how you're going to convince them you're not just another loser," Andy said. He had both his elbows on the white oval breakfast table, and he was practically leaning into his microwaved pancake-and-sausage breakfast.

"I know you don't want to hear it," he said now, "but what you ought to do is join the track team next year. Your grades have been all right"—I had a 3.9 average, which I personally thought was beyond all right—"and being on the school paper is fine, I guess, but athletics really round out your application. And you want them to think you're well-rounded, but not in the way you are now." He inflated his cheeks. "You want them to look at your stuff and think, There's a real go-getter, not, There's a big lardo. They probably already have enough of those."

I understood at once why Andy suggested track, and in a vague way, I was grateful for it. Team sports were not going to get me very far, not after the fifth grade's disastrous experiment with softball. Track, on the other hand, offered certain advantages. It was essentially a solitary sport played in proximity to others. No one was relying on me not to fuck up, at least not in the same way they would if a pop-up to right field came my way. "And, sure," Andy said, "it's not like you've ever been good at running or anything, but with a summer's worth of hard work you could at least be good enough to be the worst guy on the team."

Our house on Terrapin Way encircled a man-made pond in which nameless fish, brightly colored frogs, lumpy-billed ducks, and the occasional itinerant gator made a home, and Andy announced that he had tracked the circumference of the surrounding road at exactly one-half mile. "So, here's the deal," he said, tapping one manicured nail against his fork. "We're going to practice. Between now and when school starts, I'll give you a dollar for every mile you can run and ten dollars for every five consecutive miles you can run."

It had seemed like a nice offer. Hell, if I'm going to be honest, it was a truly generous offer, a rare moment of inspired stepparenting, though I understood it was also about Andy wanting to show just how right he was. Nevertheless, it was a good deal, even though I had never done well with running. In gym class, when the instructor sent us to do laps, I was always the first to surrender into a walk, to hold my cramping side while the other kids whisked passed me, glancing back with contempt. The money might provide motivation for me to improve my prowess, but there was something humiliating in being offered money to do what other kids could do freely and easily.

So I declined. I didn't want to go out there and sweat while Andy watched me struggle to put a half mile under my belt. I didn't want to go huffing past the house while Andy shouted an inevitable, "Keep it going, Big Booty!"

The thing was, I wanted to lose weight. I wanted to diet, but I'd been unable to do so because committing to a weight loss program would be like telling Andy that he'd been *right*, that it was okay that he'd been calling me Fatty and Lard Butt and Butterball all those months.

I knew this track business was a way out. Andy had brought it up only once, which meant going along with it was still more or less uncharged. I could diet while training but pass off the diet as a new way of eating to get in shape. And I could never accept a dime of his money for any of this. I needed to keep Andy out of my slimming.

There was no way I was going to go running around Terrapin Way. Far too many kids from school lived in Hibiscus Gardens, our subdivision, and a few even lived in houses around the pond, and I didn't want them watching—not until I could run with ease, not until I could do five miles. I needed the shield of success, since they also enjoyed calling me Fatty and Butterball, though they went with Lard Ass instead of Lard Butt, not being restrained by a stepparent's sense of decorum. Instead of hitting the road right away, I went to my room, put on my sneakers, turned on the radio, and jogged in place. At first I couldn't do more than ten minutes, then fifteen. Within a week I could do half an hour, and after a week of that I figured I was ready for actual laps.

I imagined my triumphant return to school, looking slim and fit, snappy in the new clothes Andy would have to pay for since the old ones would be too big, were getting too big already. The bullies would now have to find someone else to pick on.

I never really believed it, nor should I have. That sort of transformation is the staple of Hollywood teen movies but never allowed in real life. In the movies, the ugly girl gets new clothes and a new haircut, removes her glasses, and—*gasp!*—she's the most popular girl in school. In real life, when we bottom-feeders try to rise above our station, they pull us down, cut off our limbs, and stick us in a box. Even though I returned that September as fit as any healthy tenth grader, they still called me Lard Ass and continued to do so until I graduated.

But the fantasy was motivation enough. I started running laps while Andy was at work and my mother was off doing errands. I didn't want them to know. Not until I could run five miles without stopping. Doing so turned out to be a lot easier than I would have thought, and six weeks after my first solitary jog, I told Andy I was ready to try out for track next year.

"Fine," he said with an embarrassed shrug. It was clear that he regretted having offered me the money and now wanted to make it as difficult as possible for me to raise the subject.

As it turned out, I did fairly well at track. I made the team and acquitted myself reasonably well at matches. I didn't excel at speed, but I was good at endurance, and in some of the longer races I could outlast some of my opponents well enough to score a third, and occasionally a second, place. It would be good enough to help me get into college, and I wasn't even the slowest guy on the team.

The second good idea came a little more than half a year later, during the winter break of my sophomore year. I had been lying on my bed, reading, when the knock came at the door. It was a good two hours after dinner, and I could hear the TV going from the family room, where my mother would have nodded off on the couch, the still life with apples needlepoint pattern she'd been working on for the past nine months in her lap.

Andy didn't wait for an answer. He opened the door and stuck his head inside. "What's going on in here? Anything naughty?"

I sat up and folded the book open to my spot. Andy said nothing for a moment, just leaned against the doorjamb, grinning fiercely. His thick-framed rectangular glasses had slid down his ballooning nose.

"I think," Andy announced, "you should set your sights on an Ivy League school. Harvard or Yale, preferably, but Princeton or Columbia will do in a pinch. I guess even Brown or Dartmouth, if you had to." Andy had gone to the University of Florida himself, and to a local university of no national reputation for his law degree, but he seemed to feel he knew a lot about the intricacies of the Ivys.

"Of course," he added, "we know we can't rely on your father to help with the money."

My father was living somewhere in Jamaica now, where he worked as a tourist scuba-diving guide and, if overheard conversations could be trusted, smoked prodigious quantities of marijuana. I imagined him sitting on a beach in a circle of glassy-eyed Rastafarians, puffing lazily on a cigar-thick joint. Some of my friends had discovered reggae, but I couldn't stand the political yearnings of Bob Marley, the ganja-fueled rage of Peter Tosh, the self-aggrandizing toasts of Yellowman — not when my father was off living the life of a white rasta. Besides, he had entirely given up on paying child support, and I hadn't heard from him in two years, when he'd placed a drunken call on a warm April afternoon to wish me a happy fifteenth birthday. I was thirteen at the time and had been so since January.

"So maybe it doesn't make sense to go to a place like that," I proposed. I was confused, and presenting a counterargument seemed like the best way to draw out Andy's game. "I mean, if it's so expensive." Going to an Ivy League school had never occurred to me. I'd always believed them reserved for the movie-star handsome and privileged, charming boys and girls with trust funds and easy grins and ruddy complexions from effortless afternoons on the ski slopes.

"If you keep your grades up and you do well on your SATs," Andy prophesied, "you should be able to get a decent financial aid package. Plus this business I set up for you with the track team should help. They'll cut you a deal and you'll take out some loans. And if all of that doesn't cover everything," he announced magnanimously, "we'll work something out."

The seed was planted. I'd always thought of myself as smart, had always thought of myself as capable of doing smart-person things — but going to Harvard or Yale, that was far out of reach, like becoming an astronaut or ambassador to France. Still, Andy had suggested it, and now I wanted it. I wanted the opportunities an Ivy League degree would provide. I could become an important historian or direct movies and go into politics. Once it was on the table, I knew it was the way out, the way to a genuinely non-Floridian future.

The next summer, while visiting my grandparents in New Jersey, I had made arrangements to take a look at Columbia, Harvard, Princeton, and Yale over the course of three separate weekends. When I went to Columbia's Upper West Side campus, it was my first trip to New York City, despite the annual visit to my grandparents, who lived a light-traffic forty-five-minute drive away in Bergen County. I had been instantly seduced by the city and by the campus, and I left with no doubt that Columbia was where I wanted to go.

In fact, the moment the car crossed the George Washington Bridge, I knew that New York was the place that I must have always known about in the hidden recesses of my mind. Maybe I had already absorbed New York from television and movies. I must have seen the city depicted on the screen countless times, but it never signified much of anything but some kind of foreign and urban landscape. In reality, on the ground, with the noise and people and the gum-stained sidewalks littered with trash and teeming with the homeless, it seemed to me something else entirely. I had discovered the anti-Florida.

"Columbia's all right," Andy had assured me, "and if that's the only place you can get in, fine. But it shouldn't be your first choice. Harvard should be your first choice." He folded his arms authoritatively, though the closest he'd ever been to Harvard was Logan Airport to change planes.

As it turned out, it didn't much matter, since Yale, Harvard, and Princeton all said no. Columbia said yes, as had, improbably, Berkeley and my safety: the University of Florida. When I received the admission on a rainy Saturday afternoon, I ran to tell Andy, who was resting on his recliner in the family room, watching golf on television.

"Columbia," he observed. "At least that's something after getting the thumbs-down from Harvard and Yale."

"I just can't believe it," I said. I paced around, too excited to hold still, even for an instant. "Man, living in New York. It's going to be so cool."

Andy's face went long, a sure sign things were about to turn sour. He shook his head as he geared himself up to piss on my cornflakes. "You might want to think twice about this. University of Florida is a good school. If you go to New York, you'll probably get mugged."

"There's millions of people. They can't all get mugged."

"Some people will, but you won't? Is that it? What, you think you're exempt?"

"I don't think it's worth worrying about."

"Well, I got a pretty good education at U of F," Andy said. "What's good enough for me isn't good enough for you?"

"I don't want to go to Florida. I want to go to Columbia. You're the one who told me I should go to an Ivy."

Andy shrugged and looked over my shoulder to watch someone miss a three-foot putt. "And it was a fine idea. And you did try. I'm just saying that you may not want to go to Columbia. Harvard or Yale, sure. But they already said no. Maybe they saw something in your application and they realized you're not Ivy material. Isn't it kind of beneath your dignity to let Columbia have you as sloppy seconds?"

"That is so far beyond stupid that I don't even know the word for it."

"If you had a better vocabulary, maybe Harvard would have let you in. I think a state school education is much better. You don't want to become an Ivy League snob, do you?"

There was no way I was going to let him talk me out of it. The thing about Columbia was that no one would know me there. Unlike the University of Florida, Columbia would not have anyone from my high school or my neighborhood. Most people, when I told them where I was applying, thought I meant South Carolina. When I got there, I would no longer be the loser who had once been fat—I would be whoever I said I was. It was not only an escape from Florida, it was a clean break, maybe the cleanest break I would ever get, could ever hope for. And I knew I wasn't going to squander it.

The day of graduation, while I'd been drinking orange soda with relatives at my house before going out with friends, one of whose cousins was having a party, Andy took me aside.

"You know," he said, "I've been looking over the application material for Columbia. Maybe this isn't the best time, but I don't see how you can afford it. Even with the financial aid and the loans, you're going to need another seven thousand dollars a year. That's almost thirty thousand dollars. Where are you going to get that?"

I looked at the floor. "You said you'd help me out."

"And I have, haven't I?" I didn't ask how, since it would invariably turn into a "food on the table, clothes on my back" kind of thing, and I wasn't interested. "Come on now, Lem. I'm not your father. Your father is off smoking wacky weed and chasing topless natives. Uga buga," he added, bulging his eyes. "Maybe he should pay for it. Have you even asked him?"

"I don't know how to get in touch with him."

"So, you want me to pay for you when you haven't even asked your father?"

"You said you would help," was the best I could manage. It was my graduation, and Andy dropped this bomb as if he'd been saving it for the maximum effect.

"Come on, now. University of Florida is fine."

"I'm not going there," I said, trying to keep the whine out of my voice. "I'm going to Columbia."

Andy smiled and shook his head. "Then I guess you have a lot of money to make this summer, don't you?"

The next day I called the admissions office at Columbia and arranged for a deferment. And then I began doing research. How was I going to save $30,000 in a year? It didn't take me long to realize sales was my best bet. And encyclopedias looked like just the thing to make it happen.

Chapter 11

THAT'S REALLY ODD," Melford said. "Just not the sort of thing you expect."

Death and darkness hid her features, but I could tell the third person was an older woman with a short, fiercely coiled perm. She wore tight jeans and an open blouse, which seemed to me the same color as the darkness. Her heavy tongue protruded from her gaping mouth, like a cartoon creature caught in midstrangle. From the marks on her neck, I guessed that strangling was the way it happened.

"Who is she?" I managed.

"Beats me. But I'm thinking that this is the woman we saw when we drove by before."

"Well, what happened?" I hated how it came out like a whine, but I thought myself entitled. It was bad enough to have witnessed two murders that day, to have been close enough to smell the blood as it came out of Bastard's and Karen's respective heads. Now here was another. I wasn't built for this sort of thing, and the truth was that I had to work very hard if I was going to keep from falling apart. I didn't even know what falling apart would constitute, but I was pretty sure I'd know it when I saw it.

Melford shook his head. "I'm guessing the cop killed her."

"What?"

"Who else? We saw him with her. Now she's dead, just a few feet away from where it happened. Why would the cop leave her alone at the crime scene, where the murderer might get her? And since we know the murderer didn't get her, we have to assume the cop did."

"But it doesn't make any sense."

Melford was about to say something, but he stopped himself when we both heard the sound of wheels on dirt outside and the hum of a motor and then the cutting of a motor.

He shut off the penlight and moved over to the window. "Boogers," he whispered. He then turned to me. "Okay, listen up. The bad news is that there's two guys out there, and one of them is the cop. Out of uniform, but the cop. Now, don't panic. They're in a pickup, and they came with their headlights off, so I doubt this is official police business. We hide, and everything will be fine."

My four beers churned violently, grappling back up to my throat with little acid hooks.

I let Melford pull me by the arm into the smaller bedroom and then to a closet against the far wall—the kind with the folding slatted doors. And it faced out to the kitchen, so we had a decent view of the action. But that wasn't what I noticed about this bedroom. What I noticed was that there was nothing in here but boxes. Some had old shirts and torn jeans sticking out, some were file boxes, but most of them were sealed shut. One of them had OLDHAM HEALTH written along the side with a thick black marker. The walls were bare except for a two-year-old puppies and kittens calendar stuck on October.

This wasn't a kid's room. This wasn't even a room that had once been a kid's room and now was something else. No kids lived here. So why had Karen and Bastard lied to me?

The back door banged open, and I could see, obstructed by the slats, two figures enter, one of them swinging a small flashlight around. It was too dark to see much more than that.

For a moment I felt a fresh wave of panic. What if they had come to look for something—something that might just as well be in a closet as anywhere else? The thought made me have to piss fiercely, and I clenched my teeth as I tried to force back the urge to void my bladder.

At least there was Melford. Melford still had his gun. Melford wouldn't let us get taken. That was the measure of how much my life had changed in the past twenty-four hours. I was now depending on someone to shoot my enemies for me.

"Fucking hell," one of the guys said. "You've got a lot of dead people in here, Jim."

"I know it."

"Jesus, look at them. It was some cold mother that took them down."

"Looks like."

"And you've got no ideas?"

"I ain't got the first fuck of an idea. I mean, it's gotta be about the money. But who? Shit, don't no one know nothing about it but us, those of us in on it. Bastard's been talking, which is the only thing I can figure."

"I guess. But, hell."

"That's about right."

"Shit. Fucking Bastard. With Frank taking off last month, you're fresh out of chemists. B.B. isn't going to like that."

"Yeah, I'm working on it. But I ain't gonna put an ad in the paper."

"Jim, what the fuck was Bastard doing over here anyhow?"

"I don't know." There was something hard in the voice.

"You figure he was boffing that skank? Shit, maybe a couple of years ago, but she was like a fucking corpse, man, all that crank she was doing. I'd sooner fuck some old grandma."

A pause. Then, "Just shut the fuck up, and help me with this shit."

"Uh-oh." A laugh. "You weren't dipping your wick with that, were you? I'll tell you what. I got a couple of grandmas I could introduce you to."

"You want to stand around talking shit all night, or you want to get this done?"

I had been watching through the slat, totally absorbed, as though I were not in a mobile home closet, but in a theater watching the most compelling movie I'd ever seen. I felt strangely calm, outside of myself. And then I didn't feel calm at all. I didn't feel like I was in a theater. I felt hot and cramped and about as terrified as I'd ever felt in my life.

It was because I realized I knew both men. The cop, Jim, was the guy I'd seen at the convenience store, the one who'd given me a hard time about the ginger ale, the same bucktoothed man from the Ford who'd been hassling me outside the trailer. With the possibility of being arrested for murder, I'd managed to anger the crooked chief of police.

The other guy—I couldn't see him well enough to take a look, but I knew the voice. I was sure I knew the voice. From somewhere. I *knew* that other man.

I watched as they laid out a sheet of plastic on the floor and then picked up the body of the older woman and rolled her up. The cop grabbed one end, the familiar man the other, and they hauled her out of the house.

We listened to the near silence punctuated only by the occasional grunt or curse and then the thud of something heavy landing on a flatbed. They were back in a few minutes.

"Shit," the cop said. "The other two are gonna be messy. Wish I brung some gloves or something."

"Fuck me," said the familiar-sounding man. "Someone sure plugged those assholes. Look at the shots. Neat and clean. Looks like they were executed."

"Who died and made you a law enforcement official?" the cop asked. "You been watching too much TV."

"You sure you didn't hurt your leg?" the other one asked. "Looks like you're having trouble walking."

"I told you, I'm fine." The voice terse, grim.

"I heard you suck in your breath a second ago, too, like you were in pain."

"Forget it. Jesus."

They laid out another sheet of plastic and then lifted Karen's body. The cop complained about getting whore brain on his hands, and he wiped it off on his knee while they rolled up the body and hauled it out.

They were panting hard when they returned. "Fucking Bastard," the cop said. He kicked the body, not too hard. Then he kicked him again. It sounded like someone kicking a sandbag. "I don't know what the fuck he did, or who shot his sorry ass, but I figure he deserved it."

"Yeah, well," the other one responded. Then a pause. "You think whoever did this got the money?"

"You know, I never even thought of that, you dumb shit." He let out a derisive snort. "You think I give a shit about them being dead? It's the money. I've already looked through here and been over to his place. Tore it up, but I couldn't find jack. Not even any sign of what he was up to."

"You still think he had something going on the side?" he asked. He then turned away from me, and I couldn't quite hear what he said next, but I was sure it contained the word *Oldham*.

"Had to have been something," the cop said. "I know how much he made, and he had way too much cash, getting his wallet all fat. I just can't figure he made *that* much money doing that bullshit. But I figure he meant to rip me off, disappear with the money. And since I looked every-where else, I have to figure he was hiding it in the waste lagoon."

"You can't be serious," the other man said. "You've got to be dry-humping me. How in hell are we going to find it there?"

"I don't know. There must be a way to drain it or drag it or something. Jesus. I sure wish we didn't have to haul this dead asshole. He don't even deserve to be dumped by me."

"Let's just do it," the other man said. "No room for blanking out here."

And it must have been the term *blanking out*, because I suddenly recognized the second man. It was the Gambler. The Gambler, who ran the door-to-door Champion Encyclopedia operation for the state of Florida. The encyclopedia guru himself was in the trailer, removing the bodies of people Melford had killed. At least, Melford had killed most of them.

Melford shoved me. I must have been making noise, because he flashed a look, visible even in the near total darkness. I got hold of my breathing.

They grabbed Bastard and hauled him out, and when they returned they were gasping for air. There was the *glug-glug* of someone drinking from a bottle. Now they had a bucket and mops and paper towels and a bottle of Formula 409. They still didn't turn on the lights, but they set up a couple of flashlights and got to work erasing all evidence of Melford's crime. It took more than half an hour before they were done.

"Hard to tell with just the flashlight," the cop said, "but I think that'll do her. I'll come back in the morning and do a quick run-through in the light."

"If that fucker was screwing us over and the money's gone, we're going to be in some deep shit. B.B.'ll be in a fucking rage."

"Fuck that asshole. And fuck Bastard. Fuck me!" This last he cried out as if in sudden pain.

"You know, if your leg is bothering you, it's best to see a doctor. Why put it off?"

"Shut the fuck up about the doctor. I'm fine."

"I just think it's best to be safe. Hey! Take a look at this," the Gambler said. "Karen's checkbook."

Melford gave me a gentle tap on the back. I must have been making noise again.

"You figure she had anything in her account?" the cop asked.

"Says here the balance is almost three thousand. How did an ugly-ass skinny-skank rotten-cunt-smelling whore like that get three thousand dollars? I guess it won't hurt to write out a check, though. Make up for some losses. Maybe I can get that numbnuts Pakken to do it. He won't know any better, which will help him get away with it, and it shouldn't be a problem anyhow if he goes across the county line, I figure."

And they left.

We remained in the closet for a good fifteen minutes. They'd done a decent enough job of cleaning up. At least, Melford's penlight didn't pick up any sign of the blood. I figured the FBI could probably scare some up. They had crime labs for stuff like that. But you had to be looking for blood, and if there were no bodies, why would you look?

"All right," Melford said. "Let's get the hell on out of here."

It wasn't until we were back in his Datsun that we dared to talk about it.

"I'm fucked," I said. And I felt fucked. I felt like I was about to fall into the chasm. I felt like I was falling through the sky, just waiting for the impact of when I hit earth.

"I don't think so."

"Yeah? Why not?" I heard my voice getting shrill. "Why aren't I fucked? Tell me why I'm not fucked?"

"Because the guys who have the evidence against you are high-powered felons, that's why. High-powered felons don't seek out the law, Lemuel. They avoid it. They're not going to investigate. They won't even look to see who the checks are made out to."

Except that the Gambler would notice the check to Educational Advantage Media. He would see it in a heartbeat, and he would know who was there. But would the Gambler think it anything but a coincidence? He barely knew me by sight, but he wouldn't imagine that I'd had anything to do with this. Still, it scared the hell out of me. And I dared not say anything about the Gambler to Melford. Melford might think I was too weak a link, affiliated as I was to one of these high-powered felons. He might, quite possibly might, kill me just to be safe.

And there was something else, something that made no sense. "They weren't married," I said aloud.

"What?"

"The people you killed. Bastard and Karen. They weren't married. And they didn't have kids."

"Yeah, well, I could have told you that," Melford said.

"So why did they lie to me?"

"I don't know. Something crazy is going on. Something bigger than I realized."

"Why would the cop be hiding the bodies you killed? And what were they talking about? Bastard's business on the side? What is that? And the missing money?"

"Dunno," Melford said.

"What about Oldham Health?" I asked. "They had some mugs and stuff. Bastard told me he didn't know anything about it, but I kind of got the sense he was lying."

Melford shook head. "I don't know anything about it."

I looked over at him. Melford was lying, too. I couldn't say how exactly I knew, but I knew. We'd been talking about some heavy stuff all night, but there was something in Melford's voice that I hadn't heard, some kind of tension. Whatever Bastard had been involved with, Melford knew exactly what it was.

"The other guy who was with the cop," Melford said. "I wonder who that was."

I didn't say anything. My heart pounded and my head throbbed. I felt the urge to confess, as if it were all somehow my fault, but I kept it quiet.

"Probably just some goon." Melford saved me by answering his own question. "I'll tell you what, though. We have to find out who that woman was, the third body."

"Why do we care?" I asked.

"Because if things don't go our way and they decide they want to risk bringing the law into all of this and the cop finds us and wants to arrest us, we're going to want some leverage. If we can expose them, then maybe we can reach some sort of understanding."

"You want to figure out who that woman was so we're in a position to blackmail the criminally insane cop?"

"Pretty neat, huh?"

Chapter 12

ARLIER THAT NIGHT, Jim Doe had been in the police trailer, waiting for nothing in particular, but something bad all the same.

"How's the gonads feeling?"

Pakken sat across from Doe. His feet were up on the desk, and he was drinking from a mammoth Styrofoam cup of gas station coffee. He'd been working at it for two or three hours now, and it had to be cold as shit.

The question was apropos of nothing, since they'd both been largely still for hours. Pakken was working at one of the word finder books he liked, his pen hovering over the oniony pages. Doe was flipping through a *Sports Illustrated*, not much paying attention to an article on the Dolphins. He was still out of uniform, in his jeans and black T-shirt. Sometimes he felt like relaxing in the police trailer, was all.

Doe could tell that Pakken had just found a hard word. He liked to start a conversation after he found one. He'd talk about anything, really, but sooner or later he'd try to bring it around. "I just found 'substantial,' " he'd say with little-kid pride. These interruptions were annoying as hell under the best of circumstances, but even more so now that Pakken's favorite topic was Doe's testicles.

It had been Pakken who'd found Doe after his unfortunate run-in with that Miami bitch, Pakken who'd gone looking when Doe had not shown up the next day. It was Pakken who'd taken a guess at what might have happened, knowing about where the chief liked to take the ladies—and not a bad bit of police work for such a moron. Doe had still been passed out when Pakken had found him in the early morning. He'd peered into the car's window, a grin stamped onto his flat, wide face capped off by a single massive eyebrow and a caveman cranial ridge. Doe had fluttered his eyelids and said, "My balls. She crushed my balls."

"What happened, Chief?"

His balls were swollen and angry. It hurt even to move his legs. "Bitch attacked me," he mumbled.

Pakken let out a laugh. "Yeah, that's good. She attacked you."

Doe struggled to his feet and pain shot through his balls, but he bit his lip and climbed out of the car. Then he smacked Pakken in the face. Hard. "The fuck you laughing at?"

Pakken gingerly poked an index finger to his cheek. "Why'd you do that?"

"A woman was speeding, you dipshit," Doe said. "Risking her life, the lives of others, and now she's assaulted a police officer. You think that's funny?"

Pakken was still poking at the reddening spot on his face. "Hell. There I was thinking you was just trying to get a blow job off of her."

Now, almost a week later, they sat in the trailer, Pakken with his cold coffee while Doe leaned back in his chair and sipped at his bottle of Yoo-hoo and Rebel Yell. It was kind of a ritual, the two of them lazing around, talking or not talking, but Doe didn't want to look at Pakken's drooping idiot face. His balls were still swollen, still tender. A little bit better. He was nearly certain they were better today than yesterday. He reached into his pants with a tentative hand, and the pressure against his scrotum hurt, hurt like living shit, but maybe a little less than the last time he'd checked. And Pakken had laughed at him. It was a disrespectful thing to laugh at an officer injured in the line of duty. What kind of a sick asshole laughed?

He guessed that Pakken wasn't really sick, just young. His uncle, Floyd Pakken, had been the mastermind behind Meadowbrook Grove. He'd come up with the name, even though they didn't have a meadow, brook, or grove, but it sounded a lot better than Pigshit-Smelling Trailer Park. It had been Floyd's idea to convert the trailer park into an independent municipality, to lower the speed limit, and to watch the cash flow in. And it did. All the residents got free gas and electric, which was no small thing during the summer months of hard-humping air-conditioning. They got free water, free basic phone service. Three or four big barbecues a year, a carnival in the spring, a Halloween shindig for the kids, a Fourth of July party with an up-and-coming country star or two. They were happier than pigs in shit, which, ironically, they had to put up with to get all this. Or, more accurately, they had to put up with the smell of pigs in shit, since the city also incorporated the hog lot on Doe's adjoining family land.

Every year the Office of the Mayor, which consisted, basically, of the mayor, issued a report that detailed income from traffic violations and expenditures in taxes, services, and salaries, and everything just balanced out nice and neat. Maybe a few dollars to roll over to the next year. Why not? No one ever much looked at the report, and no one, near as Doe could tell, bothered to find out if it was bullshit or not. But of course it was bullshit.

Floyd had been a sharp fellow to devise this scam and to put himself at the helm. Doe had always figured that Floyd had something going on other than his mighty generous salary, which everyone knew about since he'd done such a good job of giving back to the city. Doe had suspected, and he'd been the obvious choice for mayor and police chief after Floyd had got himself killed, along with a couple of fourteen-year-old Cuban whores, in an explosive rollover. Two weeks into the job, looking at the records and following the money trail, Doe couldn't stop his perpetual eulogy to Floyd's genius. By two months into the job, he'd been laughing at Floyd for thinking too small. Floyd put twenty or thirty thou a year aside. Good for him. Bless his little heart. Three years later, Doe was tripling that. Easy. And it would be getting even better.

Play it right, be patient, don't be stupid, Doe could be pulling in a hundred thou a year. When he had a million put away, he'd say it was time to retire. He'd head to the Cayman Islands, where his current $130,000 sat nicely nestled. Buy himself a big house and spend the rest of his days drinking strawberry daiquiris and fucking tourists. A man could do worse for himself.

Everything had been going perfectly. The scam with the tickets, the deal with B.B.—all of it. Until now. He couldn't stand waiting around to see if the reporter from Miami turned up. The fact was—and Doe knew this from experience—most women wouldn't say shit about what happened to them. They had this kind of programming, like a robot or something, that the worse you treated them, the less they would do about it. You could overdo that, like he'd done with his ex-wife; but mostly they'd take it, because they knew what would happen if they didn't.

How many of them really wanted to bring this thing to the courts? They knew what would happen.

Tell the truth now. You found His Honor, Mayor Doe, rather handsome, didn't you?

Yes, at first. But—

And you were at least on some level flattered that he wanted to have sex with you, weren't you?

Yes, it was flattering, but—

And at any time during your interactions did you enjoy the sensation of having his unusually massive penis in your mouth? Remember, you are under oath.

I never asked for it.

Did you enjoy it? Answer the question!

Yes! Yes! I'm so ashamed, but I loved it.

Where was the woman who wanted to put herself through that? But Doe had a bad feeling about this reporter. She'd gotten away before she'd had a chance to really get into it. That she'd pounded Doe's nuts might tend to make some folks believe that she really hadn't wanted to suck him off. Plus she was a Miami reporter, and nothing would make her happier than a story on these country bumpkins up here with their speed trap trailer park.

The morning after the incident, after he'd gone home and showered—angling his body to keep the water from hitting his 'nads, keeping his head up so he wouldn't have to look at the purple, swollen horror—he'd managed to get dressed, although the underwear and pants were a bit of trouble, and had gone back to the police trailer and called up the Florida Highway Patrol.

"This is Jim Doe. I'm chief of police and mayor over here at Meadowbrook Grove."

"Is that so?" said the voice on the other end of the phone. Then there was a snicker, half-hidden. They all knew about Meadowbrook Grove.

"Yeah. Look here, this is kind of embarrassing, but I was ticketing this woman last night—"

"I'll alert the media," the smart-ass said.

"I was ticketing this woman last night," Doe continued, "and I guess I let my guard down. She was young and seemed harmless, and, well, she kind of caught me by surprise. She knocked me down with her car door and took off before I could get back up. But I still got her license and registration."

"Is that so?"

"Yeah, it's so. I don't know why she would take off that way, but she must be hiding something, I figure."

"You worked that out, huh?"

"And she knocked me down. She assaulted a police officer."

"She assaulted you *and* a police officer?"

"Now look here. I don't have no beef with you, and I'm sure if it were a highway patrolman she knocked down, you'd have the helicopter dragnet out right now."

"A highway patrolman wouldn't have got knocked down," he said.

"I'm just trying to report a dangerous person. She knocked me down, maybe she takes a gun at one of you boys. I don't know. You telling me I shouldn't have called this in?"

He let out a long sigh. "Fine. Give me the info."

Doe read off the information to them and hung up. He says she tried to get away. She says he tried to attack her. If necessary, he'll concede that it is possible that she might have, for whatever reason, believed he was going to attack her, and he'd be okay with her getting off with a warning this time. But now he'd made it so it was her word against his. That had to be worth something since, days later, he hadn't heard a thing.

Half an hour after the last inquiry. "How's the family jewels?" Pakken asked.

"Whyn't you go and get some speeders?" Doe said.

"I'm off duty, that's why."

"You ain't got no initiative."

"Maybe so, but I got 'initiate,' " he said, turning his book so that Doe could see the word ovaled in red ink.

"Get some tickets or go home."

Pakken must have figured out this meant that Doe wanted to be alone, so the kid grumbled a bit and took his time collecting his worthless shit, but finally he made it out the door ten minutes later. Doe rose to his feet and hobbled, legs wide apart, to the counter, where he took out what he thought of as his law enforcement funnel and added some more bourbon to his Yoo-hoo. He made it back to his desk—with no one around, he didn't have to try to walk as though everything were fine—and put his feet up, spread his legs, gave the injured parties a little room to breathe.

The phone rang. It was probably fucking Pam again; she'd been calling him twice a day to bitch at him about forgetting Jenny's birthday. He'd told her he hadn't forgotten, he'd been involved in some serious police work and hadn't been able to get away. Somehow that argument hadn't convinced her.

Best to let it ring, but he had responsibilities to the community, so he yanked it from the cradle.

"Meadowbrook Grove police."

"I'm looking for *Chief* Doe. This is Officer Alvarez with the Florida Highway Patrol."

"This is Doe." Name like Alvarez, Doe figured he'd have an accent or something, but the guy habloed ingles pretty well.

"Yeah, we're following up on that report you filed. Listen, we spoke to the woman in question. She said you let her off with a warning and that was the end of it."

"What?" Doe swung his legs too quickly, and he had to control the urge to yelp into the phone.

"Yeah, she says you stopped her, gave her a warning, and let her go."

When the fuck have I ever let anyone off with a warning? It almost came out, but he checked himself. "So, is that it?"

"Well," Alvarez said, "sounds to me like one of you isn't telling the truth."

"Now wait a minute," Doe began. Just then the other line began to ring. The pain in his balls, the ringing of the other line. He was going to lose his fucking mind.

"No, you wait a minute," Alvarez was saying. "One of you isn't telling the truth. We can open an investigation if you like, or we can let the matter sit. What do you want to do?"

How was he supposed to know what he wanted to do with his balls aching and the phone ringing? It was on something like its twelfth ring now. Who was it that wouldn't give up?

But the thing was, the woman didn't want to press charges. Maybe that meant she was saving her thunder for her own report. But no, that wouldn't work. She had denied to the state police that there had been an incident. To make public allegations now would be to set herself up as a liar. She'd shut herself and her story down.

"Just drop it, then," Doe said.

"You sure, *Chief*? I hear an officer of the law was assaulted."

"You heard me, señor." Doe figured he was done with this asshole, so he hung up by slamming his finger into the blinking light of the endlessly ringing line. "Meadowbrook Grove police. What's so freaking important?"

A sob and then a pause. "Jim? . . . Jim, is that you? . . . Oh, Jesus. Jim."

The voice was all broken and messed up, choking and crying. A car accident, maybe. If it happened on their turf, it was their problem, which always pissed him right off. Maybe he should buy a tow truck, have a towing service on the side, so at least accidents might be worth a few dollars. Or better yet, haul the cars over the city limits line. Let the county handle it.

Then he placed the voice: Laurel Vieland. Shit, he hadn't spoken to her for five or six years, probably. Not since she went and moved to Tallahassee. But her daughter. Now, that was something else. Karen had been fine a few years back, before the crank. And if she hadn't wanted to give it up back then, she sure had no problems nowadays. No inhibitions at all.

Laurel and Karen were the only mother-daughter team that Doe had ever fucked. Not at the same time—and now he sure as shit wouldn't want to. Still, it was something. And Karen had that daughter. The girl lived with her father up north somewhere, and he knew that the father didn't even let her see Karen, not since Karen went crazy with the crank a couple years back. But there'd be a family reunion one day. Girl would come on home to Meadowbrook Grove, thirteen or fourteen, and Doe would work his magic on her. Then he would have fucked three generations of one family. He didn't know anyone who could say he'd done that.

"Laurel, is that you, honey?"

More sobbing. "Jim. They're dead." It came out like a ghost's whisper. "Bastard and Karen. They're dead."

"Christ," he said. "Where's the accident?"

"Not that," she said. More crying. Crying, crying, crying. Jesus fucking hell, just spit it out. Of course you couldn't say things like that, because people took offense, even if it was what they needed to hear. Even if they secretly wanted you to say it, you still couldn't.

Doe was already thinking about the money. Maybe Karen a little, too, but mostly the money. Bastard had been over there again. He still couldn't believe that Bastard was stepping in on Karen. He knew, *knew*, Doe had been fucking her, and he'd moved in anyhow. Doe had seen it for himself tonight. And he'd seen Karen see him, too. Just like he planned. Let her know she was in trouble. That stupid encyclopedia kid went in there, and he figured she'd kept him inside, as if that would keep Doe from trying anything.

None of that mattered as much as the fact that Bastard had just come back from doing his collections, and he ought to have damn close to $40,000 to hand over. That was a lot of cash, and if Bastard was dead, would Doe be able to find the money? What if it had been in the car and was scattered to the winds? What if he'd hid it somewhere and now they'd never find it?

Doe told himself to slow down. Maybe he wasn't dead. Maybe he was only dying. Fucking stupid Laurel. No one was dead, he was willing to bet. Dying, maybe, but not dead. Doe could get there on time, kneel down while Bastard raised up one bloodied hand to his shoulder, pulling him close so he could whisper his dying whisper: "It's in the toolshed." Or something. Not the toolshed. Bastard didn't have a toolshed.

He rubbed his uneven teeth back and forth like a pair of opposing hacksaws. "Where's the accident, Laurel? I'll come on over." He sucked down the rest of his drink.

Sobbing. Endless sobbing punctuated by a kind of heaving and then a bit of a groan. And then more sobbing. The phone stretched far enough that he could make it to the little refrigerator/freezer unit and grab a fresh bottle of Yoo-hoo. He swallowed enough to make some room in the bottle, then, cradling the phone between his ear and his shoulder, he funneled in about four shots' worth of Yell. He got back in his chair and put his feet up.

Finally: "Not an accident," she said. "In Karen's trailer. They've been shot."

Doe swung out of his chair. Sudden movement turned out to be a terrible mistake. A stab of electric pain shot out. "You there now?"

"Yuh-yuh-yuh," she said.

"Stay there and don't call anyone." He slammed down his phone and knocked over the Yoo-hoo bottle. It gushed brown all over his desk, all over his pants. Now he'd have to change into his uniform—stress out his balls again. This was turning out to be one fucking disaster of a week.

The cruiser crunched onto Karen's driveway, its headlights illuminating Laurel, who stood puffy-eyed with her hands over her mouth. Doe shut off the lights instantly. He normally loved to flash his police lights, let the world know who made the rules, but this time something told him to keep it quiet and low-key. Bastard was dead and $40,000 was missing.

Only a couple of steps in toward Laurel, and she lunged forward and threw her arms around him. She was heaving like she'd been doing on the phone, only now he had to feel her wet tears streaming down his neck, and he felt obligated to put his arm along her back, which was all jutting bone and flesh, like wet clay wrapped in a cloth. He'd fucked her when she'd been an exciting older woman. Now she was just old, probably fifty-five, and she still dressed like a whore, even though everyone could see her tits were shaped like salamis hanging above a deli counter.

"C'mon, baby," he said. "Tell me what happened."

He knew he was in for it, so her heaves and sobs didn't piss him off too much. She finally pulled it together enough to speak.

"My casserole dish. I lent her my casserole dish last Thanksgiving. And I have company this weekend."

Doe had seen this before, and he couldn't stand it. The blubbering, the talking nonsense.

"I called her this morning. I asked if I could come by and she said I could and I wanted to come by earlier but I had to get my hair done and that took longer than I thought."

"Uh-huh." Doe tapped the tip of his shoe against a small rock.

"I said I would come by earlier, but I came by a little later. I was just going to slip in and get it, not bother her. I didn't think it would matter, but when I went into the trailer—"

What happened in the trailer he'd have to find out for himself, since all he got from her was a long wail, then more sobbing and heaving. What a mess.

"My baby," Laurel was saying. "My only baby."

Baby my ass. Karen was a grown-up whore. And it wasn't like she and Laurel were best friends or anything. Half the time they couldn't stand each other. A few months back, he'd heard they'd gotten into a fistfight when Laurel caught Karen taking money out of her purse. Now she was going off with this "my baby" garbage.

The trailer's door hung open, so Doe pushed himself away from the lamenting whore and walked up the steps. It was all gray darkness inside but one step was all he needed.

There they were, deader'n shit. Bastard the fuck. Dead. Karen the slut. Dead. What a mess. More than a mess, because Doe didn't know who had done it, which made him uncomfortable. The whole point of their business was that things like this didn't happen.

He stepped outside, where Laurel held a cigarette in one palsied hand. Her eyes widened, waiting for his professional diagnosis. Maybe she thought that somehow he could make it all disappear. As a law enforcement officer, he'd be able to tell her that they weren't really dead at all. Those were dummies. Actors. A trick of the light.

Fat chance. Doe wasn't going to make it better for her. He knew pretty clearly what was going to happen, even if he hadn't thought it through. There wasn't time for thinking it through, just for doing it.

"You call anyone else?" he asked her.

She shook her head.

"No one else knows?"

She shook her head again.

"How long was Bastard seeing Karen?"

Laurel stared at him. She didn't answer.

"How long?" he said again, raising his voice.

"Was there something between you and Karen, Jim?" she asked softly.

Jesus fucking Christ. She was about to make this personal. "Laurel, this is police work. I need to know. How long were they seeing each other?"

Laurel shrugged. "Two or three months, I guess. This time. But they been together before."

"Piece of shit," he said. He almost hit her right there. She would have deserved it, too.

He could tell she knew. He could tell by the way she was looking at him. She knew he'd been fucking her daughter, and she was jealous. He didn't have time for this crap.

Doe went back into the trailer. He walked over to Bastard and, for the fun of it, gave him a good kick in the ass. Body was kind of heavy for a skinny guy. He looked at Karen. Her head was all messed up. It had been messed up pretty good anyhow, he thought, and then tried not to laugh. Well, cheating whores get what they have coming to them. That was one thing everyone knew for a fact.

Doe let out a sigh. He nodded to himself, the signal that it was okay, and then turned toward the door.

"Laurel! Jesus! Get in here, quick! Karen's still breathing! She's alive. Holy shit, I think she's going to be okay."

Laurel came running in, right up to the bodies. Doe had stepped out of the way, in the shadow of the wall separating the kitchen from the living area. She ran up to Karen and went down on her knees, something she knew how to do all right, and put a hand to Karen's cheek.

She did not get what she had hoped for—warmth and color and movement. The cheek would have been cold and rubbery now, and even in the dark she could see that Karen's eyes were wide open, staring into the nothing that comes after life.

She started to turn toward Doe. "But. She's not—"

It was as far as she got before the handle of Doe's gun came smashing down into the side of her head, knocking her over onto her daughter's dead body. Her hand slipped into a congealed pool of blood.

No way Doe was going to keep hitting her in the head. Sometimes people went fast, or so he had heard, but not in his experience. Doe knew you might have to hit a person five or six times—good hits, too—before they'd shut the fuck up. Instead, he took advantage of her daze and wrapped his hands around her scrawny neck, her turkey neck, and pressed in good and tight. He shoved his thumbs into her bobbing throat.

She struggled. Sure she did, but not nearly so much as he expected. It was like she'd given up, she knew it was too late. More than that, Doe knew what she was thinking, and for some reason it bothered him. He wanted to clear the record.

"I didn't kill them," he told her, looking right into her bugging eyes. "I don't know who did it, but it wasn't me. The only person I'm killing today is you."

He pressed in even tighter so that his hands hurt, and he sort of liked the throbbing warmth of her throat against his hands. For an instant, he wondered if he should stop, let her up, tell her it was all a joke. He hadn't flashed his lights, but maybe people had seen them together, seen her crying. Still, what did it matter? A mother standing outside her daughter's trailer, crying. Happened every day. No one would even think twice, he told himself, and under his hands he felt something like a chicken bone snap.

Chapter 13

D ESIREE SAT ON HER BED, cross-legged, wearing only her panties and her bikini top, a gray copy of the *I Ching* in her lap. For the past three weeks, she'd been coming to the same symbol again and again. No matter how she asked the question, no matter how she sought her answer, she kept coming back to the *hsieh*.

She drew it on the back of her left hand with a Sharpie so she would think about it constantly. Meditate on it. When it finally faded away in the slow tide of flaking skin, she would redraw it. Last week, she had passed a tattoo parlor on Federal Highway, and she thought about having it placed on her hand permanently, but she decided there was no point being permanent with a symbol of change.

B.B. saw it on her hand and said it looked like a bunch of lines, and she guessed they all did, but this pictogram, she knew, derived from the image of two hands holding on to the horns of an ox. It signified transformation, addressing and fixing a problem. It was her symbol. She had to fix the problem, and the problem was her life with B.B.

She was now twenty-four, and she'd been with him for three years, fixing his meals and driving his car, organizing his calendar, reserving his tables in restaurants. She bought his groceries and paid his bills, answered his door, mixed his drinks. He needed her, and she knew that, she loved that. She felt grateful, too. She'd been about as lost as you could get when he'd taken her in. He'd done it for his own reasons, to exorcise his demons, but he'd still done it.

Those first few days, weeks, even months, she'd slept lightly, watching the door handle, waiting to see B.B. slink in under cover of darkness and claim his due. Maybe not that first day, when her stench had been so bad that even she had had to breathe through her mouth not to gag, but once she'd cleaned up, got off the crank, bought some new clothes—different story then. Her old face started to come back in the mirror. Flesh grew on bone, cheeks reddened and rounded, her nose became less narrow, less sharp, her hair less brittle. She had become herself.

B.B. had told her that no matter what happened, no matter how clean, how happy, she became, she'd never stop wanting to use. The crank would always call to her. It would be a shadow that would haunt her; it was a rope tethered to her neck that would never stop tugging.

He was wrong. He was wrong because Desiree already had a shadow, she already had a tether. The crank had obscured it, hidden it—and God help her, that was what she had loved about it at first. But when she was clean, as she lay in the bed in B.B.'s Coral Gables house, staring at the endless rotation of the ceiling fan, listening to the distant sound of lawn mowers and car alarms, she found her way back to her sister.

Aphrodite had died during the procedure that had separated them. The girls hadn't reached their second birthday when they'd performed the operation, which her mother had known was complicated, which risked the lives of both girls. The doctor had urged her on, however, telling her that his university would cover the costs. It was a great opportunity for the children and for science.

They'd separated the girls, who were linked from shoulder to hip, in what the doctors referred to as a "minor" omphalopagus. Yes, the girls were joined, but mostly by muscle and vascular tissue. Of the organs, only the liver was shared, and they believed they could separate the livers with a chance that both girls would live. The doctor had been clear: It was *possible* that they would both live, likely one would die, and unlikely neither would make it.

Aphrodite died. During the operation, not afterward, which maybe, the doctors had said, was better since it spared her days of painful lingering. But the prognosis for Desiree was quite good. She would have a scar for the rest of her life, and quite a large scar at that, but she would have a normal life.

Desiree learned that it was all a matter of what you called normal. Jeering in school locker rooms, every year settling into the role of de facto freak, fear of wearing a bathing suit, for example? Were these things normal? They were not, of course, beyond-the-pale odd. Lots of fat, ugly, and misshapen children had similar experiences, and they weren't ready for the sideshow, but the whole world knew about Aphrodite. They knew Desiree had been a *Siamese* twin. Kids at school, for as long as she could remember, would pull back their eyes with their index fingers and sing that cat song from *Lady and the Tramp*. Somehow, inevitably, they learned Aphrodite's name and asked after her as though she were still alive, still joined to Desiree. Every single year of middle and high school there was always at least one pair of kids—and once as many as four—who came for Halloween as conjoined twins.

Then there was her mother, who always claimed to have favored Aphrodite. Even before she was out of elementary school, Desiree had begun to wonder if it was true, if it was just something hurtful to say, but wondering that, even believing that, didn't diminish the sting. Her mother loved to cry, to hold her head in her hands and say, "Oh, why wasn't Aphrodite spared?"

And there was Aphrodite herself. Desiree started hearing her voice around her twelfth birthday. Her mother was out of town that week, gone to Key West with a new boyfriend, though the relationship—big surprise—never went anywhere but the emergency room. Even calling it a voice was suggesting too much, she supposed. Aphrodite was there, a presence, a sensation, a compulsion, even a stream of intuitive information. When she met someone and she took an instant like or dislike, she could feel her twin's push or pull.

At first it had been welcome, a balm in the loneliness of her life, but by the time she was fifteen, things had begun to change. She met people who didn't care about her scar, who wanted to hang out, listen to tunes, smoke cheeb. Aphrodite didn't like these people, but they liked Desiree plenty. Then Desiree discovered that crank made Aphrodite's voice quiet. It stung at first, made her nose burn with such incendiary pain that she snorted up water and blew it out like a whale. The next time it didn't burn so much. The time after that, if it burned, she didn't notice.

That was how it went until B.B. had found her. Or she had found him. He was driving on the Ft. Lauderdale strip, stopped in his Mercedes at a light with the top and windows down and Randy Newman blasting as if it were Led Zeppelin.

This guy had what she needed: cash. She needed cash because she needed to shoot up so fucking bad that it killed her. Once it had jolted her from the normal world to a place of power where she could do anything, say anything. She felt whole and finished, no longer subject to the whims of her mother or teachers or dead twin.

Now it was something else. The crank still lifted her up, no doubt about it, but not to such heights. And the lows—the lows were more than she could ever have imagined. Under the earth lows, buried under your grave so you were scratching the bottom of your own casket lows. She was dry and evacuated, a squeezed-out and tattered sponge, and she would do anything to get back up, if only she could begin the cycle again. Even go over to a stranger on the Ft. Lauderdale strip. Whatever restraints had once governed her routines had been eroded by endless fatigue and sleeplessness, as far back as she could remember, which wasn't very far since her memory didn't work so well in those days. A low level of panic hummed perpetually just under her consciousness. Her mouth felt dry no matter how much she drank, and she never felt hungry no matter how little she ate.

For all that, she'd never done anything quite like this before. She fucked and sucked for crank, but always guys she knew; but the more she thought about it, the more she saw that it didn't matter. It was just a few minutes. Of what? Sex? Big deal. They tried to make a big deal of sex, but it was nothing. A few minutes, and she'd have some money and she could score.

Even then, with the pound of need and terror in her ears, she could hear her sister's muffled voice. She couldn't make it out, but she knew it was there, a distant pleading. But the guy, he seemed like he would go for it. He was nicely dressed, hair neatly combed, neatly dyed. He had a few pieces of tasteful but expensive jewelry—her time in the pawnshops had taught her to tell the difference. He didn't look like just another rich

Florida doctor or lawyer or real estate developer in a convertible. He was that other kind. He had the mark, the sign, the vibrating tone audible to crankheads and dogs. He lied on his tax return, cheated on his wife, fucked over his partners. Something. The guy in the Mercedes was crooked, and he had money.

She walked over, smiled at him. She used her best smile, which was radiant. At least it had been once. If she'd known how she looked—cancer thin, sunken eyes, thin lips, red welts on her face and hands—she never would have offered, never would have thought anyone would want her. But she didn't know, so she smiled, and he turned to her.

"I'll blow you for ten dollars, sweetie," she said.

He started to roll up his window—a defense of minimum value with the convertible's top down—and she pulled away from the rising glass, about to swear. Then he stopped. The window came back down.

"What are you using?"

"Fuck you," she said, starting to turn away—but slowly. She knew they weren't done.

He took out a twenty and showed it to her. "What are you using?"

She paused. She could hear Aphrodite, the voice that had been muffled and muted for years. She could hear it now, hollow and echoing, the trickle of distant water in a cave. A feeling so strong that she could almost sense the words: *Don't tell him.* And that was why she told him. "Crank," she said.

He studied her for a minute longer and then unlocked the doors with a flick of his finger. "Get in," he said.

She got in. Why not? He was okay looking for an older guy. Probably clean, certainly rich. That other thing—the vibrating something that told her she might die, might end up dumped in a vacant lot, tossed off an airboat into the Everglades—that didn't matter right now. The need called to her, the need. The need. Ripping her in half, pulling her, crushing her, knocking her off her feet and dragging her through the dirt. So she got in.

But the man in the Mercedes didn't want a blow job. He wanted to clean her up.

B.B. never came for sex. After a couple of months, by which time Desiree had become a kind of live-in maid, it was clear that he wasn't going to. He didn't like women. He didn't look at them when they passed on the street or in the mall, not the charming or the cute or the beautiful. The slutty and the sexy he looked at, but not with desire. It was more like a vague hostility, or maybe amusement.

At first she assumed he was gay, which was okay by her. She'd known plenty of queens on the street, and even if she hadn't, she'd spent too much time as the object of derision to judge anyone for being in any way different or out of step with the idea of normal you got on TV. Still, it never rang true. B.B. didn't much look at men, either. Not even those who were both beautiful and obviously gay.

It was entirely possible that he was asexual, but Desiree's gut and Aphrodite's voice doubted it. He was maybe asexual and maybe not, but he was something else, too. Something the twins could not put their respectively fleshly and ephemeral fingers on. There was a blankness to him. He seemed in a daze half the time. He'd rescued her, but he never acted like the sort of person who would rescue a drug addict. Only when he was doing charity work with one of his kids did he come fully alive. Or sometimes when he was watching a boy. They'd be in a restaurant or walking on the beach or shopping, and his pupils would dilate and his posture would grow straighter without getting stiff, and he would flush a healthy pink, as if he were in love. Each time he seemed to fall in love.

Once she brought it up. Only once. Because the thing of it was, there was something almost admirable about B.B.'s desire for boys. He wanted to be with them—she could see that. On the street, she'd seen men who went for boys, for girls, for children so young that they didn't know what sex was. They were predators, monsters, and she regretted not having killed them all. B.B. was like them, but also not. He turned his desire into charity; he hid from the world, maybe even from himself. Instead, he helped them. If there was a way to be admirable in such a desire, surely this was it.

She'd been with him more than a year, made herself as much a part of his life as his limbs, when over dinner she decided it was time. It was B.B.'s birthday, and he'd taken a little too much of a few bottles of red he'd been saving. Maybe she'd had a little too much, too.

"About you and your boys," she'd said.

"Yeah?" He chewed at a piece of perfectly rare choice triple-trimmed filet mignon that she'd grilled for him. On his plate, along with a pile of asparagus, were two pools of dipping sauce—a delicate au poivre and a garlic cream.

"I just wanted to let you know that I understand, okay? I know why you do what you do, B.B., and I think it's very brave. If you need anything, any help, you can be honest with me."

He set down his fork and stared at her. His face reddened and veins bulged in his neck, and for a moment she thought he was going to burst, explode, throw his plate at her, order her out. Instead he let out a thick, throaty laugh. "Not you, too," he said. "Oh, Desiree. I know that people love to imagine the worst, but I thought for sure you would understand."

"I do understand," she said.

"I just want to help them. I had a rough time when I was a boy, and now that I can, I want to help other boys. That's it. I'm not a pervert. If you don't understand that I might want to help someone without wanting to fuck them, then no one will."

He wasn't angry, not even sad. Mostly he seemed weary.

"Okay, B.B.," she said. She knew better, but she nodded. He could hide his impulses from the world as long as he hid them from himself, too.

So at least she didn't have to worry that her friend and boss and companion might go around fucking boys. He might do a lot of bad things, be a lot of bad things, but he had this in check. Even so, Aphrodite would not be appeased. Yet dead twins can rant only so much before even they give up, and her objections quieted down after the first few months. Yes, it was probably wrong to work for a man who made his money, his loads and loads of money, the way B.B. did, but someone was going to, and if she stopped working for B.B., there would be just as much trouble in the world, but no food and shelter for poor Desiree. She could hardly get a job with no high school diploma and her only prior experience being personal assistant to a criminal.

Besides, B.B. wanted her around, valued her, deferred to her opinions. She owed him her life, so she could turn a blind eye to the pleasure he took from setting his hand on a boy's shoulder, from the way his eyes lit up when he saw one of his charity cases in a bathing suit. She could live with being his beard, his disguise to the world.

Then things took a sharp turn. Last month, they'd been driving back from a dinner meeting with a guy who ran an encyclopedia operation in Georgia. B.B. was thinking—more like half thinking—of expanding, and maybe that would have bothered Desiree if he'd been serious, but he would never expand. He made all the money he needed now, and he hated hassles; why risk new territory and cross state lines?

The meeting went badly, and both he and Desiree didn't like the Georgia guy, didn't feel they could trust him. Desiree felt relieved, and she suspected B.B. did as well. It was almost as though he were looking for a way to celebrate, and when they saw a kid walking along the beach, something shifted visibly in B.B.'s face.

The boy looked maybe eleven, cute, clean-cut but staggering. As if he were drunk—maybe for the first time. He had a stupid, happy grin on his face, and he sang something boisterous to himself, occasionally breaking into air guitar as he walked.

"Why don't you stop the car," B.B. said. "Let's give that boy a lift."

Desiree didn't want to stop, but the light turned red and there was no choice. "Where do you want to give him a lift to?"

B.B. grinned at her, like whatever had broken in him must have broken in her. "Our house."

Desiree kept her eyes straight ahead. "No."

"No?"

"No. I'm not going to let it happen."

B.B. bit on his lip. "What exactly are you not going to let happen?"

"B.B., let's just forget it. Go home."

"If I say we give the kid a lift, then that's what we do." His voice had turned loud. "You don't tell me no, and he doesn't tell me no. No one tells me no. Stop the car and sweet-talk that kid into the car, or you'll be on the street tomorrow and whoring for crank in a week."

"All right," she said softly. She chose her words deliberately, because his cruelty demanded treatment in kind, and she wanted him to think, if only for a second, that he had won. "Okay, fine." The light turned green, and she sped past the boy.

The next morning, her packed suitcase and gym bag were met with flowers and chocolates and an envelope with cash. He didn't apologize, didn't say he was sorry he'd tried to turn her into a pimp, but she knew he was sorry. For all it mattered. She knew she would stay, but as she unpacked, Aphrodite made it clear that this was a reprieve, not a stay. Desiree didn't resist or disagree or shrug it off, because it wasn't a suggestion. It was fact.

They both saw it. The urge inside B.B. was coming out, and sooner or later bad things were going to be happening under her roof. Maybe she could keep him in check, but for how long? Forever? It seemed unlikely. What frightened her, however, was not the thought that B.B. would give in to his worst self, that he would become the monster he had resisted; it was that she would lack the strength to fight him. She would convince herself that it would be worse if she wasn't around, that she helped him from hurting even more boys. She would help him with this, like she helped him with his business. How long could a person participate in evil without becoming evil herself? Or had she been guilty the moment she'd accepted B.B.'s charity, the moment she'd chosen to stay after learning who and what he was?

She had to get out. She had to move on. Aphrodite whispered it to her in a mantra so perpetual, it was like the sound of breath. Even the I Ching couldn't stop telling her so.

That B.B. would panic if she left hardly mattered. That she had nowhere to go hardly mattered. She had what she needed. She had money she'd saved—enough money that she could live for a year or two while she figured things out. And she had information on B.B.'s trade. Not that she wanted to extort him or threaten him, but she had a feeling that once he realized she wasn't coming back, once he realized she was gone for good, B.B. was going to be very, very angry.

And when a man is very angry, and he has a bunch of people like Jim Doe and the Gambler working for him, things can get tricky.

Chapter 14

THE PHONE CALL came in the middle of the night. B.B. never answered the phone himself; that wasn't his thing. But he liked to keep the phone near his bed. It was one of those office phones with a shrill office phone ring and the multiple buttons so you could see which line was in use. They had only one line, but he liked the idea of having several.

And he liked to keep an eye on when the line was in use. It wasn't that he didn't trust Desiree. Of course he did. He trusted her more than anyone, but why take chances?

The TV was on, but there was only snow. B.B. looked over at the digital clock: 4:32. A phone call at that hour couldn't be anything good. He sat up and turned on the bedside lamp, which was shaped like a giraffe reaching up to eat leaves. The shade was over the tree. B.B. sat still, staring at the blue and pink of the rococo wallpaper until he heard the light tap at the door.

"Who is it?"

The door opened a crack. "It's the Gambler."

"Fuck." He picked up the handset and punched the button to switch over to the right line. He always kept the phone on one of the dead lines, since he liked the feeling of pushing the button when he took a call. It made him feel like he was an executive. Which he basically was, just an unconventional sort of executive.

"So, what's the status?" he asked the Gambler. "Everything in line?"

There was a pause. It was the sort of pause that B.B. did not much like.

"Not really." The voice was flat. "Wouldn't be calling now if it were."

"What does that mean?" He looked over at Desiree, who was leaning against the door with her arms folded, studying him. She wore a white bathrobe and probably nothing else underneath. A lot of guys, scar or no, would find that pretty sexy, he figured. And the fact that it might be kind of sexy seemed, for an instant, kind of sexy. Then the feeling passed.

"It means," the Gambler told him, "that there's a serious problem, the sort I may not be able to get resolved."

B.B. hated having to talk in code on the phone, but even though there was no evidence the feds gave the slightest shit about his dealings, you had to assume they were listening, which meant you had to spend a lot of time talking around the issue, and that got awkward when you didn't even know what the issue was.

Who needed these hassles? Wasn't all of this supposed to be hassle free? Not really, but it was supposed to be easy, and he guessed it was. B.B. had inherited his hog lot outside Gainesville from his father's father, a red-faced old man with wisps of white hair that stuck out of his head as though they'd been rammed in by a vengeful enemy. He was so ornery that he was like a parody of an ornery old man, cursing and spitting tobacco in a rage and slapping away kind hands, grandchildish hugs, bologna sandwiches—anything anyone might offer. Visits to the farm had been an unrelenting torment. The old man would put him to work shoveling hog shit, mopping up pools of hog piss, dragging dead hog carcasses by their hooves.

If he even gestured toward an expression of complaint, his grandfather would tell him to shut the fuck up and smack him in the head, sometimes with his hand, a few times with a mostly empty sack of feed, once with an old-fashioned metal lunchbox. There were other punishments, too, in the empty barn, when B.B. broke "the farmer's code," a fluid list of regulations that had been omitted from the *Poor Richard's Almanac*. B.B. never learned the code, understood its rules or parameters, but a few times a year his grandfather would come up on him, looking especially tall and dirty. He'd spit a wad of dip in B.B.'s direction and tell him he'd broken the farmer's code and he needed to be mentored in the old barn. He had no idea what the word meant, had no idea what it was to mentor a boy. He was a monster, and by the time B.B. became old enough to make decisions for himself, he vowed never to see the old man again.

Then, ten years ago, the old man died. He'd reached ninety-seven, kept alive by free-floating Achilles-like wrath and a similarly quasi-divine hatred of do-gooders, women, television, politicians, corporations, changing fashions, and a world turning ever more youthful while he turned ever older. B.B.'s own father had died long before in a drunken and coke-fueled motorcycle accident, the helmetlessness of which smacked of suicide. After his grandfather's death came the registered letter from the lawyer telling him he'd inherited the farm, and at just the right time, too, since things had not been going so well for B.B. in some of the various careers he'd been trying on, including car salesman, unlicensed real estate agent, landscaper, security guard, and a stint as a Las Vegas poker player.

This last had involved long and delirious runs under casino lights that obscured the difference between night and day, drunkenness and sobriety, winning and losing. He now remembered hyperbolic laughing, raking piles of chips toward his chest, and he remembered that the next day he'd mysteriously have no money. But those weren't the memories that came to him most often. When he thought of Vegas, he thought of the shirtless Greek he owed (and still owed) $16,000 sending a thug to beat him so hard with a broom handle that his ribs still ached when he sneezed more than ten years later. He thought of his shameful retreat from town, sitting on a bus and disguised as an Eastern Orthodox priest, the only plausible costume he could get on short notice. It was that or flee town as a pirate or a mummy.

With no other options, he took on hog farming. It paid the bills, though barely, but it stank and filled him with a vile repulsion toward animals, animals that stank and shat and demanded food and bellowed in pain and misery and deserved to die as punishment for being alive. And the land itself—that god-awful farm with its memories of his fucking grandfather, for whose sake alone he sincerely hoped there was such a place as hell. The barn by its simple proximity so disturbed his sleep that he convinced a trio of potbellied and thick-forearmed locals to take it down for him. He paid them in beer and a whole roasted pig.

Going back to the farm, working his grandfather's lots, had been degrading, a waking nightmare, but he'd been broke, beyond broke, and the farm kept him afloat. There was money for food and a roof over his head and occasionally the wines he'd learned to love in Vegas.

Then this guy he almost knew—spoken to a few times in a local bar, a friend of one of the men who had taken down the barn—a biker in a gang called the DevilDogs, came to see him one night. How would he feel if a couple of the boys set up a small lab on the property? No one would know, since the smell of the pigs would hide the smell of cooking meth. B.B. wouldn't have to do anything except keep quiet, and he'd get $1,000 a month.

It was a good deal. After a month or so of not wanting to know about it, B.B. began to hang out with the meth cooks, learn how they did it, learn how easy it was to turn a few hundred dollars' worth of over-the-counter cold medicine into speed so potent that it made coke look like a watery cup of Maxwell House. Then the guys who worked the lab were busted while distributing. He figured they'd roll on him, but they never did. He figured other guys from the operation would come by and take over the lab, but they never did. There it was, a fully operational moneymaking machine on his property. He'd be crazy to ignore it.

The problem was, B.B. hadn't known the first thing about distributing drugs. Had no idea how to go about it. He couldn't see himself on the corner, wearing a trench coat, *pssting* to any skinny, trailer-trashy redneck with an oversize shirt and a dull look in his eyes. He continued to make the meth—not large quantities, only an ounce or two a month while he got the hang of it. It seemed like a good idea to keep the quantities small, since making meth when you didn't know what you were doing was like holding a jar of nitroglycerin on a roller coaster.

He made it and he stored it. Just a hobby, really, like putting ships in a bottle. It took only a couple of days of work, and then there it was, this lovely yellow powder. He got better, more confident, made more, learned how to dispose of the waste, which was so toxic that it ate through the ground. Within a year, he had thousands of dollars' worth of stuff and no idea how to unload it.

When he read in the business section of a local newspaper that Champion Encyclopedias was looking for someone to run an operation in the state, it all began to come together for him. He convinced them he was an entrepreneur, that he could run the book business as well as he ran his "agricultural concern"—his term. But enthusiasm was wasted on them. They cared no more for his acumen than his crew chiefs cared for the acumen of new bookmen. You hire everyone you can, you cast them to the waves, and you see who's still floating.

This happened three years after Vegas, and when B.B. met with the top crew chiefs in the state, he knew one of them. A guy by the name of

Kenny Rogers, called himself the Gambler. He didn't recognize B.B., but B.B. recognized him. The Gambler was the thug who'd beaten B.B. with the broom handle in his Vegas apartment. B.B. down on the ground, hands over his head, the sounds of the neighbor's dog barking, the neighbor's TV turned up loud to pretend he couldn't hear, and B.B.'s own sobbing filling his ears.

B.B. had been thinking only of revenge, of exorcising his demons, when he'd hired the Gambler. Let him work for B.B. Let him think he was doing a great job, in on the deepest secrets of the organization, part of the whole planning process. B.B. was keeping the Gambler close, figuring out where and how he would get even, make things right in the universe. As time went by, however, the revenge never happened. The Gambler made B.B. money, way too much money to remove him so thoughtlessly, and the greater truth was that if B.B. did take revenge, then he would no longer have the pleasure of anticipating the sweetness of payback. So B.B. had kept the Gambler where he was and occasionally thought about what he might do to him.

Things had gone so well for so long, he should have expected something like this.

"Can you get me the thing I asked for?" B.B. said. He tap tap tapped a pencil on the night table.

"I don't know." The Gambler kept his voice devoid of content. "Right now it's missing."

"Missing? Jesus Christ. Where's, um, the guy who is supposed to have it?"

"He's gone. Gone in a permanent and messy way, if you know what I'm saying."

"What the hell is going on there? Who caused him to get gone?"

"No idea," the Gambler said. "We're working on it."

"Yeah, you working on getting me my stuff, too?"

"We're working on it, but right now we don't have a whole lot to go on."

"Am I going to have to come out there?" B.B. asked.

"I don't think that's necessary," the Gambler said. "We can take care of everything. I'll keep you updated."

B.B. hung up the phone. He'd keep them updated. Great, with their little "I spy with my little eye" games?

He turned to Desiree. "Get dressed. We're going to Jacksonville," he said.

She scrunched up her nose. "I hate Jacksonville."

"Of course you hate Jacksonville. Everyone hates Jacksonville. No one goes to Jacksonville because they like it."

"Then why do people go to Jacksonville?"

"To find their money," B.B. said, "and to make sure their people aren't trying to rip them off." And maybe, he thought, to take care of the Gambler. If he'd lost the payment, then there was a pretty good chance he'd outlived his usefulness. Maybe even if he could find the money.

The Gambler hung up the phone. The asshole was going to come up here; he just knew it. The last thing he needed was B.B. and his freak-show girlfriend messing around with the business. Technically, of course, it was B.B.'s business, but that struck the Gambler as more a matter of happenstance than anything else. He'd stumbled into this deal. Met some people. Formed some alliances. Whatever. The money came in not because B.B. was so smart, but because people were willing to buy crank, crank was cheap to make, there wasn't much competition for the market, and the cops were too busy chasing after cocaine cowboys to pay much mind to homemade meth. They could sell it out of ice-cream trucks—hell, they practically did—without the feds or local law taking notice. They had bigger fish to fry than some homemade bullshit that you could cook up out of over-the-counter asthma medicine.

The truth was that there was a lot more money to be made, and the Gambler was sick and fucking tired of baby-sitting this encyclopedia zoo. He wasn't going to have the strength for it much longer, and he was ready to move on, to help expand the empire. He needed something less physically taxing, something that would enable him to sit and think. And make money. He'd told B.B. as much, though he left out the part about worrying about his strength. B.B. hadn't been interested.

"Right now," he'd said, "we're all making money, the cops are oblivious, and everything is just fine. We get greedy, everything could fall apart."

It was easy for B.B. to be happy with the status quo. He didn't have to hang out with these door-to-door fuckos and assholes like Jim Doe. He didn't have to perform for the sales monkeys twice a day. And he didn't have to worry about the day coming—and it could be in a couple of years, maybe even next year—when he wouldn't be able to do it anymore, when the medical bills would begin to pile in, when he would need the cash to make sure someone was taking care of him so he didn't end up with psychopathic orderlies who would stick pins in his eyeballs just for the fun of it.

The Gambler had never been anything but effective and loyal, and he was getting sick of B.B.'s ingratitude. Not just ingratitude—there was something else. B.B.'s new residence in the land of oblivion. He was checked out. On another planet. That was no way to run this kind of operation. The Gambler had worked with guys in Vegas who could run six operations at one time, have three phone conversations, and handicap a weekend's worth of football games—and give them all their full attention. Fucking B.B. couldn't figure out if a yellow light meant speed up or slow down without fucking Desiree to tell him.

And sure, the money was good, but it wasn't going to be enough—not when he began to decline.

He'd been forced to leave off working for the Greek in Vegas when the freezing started. He probably ought to have gone to a doctor right away. You're in the middle of kicking someone's ass and you just freeze, bat over your head, like you've turned into an action figure—that's usually a sign to head for the doctor. But it was an isolated incident, a freak thing, so he forgot about it. Then it happened again three or four months later, out on a date with a showgirl. Ruined the whole thing. Then three months after that, this time while playing golf. Midswing—and frozen, just like that.

He'd been with the Greek that time, and the Greek had wanted to know, reasonably enough, what the fuck was going on.

Five doctors later, it was confirmed. ALS: amyotrophic lateral sclerosis. Lou Gehrig's disease. A form of muscular dystrophy. He was now one of Jerry Lewis's fucking kids. It could start in any number of ways—muscle spasms, loss of coordination, slurring of speech, clumsiness, and the Gambler's own freakish freezes. It would progress until he was a complete physical nothing, unable to move, even to breathe or swallow on his own, while his mind, meanwhile, remained in perfect working order.

It could happen slowly or it could happen quickly. No one knew. In the Gambler's case, the progress appeared to be slow, so that gave him time to get his shit in order. It wasn't the death he feared. He knew that death wasn't the end; he'd seen those pictures of ghosts, heard the recordings of voices from the other side, even been to a medium who let him speak to his dead mother. Knowing that the body was but a shell and the soul lived on had helped him in his enforcement work in Vegas. It's not so hard to beat someone to death if you know you're not doing any permanent damage. What scared him was the time leading up to death, when he was alone and helpless, and the only thing that was going to keep him from being abused and tormented was money. He needed money.

If he told B.B. the truth, B.B. would be sympathetic, understanding, and he would send him on his way. Maybe with a nice little bonus, but not nearly enough. The Gambler needed money, piles and piles of money, enough money to pay for the bills, to pay for a personal nurse and pay the nurse so well that she would do anything to keep him happy and healthy.

The way things were going, the cause was in trouble. In the last six months, B.B. had been more distracted than ever. Business was falling off, and he didn't seem to care. And Desiree, that sneaky bitch, was up to something. He was sure of it. Maybe she was planning a takeover, to cut out the Gambler entirely. But there was no way he was going to work for her, and he sure as hell wasn't going to let her get rid of him. If anyone was going to take over for B.B., it would be the Gambler.

Desiree kept her eyes straight ahead. Next to her, in the passenger seat, B.B. sat quietly, his head tilted slightly away from her. She couldn't tell if he was asleep or not or maybe pretending. His tape of Randy Newman's *Little Criminals* had finished playing a minute ago, and now there was only the hissing silence of the radio. She wanted more music, the radio, anything to help keep her awake. Her fatigue, the darkness of the highway, the glare of oncoming traffic, lulled her into a hypnotic stupor.

"You had a good time with Chuck?" she asked at last.

B.B. stirred. "What do you mean?"

"I mean, did you have a good time?"

"We had a productive dinner," he said. "He's a good kid. Bright. Ready for mentoring. Could be more if, you know, he's willing to open himself up."

She let that hang there. "Okay."

They said nothing for a few more minutes. Desiree winced when they passed a pair of squashed raccoons in the roadside.

"I never wanted to be like this," B.B. said.

Desiree felt herself suck in her breath. In a way, she'd been waiting for this, the big confession, and she'd been dreading it. Once he told her of his shame, of how his desires controlled him, of how he had been victimized as a boy—whatever it was that he would say—she was afraid she would feel pity and sympathy, and the will to leave would be lost in a tangle of guilt and obligation.

"I never wanted to be in this business, you know. It just happened to me."

Relief passed over her. He didn't want to talk about his thing for boys, he wanted to talk about being a supplier. "I'm in no position to judge anyone, B.B."

"I never wanted to do this," he said again. "I don't like it. I'd live off the hogs if I could, except I've gotten used to the money now. But it's like a stain on my soul, you know? It's a blackness. I keep thinking that I want to get rid of it."

"So walk away," she said. "Just walk away. No one is stopping you."

"I was thinking something else," he said. "I was thinking that maybe someone could take over for me. That *you* could take over for me. I'd cut you in on the profits, and I could retire from it all, work at the Young Men's Foundation full-time. Live a decent life."

"That's very flattering," she said. "It's really incredible that you trust me so much, B.B. But I need to think about it."

"Okay," he said. And he fell into silence again.

Desiree had no desire to think about it. B.B.'s idea of cleaning the stain off his soul was to hand the dirty work to someone else and just take the profits. Ever so slightly, she shook her head. She didn't want him to see it, but she felt she needed to offer the universe a gesture. Her decisions were getting easier all the time.

Chapter 15

THE ALARM WENT OFF AT SEVEN A.M. Normally, after hanging out by the pool, people would begin to drift off to sleep between one and two, and hardly anyone was left by three. That meant you could get four hours of sleep easy, which Bobby said was all you needed. He ought to know. He was always among the last to leave the pool area, and he never once looked tired. I couldn't remember ever having seen him yawn.

I had grown used to the fatigue in the way you might grow used to having a tumor on the side of your face—you never forgot about it, but not forgetting about it didn't mean you were actually thinking about it. I woke up each morning exhausted, fuzzy, slightly dizzy, and the feeling never quite went away.

Bobby tended to breeze into our room about twenty after seven, swinging the door wide and bounding in like a character in a musical about to break into song. He would make sure everyone was awake and chitchat with whoever had been the first to shower and was by then usually dressed, since they had to rush if four people were going to get showered and have breakfast in time for the prep meeting at nine.

As it turned out, I was the first to hit the showers, though I was the last to go to bed—bed being a euphemism for a spot on the floor. I'd crawled into the room just before five in the morning, undressed quietly, and gone to sleep in the space between the television and the doorless closet, resting my head on a dirty undershirt. No one had left me a spare pillow.

I'd slept, I was almost certain of it, but it had been a fitful sleep in which I dreamed, mostly, of lying awake on the floor and trying to sleep. At least I hadn't dreamed about selling books, and it was the first time in weeks that I could say that. And I hadn't dreamed about Bastard's and Karen's bodies, which was some kind of mercy.

When the alarm went off, I jumped up as only someone who's had chronically little sleep can, and headed for the bathroom. By the time I showered and put on my other pair of khaki pants, a light blue button-down and a narrow tie, noontime sun yellow, I was feeling almost like myself again. I could forget what happened in the trailer, the evening with Melford, and the events back at the trailer. I could almost forget that I had been involved in a double murder, a third murder implicating a crooked cop and the head of the company for which I worked.

I sat on the bed, staring at my vaguely trembling hands, trying to summon the desire for breakfast, when the door opened and Bobby came bobbing in.

"Up first, and I'm not surprised," he said. "Glad to see it, Lemmy. I scoped out today's area already, and I have a moochie spot for you. But you've got to promise me a double. You're getting out there by eleven this morning. You'll have twelve hours. You think you can promise me a double? At least, that is. A double at least."

"I can try," I said lamely.

"Hell, he's too tired," Scott said. He was lying on the bed, shirtless, and his pale gut and pale tits were hanging out at us. "I don't know how much sleep he got last night. Maybe you should give that moochie area to someone else, Bobby. Someone who ain't gonna let it go."

Bobby grinned at him as though Scott had just told him that he liked his haircut. "Lemmy here has earned the mooch. You produce like Lemmy, you'll share the spoils like Lemmy."

"Now, how's that gonna happen if you're every time giving him the best areas?"

Bobby shook his head. "A good bookman can sell anywhere. And when Lemmy came up, he didn't get the cream, just like none of the green guys get the cream. You didn't get any special treatment when you came up."

"And I still don't," he mumbled.

"That's where Lemmy proved himself. You want a share of the mooch, you have to show me you deserve the mooch."

"All he done was get lucky," Scott said. "Ain't nothing but a rich Jew that wants more money for hisself."

"C'mon, Scottie," Bobby said. "Lemmy's a good guy."

"Yeah, good at what? Butt fucking, I guess," said Ronny Neil, lying still on the other bed, his arms and legs out as if he were making a snow angel. "You good at butt fucking?" he asked me.

"Define 'good,' " I said.

"Holy bananas, you guys are cranky this morning," Bobby said. "But I'm glad you're dressed, Lemmy. The Gambler wants to see you."

Ronny Neil, who had been sprawled out dreamily, suddenly shot up-right. Like Scott, he slept shirtless, but unlike Scott, Ronny Neil had a tightly muscled body. He had small but hard pecs, and his back muscles shot out like wings. On his left shoulder he had a cross tattoo—it had been done by hand and in ink, the kind prisoners give each other.

"What's the Gambler want with him?" Ronny Neil demanded.

Bobby shrugged. "I guess you'll have to take that up with the boss yourself, Ron-o."

Ronny Neil narrowed his gaze at Bobby. "He don't have nothing to do with the Gambler. I ain't gonna stand for the Gambler bringing him in."

"Bringing him in to *what*?" Bobby demanded.

"I don't want him talking to the Gambler," Ronny Neil said. It wasn't quite sulky, more like a growl.

The fact that I didn't want to talk to the Gambler either didn't seem to count for much. I felt a wave of dizzying panic. Had the Gambler some-how learned that Melford and I had been hiding in the closet? He had the checkbook, which meant they knew someone from the company had been there, and by now he'd probably figured out that the someone in question was me.

"Let's go, Lemmy," Bobby said. "Don't want to keep the big boss man waiting."

"He gets too cozy with the boss," Ronny Neil said, "I'll stick a knife up his ass."

"Does that count as being good or bad at butt fucking?" I asked.

"Oh, don't be that way, Ronster." Bobby put a hand to my shoulder and led me out the door.

I couldn't believe he was going to leave it at that. Maybe he thought that if he came down harsher on them, it would be worse for me. Maybe he thought that leaving it alone wouldn't affect how many books were sold. Maybe he was off on Planet Bobby and didn't understand that Ronny Neil was a scary asshole and Scott was a scary and pathetic asshole.

Was such a thing possible? Had Bobby skated so blithely through life with his salesman grin and good cheer that he didn't know what it meant to be picked on, to be humiliated by bigger or meaner guys who got their rocks off by reminding you that you walked around unscathed at their pleasure? Was Bobby like Chitra, insulated from the cruelty of the world, not by his looks but by an impenetrable armor of optimism and generosity?

If that was the case, it meant that Bobby and I lived in entirely different places—the same to an outside viewer, but utterly unalike to our particular perspectives. Where I saw danger and menace, Bobby saw only innocent ribbing—a little on the harsh side, perhaps, but still innocent.

What if Bobby lived in this wondrous world precisely because he believed in it? I had seen how Melford had defused a certain whumping the night before in the bar, but he'd done it consciously. What if Bobby did that sort of thing all the time, only he didn't know he was doing it? He assumed the best in people, and he got kindness and leeway in return.

If that was true, it meant that I was in some way responsible for Ronny Neil and Scott hating me so much. I assumed the worst about a couple of ignorant rednecks, they picked up on it, responded to it, acted on it. Did it work that way?

What troubled me about this idea, truly troubled me, was not so much that I had to shoulder the blame for Ronny Neil threatening to stick a knife up my ass—though that was undeniably distasteful—as that it seemed to be too much like what Melford had been talking about last night. We all see the world through a veil of ideology, he'd said. Melford thought that the veil came from outside of us, the system or something, but maybe it was more complicated. Maybe we made our own veils. Maybe the world made us, and we, in turn, made the world.

Surely Melford couldn't be the only person thinking about this stuff. He'd mentioned Marx and Marxists, but there had to be others—philosophers and psychologists and who knew what. If I had been on my way to Columbia, instead of being on my way to see the Gambler, the dead-body-hiding and evidence-concealing Gambler, I might have a hope of finding out someday. But unless the sample volume of the *Champion Encyclopedias* I carried around with me took up the issue, I'd probably not find out anytime soon.

Chapter 16

W E WALKED ALONG the motel balcony as if it were the corridor to the electric chair. At least I did. The morning was bright and sunny, with only a few wispy streaks of white in the sky, and the extreme, mind-numbing heat hadn't started to get going yet, so Bobby appeared to be in a good mood. He had his hands thrust into the pockets of his khaki chinos and his lips pursed in a soft whistle. Maybe something by Air Supply.

"So, what does the Gambler want with me?" I ventured.

"I guess you'll find out soon enough," Bobby said. "I sort of figured you'd know."

Fat chance. I was about to ask something paranoid and foolish: Did he seem angry when he asked you to get me? Did he say that he found something, perhaps? Something in a checkbook he took from a dead person's trailer? I choked back all those questions. What would Melford do? I wondered. Melford, I decided, would tell himself that the Gambler was not about to kill me, not when there were half a dozen people who knew I was going into his room. Melford would figure that the Gambler was looking for information. Melford would see this as an opportunity to get some information for himself.

We were only about four doors down from the Gambler's room, so I stopped. "What's the Gambler's deal, anyhow?"

Bobby stopped, too, but reluctantly. He looked at me and looked at the Gambler's door, as though he couldn't believe I was in one place and not the other. "What do you mean?"

"I mean, he works for this company Educational Advantage Media, right? But they're not part of Champion Encyclopedias. How does all of this work?"

"There's no time for a civics lesson, Lemmy. The boss man is waiting."

"Come on," I said, trying to sound relaxed. "I just want to know how all of this works."

"You want to know *now?*" But he must have decided it would be more expedient to answer than argue, so he pursed his lips and emptied his lungs. "Educational Advantage Media contracts with Champion, okay? They contract for various cities and their surrounding areas, and in Florida, they contract for Fort Lauderdale, Miami, Tampa, Jacksonville, and Gainesville. That's why we go to those places over and over again."

"Who owns Educational Advantage Media? The Gambler?"

Bobby shook his head. "No, but he's high up, maybe even the number two guy. The boss is a guy named Gunn, who I've never met. The Gambler talks to him all the time, and he's been out to visit us on the road a few times, but he never bothers to meet with us little people."

"So is this guy, you know, okay?"

Bobby shrugged. "Probably. I guess. I'll tell you one thing, though." He looked around conspiratorially. "He's got this woman who works for him. She's kind of hot, and she always wears a bikini top, but she's got this nasty scar down her side, like she was in a motorcycle wipe-out or something. It's really pretty ugly, but she loves to show it off. I don't want to judge someone for being unfortunate or anything, but ouch. Don't show the world. You know?"

I said I knew, though I didn't know at all.

"Okay, enough piddling." Bobby clapped his hands together with cheerful finality. "Let's go see the boss."

The Gambler sat at the peeling particleboard desk in his room, looking over some credit apps. He wore greenish-tinted chinos, a white oxford with no tie, and brown loafers. He had perched on his nose a pair of glasses that made him look like a nineteenth-century accounting clerk, an effect only increased by his hair, straight and thick and just a tad long. All he needed was a high collar and some muttonchops.

"Sit," the Gambler said. He gestured with his head to a chair by the window.

I walked over and sat. The chair rested on thick wooden legs and was upholstered with a leather worn so thin that it threatened to burst like a soap bubble. My heart thumped violently, and my hands shook. I stared up at my boss, having no idea what to expect. I probably should be trying to think of what sorts of things the Gambler might ask so I could come up with good answers, but I couldn't think clearly. Everything swirled around me in gray eddies.

"You can leave us alone now," the Gambler said to Bobby.

"Okie." Bobby bounced on his feet, almost a heel-clicking salute, and then walked out.

The Gambler continued to peer at the paperwork, gazing over his perched glasses. What were they there for if not for reading?

"How have you been, Lem? Everything all right?"

"Terrific," I said, though I didn't sound terrific. I sounded like I knew I was in trouble.

"Terrific, huh? I guess we'll see." He stared at me until I looked away. "You know, Bobby says you're a born bookman. A real power hitter. You got that grand slam that fell through a while back, didn't you?"

"That was me."

"Shame about it. I mean, you do good work, you should get your reward, right? A more experienced bookman might have seen those guys for deadbeats, but you can't blame yourself for not knowing what only years on the job can teach you."

"I guess not." I hadn't been blaming myself, and I couldn't think of what a more experienced bookman might have picked up on. Sure, Galen had lived in a relatively run-down place, but he'd had a pretty nice truck, his wife had some decent jewelry. His friends all looked okay, too. None of them were going to be extras on *Knots Landing*, but nothing suggested that they were off to the welfare office the next day, either.

"But I'm more concerned about this," the Gambler said. He now held up a credit app: Karen's. Not that I could read it from across the room. But I knew what it was. "Bobby tells me you got all the way through and they balked at the check. Is that right?"

"Yeah."

"That shouldn't happen."

"I know."

"You get that far, you should close. You should have been closing the minute you walked through that door. The check should have been a formality, not a deal breaker. You understand what I'm saying?"

The Gambler's voice remained calm through all of this, but there was an urgency there, too, a kind of growing gravity. And anger, too, maybe.

"I understand what you're saying. The words, the ideas behind the words. The whole thing." I had the distinct feeling that I was talking too much, but I didn't know what he wanted from me, and my mouth switched into running mode.

"If you understood," the Gambler answered, "then we wouldn't be having a talk about this bullshit, would we?" He smiled thinly. "So I want you to tell me what happened with these people. You had them, they filled out the app, they were ready to go, and then what?"

"They balked." I sounded a little shrill, so I looked at my hands to hide my embarrassment. And my fear. This Gambler, the Gambler in front of me, had nothing to do with the old-time revival preacher who sermonized to us about selling. This was not the supersalesman Gambler. This was the Gambler who disposed of corpses in the middle of the night.

"They balked. Tell me something I don't know. Why? Why the fuck did they balk?"

Maybe anger wasn't the right way to go when speaking to an accessory to murder, but there it was. Besides, I was myself an accessory to murder, so I had to figure that leveled the playing field. "Look, Bobby told you I'm a power hitter, and I am. I sell a lot of books. I've never had people balk at the check before, and there's no reason to think it's going to happen again. It was just one of those things."

"Just one of those things, huh? Well, how about we don't do anything about it, Lem, and then it becomes two of those things and then three of those things? How about you tell me how many sales you have to blow before I'm supposed to care about it? How many? Tell me."

I let it hang in the air for a moment before I spoke. "More than one." I wanted to look away, but I told myself to keep my eyes steady. This was his problem, not mine.

"More than one? Okay. More than one. But I don't want it to be more than one. I want it to be less than one. It's a little late for that, I know, but I'm thinking—and maybe I'm crazy here—I'm thinking it might be better to stop this in its tracks so you don't sit in someone's house for three fuck-ing hours, have them fill out the app, and then fuck up the close. That's what I'm thinking, Lem. So tell me what happened."

I bit my lip. This wasn't the principal's office. I wasn't in danger of my mother getting a phone call. I was in danger of being executed, like Bas-tard and Karen. I had seen it. I knew what it meant, and I had to come up with something.

Based on the conversation I'd overheard, I could feel reasonably con-fident that the Gambler had known Bastard and Karen, knew something of their personalities, so whatever story I came up with would have to sound plausible.

"When the wife was filling out the app, the husband was making trou-ble. He was kind of a clown, you know, trying to distract her, insult her, in-sult me. With him carrying on, I could see the wife was having problems. She looked nervous. She started talking about money."

"What money?" the Gambler demanded. "How much money?"

I knew I'd hit a nerve. He and the police chief had been looking for money. From what I could tell, a lot of money. I took a deep breath and concentrated on acting as though I had no idea what he was talking about. "Just money. You know. Then when it came time for the check, she said she didn't want to do it."

"Yeah?" the Gambler said. He took off his glasses and rubbed his eyes with the back of his hand.

I felt pretty sure I was bombing. "So I, uh, tried again. I went over all the stuff they'd seen, I told them about how I had asked them to let me know if they weren't interested. I did all the things we've talked about in training, but she still wouldn't budge. I guess the husband got angry, and then I knew it was pretty much lost."

"This is bullshit," he said. "Why the fuck would they want encyclope-dias?"

I stared at him. "Um, I don't know," I said. "Why would anyone want encyclopedias? I mean, they're great books and all—"

"Spare me the bullshit. What did you do then?"

I shrugged. "I left."

"You left?" the Gambler repeated. "You just walked out of there? Did you say, 'Hell, I don't need two hundred dollars. I made me that already, so I don't need it again.' Is that what you told them?"

"Do you think that would have been helpful?"

His face reddened, but he didn't say anything. It was clear now that the Gambler wanted some other kind of information, information he didn't know how to excavate. So I bit back my irritation. The thing to do, I realized, was to use his confusion, his desperate fishing. I needed to figure out a way to make all of this work for me.

"I didn't know what else to do. I got the feeling they wanted me to leave, like I was getting on their nerves. I didn't know how to turn it around." I sighed. "So, can you tell me what I should have done?"

"What?" the Gambler sneered at me, astonished at the audacity of the question.

"I mean, if this is about keeping me from losing them at the check ever again, I need to know how to handle it. How would you have handled it?"

The Gambler's eyes narrowed, and his face pinched inward. "You tell me, Lem. You think about it for a while, then you come back and tell me. Right now I'm more interested in what you did. So you left? Were they doing anything when you left?"

I felt like I was gaining some ground, so I pushed it further. "Why? What does that have to do with my having lost the sale?"

"Just answer the question, would you?" The Gambler looked away.

"I don't think so. They were sitting at the kitchen table, smoking, too angry with each other to talk."

He stared at me blankly. Then I felt the smack of inspiration. Ideally, I would have had more time to think it through to be certain it wasn't an amazingly stupid idea, but I didn't have time, and I decided to run with it.

I paused and peered away as if in thought. "Before I went in there, I saw this creepy guy hanging around."

The Gambler now sat up straight. "What creepy guy?"

I shrugged, as if the story were no big deal. "Just a guy who stopped me, wanted to talk to me. He drove a dark Ford pickup and he had a strange haircut—short all over, but longish in the back. He had weird teeth, too. I think he might also have been the guy who was hanging around in the dark outside the trailer when I left, but I'm not sure. I didn't see whoever it was lurking around the trailer, but it was just a feeling I had, you know?"

I tried to look more puzzled than pleased with myself. The Gambler and this other guy, Doe, were clearly working together on this—and had been working with Bastard and Karen. Now I had the Gambler suspecting Doe. If I could cook up enough *Treasure of the Sierra Madre* tension between the two of them, they'd forget all about me and the check that never got written.

"All right," the Gambler said. "Get out of here."

I stood up and started to walk toward the door. "I won't let it happen again," I chirped like a good little bookman.

The Gambler didn't even look up. "That's just fucking great."

Chapter 17

H E'D BEEN DREAMING about the bodies, about moving them, which was why he believed you should never do anything too unpleasant right before going to sleep. It always stuck with you. In his dream, Doe had Karen's body, thin and light, like a department store mannequin, draped over his shoulder. Next to him, with Bastard in tow, was not the Gambler but Mitch Ossler, that fat bumbler. In the dream, Doe was just waiting for him to drop Bastard. And he would have. He'd have dropped the body and it would have come out of its impromptu bedsheet shroud, and it would have rolled away from them, even though they were on flat ground.

Mitch Ossler was like that. He'd taught the other guys how to cook meth, and he knew his stuff. No doubt about it. Mitch could cook fast, and he could cook reliably. He had his ear to the ground and came up with new recipes. He was the one who found out how to turn crankhead piss back into meth. But Mitch never had a mind for the details, little things like safety and staying alive. No one had been surprised, really surprised, when the accident happened. Something like that was bound to happen, and Mitch was exactly the sort of guy it would happen to. The asshole had been setting up a new lab; he let a batch get too hot, and it vomited out a violent blast of vapor right in his face.

No one else had smelled anything, but Mitch, whose face had gone all red and puffy from the wallop of heat, said it was mustard gas. Invisible, almost odorless, and in about twelve hours his organs would start to rupture. He had to go to a hospital.

Thing was, Doe couldn't let Mitch go to the hospital, couldn't let him make up some bullshit story about how he got exposed to mustard gas. It wasn't exactly like he could have been defending his trench against an offensive by the Germans. So they'd burned down the new lab, and Mitch had been the first guy to end up in the waste lagoon. Too bad, because he knew a lot of useful things.

Doe was up earlier than he would have liked and later than he should have been. He forced himself out of bed and hobbled around his bedroom, moving from closet to dresser and back again, keeping his legs wide apart to ease the pain. He wasn't going to look at his balls anymore. He'd decided he would just not look. He'd wait a week and then look again, surprise himself by seeing a normal sack. That was much better than checking them every day like some sort of hypochondriac.

No one would have guessed from looking at his trailer, from looking at the stuff in his trailer, that he had a fat and fast-growing account in the Caymans, and that was just how he liked it. Sure, his trailer was a little bit bigger than most of the others in Meadowbrook Grove, a little bit more nicely kept. He had a girl come twice a week to pick up for him, so he didn't need to bother with crap like laundry and putting away dishes. That's why most people lived badly. They had to choose between the freedom of laziness and the tyranny of neatness.

Doe knew that a cleaning girl was the third way. In his case, he had a chunky sixteen-year-old with bad acne and droopy eyes. Her mother said she was slightly retarded, and Doe had no problem believing it, the way she hulked around, mumbling cheerfully to herself. But she cleaned with a thoroughness that bordered on obsession, and she didn't steal or nose around. Even better, he almost never felt the urge to fuck around with her, ugly thing that she was. One time he thought about throwing her down and shoving it right into her asshole, purely on principle, because he could get away with it. Give her a cookie or a lollypop or something, and she'd be all right. But the phone rang or someone knocked on the door, and he was distracted.

First thing that morning, he staggered into the shower, angling himself so the water didn't hit his balls. He stayed in there for a long time, maybe too long, but finally forced himself out, and after a cursory pass with the towel, he stumbled into loose-fitting jeans and a Tampa Bay Bucs T-shirt. With breakfast in hand, a bag of Doritos and a Pepsi from the fridge, he hit the truck.

Bastard was dead, and that was going to be a problem. Now he had to see to it that there were no other problems. He needed to do the rounds, make sure everything looked normal. Bastard had a family emergency, he might say. He had to take off, visit his dying mother, fuck his dying sister, it didn't matter. Bastard found out he had colon cancer and had to go off for treatment. That might be good. Serves the fuck-stick right for messing with Karen. He deserved to have the world thinking he had ass cancer.

Meanwhile, Doe would have to get someone else real soon, because if production dried up, there was going to be trouble. Even if Doe understood in principle how to cook, he wasn't about to risk getting an organ-melting blast of mustard gas. So until they could recruit a new cook, it would be business as usual. A great deal of the distribution went through the encyclopedia kids—those two assholes the Gambler kept close—so that wouldn't be a problem. Same as always, they'd come to town once a month, go into neighborhoods, pass off to their dealers. Nice and neat. Cops didn't look at them twice.

They weren't the problem. The problem was the extracurricular product that the Gambler and B.B. didn't know about. Things had been growing lately, and Doe had begun to move beyond the cover of bookmen. There were other distributors now, and if they didn't get what they wanted, they'd whine. If their tweaking crankhead buyers didn't get what they wanted, they'd do more than whine. They'd make trouble, they'd break into houses and knock off convenience stores and old ladies in the street to get their ten fucking dollars for their fix. They would get themselves arrested, and once these assholes were sitting across the interrogation table from the cops, too stupid to ask for a lawyer, they'd talk.

Doe drove out to the hog lot and parked his truck out back. He was alone, no chance he wasn't, but even so he looked around carefully. He saw nothing but the pines, the undulating waste lagoon, a few egrets passing overhead, and a waddling trio of ducks—the ugly kind with gnarled red knobs on their beaks. An enormous toad, almost the size of a dinner plate, sat glumly in his path. It was low and fat and sprawled out as though its own size had been a horrible mistake. Doe gauged the distance to the waste lagoon. It might be possible, just possible, to punt it all the way over there, watch it splash into a shitty death. But he didn't do it. Letting it live was punishment enough.

Mitch had designed the door to the lab so that it was practically invisible from the outside if you didn't know where to look—just slats in the corrugated metal exterior of the hog lot. Doe slid his fingers inside and pulled the hidden latch outward. The door swung open and a blast of cool air hit him hard. He always winced. Always. Like the cool air might contain the same toxic cloud that killed Mitch. But it was just the AC, cranking hard. Unlike the hog lot proper, which he kept just cool enough to keep the hogs alive, the lab was downright chilly. If it went over sixty-five degrees, alarms went off to warn them. He had a special receiver in his house, in his car, in the office. It seemed like a good idea because of all the shit they had in there; if it got too hot, the place would erupt into a toxic mushroom cloud. So he kept it under sixty-five degrees.

Christ, he hated the place, and he avoided it as best he could. Bastard had made it easy. Piece of shit though he was, he had been good at his job, had been able to make sure everything went as it should, and he could cook quickly and safely. All of that freed Doe from having to do more than the occasional spot visit. Say good-bye to that for a while. He'd be practically living in this shithole until he felt he could trust their new cook—as soon as they could find one.

After the cool, the first thing that hit him was the stench. An impressive trick considering that he'd been walking along the shore of the waste lagoon. But that was what the waste lagoon was for—it disguised the stink, the gripping, knife-sharp, gut-churning stink like cat piss that rammed through his eyes and up into his brain the instant he crossed the threshold. Doe grabbed at one of the face masks, the kind favored by workers removing asbestos, hanging near the door. It helped a little, but he could still smell it, and he could hear, softly through the wall, the low, pathetic grunting of hogs.

The cooking gear lay everywhere—empty containers of stove fuel, starting fluid, ammonia, iodine, lye, Drano, propane, ether, paint thinner, Freon, chloroform, and sinisterly marked containers of hydrochloric acid, more skull-and-bones symbols than a pirate hideout. There were open boxes of cold and asthma medicine, crap they bought by the caseload from Mexico. In one corner were hundreds of empty wooden matchboxes, and scattered around lay thousands, maybe millions, of little wooden sticks whose red phosphorus Bastard would spend hours scrapping into a metal mixing bowl while listening to Molly Hatchet. Every once in a while, he was supposed to destroy as much of this stuff as he could, take it somewhere out of town and burn it. Holy Jesus, they didn't risk dumping it, but it looked like Bastard might have been a little lax on that point of late. That he had been lax about the trash suggested he'd been lax about other things, and that was about as disturbing a thought as you could reasonably have.

Doe walked around a large wooden table with three hot plates, half a dozen coffeemakers, and a huge, tipped-over box of rock salt. He maneuvered around the pit—a hole ten feet in diameter, maybe eight feet deep, dug right into the dirt floor, where they poured the used lye and acid. Then he made his way back past the hulking old ice machine. The cooling process demanded a lot of ice, and Doe had decided it was too suspicious to keep buying their own. He'd heard about a couple of guys in California, where the cops were starting to pay attention to crank, who got nabbed because they bought a twelve-pack of beer and twenty bags of ice to go with it. A sharp-eyed cop saw the transaction, figured something was up, and followed them to their lab. So Doe had bought this used machine out of state. One more reason why he would last while the others fell before his mighty empire.

Behind the ice machine, which he wheeled aside, he found the spot on the particleboard covering of the wall. A quick push and the flap opened, revealing the safe. Two thoughts shot through Doe's mind. One was that he would find the money in there, that Bastard had been keeping the money in the safe, even though he knew he wasn't supposed to keep cash and product together. The other thought was that the safe would be entirely empty. Neither turned out to be true.

Inside the safe he found a brown Publix shopping bag filled with dozens of little plastic bags of yellowish powder. All in all, about a pound of nicely diluted meth. Without factoring in overhead, it had cost a couple of hundred dollars in ingredients to cook. He would be able to sell it for close to five thousand.

Doe did another quick pass-through. He wanted to make sure nothing was cooking, nothing hot, nothing in the works when Bastard had got himself killed.

That was the problem with this stuff. It was gold, pure profit, and the cops didn't give a shit about it. But it could explode if you looked at it funny. You made the stuff by soaking over-the-counter cold medicine in toxic chemicals, reducing the ephedrine out of it; and the process required—and produced as by-products—shit so deadly that you could fight a war with it. He'd heard countless stories—meth labs exploding, the cooks all found dead or worse than dead from acid and lye burns, searing chemicals in their lungs that made them pray for a bullet in the brain.

Everything looked turned off, cool, and nonexplosive—no frothing chemical reactions, no smoke or burning smell or hiss of seeping chemicals. Doe got out of there, got out right quick, shut off the light, and didn't take off the mask until he was outside and could breathe in the pure shit stench of the waste lagoon.

Back in the truck, he predicted he could have everything taken care of within a few hours. Drive off to Jacksonville, unload the product to the distributors. At a couple of places, he would need to pick up twenty-gallon containers of urine. It had been Mitch, stupid dead Mitch, who had discovered that crankheads processed meth very badly, and you could recycle their urine. They'd been giving good deals to anyone who provided a healthy quantity of the stuff, and there was a certain pleasure in getting people hooked on meth and then harvesting their own piss to keep them hooked.

Bastard had loved that part. Now the asshole was dead. Doe didn't know what it proved, but he was sure it proved something.

Chapter 18

EVERY TIME WE WENT OUT on the road, we ended up in a motel near a Waffle House. Maybe Florida law stated that motels had to be built near a Waffle House. Anything, I was coming to understand, might be as true as anything else. I wasn't particularly hungry, but I thought I should eat something, so after I got out of the Gambler's room I headed over. It was probably where most of the bookmen would be eating—including, I hoped, Chitra, who I had not forgotten seemed to think I might be cute.

The Waffle House sat on the other side of the highway off-ramp, and to get to it you had to cross an empty lot full of sandy dirt and thorny weeds and huge, undulating fire-ant mounds. Fat crickets and toads the size of my thumbnail hopped out of my way as I walked slowly, making certain I didn't step in anything that would bite me. Litter from the highway punctuated the field, and there were piles of broken green and brown beer bottle glass, and a run-down wooden shack about as long and as wide as three Jiffy Johns placed side by side. I decided to plot a course far around it in case a derelict had set up camp there.

I had nearly reached the Waffle House when I heard footsteps behind me. Ronny Neil and Scott.

They both wore newish 501s and button-downs—Scott's was a pale, faded yellow of a heavy cotton weave, far too hot for this weather. Ronny Neil's was white, but with stains the color of Scott's shirt under his arms. Both wore old pattern ties that had certainly belonged to their fathers, though Ronny Neil's was wide and short enough that it might have been his grandfather's.

"Where you going?" Scott said.

"Breakfast," I told him.

"Is that fucking right?" Ronny Neil asked.

I kept walking.

"Didn't you hear him?" Scott asked. "He was talking to you."

"How rude of me," I said. "Yes, Ronny Neil, it is, in fact, fucking right."

"You watch your mouth," Ronny Neil said. "And I'll tell you something else. You ain't as smart as you think you are."

"Look, I'm going to get something to eat," I said, trying to soften things up a little.

"So are we." Scott flashed a crooked grin. "Why don't you buy us some breakfast?"

"You can buy your own breakfast," I told him.

"You being a cheap Jew?" Scott asked me. "Is that it? Pinching your pennies?"

"I'm not the one asking for a free breakfast."

Ronny Neil smacked me in the back of the head. It happened so fast that someone looking might not have been sure it had happened at all. But there was no mistaking the sting. Ronny Neil wore a ring on his finger, maybe not turned around, but he knew how to smack ring first. It hit me in the skull with a sharp crack that brought tears to my eyes.

I went stiff with disbelief and anger. I was out of high school. This sort of thing wasn't supposed to happen anymore. Despite the long hours and grueling conditions, and aside from the money, I had loved selling encyclopedias because it put me beyond high school. No one could see that I used to be heavy, that I used to be easy pickings. All they could see was the new Lem, fit, slim, good at selling. Now, with Ronny Neil and Scott, the feeling of powerlessness so infuriated me that it took all my will to keep from lunging at one of them. Both of them. Lunging haplessly and ineffectively, no doubt, but I wanted to lunge all the same.

"I keep a Buck knife in my pocket," Ronny Neil told me. "Now, my brother's in jail for armed robbery, and I have two cousins in there, too. One for grand theft auto and another on manslaughter, though it was really murder and he got pleaded down. That's what happens on a first offense, which my killing you would be. You think I'm afraid to sit a few years in jail, you go on and try me."

"You think maybe you want to buy us some breakfast now?" Scott lisped.

"Yeah," Ronny Neil said. "You ready to buy uth some breakfath?"

When we walked into the Waffle House, there were already groups of bookmen in some of the booths. Under certain circumstances—the post–sales pool gatherings, mostly—the bookmen could be a gregarious lot, but for the most part we stuck to our own groups. The Ft. Lauderdale crew socialized with the Ft. Lauderdale crew and Jacksonville with Jacksonville. No particular reason for it, and it wasn't a segregation in any way promoted by the crew bosses. But there was an inherent competitiveness among the crews, and no one ever got too friendly.

People glanced at us as we walked in, offered a few friendly nods, but no waves, no one shouted, "Hey, come over here and join us." All of which was fine by me. I didn't need my humiliation to go public.

They led me to one of the booths and pushed me in. Scott blocked me, and Ronny Neil sat across. He immediately picked up a laminated menu and began to study it intensely.

"Most important meal of the day," he said. "There's a lot of people don't know that."

The waitress, a plump blonde in her late twenties, came by and began to put down the table settings.

"How you doing this morning, darling?" Ronny Neil asked.

"Just fine, baby."

It was going to be one of those god-awful polite exchanges, full of empty endearments, and somehow that infuriated me more than my near abduction. "Only two," I said to her. "I won't be staying."

"Yeah, you will," Scott said.

"No, I won't. Get up and let me out of here."

"Don't mind him," Ronny Neil said to the waitress. "I think he's forgotten what my good friend Buck told him."

I shook my head. "Scott, get out of my way."

"Just sit and shut," he said.

"Juth thit and thut," Ronny Neil echoed.

I turned to the waitress. This was a big and enormously dangerous gamble, but I couldn't live with myself if I backed down now. I was done with backing down, at least for the moment. "Call the police, please." I hardly wanted the cops around, but I wasn't in Meadowbrook Grove, so it was worth at least conjuring the idea of law enforcement.

Her eyes narrowed. "You serious, hon?"

I nodded. She nodded back.

"Now, hold on," Ronny Neil said. He held his hands up in the air in the universal gesture of lighthearted surrender. "No need to get all threatening on me. We're just having some fun." Then, to Scott: "Get your fat ass up. Can't you see he's trying to get out?"

I pushed my way out and past Scott, avoiding eye contact with the waitress or any of the other bookmen. I didn't know how they read this exchange, and I didn't want to know. Instead, I turned to Ronny Neil. "Don't fuck with me." I said it quietly and slowly.

Maybe if it had been a movie, something dark would have crossed his face. He would have recognized he'd gone too far, and he would have winced, pushed himself back into the padding of the booth. That was the myth: Bullies are cowards, and if you stand up to them, they'll back down. It was the most insidious of fables, of course. It was the lie that parents told their children because they liked to tell it to themselves; it was an excuse to avoid the social awkwardness of getting involved, of standing up for their kids, of facing the bullies' parents, surely as frightening and unhinged as their issue.

Ronny Neil turned to Scott, and the two of them snickered.

"I guess we'll just see you later, then," Ronny Neil said.

Inside the Waffle House, everything had been cold with air-conditioning and vibrant with energy. There had been loud conversations, music, the sizzle of the grill, the ring of the cash register, the clink of coins dropped on a table for tips. Outside, the world was hot and still and sticky. I trembled in tight little spasms, fight or flight pounding through my system, but it had suddenly become distant, as though the conflict with Ronny Neil and Scott, then telling the waitress to call the police, were a vague memory or a story I made up.

There would be consequences. I knew it. I knew that my situation had grown almost inconceivably dangerous. This was no longer a matter of boys calling one another names or the occasional fingers flicked hotly against earlobes. This was deadly and dangerous. Anything could come at any time and from anywhere.

I squinted across the parking lot and saw Chitra making her way toward the restaurant. She walked with her head down, slightly slouched, and her gait tended to be a bit shambling. It was quite possibly unsexy, but I found it remarkably endearing—and therefore utterly sexy. Funny how that worked.

She caught my eye and smiled. "Oh, you've eaten already?"

I was sure she was looking for company, and I might have been as acceptable a companion as any of a dozen others. Or I was nearly sure, because Melford had said she'd thought I was cute. "No," I said. "There's an IHOP about a quarter mile up the road. Let's go there?"

"What's wrong with the Waffle House?"

"I can't believe that's a serious question," I said with a forced grin. I didn't want to tell her about Scott and Ronny Neil. I didn't want to look weak in front of her. And I didn't want to have to explain what it was all about. I didn't know what it was all about.

Chitra didn't actually say that she wanted to go down the road, but somehow we were walking there, keeping to the ragged side of the street, trying not to stray too much into the weeds unless a car or a mammoth truck came barreling past. Every ten paces or so, I would sneak a look at her profile, angular and dark and breathtakingly beautiful. A couple of times she caught me, gave me a half grin, and then looked away. I didn't know how to take it, but I had a feeling that maybe those little half grins would be enough to get me through this mess.

Inside the restaurant, which smelled deeply of maple syrup, we sat down and watched our waitress place before us coffee in thick white cups with droplets spilled over the side. It felt like permission to start talking in earnest. I didn't know what I had to say.

"This is the first time we've been alone since last week," Chitra said.

That sounded promising. "I guess it is." *Think of something clever. Something witty and seductive and disarming.* "It presents all kinds of opportunities."

Her eyes narrowed. "Such as?"

Had I gone too far? Had I been cheeky? Too suggestive? I needed to make a quick recovery. "For conversation. I mean, not to be critical of anyone, but you're not like the other book people."

"Neither are you."

"How do you mean?" I asked.

"How do *you* mean?" She smiled slyly at her coffee cup.

My cheeks burned. "You just seem, you know, more together than a lot of the others. You're going to a women's college and all."

She gave me a look of pleasant surprise. I'd scored a point, thanks to Melford's sensitivity training.

"I expect it will be a friendlier place for me than the world of book sales," she said.

"I'll bet. You know, I never asked you. How does someone like you end up here?"

She shrugged, maybe not very comfortable with the question. "Summer came around and I needed extra money, and more than I could make working at a store in the mall."

"I know how that goes." I had already told her about my quest to raise money for Columbia.

"I wish I could have taken a year off like you. My father owns a dry-cleaning business, and he had a problem with his crooked landlord, and that ended up with my father having some debts. But he refuses to let me offer him any money from my college account. So I'm trying to earn extra cash and take the burden off them."

I laughed. "I have the opposite problem. My parents have the money, but they won't give it to me."

"Well, believe me. I have problems of my own with my parents. They think I'm far too American, they hate the way I dress, the music I listen to, my friends, my boyfriend."

I took a casual sip of my coffee and forced a smile that must have looked grotesque. I felt like I was trying to get the corners of my mouth to touch each other somewhere behind my head. "Yeah?" I somehow managed.

Her eyebrows knit together. "Ex-boyfriend, really. Mostly. Anyhow, people in my family are pretty good about getting, you know, feelings about people. My father had a feeling about Todd. My boyfriend."

"Ex-boyfriend," I said. "Mostly."

She gave me one of those sly, sideways looks. "Right. Ex-boyfriend. Try telling him that. Things in that department haven't been so smooth. Anyhow, my father was sure that Todd was bad news, and he wouldn't let up about it."

"You said those feelings run in your family. Didn't you have a feeling about Todd?"

"Yes," she said. "I did."

"But you had a different feeling."

"No, I also had a feeling he was bad news. But sometimes a girl likes a little of that. Maybe," she said, "in your own way, you're sort of bad news, too, Lem."

The waitress arrived just in time to keep me from trying to figure out what the hell she was talking about. I could instead occupy myself with figuring out what to eat for breakfast. It occurred to me that I didn't really know how to order breakfast, not if I was going to be a vegetarian. And when had I decided to become one? I didn't even know, but it seemed to me odd now to think of eating meat, and I figured it might be best to hold off until I had a chance to think things through a little more. So I ordered oatmeal to play it safe, and I asked the waitress to keep milk and butter out of it.

Chitra ordered a cheese omelet.

"Are you a vegetarian?" she asked once the waitress had gone.

I don't know why, but I blushed. Given her discussion of her attraction to guys who were bad news, a category to which I now inexplicably belonged, I didn't know why my possible vegetarianism was so touchy. But it seemed to be. "Sort of, maybe. I'm pretty new to it, but my friend Melford, who you met—he's been trying to talk me into it. And I guess once you hear certain things about how animals are treated, it's hard to go back to pretending you don't know."

"Then don't tell me," she said. "I enjoy chicken too much." Maybe I looked disappointed, because she smiled at me and shrugged. "How long have you been a vegetarian?"

"Not long," I said.

"How long is not long?"

"Since last night."

She laughed. "Anything special happen last night? You didn't meet a nice vegetarian girl, did you?"

And there I was thinking I couldn't get more nervous. "Not really. I mean, no. No girls. I was just talking to Melford, and he has all these arguments. They're very convincing."

"So is Melford," Chitra observed. "I didn't talk to him long, but I could tell he's very charismatic. You get to talking to him, and you feel like you've known him a long time, and it's easy to open up. I said some things to him, and maybe I should have kept quiet."

Like finding me cute, I thought. In fact, I almost said it, but I caught myself in time. I wanted her to like me, not to see how clever I could be at her expense. "Yeah, he's charismatic."

"How long have you known him?"

"Not that long," I said.

"Longer than you've been a vegetarian, I hope."

"A bit longer," I said, trying to sound playfully casual but hating the half lie.

"He's very likable," she said. "But, to be honest, I sort of didn't like him anyway. I mean I did, but I didn't trust him. I don't know, I don't want to be down on your friends or anything, but if you don't know him that well, I thought maybe you might want to be careful, because the truth is, as far as feelings about people go, I had one about Melford."

"Oh?" My casual oh.

"I had a feeling that he's bad news himself. But in a real way. Not like with Todd, who could end up in jail as easily as community college. Or with you, in your interesting kind of messed-up way. I mean real bad news."

There was so much to say, really, that I hardly knew where to begin. Her sort-of-ex-boyfriend who might end up in jail. Did I ask why? How, precisely, was I interesting and messed up? Beyond all that, she had pegged Melford. Did she have these vibes like, oh, maybe he might have just killed some people?

"What does that mean, exactly? Real bad news?"

She held up her hands. "I'm sorry I said anything. It's not my business. I worry, is all."

I couldn't help but smile. She was worried about me.

I picked up a packet of sugar and began to tug lightly on the opposing corners. "Since we're talking about trust," I said, "there's something I've been meaning to bring up."

"Oh?" She leaned forward, and her large eyes grew larger.

She liked me. She had to like me. She was flirting with me. Wasn't she?

"The thing is . . . ," I began. I tugged on the sugar packet again, this time almost hard enough to rip it and send sugar sprawling over the table. That would be bad. "The thing is, I kind of get the feeling that Ronny Neil is interested in you."

"Ronny Neil Cramer," she said wistfully. She put a hand to her chin and let her eyes roll upward in delight. "Chitra Cramer. Mrs. Ronny Neil Cramer. What colors do you think for my bridesmaids?"

"You're teasing me," I observed.

"Can you seriously think that I would need to be warned off a fellow like that?"

"I don't know. I figured, you know, you're not American, and he's such an American type. He might not be as obvious to you as he is to me."

"Mmm," she said.

"Have I offended you?"

She said nothing for a moment. Then, a massive, dazzling smile, white against the vibrant red of her lips. "No. Not at all. I only wanted to make you squirm a bit."

On the way back to the motel, Chitra kept glancing over at me and grinning in a way that felt absolutely wicked. It was driving me crazy in virtually every way.

"What exactly is so funny?" I finally said.

"I grew up in a family of lapsed Hindus," she said. "My parents aren't religious, and we ate fish and chicken, but never red meat—out of habit, I suppose. I've never had a hamburger."

"You're kidding."

"No, I've never had one. Do you think I should?"

"Well, they taste good, but as a new vegetarian, I can't really endorse a move like that."

"You know what?" She was now twirling a little strand of hair above her right ear. Her ears were unusually small. "I think we should go out for hamburgers."

"Except that I'm a vegetarian. You're forgetting that part."

"I've never had one, and you're not supposed to have them. That's what will make it fun. Don't you find the forbidden exciting?"

I could think of no way to tell her that I'd had enough of the forbidden in the last twenty-four hours to last me some time. "Hamburgers aren't forbidden to me. I've given them up."

"Well, now you're challenging me, aren't you? I'm going to make it my mission to cause you to lapse."

"I have pretty good willpower."

"We'll see."

"What does that mean?"

"It means that everyone has a breaking point."

"Not me," I told her. "Once I decide to do something, that's it."

"Oh? Suppose I offered to sleep with you if you eat a hamburger?"

I stopped in my tracks.

She let out a laugh, playful and strangely innocent. "I'm not actually offering to sleep with you," she said, not stopping so that I had to dart to catch up. "I'm just making a point. You think you have an iron will, but we'll see."

"You're assuming I want to sleep with you." I had no idea why I would say such a thing, but I felt exposed.

"I suppose I am," she said.

I had no response, and we walked for a moment in strained if amicable silence. I decided it was time to change the subject and raise the question I'd wanted to ask. It needed to seem casual, relaxed. "So, what's it like being in the Gambler's crew?"

She studied me as we walked. "Why?" Her voice was strangely flat.

"No reason. I'm just wondering. I work for a nice guy, but you work for the big boss. I was wondering what it was like."

"Oh, I'm sure it's pretty much the same as anyone else's. Or maybe I haven't been around long enough to know."

"Is he always like he is in the meetings? You know? So vibrant?"

"Sometimes."

"Does he ever talk about his own boss?"

There was a pause now. A long one. An unnaturally long one, as if she were trying to think about how best to answer. "Why are you asking me all of this?"

"I'm a curious guy."

"Well, there are better things to be curious about."

"Like what?"

"Like me," she said.

And that pretty much killed my line of questioning.

Chapter 19

SETTING UP A PLACE TO MEET was the tricky part, since the Gambler didn't want to be seen with Jim Doe in public, and he figured the feeling was mutual. That meant that the police trailer and restaurant were out. So more often than not, they met in the Gambler's motel room. Doe had complained about the arrangements, finding them too gay, but as he'd been unable to come up with an acceptable alternative, the arrangements had stuck.

Now he sat in the Gambler's room, drinking a cup of Dunkin' Donuts coffee, with a little Rebel Yell splashed in for good measure. It helped him to keep his head clear.

The Gambler gazed at him, looking in that high-and-mighty way that made Doe want to stick his fist through the Gambler's face. Doe saw how this was shaping up. The dust had cleared, all of Doe's hard work was getting lost in the haze of greed, and now that asshole was trying to figure out who was looking to rip him off and how.

"You're still walking funny," the Gambler said. "You should see a doctor about that."

"I just pulled something moving the bodies."

"You were walking funny before we got to the bodies. If you're having leg pain or something, you shouldn't ignore it. Have a doctor check it out."

Doe didn't need this bullshit. "It ain't nothing. Jesus. I got enough problems without you trying to be my mother."

"Okay, fine. I'm just saying to see a doctor, is all." He paused for a minute to recover his momentum. "I talked to the kid."

"Yeah?" Doe asked. "What he have to say?"

"Fuck-all. They were going to buy, but balked at the last minute. What I don't get is, why would they invite him in, let him sit there for three hours, pretend they had kids?"

"Karen has kids," Doe said. "Had them, anyways. From her first husband. Little smart-ass fucker named Fred George, if you can believe that. Two first names. Worked for the bank and seemed to think that was some sort of big deal, something everyone ought to just marvel at, like being a pro football player or something. He took off and grabbed the kids when Karen first started doing meth."

"Why would she pretend she wanted to buy encyclopedias? She didn't know about the arrangement with me, did she?"

Doe didn't know the answer, but he knew that the Gambler *thought* he knew the answer, *thought* he was being clever, getting the best of the conversation. "I don't fucking know, Gamb. I don't think she did. And as for why, I can't guess what went on in her head. I don't know what she was doing there with Bastard. Maybe he was looking to rip us off, you know. Maybe he had a plan to stash the money there, maybe he was doing a deal with that money and it went bad. Could be a lot of things."

"Kid said something else."

"Yeah?" He took a sip of the coffee. It could have used more Yell.

"Said he saw you hanging around outside."

"He don't know me. How's he gonna say he saw me?"

The Gambler clucked his lips impatiently. "He gave a description that matched you."

"Handsome guy?"

The Gambler stared. "What?"

"That's a description that would point you right to me. Handsome guy?"

"Fucking hell, Doe. Is this all a big joke to you? We got dead bodies piled up to our dicks, we've got missing money, and I've got B.B. on my case."

"B.B. is always on your case."

"Yeah, well, he isn't always on my case so much that he's even as we speak in a car on his way here to find out where the fuck his money is."

Doe felt himself blanching. "Jesus, he isn't bringing that freaky cunt, is he?"

"He brings Desiree everywhere, and since he's coming here, I guess he's bringing her. Makes sense, don't you think?"

"That girl is weird. And that scar is nasty. But you ever think she's also kind of, you know, sexy? Like you wouldn't want to fuck her, but if she came up to you and was, like, Come on, let's go, you'd probably end up fucking her. You know what I mean?"

"You're going to get fucked, and not by Desiree, if you don't start working with me."

Doe stood up. "Wait a second there, Gamb. I don't much like the way you're talking. Are you *blaming* me for something?"

The Gambler kept his expression blank. "I'm just trying to find out why Bastard was acting so weird, letting one of my bookmen pitch him for three hours. And I'm trying to figure out why you were skulking outside the house the whole time."

"I saw the kid on the street, gave him some lip. That's all. I don't fucking know why Bastard would invite him in. Maybe it was all a big joke to him."

"You want to hear my theory?"

Doe didn't especially want to hear his theory, but he figured he'd have to listen to it if he protested or not, so there was no point in griping. He sat back down.

"My theory," the Gambler said, "is that Bastard invited the kid in because he was scared that something was going to happen to him, and he thought he needed a witness. Since you were slinking around outside, it's going to look to some people like he was afraid of you. And since you and he seemed to be fucking the same crankhead, and he ends up dead with our money missing, it's going to look to some people like you killed him and you took his money."

Doe slapped his coffee cup down, spilling it on the particleboard table. "You want to tell me which people exactly are going to see it that way?"

"B.B.," the Gambler said. "And if you don't find that money, you are going to be in some deep shit, my friend."

That took some of the anger out of Doe. It was true enough. The Gambler was a smug old fucker, but he knew how to call it. If B.B. was coming to check on the money, it meant he didn't believe that Doe could handle the situation. If the money didn't show up, the arrangement could be in trouble.

Still, it didn't seem inevitable that B.B. would blame Doe. All this business about how people were going to see things was crap. The Gambler was going to make sure that B.B. saw it a certain way to cover his own ass.

The fact was, Doe could come up with the money himself if he had to. It would mean a trip over to the Caymans, and it would hurt, but he could do it. He had to admit the money *had* been lost on his watch. Still, he'd only consider that option when all others were exhausted.

"So what do you think happened to it?" he asked.

"I don't fucking know," the Gambler said. "It beats the shit out of me, but you'd better find out."

"Yeah," Doe said. He finished his coffee and set down the cup, leaving it in a film of spillage on top of the table. With all the weight the Gambler was putting on him, Doe was starting to think that maybe the Gambler had the money himself. Maybe he'd killed Bastard and Karen and taken the cash. Doe had never seen the Gambler kill anyone, but he'd seen him beat the shit out of some crankheads trying to rip them off. It might well be that he'd gone over to see Bastard on some ordinary business, things had gotten out of control, and the next thing you know, Bastard and Karen are dead. Now he was either trying to cover his tracks or find some way to take advantage of the situation.

It was possible that the Gambler was setting him up not just in case — but setting him up, period. And that meant Doe was going to have to do some clever thinking to get out of this.

Once Doe had left the room, B.B. came out of the bathroom, where he'd been hiding in the tub behind a tan shower curtain streaked with a Milky Way of mildew. Now he walked into the room and took a seat at the foot of the bed. He dusted off his linen suit and flattened out his pants as he walked.

B.B. sat in the armchair but shot up almost at once. "The chair is wet," he said.

"It's just water," the Gambler said. "I spilled some ice last night."

"You saw I was going to sit in a wet chair, and you didn't say anything?"

"Jesus. I spilled the water last night. I forgot about it."

B.B. went into the bathroom and got a hand towel, which he dabbed repeatedly against his ass.

He'd always been a little off, but this was how it had been going lately—fussing over his clothes, his hair, and his shoes like a woman, obsessing over the smallest and strangest details of the operation, having his crazy scarred bikini girl do all the important work. Lately he'd been distracted, as though the business were taking him away from something more important.

That morning, while they'd been waiting for Doe to show up, after agreeing that B.B. would hide in the bathroom, he'd wandered off without telling the Gambler where he was going and when he'd be back. Next thing you know, there's no B.B. The Gambler had stuck his head out the door and seen him, on the balcony, staring at a couple of shirtless boys by the pool. If Doe had come by, the plan would have been shot to hell.

Not that the Gambler cared. If B.B. wanted to go around fucking boys or chickens or accident fatalities, that was his problem, but don't forget you're running a business. That was the thing. You took care of business first, and you kept your eye on the ball.

It was at that moment—when he saw B.B. leaning against the rail, leering at a couple of boys like a drunk in a strip club—that the Gambler knew he couldn't let things go on this way. For everyone's good. The only problem was that he had no idea *how* to take over. This wasn't *The Godfather.* He couldn't have his boys whack B.B.'s boys. There were no boys to speak of and no whacking. Their operation didn't work that way. They kept it low-key, what with the encyclopedia front and the hog lot front.

Now B.B. was staring at him, slightly red in his smooth, babyish face, wiping at his ass as though he'd just taken a shit. "Next time be a little more mindful."

"Sure. Fine. Whatever." The Gambler held up his hands in surrender. "I'm sorry you sat in my wet chair. Let's move on."

B.B. tossed the towel on the Gambler's bed. "I just don't like to sit in wet things."

"Let's move *on.*"

Pressing a hand to the corner of the bed, testing for hidden wetness, B.B. considered for a moment and then sat very carefully, as though the bed might turn into a fountain if he weren't careful. "Those two kids by the pool. You know them?"

"Why would I know anything about kids by the pool?"

"They looked, I don't know, familiar or something. You seen them with their parents?"

"What does it matter?"

"You know I run a charity for neglected young men. I'm just wondering if they need help. You see them with their parents, you let me know what the parents are like, okay?"

"Fine, but can we get back to Doe? What did you think?"

B.B. shook his head. "I think the guy is full of shit, but that doesn't mean he took the money."

"Then what does it mean?"

"Mostly it means that he's full of shit. But he knows he'd better come up with the money. I'm glad that Desiree wasn't with me to hear what he had to say. She doesn't like that kind of talk. He mouths off like that in front of her, I'll kill him."

"Somebody might have to kill him." The Gambler didn't know if it was true or not. Even if Doe had taken the money, he was still essential to keeping the Jacksonville operation alive. And the Gambler knew that he himself was necessary for keeping the book operation running smoothly. The only person who didn't pull his weight, it seemed, was B.B.

B.B. glared at the Gambler. "You're awful quick with the violence, aren't you?"

"I'm just saying."

"I'm the one who just says, okay? Remember that."

"What? I'm not allowed to make suggestions?"

"Make good ones, and you'll be allowed."

"Christ, you're touchy today. Let's forget it." He looked out the window. "You think having Desiree follow the kid is worthwhile?"

"No, it's a waste of time. That's why I'm having her do it."

The Gambler shook his head. "Okay, B.B. Whatever you say."

"That's right. Whatever I say."

The Gambler didn't answer. There was no response that didn't involve kicking the crap out of him.

Back in his room, B.B. sat on the side of the bed and picked up the phone. He dialed the number he had memorized but not yet called until now. For an instant he felt the hammering in his chest might be the sign of something serious. He might look like a young man, but he was in his fifties, and people his age, seemingly healthy people his age, dropped dead from heart problems all the time.

It was only nerves. Odd he should feel so nervous, like a kid asking a girl out on a date. He was just calling, that's all.

He heard the click of an answer, and he prepared to hang up until a familiar voice spoke.

"Hello?"

"Chuck?" B.B. said.

"Yeah?"

"It's B.B."

"Oh," he said with cheer, wonderful, heartening cheer. "Hi."

"Hi," B.B. said. He was silent for a minute while he gathered his thoughts. "Listen, I was just calling to tell you that I, you know, had a good time with you last night." He hoped it didn't sound stupid.

"Yeah, it was fun," Chuck said. "The food was good."

"And the wine?"

"Yeah. I didn't tell my mom about that, but it was good, too."

"Maybe you'd like to try some more," B.B. said.

"That would be neat."

"I have a nice collection at my house."

"Okay."

The boy sounded hesitant. Did he not like the idea of being invited over, or did he not know exactly what having a wine collection meant?

"Maybe you'd like to come over sometime next week. See the collection. Sample a few choice bottles."

"That would be cool. Thanks, B.B."

He felt himself suck in a breath. Chuck wanted to come over. He wanted to drink wine with him. Desiree wouldn't like it. She would think he was up to something. B.B. would deal with that later, because Chuck was a special boy, maybe the most special boy he'd come across, and there was much to teach him and show him. That was what it meant to be a mentor.

In the distance, he heard Chuck's mother call his name in her shrill, gnome voice.

"Listen," B.B. said, "I have to go, but stop by the foundation early next week, and we'll set up a time." He'd have Desiree out on a wild goose chase that afternoon. Something.

"That sounds great. I'll see you later, B.B."

He hung up the phone and shook his head against the power of it all. Here it was, the boy B.B. had always known was out there. The one he could show things and educate and enlighten, and together they could tell the world to fuck off with their narrow-minded suspicions.

Maybe everything was changing. Maybe it *was* time to move on, hand the business over to Desiree. She'd been overwhelmed by the idea, of course, but he only needed to help her gain the confidence. That would get her out of the house, certainly.

There was one last thing, however. He couldn't hand things over to Desiree with the Gambler still running the operation. Desiree wouldn't be the new B.B.; she would be the new Gambler, only with more responsibility. And that meant it was finally time. He'd kept the Gambler around long enough, savoring the opportunity, enjoying the feeling of toying with him. Now it was time to get rid of him.

That he had no idea how he would do such a thing bothered him hardly at all.

Chapter 20

I SAT GLOOMILY in the car while Bobby drove us around, getting us pumped up for the selling day. He would point at moochie houses, point at lawn furniture and Slip 'N Slides and volleyball nets. Finally, he let me out at a little after eleven. He would come by the Kwick Stop to get me in about twelve hours.

There had been times when I enjoyed it, this feeling of the day being all before me, every house a potential sale, a potential $200. Some days the unanswered knocks with the low barking behind thin metal doors didn't even bother me. Some days I all but smirked at the people who stared at me blankly as I went through my introductory speech, and I judged them. I judged them for their apathy. That's why you live in this shithole. That's why your kids will live in a trailer, just like you, when they grow up. Because you don't care.

Not that the encyclopedias mattered. Sure, it was possible that they'd make a difference in someone's life, but if a kid wanted to know some detail about the population of Togo or the history of metallurgy, he'd find out at school or in the library. On the other hand, the parents' willingness to buy the books, to invest the money, signaled something, and there were times when I actually believed in the importance of the work.

Not this morning. I skipped houses if they didn't look moochie. I knocked listlessly, mumbled my lines. Half an hour into the day, I'd had a smallish woman, pretty but ferociously freckled, just about primed. She was ready to bite, I could feel it, but I eased up on the pitch, excusing myself from going inside.

I knew that my days as a bookman were over. I'd go back to Ft. Lauderdale on Sunday night and I'd quit, and the thought of my impending freedom both excited and enervated me. What would I do with the rest of my day? If only there were a movie theater around here. A good bookstore, a library. A mall. Someplace I could go to cool off.

But for twelve hours? Suddenly the day stretched out endlessly. The heat hammered down on me, and I felt the sting of perspiration in my eyes. The endless expanse of time blanketed me, smothered me like the humidity. I wished I could gear myself up into book mode, just for the next couple of days. I'd still quit, I'd still walk away from this and never come back.

By twelve-thirty I was walking along a main road, not even bothering to look at the houses I passed, when I heard a car slowing down behind me. I turned and saw Melford's old Datsun, a faded dark green in the sunlight.

He rolled down the window. "Hop in."

I continued walking, with Melford keeping up with his slow pace. "I don't think so."

"Come on. What, are you going to kick rocks all day? I've got air-conditioning, tunes, witty conversation."

I told myself that I had no choice, that the guy was a killer, and a person was smart to do what a killer said to do. But I'd stopped being afraid of Melford. Not entirely, maybe— I wouldn't want to provoke him or even be around him when someone else had provoked him, but for all his killing he wasn't like Ronny Neil and Scott, whom I actually feared.

I sighed and nodded, so Melford stopped. I went around to the passenger side and got in. He did have the air conditioner going pretty strongly, and it felt good. We sat in silence for a few minutes while Melford drove past houses and mobile homes and a shopping plaza with a Kmart and a sporting goods store and an Italian restaurant. Coming out of the Kmart, I was sure, was Galen Edwine, the man at whose house I'd sold the grand slam that didn't work out. Not so far from where I'd been selling the day before, in fact.

Melford saw me looking at the strip mall. "God, I love Florida," he said.

"You're kidding. I hate this place. I can't wait to get out of here."

"I think you're the kidder. This is the land without art or values or even the most basic cultural orientation. Nothing matters but real estate and shopping malls. There are more golf courses than schools, prefab housing subdivisions growing like cancers, an aging and dangerous driving population, the Klan, drug lords, hurricanes, and twelve-month summers."

"Those sound like bad things to me."

He shook his head. "In Florida, you get to live in perpetual irony. It keeps you from settling into false consciousness."

"I just want to get out and never come back," I said.

"Well, there's that position, too, I guess."

We rode in silence for another ten minutes until I asked where we were going.

"You'll see."

"I want to know now." While I might have felt a strange liking for Melford, despite all I had seen, I couldn't stand this. I couldn't stand being boxed out and left in the dark.

"You're awful curious, aren't you?"

"I just don't want to be shot in the head or anything."

I regretted it the instant I said it—not because I had endangered myself, but because it seemed to hurt Melford's feelings. His eyes narrowed and he looked away.

"Surely by now you realize I don't solve all of my problems with violence," he told me. "Violence is a tool. It's like a hammer. It has its uses, and it is great for those uses. But if you use a hammer to change a baby's diaper, there's going to be trouble. I chose to use violence with those two because I thought it was the right thing to do."

"Okay," I said. "I understand." I didn't, and it was clear from my tone that I didn't.

Melford shook his head. "I don't enjoy hurting anyone, Lemuel. I only do it when there's no choice."

"But you won't tell me why."

"I'll tell you why when you can tell me why we have prisons."

"I don't have the energy for your prison riddle. I want to know why."

"And I want to tell you, but until you're ready, there's no point. It would be like telling a four-year-old about relativity. There may be a will to understand, but not a capacity."

I thought to blurt out something defensive, like he thought I was no smarter than a four-year-old, but I knew that wasn't what he meant.

"For now," Melford was saying, "what's important is that we're in this together. You are in serious trouble, my friend. We both are. There is dangerous stuff going on around here, and we've had the bad luck to land in the middle of it."

"But I don't have anything to do with it. It's not my fault."

"That's right. It's not your fault. And if your house was hit by lightning and started to burn, that wouldn't be your fault, either. So do you stand there and shout at the flames, or do you do what you can to save yourself and put out the fire?"

I didn't have an answer because he was just convincing enough to piss me off.

Melford stopped outside a Chinese restaurant and announced that it was time for lunch. I was reasonably hungry, not having eaten much of my breakfast. The dairy-free oatmeal had tasted like Elmer's glue, and I'd been too nervous about talking to Chitra to try to force it down.

"Chinese restaurants are great for vegetarians," he told me as we sat at a table in the smallish dining room lined with red wallpaper flocked with gold Buddhas. There were an additional two Buddha statues by the door, a tank full of white and orange koi, and a small fountain. "They tend to have lots of nonmeat options, and they don't traditionally cook with dairy." He poured tea into white cups with cracked enamel.

Eating breakfast with Chitra, I'd been determined to abandon all animal products. Now, here with Melford, I wanted to be a carnivore. This morning, I'd wanted to impress Chitra with my sensitive soul. Now, I wanted to impress Melford with my defiance. I needed to decide if I agreed with the principle or not—if I wanted to be a vegetarian or if I just wanted to stay away from meat when I thought it might impress the ladies.

I looked at the menu. "What about fish?"

Melford raised an eyebrow. "What about them?"

"Do you eat fish? The sea bass with black bean sauce looks pretty good."

"Do I exclude fish from my moral calculus because they live in the water instead of land? Is that what you're asking me?"

"I think I get the answer," I said, "but come on, we're talking about fish here. Not fluffy bunnies or Bessie the cow. They're fish. We put hooks in their mouths every day."

"So, cruelty justifies itself. You, of all people, ought to know better than that."

"What does that mean?"

"It means that when I came up to you with those two guys at the motel last night, I had the feeling that it wasn't the first time some mindless ass-holes decided to turn you into a pincushion. The fact that it's happened before doesn't mean it's okay for it to happen again. The fact that we're cruel to fish doesn't mean we should be cruel to them. Just because they live underwater and have scales instead of skin or fur doesn't make it okay."

I sighed. "Fine." When the waitress came I ordered the vegetable lo mein. Melford ordered vegetable dumplings.

"I'm not especially hungry," he said.

"Then why are we here?"

Melford shrugged. "Mostly I wanted to see if the woman following us would come in with us."

"What woman?"

"She was driving a Mercedes, and now she's at the table behind you. Don't turn around. Actually, no need to bother, since it looks like she's heading over here."

The woman came around and stood between us and looked us over as though deciding which of us she might choose to bring home. She was pretty and tall, dark blond shoulder-length hair, rounded features that would have once been considered hyperfeminine and now seemed girlish. As if to offset that effect, she dressed to draw attention, wearing tight pink jeans and a nearly translucent white blouse that exposed her black bra underneath. "You don't want to let him eat fish?" She was now looking over sunglasses at Melford, her eyebrows knit together. "Why do you make him miserable about his lunch—boss your friend around like that?"

We were silent for a moment. Finally I ventured, "He's not really mak-ing me miserable."

"He's giving you a hard time, isn't he?" She then looked at Melford. "Are you a bully?"

"He's not a bully," I said, not sure why I should stand up for Melford or defend him to this woman, whoever she might be.

"Sometimes people are so bullied that they don't even know they're being bullied," she told me. Then she looked at Melford. "Isn't what people eat a matter for their own choice?"

"No," said Melford, nothing but kindness in his voice. When I said no it came out blunt and hostile and defensive. He made it sound like an invitation. "Whether or not to wear clothing that exposes our underwear is a matter of choice. Whether or not to apply lipstick or go to the movies or enter the goofy golf tournament are matters of choice. When you do something that inflicts suffering on another, then it becomes a moral question."

The woman looked at him in a way that seemed both sly and appraising. "You know what?" she said. "You just might be more interesting than I thought at first. Can I join you?"

"I'd be delighted," Melford said.

She sat down and angled her chair slightly toward Melford and put her sunglasses in the breast pocket of her diaphanous blouse. "I'm Desiree," she said. And as they shook, Melford glanced at a series of lines drawn on the back of her hand. He gently kept hold of her fingers for a moment, almost as if he were getting ready to kiss her hand. "*Hsieh?*" he asked.

She nodded, not bothering to hide her surprise. "That's right."

He let go of her hand. "Are you considering making a break with the past?"

She tried to look neutral. "I guess so."

"Me too." He folded his hands. "So, you're interested in becoming a vegetarian?"

"I'm not," she told him. "I like eating what I eat. I'm interested in why you care so much."

"I care," Melford said, "because when we see something wrong, we ought to try to make it right. It's not enough to silently condemn evil, to congratulate ourselves for not participating. I believe we all have an obligation to stand against it."

Something darkened in her face. At first I thought he'd made her angry, but then I realized I saw a pang of sadness, maybe even confusion and doubt. "How exactly is this a matter of ethics? Animals are here for our use, aren't they? So, why shouldn't we use them?"

Melford picked up an empty teacup. "This was put here for our use, right? It was designed to make our lives better and all. What if I were to hurl it across the room? That would be considered an impolite act at best, but also violent, antisocial, unkind, and wasteful. The cup is here for my use, but I'm not free to use it in any way I see fit."

She shrugged. "Sounds reasonable."

"But not so reasonable that you'll change how you eat?" Melford said.

"No, not that reasonable."

He turned to me. "It's interesting, isn't it. You convince someone that everything you say is right, make them understand that eating animals is wrong, but they still won't change."

"Ideology?" I asked.

"You got it."

"So, what are you fellows up to today?" she asked.

"Oh, you know. This and that," Melford said.

She leaned a little closer to him. "Can you be more specific?"

He leaned closer, too, and it looked for an instant as though they might kiss. "Can you maybe give me a reason why I ought to be more specific?"

"Because," she told him, "I'm a curious, curious woman."

"Are you curious enough to wonder what it would be like to stop eating animals?"

"Not that curious."

Melford leaned back a few inches and then reached out to her hand and touched the black marks she'd penned onto her flesh. "You can tell yourself that your actions, alone and weighed against the balance of the universe, don't matter, but I think you know better. How long can you wink at evil because it is easy and gratifying to do so? You're better than that."

She pulled her hand away, but not violently. It looked to me more like embarrassment—or surprise. "You don't know me. You don't know anything about who I am."

Melford offered the ghost of a smile. "Maybe not. But I have a hunch."

She said nothing for a minute. She unwrapped a tube of disposable chopsticks, separated them, and tapped them together. "Does it make you happy to crusade for animals?"

He shook his head. "Does helping the sick, caring for the desperate, make someone happy? Would giving comfort to lepers in the Sudan make me happy? I don't think so. Happiness isn't the issue. These things make us feel balanced with the world around us, and that is something much more important than happiness."

She nodded for a long time, still tapping her chopsticks together. Then she dropped them, as though they'd suddenly grown uncomfortably warm. She stood up. "I have to go."

Melford held out his hand for her to shake. She looked surprised, but she took it anyway.

"You want to tell me who you're working for?" he asked. "Why you're following us?"

"I can't right now." She looked genuinely sad about it, too.

"Okay." He let go and she turned away, but he wasn't entirely done with her. "You know," he said, "you're much too smart to be working for them. You're not like them."

She reddened slightly. "I know that."

"*Hsieh*," Melford said.

She looked at her hand and nodded.

Chapter 21

S O, WHO WAS SHE?"

"I don't know. Someone who works for them. Whoever they are."

I sat in the passenger side of Melford's Datsun. I'd eaten the lo mein and put back five or six little cups of tea. Desiree's little visit that afternoon had left me stunned, but Melford appeared unperturbed. He'd eaten his green-tinted dumplings with splintery chopsticks and talked for a while about a philosopher named Althusser and something called "the ideological state apparatus." Only once we were back in the car did I try to talk about the woman.

"Doesn't it bother you that a strange person in peekaboo clothing is shadowing us?"

"Peekaboo clothing isn't without its pleasures. Don't you think? I noticed you inspecting the lace of her bra. Maybe you were thinking about buying a gift for Chitra."

I hated the feeling of being caught. "I do have to admit it. She seemed less scary and more . . ." I let my voice trail off.

"Sexy?"

"Sure," I agreed cautiously. I didn't know that Melford would be the world's best judge of which women were sexy and which were not. "But, still. We've got someone following us. What are we going to do about it?"

"Nothing," Melford said. "She's not following us now, and to be honest, I don't think she means us any harm."

"There are dead people floating all over the place. I know you killed *some* of them, but isn't it a bit naïve to assume they don't mean us harm?"

"I can't speak for *they*. I'm sure *they* do mean us a whole truckload of harm, but I don't think Desiree does. You could see it in her eyes. She is straying from them. She doesn't want to hurt us, or even report back about us. I have a feeling."

"Great, you have a feeling. Fine."

"It's the best we have until we know who *they* are."

I thought about telling him what I knew, that the Gambler was involved, but I hadn't told him last night, and now it would look weird, as though I'd been holding out on him and that maybe he ought not to trust me. There would be a way, I decided, to steer him in that direction if it became necessary, or to *discover* something that would point to the Gambler. In the meantime, I felt safer with his not knowing, even if it meant keeping a huge secret from a guy who was known to resolve his grievances, from time to time, with a silenced pistol.

"So, where are we off to now?" I asked.

"You'll recall that we have a task to do," Melford said. "We have to figure out who that third person was, the body in the trailer."

"What about the money? They're looking for a ton of cash. Maybe we should find out about that."

He shook his head. "Forget the money. It's a dead end. Let's think about finding the body."

"And tell me again how we do that?"

"The first thing we want to do is look at the body. Who knows. Maybe they were dumb enough to leave identification on her. Long shot, I know, but it's worth trying."

"Sure," I said. "That's a great idea, poking around at a dead body, looking for a wallet. But, and I may be being dense here, shouldn't we know where the bodies are first?"

"It so happens, smart guy, that I have a pretty good guess where they put the bodies. You catch that bad odor in the trailer park? You know what that was?"

"The smell of trailers? I don't know."

"It was a hog lot, Lemuel. The city of Meadowbrook Grove is mostly just that trailer park, which raises the bulk of its revenue through speeding tickets. Behind it is a small factory farm that raises hogs. Intensive hog farming produces a ton of waste, and that waste has to go somewhere. That bad smell in the trailer park comes from the waste lagoon, a nasty, environmentally hazardous seething pit of pig piss, pig shit, and pig remains. It also happens to be the single best place I can think of to hide bodies. So that's where we're off to."

"And we just waltz onto this property and start digging around through pig crap and no one will mind? Is that it?"

"No one will be there. There's no Old MacDonald. There's no oink oink here and oink oink there. The evil brilliance of these things is that they require virtually no maintenance. Just someone to stop by once a day to make sure the animals are fed."

"How do you know that the guy who feeds them won't be there?"

Melford shrugged. "Because I killed him yesterday."

I sucked in a breath. I felt the painful jolt of realization. "Is that why you killed Bastard? Because he worked at a pig farm?"

"Relax. I'm nowhere near that arbitrary. That had nothing to do with it. I feel sorry for most of the employees at these places—they're exploited just like the animals are. They earn low wages and labor for employers who neglect their health and safety. They're victims. The owners deserve to die, not the workers. No, this is a coincidence." He paused thoughtfully. "Sort of."

Melford pulled off the main road and drove behind the trailer park, then made a sharp right onto a dirt road that I might never have noticed even if I'd passed by a dozen or more times. It cut through a dense wood of scraggly pine and wayward Florida shrubs and white rock. We followed this path for a good mile or so, and all the while the thick stench of sulfur and ammonia became stronger until it felt as if someone had fashioned an ice pick out of bad smells and was shoving it into my sinuses.

We arrived at a fence and Melford stopped the car, hopped out, and removed a key from his pocket, which he used to open a padlock. When he got back in the car, he was still grinning.

"Where did you get the key?" I asked.

"I have my methods."

Back in the car, and after a little more wood-lined road, we pulled out into a clearing and I could see in front of us a large, flimsy-looking building with no windows. It was maybe two stories high and made out of what appeared to be aluminum sheets. The thing vaguely resembled a warehouse, but a nightmarish one, all alone in the clearing like it was. Or maybe it resembled a prison. I figured Melford must be getting to me.

He parked behind some pines so it wouldn't be visible if someone happened by—better safe than sorry, Melford explained—and we got out and began to walk toward the building. I thought it smelled bad in the car, thought I was getting used to it, but it grew stronger, harsher. The stench in front of us was like a physical weight in the air. Walking into it was like walking against the force of a wind tunnel. How could anyone work here? How could people stand to live nearby? And the pigs themselves—but I decided not to consider that. I had bigger things to worry about, and I was determined that Melford's obsession would not become my own.

Around the back of the warehouse, the grass and brush faded into a thick black dirt from which sprigs of grass shot upward intermittently. This beach extended maybe thirty feet, and then the lagoon began abruptly— so abruptly that I thought it must not only be man-made, but concrete lined. It was smaller than I imagined, the word *lagoon* suggesting tropical excess, lush green, misting waterfalls, flocks of shrill tropical birds exploding into flight. Waste lagoon turned out to be a euphemism, and when your euphemism has the word *waste* in it, you're starting from a pretty bad place. I found not a lagoon but a ditch, the worst, most horrible ditch I could ever have imagined, maybe three hundred feet in diameter. Nothing grew near except a scattering of the most ragged of weeds—and the strangely miraculous exception of a single black mangrove tree, whose gnarled roots looped in and out of the soil and into the lagoon.

I expected to get mud on my shoes as we approached, but the dirt was as dry and crumbly as a moonscape. With each step, however, the stench grew worse, impossibly and exponentially worse. The stink, to my surprise, seemed to possess mind-altering qualities. My head grew light, my steps unbalanced. I held out my hands to keep my balance.

I kept my eye on the lagoon, as though a monster might emerge to devour us. At first I had thought it was a trick of the sunlight, but the contents were not merely shaded, they were brown. It was a brown pond of viscous sludge that undulated its bloated waves against the slick shoreline. Pond is to waste lagoon, I thought, my mind lapsing into SAT analogy, as human being is to zombie. A seething nimbus of insects hovered above, buzzing with mutant menace.

Melford stopped outside the perimeter, marked by a series of metal rods around the pond, linked by string with Day-Glo plastic ribbons that fluttered sickly in the mild breeze. "They're probably in there," he said, gesturing toward the pond.

"So that's a waste lagoon?"

Melford nodded.

"That is all pig shit and pig piss?"

Melford nodded again.

"They all this vile?"

"Probably. I've never seen one close up before."

I stared at him. "You've never seen one?"

"Never. It's worse than I thought it would be. Bigger. More impenetrable."

"It looks like a good place to hide bodies," I said. "So, how do we find them?"

Melford shrugged. "We don't. This was a stupid idea."

"I'm sorry about the waste lagoon business," he said. "It seemed like a reasonable plan when I came up with it."

I shrugged, not quite sure what to say when a thoughtful assassin apologizes for the fact that his scheme to exhume the one body he didn't kill has ended up so badly.

Toward the far side of the warehouse, we approached a pair of large double doors, imposingly sturdy against the rest of the building, which close up looked as if it had been made from punched tin. A massive padlock held the doors together.

"Next stop," Melford said. He took out a key chain and opened the lock.

"How do you get these keys?" I asked.

He shook his head without looking up from the lock. "Lemuel, Lemuel, Lemuel. Have you not yet learned that Melford is a man of wonders? All doors yield to Melford."

He pulled open a door, hung the lock on the latch, and gestured for me to enter.

I didn't want to go inside. It was dark—not pitch dark, but gloomy. The building had no windows, and the only lights came from four or five nakcd bulbs that dangled from the ceiling. They were interspersed with slow-moving fans, which created a disorienting strobe effect, turning the space into a nightmarish nightclub of the damned. It smelled far worse than anything outside, worse than the lagoon, worse than a hundred lagoons. It was a different smell—mustier and muskier, thicker and more alive. A blast of cool air wafted from inside—not cool, really, but cooler than the scorching temperature outside. And there was the noise.

It was a low chorus of moans and grunts. I had no idea how many pigs were in there, but it had to be a great deal—dozens, hundreds, I had no idea.

Then Melford took out his pocket flashlight and pointed it forward, looking suddenly like Virgil in a Gustave Doré illustration from *The Inferno.*

I still couldn't see very well, but I could see enough. Dozens and dozens of small pens were staggered from the entrance to the far end of the warehouse. Each pen could hold four or five animals comfortably, contained fifteen, possibly twenty. I couldn't be certain because of how tightly they were packed. I watched the pen where Melford pointed his light. One pig was trying to move from one end of the pen to the other. As it pushed its way forward, it created a space that another pig had to fill. It was like a Rubik's Cube. Nothing went in or out, and if one was going to move, it had to trade spaces with another animal. The floor was slotted to let their urine and feces pass through to a drainage system that would flush it to the lagoon, but the slots were too big, and the pig's hooves kept getting caught. I saw one animal squeal as it yanked its leg free, and then it squealed again. Even in the gloom the blood on its hoof was clearly visible.

I took the light from Melford's hand and approached the nearest pen. The pigs, which had stood in a kind of trance of labored breathing, woke at my approach and squealed. They tried to push back, away from me, but there was nowhere for them go to, so they squealed more fervently, more shrilly. I hated to frighten them, but I needed to see.

What I thought I'd observed in the sporadic flashes of the strobing fans was now all too clear. Many of the pigs—most, perhaps—had heavy red growths erupting from under their short hair. Ugly, knotted, red tumorish things that jutted with malevolent force like misshapen rock formations. Some of the growths were along their backs or sides, and the pigs appeared to more or less ignore them. Others had them on their legs or near their hooves and so had trouble moving. Some had them on their faces, near their eyes or on their snouts, so they couldn't close their mouths or open them fully.

I backed off. "What's wrong with them?" I asked Melford. "I mean, holy shit. It looks like a medical experiment or something."

"It is, in a way," Melford said with the clinical calm I was coming to expect of him. "But they're not the test subjects. We are. No animals, except maybe social insects, were meant to live in such close quarters, but the hog farmers pack them in because the closer you can get them, the more hogs you have to raise in a single space. It's a matter of being cost-effective. But the pigs—and let's forget about their pain and misery. Most of them are probably insane by this point anyhow. But on a purely physiological level, the pigs can't stand it, their bodies can't take the physical stress, and that makes them vulnerable to disease. So they get pumped full of medicines, not to make them healthy, you understand, but to allow them to survive their confinement and reach slaughter weight. I'm talking about mammoth quantities of antibiotics."

"I don't get it. Isn't there like an inspector or something who will say they're too diseased for human consumption?"

"That would be the USDA—the same agency that's in charge of making sure that we don't eat diseased animals is also in charge of promoting the consumption of American meat. It's bad business to make meat safe and treat the animals humanely, because that costs money. If the meat costs too much, well, that makes voters unhappy. So if an inspector actually gets it in his head to try to stop this craziness, the farmers—the guys they are supposed to regulate—file complaints, and next thing you know, that inspector is reassigned or out of a job. The result: No one opens his mouth, and sick animals get sent to the slaughterhouse, where they are often dismembered while still alive, the visibly diseased bits are cut off, and their flesh, steeped in antibiotics and growth hormones, arrives on the dinner table."

"So, what are you saying? That our food supply is tainted and no one knows but you?"

"Lots of people know, but people don't worry about it because they are told everything is fine. But the statistics are staggering. Seventy percent of the antibiotics we use go into livestock—meat and dairy animals that people end up consuming. Most of the population is walking around with low dosages of antibiotics in them, allowing bacteria to evolve into antibiotic-resistant strains. Even if I didn't care how the animals are treated, I would still have to worry about the plague that's coming to wipe us all out."

"I don't believe it," I said. "If it were really that dangerous, then wouldn't someone do something about it?"

"Things don't work that way. Money greases the wheels. If there were a plague and it were linked back to factory farming, then someone would do something about it. Until that happens, too many people are making too much money. Our senators and representatives from farm states say that there's no evidence that intensive farming hurts anyone. Meanwhile, they're taking zillions of dollars of campaign contributions from these giant agribusinesses that destroy family farms and replace them with Nazi monstrosities."

"It can't be that bad," I said.

"It's amazing. You're like a walking poster child for ideology. How can it not be that bad? You are looking right at it. It *is* that bad. And if your own eyes don't convince you, how can you ever be convinced of anything ever except what you already believe?"

I had no answer.

"Look," he continued, "even if you have no sympathy for the suffering of the animals, even if you're too shortsighted to care about the long-term health risks of tainted meat, then think about this: There are consequences, terrible, human consequences, soul-crushing consequences, from being asked to not think about something as basic as our own survival because big corporations need to keep up their bottom lines."

It was a good point, and I didn't have a response. "Let's get out of here."

Outside, even in the midst of all that stench, I didn't feel like moving. We stood in the clearing while I stared at the building in numb disbelief.

"Imagine what you've just seen," Melford said, "only multiply it by millions. Billions. It makes you wonder, doesn't it."

"Makes me wonder what?" I asked. My voice sounded hollow.

"If it is ever ethical to sacrifice human life for the sake of animal life."

Even in the face of what I'd witnessed, I didn't hesitate. "No," I said.

"Are you sure? Let me ask you something. Say you come upon a woman being raped. The only way to save her from rape is to kill her attacker. Is killing him the right thing to do?"

"If I had no other choice, of course."

"Why? Why is that morally acceptable?"

"Because I value the right of a woman to escape rape over the right of a rapist to live."

"Good answer. But what about the right of an animal to escape torture? You don't value that right over the right of a torturer to achieve pleasure or profit?"

"No. Look, what goes on in there is terrible, Melford. I would never say otherwise. But there is still a basic divide between people and animals."

"Because animals have a lesser sense of themselves?"

"That's right."

"And what about a severely retarded person—one who, as far as we know, is not any more aware than a monkey? Does he only have the rights of a monkey?"

"Of course not. He's still a human being."

"And receives the rights thereof, yes? The umbrella that includes the imagined or the typical person must also include the lowest of us. Is that it?"

"Yeah," I said. "That's it."

"But is that umbrella natural and right and just, or is it just what we tell ourselves for our ethical and economic and sensual convenience? Why shouldn't that umbrella include all creatures who are capable of feelings and emotions? If it's wrong to torture a pig, then it's wrong. To say that it is no longer wrong when it's lucrative—because we want valuable exports and cheap meat at the supermarket—is insane. Ethics cannot be bound up with profit. It's like permitting contract killing while making murders of passion illegal. Is cruelty motivated by capital less evil than other kinds of cruelty?"

"I understand what you're saying, but you can't convince me that there's no hierarchy. Animals might feel emotions, but they don't write books or compose music. We have imagination and creativity, and that means human life is always more valuable than animal life."

"Always? Let's say there's a dog, a heroic dog. A dog who has saved the lives of countless people through acts of bravery. Maybe a firehouse dog who rescues babies from a fire. And let's say there is a convict on death row, one you know is guilty of horrible murders. He's escaped on the eve of his execution and he's taken the dog hostage. The next morning, the authorities discover his hideout. They know they can recapture him, but in doing so, the dog will surely be killed. Or they can have a sniper take out the convict and save the dog's life. What's more important, the convict who has killed numerous people and who would already be dead had he not escaped, or the dog, who has only done good?"

"Come on. It's an extreme case," I said.

"Agreed. It's the most extreme case I could devise on short notice. Now answer the question."

"You save the man," I told him, not entirely convinced I believe it. "Once you go down the road you're talking about, it's a slippery slope."

"So human life, no matter how evil, must always take precedence over animal life, no matter how exalted?"

I shrugged, playing at an apathy I didn't feel, didn't come close to feeling. The truth was, I had no answer to his line of questioning, and it bothered me. If Melford was right, then there were no absolutes, not like I'd always believed, and it put me in an ethical free fall. The example *was* extreme, and I understood that was Melford's point. I wasn't willing to admit that you probably save the dog, however, since that meant that the question was no longer black and white, but a matter of degree. It wasn't if you value human life over animal, but when and under what conditions. "I don't know. Can we go now?"

"Yeah, head over to the car. I haven't quite figured out how I'm going to save these pigs, but in the meantime, I need to feed and water them. It will only take a few minutes."

"You want help?"

"Nah, don't worry about it."

I did worry about it, but I obeyed, because with Melford it was my lot to obey. So I put my head down and shuffled toward the car, trying to blank my mind, trying to think of nothing at all rather than think about those pigs with their ugly red tumors and the hollow looks in their eyes. I couldn't make my mind go blank, though. Instead, I thought of Karen and Bastard, cold and dead and wide-eyed.

When I was halfway to the car, I looked up from my miserable reverie. Something must have attracted my attention, and when I peered in the glaring afternoon, with everything hazy from the sun blasting the land with oven-hot intensity, I saw something that made me freeze with terror. A cop car was pulling onto the grounds and pivoting right at me, as if it were lining me up to run me over. There could be no doubt. Whoever was behind the wheel had seen me.

I craned my neck in search of Melford, but there was no sign of him. The cop probably hadn't seen him, either. As far as he knew, I was there all alone.

I recognized the cop at once. It was the guy from the dark Ford outside Bastard and Karen's trailer, the guy who had helped the Gambler move the body. The police chief of Meadowbrook Grove.

Chapter 22

T HE COP STEPPED OUT of his car, shut the door, and leaned back
against it. If he'd been a smoker, he'd have lit up. The car was clean;
I noticed it right away. It looked newly washed, the kind of car you
wouldn't mind leaning against.

He waved me over as if we were old friends, and I obeyed the command. I wanted to run, figured I probably ought to run, but I knew I wasn't
ready for an instant metamorphosis from working teen to outlaw. Besides,
Melford was nearby, and I figured I was probably safer with him lurking
somewhere around here than I would be running through the trees with a
cop of pretty questionable ethics on my tail.

I walked over slowly, trying to keep my head up, to smile, to look as
though I'd done nothing wrong. I'd learned that much from Melford. Act
like everything is cool, and maybe everything will be cool. Of course,
Melford was also willing to start shooting people in the head if things
ended up leaning toward the not cool.

"Good afternoon, Officer," I said.

"Well, now," the cop said. "If it ain't the encyclopedia salesman. You
sell any encyclopedias to them pigs?" He grinned, showing me his twisted
teeth.

I recalled that I had never told the cop what I'd been selling. "I never
thought to try," I said. "I was getting out of the heat in those trees, and sort
of wandered around and came out here. I was curious about what this
place was, the smell and all that, so I thought I'd look around. Am I trespassing or something?"

The cop, Jim Doe by Melford's account, squinted at me. He rubbed at his nose, and his fingernail clawed for one unconscious instant at a hard booger encrusted at the tip of his nostril. "What the hell you doing wandering in the woods when you're supposed to be selling books? Your boss gonna like that?"

"It's a long day," I said. "I wanted to take some downtime before heading back on the road. You can understand the value of resting a bit before hard work, I'm sure, Officer."

"I don't see how trespassing on a hog lot is downtime," he said. "In fact, it seems to me that what you were doing was breaking the law. Not a whole lot else besides, either."

"I'm sorry, but I didn't see any signs telling me I couldn't be here."

"I guess you didn't see that big yellow sign saying NO TRESPASSING, did you? Didn't see that gate that keeps folks out?"

"I came through the woods," I said, not knowing if such a thing were possible. "Anyhow, I was just leaving. I think you can understand my mistake, can't you?"

The sales technique didn't seem to be doing the trick. "I'd better look around to make sure you didn't fuck anything up. Then I'm going to take you to jail on trespassing charges." He stepped toward me. "Now turn around and face the car. Hold your hands behind your back."

"I don't think this is really necessary," I said. My voice wavered as panic began to set in.

Doe grabbed my shoulders, digging into the flesh hard enough to bruise. He twisted me around and shoved me into the side of the cruiser. If I had not yanked my neck back, my head would have slammed against the passenger-side window, and for a dizzying moment I thought I would fall down. Somehow I managed to maintain my balance, but Doe gave my head a shove, and my nose hit the window hard. The blood began to trickle out of one of my nostrils.

There was only a moment to process this pain before the next wave began. Doe slapped the cuffs down on my left wrist and then the right. The cold clamping of metal cut into me, and then a curious combination of sharp, tearing pain and a growing numbness shot up my arms.

Another claw on my shoulder, and I was spinning around again to face Doe.

"These cuffs are too tight," I gasped. "You're cutting off my circulation."

"Shut your fucking hole." Doe punched me in the stomach.

The air went out of me, and I bent over and let out an *oof* but then straightened myself up. Vegetable lo mein churned in my stomach. As much as it hurt, I knew that Doe had pulled his punch, and I knew I didn't want to taste the real thing.

"Now," Doe said, "you cut out the bullshit and tell me what you're doing here."

"I told you," I said, wincing at how feeble I sounded. Blood trickled out of my nose and into my mouth. A *whoosh*ing noise roared in my ears.

"You haven't told me shit. You keep showing up in the most fuck-all places, boy, and your story about wandering onto this property ain't going to convince me of nothing."

"Am I under arrest?"

"You ain't that lucky." Doe opened the door to the backseat. He shoved me inside, making sure to knock my head against the roof on the way in. "You're going to sit in here while I go look around to see if I can tell what you were up to. You better hope I don't find nothing, either, or you may be getting a better look at that there shithole." He gestured toward the waste lagoon and then shoved the door shut.

I wasn't going to cry, despite the watering of my eyes and the growing mass in my throat. This wasn't Kevin Oswald from gym class knocking me hard in the locker room so I fell backward over the bench and smashed my head into Teddy Abbott's locker. This was a cop clearly operating outside the law, possibly guilty of murder, who was intent on doing something really terrible to me. I concentrated on licking away the salty blood that trickled slowly out of my nose and settled on my upper lip.

I tried to wiggle, but it hurt too much, and my hands felt like overfilled hot-water bottles, ready to burst. I wondered if the cuffs were going to do any permanent damage, and I wondered if permanent damage was even something I needed to be concerned about. Just what were the chances that I would have the opportunity, say, ten years from now, to rub my wrists and think that the old cuff injury was acting up again?

Where the hell was Melford? Surely he would take a little time off from tending to the livestock to come back to rescue me. Melford would not be intimidated by a little thing like going up against a policeman. He had removed himself from the ideological state apparatus, or so he claimed, so he would have no compunction about sneaking up on a cop and bashing in his head. That's what I was hoping, because I also had to wonder if Melford would take advantage of the opportunity and leave me holding the bag for everything that had happened.

I looked out the window and saw Doe walking slowly, legs wide like an old-time cowboy, toward the barn. Was Melford still in there, making clucking noises while casting hog chow to diseased pigs? Or was he at that moment planning a covert attack? Had he covered himself with leaves and twigs and taken a slow crawl along the ground so he could leap up and slit the cop's throat?

I didn't want to be party to another murder, particularly a policeman's murder. Though I was now well convinced that Doe was the kind of guy who needed killing, the kind of person I would gladly sacrifice to save a dog of even moderate bravery, I still had more significant qualms about murder than Melford did. I sure as hell didn't want to be a fugitive from a cop killing. Doe could be a baby raper, but if he was killed, every cop in the world would pursue the murderer with unceasing rage.

All of that became irrelevant, because just then I saw another cop car coming down the dirt road and out of the thick of pine trees. That meant Melford was now outnumbered. Doe had backup, and the cops back at their station knew about the call. If something happened to these guys, we would be world-class fugitives.

Then I noticed something about the second cop car. It wasn't navy blue like Doe's; it was brown. Instead of CITY OF MEADOWBROOK GROVE along the side, it had GROVE COUNTY SHERIFF'S DEPARTMENT. I glanced over at Jim Doe, who had also turned to look at the car, and even from the distance I could see him mouth a single syllable. It looked a lot like "Shit."

Doe started power-walking back to his car, one arm swinging hard, one hand pressed to the crown of his hat to keep it from falling off. The brown sheriff's department car pulled directly in front of Doe's, and a woman came out, dressed in an unflattering brown uniform.

It was hard to say what might have been flattering on her. She wasn't ugly, but she was stocky and rugged, with a mannish build and a slightly flattened-looking face. Her short, walnut-brown hair was pulled back into a sensible ponytail—the sort that wouldn't get in your face while hopping fences and darting into alleys in pursuit of bad guys.

She glanced at Doe and then into the back of Doe's car, making eye contact with me for a moment. She then reached into her own car to pull out her radio mike.

"Hold up there," I could hear Doe say, though his voice was muted by the glass of the car. With one hand still on his hat, he speed-waddled toward her. "Let's just hold up a second."

The woman put the mike back. I suspected that it might have been a bad move, but I wasn't about to start shouting or knocking on the window with my skull. I couldn't even decide if the presence of this new, potentially uncrooked cop was good news or bad news.

"No need to call in nothing," Doe said, slightly winded from his jog. He offered a smile certainly meant to be friendly, but it looked grotesque to me. "What's the hurry, Aimee?"

She glanced at me. I tried to plead with my eyes. "What the fuck is going on here?"

"I don't like it when a lady swears," he told her.

"What are you, my minister? I don't give a rat's shit bag puss fuck tit what you like. I want to know what's going on here."

"Got me a trespasser," Doe said. "That's all. Maybe more than one. Still got to check out the grounds. And this here is Meadowbrook Grove's jurisdiction, not to mention my own personal property. So if you don't mind staying out of our business, I promise not to stick my nose in yours." He unveiled another grin. "Nope, I won't stick nothing in your business."

She met his gaze. "Jim, you know perfectly well you can't order a county cop out of a municipality, and if I think you might be up to something, I can have a look around. It's a little something called 'probable cause'—a concept pretty well-known among cops. And let me tell you, that sad-looking boy in your car, licking the snotty blood off his face, gives it to me."

Doe turned away from her, pressed one finger to his left nostril, and blew out a wad of snot onto the ground. "You want to play hardball with me, sugar?"

"What I want is to know what's going on. So how about you stop jerking me around."

"Maybe you want to jerk me around a little?" Before the county officer could speak, Doe let out an exasperated sigh and pointed toward the hog lot. "I came to check on my property, and I happened to notice this suspicious-looking fellow prowling around, looking to break in, I guess. What should I have done? Called the police?"

"Yeah." She nodded. "That's what you should have done. Get him out of that car."

"I don't much like the tone of your voice."

"You're not going to like the tone of the county jail, either. Get him out of there."

He put his hands on his hips. "What crawled up you? Is this because I forgot Jenny's birthday? Is that what this is about? Because if Pam told you to give me a hard time about that, why, that's nothing but harassment, is what that is. I might file me a complaint."

"You don't want to play it this way."

"I don't understand why you folks at County don't have more respect for your fellow law enforcement officers from other jurisdictions."

"We have plenty of respect for other law enforcement officers," she told him. "We just don't respect you. Get him out of there now, unless you want me to radio for backup. Because if that happens, things are going to get ugly."

"It got ugly the minute you showed your face," Doe mumbled.

He opened the door and yanked me out, sending another wave of pain through my arms. "Don't make me mad," he whispered, hardly more than a hot breath, into my ear. "Don't think for a second you're getting away with anything. I know who you are, boy."

The other cop gave me an appraising, almost sympathetic, once-over. I couldn't figure out my move. Cops were no longer my friends, but I had to believe that she would be a better bet than Jim Doe, a better bet by a long stretch. Frankly, at that moment I believed I'd be willing to face charges and trial and testify against Melford if I could get away from Jim Doe. Maybe not very loyal, but I hadn't seen Melford running to my rescue, and I wouldn't be involved in any of this if Melford hadn't killed Bastard and Karen for reasons he still wasn't talking about.

"Jesus fucking Christ," swore the county cop, looking at my bloodied nose.

"I found him that way," Doe said.

She ignored him. "What's your name, son?" she asked, even though she was still in her twenties, possibly even early twenties, and had no business calling me "son."

"Lem Altick." No point in lying when she could, and certainly would, pull my license.

"What were you doing here?"

I told her the same story I'd told Doe, about looking for shade and then just wandering around in the absence of NO TRESPASSING signs. It found a more sympathetic audience with her, perhaps because of the blood.

"You resist the man in any way?" She gestured toward Doe with her head.

"No, ma'am. I explained myself like I did with you."

"Turn around," she told me.

I did.

"Jesus fuck," she whispered. "Take those off of him now."

"I got a right to handcuff a perp."

"Doe, I'm going to count to three, and if those cuffs aren't off, then you're going to be the perp here."

He grumbled but took out his keys and unlocked the cuffs, getting in a few rough jerks while he fumbled to fit the key in the lock.

"What a bullshit move, putting them on too tight. What, did you knock his head against the door when you put him in the car, too?"

It had been a rhetorical question, but I answered for Doe. "Yes, ma'am, he did. Punched me in the stomach, too."

"This fucker is lying," Doe said as the cuffs came off.

I felt a rush of pain as the blood began to flow. It stung horribly, and I winced as my eyes watered, but I was determined to show nothing more than the wincing. I kept my hands behind my back, not wanting to see them until the pain dissipated.

"It sure doesn't look that way, Jim. I'm going to have to bring you up on charges."

But she didn't move. She didn't go to cuff him. Instead, she smiled thinly and stared at him, waiting to see how he planned to take it.

"Is this because I wouldn't fuck you?" he asked. "Is that what this is about? It's just that I don't like women without titties."

"Unless you have something useful to say that would make me view this matter in a better light, I'm going to have to take you over to the station."

I didn't know I was going to say it until it came out. "I don't want to press charges."

The cop turned to me so fast, I was surprised her hat stayed on her head. "Why in hell not?"

I shrugged. "I don't want any trouble. I don't live near here, and I wouldn't be able to come back for the trial or anything. And I guess I was trespassing, even if he got a little mean about it. I'd just as soon forget the whole thing."

Doe grinned at me as though we were co-conspirators. Or something else. As though he hadn't been appeased, and this effort to get on his good side would only hurt me in the end.

Still, it was the right move. Best to let the whole thing disappear. Get the cops and the courts and maybe the media involved, I might end up in jail. Way things were now, it might just turn out okay. It was a long shot, but it was something to hope for.

"You sure about that?" she asked.

I nodded.

She turned to Doe. "This is your lucky day. Why don't you get on out of here."

"Why don't I get on out of here?" he asked, scratching his head. "Let me think about that one. How about this? Because it's my fucking land. How about you get out of here?"

"Do us both a favor and take a hike. And let me be clear about something. If anything happens to this boy, Jim, anything at all, I'm coming after you, so I suggest you be careful."

"I ain't never seen a woman with such small titties," he answered, and then got into his car. The engine came on with an angry growl, and the car pulled out at about fifty miles an hour.

The county cop watched it go. "I ought to give him a speeding ticket," she said. "See how he likes it." The she looked over at me. "So, what *were* you doing here?"

"Just like I said," I told her. "I was wandering. I sort of plan to quit selling encyclopedias when I get home, and I didn't have the energy to work today. So I was walking along, and I came here."

"Come on, there must be more to it than that. You smoking pot or something? I don't care. I just want to know."

I shook my head. "Nothing like that. I was walking is all."

She shook her head. "Fine. Let me give you a ride."

I thought about the offer for a minute. Melford was back there somewhere, but what had he done for me but hang me out to dry? Either he hadn't seen what was going on, which showed he couldn't be trusted to watch my back, or he had and decided not to help me. Either way, I figured I ought to have no problem washing my hands of him.

For want of anyplace else to go to, I asked her to give me a ride to the motel, then I climbed into her car, fully aware that sitting in a cop car, front seat or back, was just about the last place I wanted to be. As we pulled out along the pine-lined road, and I caught a glimpse of Jim Doe's car hidden behind a few trees, I knew taking the ride had been the smart move.

The cop, Officer Toms according to her badge, decided the silent treatment was the best way to go. She handed me a tissue for my nose, which had already stopped bleeding, but I dabbed at it anyhow because it seemed the polite thing to do. Finally, without turning to look at me— though she might have given me a sidelong glance behind her mirrored sunglasses—she said, "You're in some kind of trouble, aren't you."

"Not anymore."

"Yeah, you are."

"What makes you think that?" I tried to keep my voice steady.

"Because you were the victim of an asshole cop's brutality, and now you're happy to forget it ever happened. In my experience, only people who are afraid of the law are content to look the other way when a cop steps over the line."

I shrugged, and then the lies started flowing. I'd never been a saintly paragon of truth, but I wasn't a habitual liar, either. Still, it was getting to be pretty easy. "I'm scared of the guy. I'd rather he forgot I exist. I've got nothing to gain by trying to beat him in some legal contest. All I wanted was to get away from him, which I did thanks to you."

"What's he up to, anyhow?"

She had a distant tone in her voice. I knew she wasn't talking to me, so I didn't have to tell her that he was up to hiding dead bodies and searching for a whole bunch of money.

"We've been trying to get a search warrant on that lot for months," she told me, "but I think he's got connections at the courthouse. The judges keep telling us there's no probable cause. But I sure as hell don't think he's doing nothing more than raising hogs."

I was about to say something nondescript, like "I wouldn't know about that," but I thought better of it. Instead I opted for a Melfordian strategy. "Well, what do you think he's up to?"

She turned her head, but her eyes were invisible behind the glasses, so her face was illegible to me. "Why do you want to know?"

"I'm just making conversation with the nice police officer who rescued me."

"Good for you," she said.

"Good for me what?"

"Police 'officer.' Mostly I get police 'woman,' like I'm Angie Dickinson or something."

"True equality can only be achieved through gender-sensitive language," I told her.

She glanced at me again. "Right you are."

I'd never seen a car drive away skeptically before, but that's how Officer Toms did it. One last dubious glance, and she eased her cruiser away. And there I was, back at the motel. It was a few minutes before two now, and I didn't know what to do with myself.

Then a remarkable idea occurred to me. I could sleep. I could go back to my room, sleep for hours, and then wake up in time to hoof it over to the Kwick Stop and claim to have blanked. I could make the tedium of the day disappear, get some sleep, *and* remain hidden from rednecks, crooked cops, and compassionate assassins. Opportunities like that didn't come along every day.

I climbed the stairs to my room, already full of sleepy satisfaction. I passed Lajwati Lal, Sameen's wife. She wheeled her cleaning cart along the balcony, her face impassive, hard, and lined. But she smiled at me when I passed by, giving her a little wave.

"Good afternoon, Mrs. Lal," I said, thinking myself enlightened because I cast a friendly greeting at an immigrant busy toiling over a stranger's bed.

She nodded agreeably in my direction. "I hope you're staying out of trouble."

My stomach flipped. What could she know? "Trouble," I said, my voice a rasp.

"My husband told me about those very wicked boys," she said with a sympathetic smile.

I let out my breath. "He was great to help me."

"Oh, yes. He fancies himself a real hero with his cricket bat," she said. "But I think he only wanted an excuse to teach those fellows a lesson."

I asked her to thank him again for me. Once inside my room, I turned up the air conditioner and sat on the edge of the newly made bed. The stillness, the dark of the room with its reddish orange curtains drawn—all of it felt too luxurious for words. I would at last sleep.

After splashing water on my face and rubbing off the last of the blood, I was happy to see I didn't look like someone who had been beaten up. A little red but nothing more. I lumbered over to the bed and lay down, fully dressed, arms stretched, ready to fall asleep. Then I sat upright. How could I afford to sleep when I was a potential murder suspect? If I were arrested, tried, and convicted and had to spend the rest of my life in jail, I'd spew curses at myself forever for having squandered this time. Time I could have used for . . . For what, exactly?

For trying to figure out what the hell was going on, I supposed. Melford seemed absorbed by the mystery of the third dead body, but that bothered me less than it did him. I was more troubled by the Gambler's involvement in all of this. Of course, I *knew* about the Gambler's involvement and Melford did not. Best not to think about Melford too much, since for all I knew he was sitting in the back of Jim Doe's police car with a bloody nose and his hands cuffed tight behind his back.

I, however, was at the motel, and the Gambler was not. It occurred to me that being here at the motel presented a golden opportunity.

I stood up and headed out of my room, very slowly. Down the hall I saw Lajwati's cleaning cart and no sign of Lajwati herself. I walked slowly along the balcony, trying to look anything but furtive and probably failing miserably. When I got to the cart, I saw that luck was on my side—or perhaps fate was simply setting me up for an even greater tumble. There, hanging on a hook on the side of the cart, were the extra pass keys, the ones Ronny Neil and Scott had stolen in order to wreak havoc. I could take one and Lajwati would never notice—or, at the very least, never suspect me.

I heard the sound of running water coming from the open room, and when I peered in, there was no sign of Lajwati herself—except for one small, white-sneakered foot protruding from the bathroom. She was in there, scrubbing with the water running. With a casual swipe, I took one of the keys and kept on walking.

I went around to the side of the motel to the Gambler's room. There was no one around and no sign of lights on in the room. To be safe, I knocked and then ducked around the corner to watch. But the door didn't open. I went back, looked both ways, and stuck the key in the door.

It worked. I'd been half hoping it wouldn't. If the key had failed me, I could tell myself I'd done my level best but the black bag operation simply wasn't in the cards. Now I had no choice but to go forward. I sucked in my breath and pushed open the door.

And that was it. I'd broken into the room of a dangerous criminal. I couldn't imagine having done this twenty-four hours earlier, but twenty-four hours earlier I'd been a different person, living a different life.

I looked around the Gambler's room. Lajwati had already cleaned here, too, which was good since it meant I didn't have to worry about her barging in. It also meant that I didn't have to be paranoid about putting everything back exactly as I found it. Things would have been moved anyhow, giving me the freedom to look around as I pleased.

But what was I looking for? Some clue to who the Gambler really was, why he would be involved in covering up a triple homicide.

His burgundy garment bag was entirely unpacked, but I went through it anyway. Nothing. He had a few shirts and pants hung up and a pile of dirty laundry shoved in the bottom of the closet. I poked at it with my shoe, in case his dirty underwear was meant to disguise something of consequence, but a little shifting around revealed nothing. I went through the drawers, carefully lifting the undershirts, T-shirts, briefs, and socks, but found nothing of interest there, either. Nothing under the newspaper on the nightstand. A whole lot of nothing.

In the bathroom, I discovered the Gambler used cheap disposable Bic razors, off-brand shaving cream, and Crest. But I discovered little else except that he took three prescription medicines, none of which I'd ever heard of.

This was turning out to be a big bust. But then I saw it, hiding in plain sight. Hell, it was so obvious that it was a miracle I saw it at all. Right in the middle of the glass table toward the back of the room, next to the clean ice bucket with fresh plastic liner. His date book.

It would have *everything* in there. It was one of those date books that was about as broad as a paperback novel and almost as long. It had a little clasp and pockets on the inside and outside jackets. The pages were disposable, to be replaced each year, and there were too many of them shoved into a small ring, which made it hard to turn them. As I flipped through, I began to see that this wasn't the gold mine I'd been hoping for, it was a barely legible scribble mine. Each spread of two pages represented one week, and there was an entry for at least one day each week, generally more. The problem was that the entries didn't mean anything to me. "Bill. 3:00. Pancake." Somehow this tidbit didn't exactly clarify things.

Then I noticed that one name appeared over and over again: BB. "Expect BB call PM." "Get instructions BB." "BB 9AM Denny's." This was surely something, I thought. I checked the back of the date book, which had an alphabetized section for addresses. It was pretty well maxed out, so I concentrated on the Bs but found nothing that looked right. Then I checked the front and back pockets, overflowing with business cards. Anything, I thought, with the initials B.B. But nothing. Salesmen, lawyers, real estate agents, doctors, appointment cards. It was all crap. I was putting them back, trying to remember the right order, when one card grabbed my attention. It read, "William Gunn, livestock wholesaler."

Bobby had mentioned Gunn as the owner of Educational Advantage Media. So what was with the livestock? There was nothing else in the book to suggest that the Grambler had anything to do with livestock. Jim Doe, however, did. Then there was the name. William Gunn. B. B. Gunn, I thought. An inevitable nickname—as inevitable as the Gambler's. I ran over to the desk, took out a motel pad and pen, and copied the information. I put everything back carefully, then did a quick run-through to make sure all was as I'd found it.

Nothing to do now but make a clean getaway and I'd be home free. I parted the curtains slightly and looked out as best I could. The angle left a lot of room for blind spots, but I felt moderately comfortable that I could escape unseen, so I opened the door and stepped into the light and heat.

As it turned out, there had been a pretty serious blind spot. Standing fifteen feet down the balcony, hands in his pockets, was Bobby.

Chapter 23

DESIREE STOOD BY THE PAY PHONE, running her neatly manicured but unpolished thumbnail along the receiver. She really
ought to have called in by now. B.B. would be waiting. He'd be wondering
and very likely worried. He worried about her easily. If she was half an
hour late, he'd be a wreck when she got back. She liked to think it was just
need—he needed her, and if she'd been killed in a car accident, who was
going to make his dinner? But it was more than that. In his own self-
absorbed way, B.B. loved her. She knew he did. And that made it harder.

She hadn't been following the kid and his friend since the Chinese
restaurant. Why bother? It was clear to her she wasn't going to tell B.B.
anything. Aphrodite seemed to like them, she had that feeling from her
long-dead twin, and she especially liked the friend, Melford. That just
went to show that she and Aphrodite were agreeing on things more often,
because Desiree liked him, too. Following them, giving B.B. what he
wanted, would feel like a betrayal, and that meant that in the end she was
going to have to betray someone.

What Melford had said about sitting by idly, about winking at evil because it was easy to do so—it had felt like he was talking about her. Like he
knew about B.B., what he did, what he was likely to do when the pretense
of mentoring could no longer keep his desire caged; like he knew how
she'd been helping B.B. peddle crank, the same poison that had nearly
killed her. Of course, he didn't know. He was talking about how he wanted
to make the world safe for little lambs and piggies, and that was sweet,
naïvely sweet. She'd been surrounded by the taint of crime and drugs and

human destruction for so long now, the thought of involving herself in something as kind and hapless as helping animals might be just what she needed.

B.B. might not bloody his hands directly, but she knew—and she'd known all along—that his little empire had left more than a little carnage. Lives ruined, pain and suffering and death, all in the service of meth. That he'd been kind to her might make it easier to sympathize, to care, to have feelings, but it didn't mean that what he did was right or that she ought to help him.

"Hey there, sweetness. I like what you're wearing."

Desiree looked over. Standing no more than three feet away was a wide man in his forties, longish beard and hair, jeans, and boots of a biker. He cradled a six-pack of Old Milwaukee under his arm.

"You about done with that phone?" he asked her. "Because I need to call my mama and tell her that I'm in love."

"Do I look like I'm your private peep show?" Desiree said. Her voice was calm, almost absent.

"Whoa there," he said, taking only half a step back. He raised one hand defensively and flapped up the other, since the arm was still primarily committed to holding the beer. "Don't be so uptight, baby. Can't a man tell you he thinks you're pretty?"

She was out of the booth and facing him, her switchblade out, the blade extended, before she even had time to think about it. "No," she said. "He can't."

"Jesus. All right." He took another couple of steps back and gave a half shrug to tell anyone who might have witnessed the exchange that it didn't bother him.

Desiree watched to make sure he was gone. Then she picked up the phone and started to dial the motel. She hung up before it rang. The time had come to sever ties with B.B.—now, not some point in the near future. She'd been guilty and complicit too long.

That's what their fight last month, over the boy at the roadside, had really been about. She'd been asked to draw a line. For as long as she'd been with him, there had been a line somewhere on the horizon, and now she'd come to it, stood over it. And once you get there, she thought, you can see what's on the other side, and you can see what you've left so far behind that it's lost in the blur.

No more. She had hardly exchanged more than a few sentences with him, but she was sure that Melford had come to tell her that. Things happened for a reason, accidents were part of the order of things, coincidence a manifestation of cosmic design. It was time to move on, and maybe, she thought, to make up for her mistakes, too. There had to be balance in the universe. She'd done harm, and now she had to do good. But what, exactly? Hurt B.B.'s business, slow down his crank trade? That didn't feel right. B.B. was what he was, and he'd helped her. She would have to find something else. She would figure it out. Or maybe she could get some help.

For the second time that day, B.B. picked up the phone with his heart pounding. In his mind he'd always imagined having a hand in the Gambler's destruction, but in the end he would almost certainly have to skip that. Why not turn things over to the mechanisms so readily available?

The ringing ended. "Meadowbrook Grove police."

It wasn't him. "Chief Doe," B.B. barked in a staccato voice, base and forceful, entirely unlike his own.

"Hold on."

There was a brief pause. "This is the chief."

"Chief Doe," B.B. said in his disguised voice, "I am calling to warn you. Ken Rogers, the Gambler, is setting you up. He had your meth cook killed to frame you. He is out to get you and take over your cut for himself. You've been warned."

"Yeah? Who is this?"

"Someone who works with him," B.B. said.

"And why are you telling me this?"

The question stumped B.B. Why *would* someone tell Doe? "Because," B.B. said, deciding to stick to the truth, "the Gambler's a fucking asshole who deserves what he gets."

"Can't argue with that logic," Doe said.

B.B. hung up the phone. Now things would follow their course. Doe was a ruthless bastard, and he wouldn't hesitate to take out the Gambler. He'd deny it to B.B.'s face, but that was okay. In the vacuum, Desiree would step in, and B.B. would be able to toast his success with Chuck Finn over a glass of Médoc.

Doe slowly hung up the phone.

"Who the heck was that?" Pakken asked him.

"A guy who was disguising his voice."

"That's what I thought, too," Pakken said. "What'd he want?"

"To tell me the Gambler is going to fuck me over."

"You think it's true?"

Doe pushed himself down into his chair. "I don't think so. I mean, he would if he could, but I don't think that's what's going on right now. But I'll tell you that whatever is going on, it is highly fucked up because a disguised voice don't mean shit to me. I recognized him."

Chapter 24

ON THE BALCONY, standing in Bobby's massive shadow, I watched a
wounded palmetto bug the size of an egg limp toward the Gambler's door and force its way in through the crack. I'm sure there was something very clever I might have said to Bobby to defuse the situation, to
make it disappear in a puff of smoke, but I didn't know those words.

"Bobby," I said. My voice felt heavy and stupid. "What's new?"

"What were you doing in there?" he asked me, pointing to the Gambler's room.

The words just tumbled out of my mouth. "The Gambler asked me to
get something for him." Why not? Bobby was already puzzled about my
earlier meeting.

He continued to stare. "Shouldn't you be out selling?"

I shrugged. "You'd think, wouldn't you? But you know. The Gambler
and all. Anyhow, what are *you* doing back here?"

"I just needed to get some Tums," he said absently. "My stomach's
bothering me."

"Hope you feel better. I'll see you at the pickup later, okay?" And I
dashed off, leaving him in what I hoped would be a state of such perplex-
ity that he wouldn't say anything to the Gambler before the end of the
weekend.

Back in my own room, still shaken from my run-in, I stared at the information I'd copied down and tried to figure out what I was going to do with it.
Then, all at once, I knew.

I took out the yellow pages and flipped through it in search of "Private Investigators." Nothing, but I was redirected to "Investigators." There were perhaps two dozen listings, but only three ads. I wanted someone who had taken out an ad, because I couldn't risk some small-timer running a scam—not the way I was planning on handling this. After examining the ads, I went with Chris Denton Investigations. The quarter-page ad featured the silhouette of a man crouching and taking a picture with a telephoto lens. The text assured me that Chris Denton excelled in surveillance, criminal investigations, check-mates (which I assumed had nothing to do with chess), preemployment screening, process serving, employee fraud, missing persons, child custody evidence, contested wills, and loss prevention, whatever that was. More to the point, he could do background checks and record retrieval, which I guessed might be exactly what I wanted.

It was a local number, so I didn't need my phone card, yet it didn't seem like a good idea to me to talk in the room, thereby leaving evidence of the call on my bill. So I wrote the information on the same sheet of paper on which I'd copied everything from William Gunn's business card and headed outside. I'd seen a phone booth behind the motel, where the parking lot met the highway, so I strolled over to the phone booth.

A shrill voice answered on the first ring. "Denton."

Here I was mouthing off to Officer Toms about gender equality, and it had never occurred to me that Chris Denton might be a woman. "Oh," I said stupidly. "I thought you would be a man."

"I am a man, you asshole," the voice shot back. "I'm a man who sounds like a woman, okay? Everyone thinks I'm a woman on the phone. Can we move the fuck on?"

"Yeah, sure. Sorry."

"Don't sorry me, douche. Just state your business."

"Okay, can you do a background check on someone for me?"

"How'd you get my number?" he asked.

"From the ad in the phone book."

"Did the ad say I could do background checks, Sherlock?"

"It might have alluded to something like that."

"Then you've got your fucking answer, don't you? Look, I'm just finishing up some paperwork. Be at my office in an hour."

"I can't," I said. "I'm sort of in a tight spot, and I need to do this over the phone."

"You gonna shove my fee through the phone, too?"

"I'll give you a credit card number. You can run it first, if you like, just to make sure everything is legit."

"Can I now?" he snorted. "Thanks so fucking much for the permission. Okay, give me what you have."

I read him the info off my piece of paper. "I'm looking for anything in the public domain about this guy. Does he have a criminal record? Are there any press articles about him? That sort of thing."

"Fine," Denton said.

"I need it pretty fast."

"Said the priest to the whore. How fast?"

"Today fast," I said.

A brief pause. "I need four or five hours, but a rush job will cost you. Two hundred."

It was more than I wanted to spend, and certainly more than I wanted to put on my credit card. I knew I was going to get it from Andy. Even if I told him in advance, gave him the money in advance (which I wouldn't do, since the last time I did that, he claimed I hadn't given him anything when the bill came), he'd still give me a hard time, tell me I was wasting his credit (as though credit were like the elastic on a pair of briefs that could get stretched out). But the money had to be spent, so I read him the credit card information and hung up.

When I turned around, Melford's car was parked directly in front of the booth. I hadn't seen him pull up. "Howdy, stranger," he said through the rolled-down window.

The truth? I was happy to see him. Clearly he'd had no problems with Doe and made a clean escape. But that didn't mean I was ready for more adventures. "No thanks," I told him.

"We've been through this," Melford said with mock gravity. "Let's cut to the place where you get in the car."

"Forget it," I told him. "I've seen people killed, I've broken into buildings, I've been harassed and hurt by cops and nearly arrested. And you know what the worst thing is? You hung me out to dry, Melford. You were going to let me go down for your crimes. So, if you think I'm getting back in that car with you, you're crazy."

"I hung you out to dry?" he asked. "Lemuel, I was right there, every step of the way. I wasn't going to let anything happen to you."

"Yeah, what were you going to do about it?"

"Who do you think called the sheriff's department in the first place?" he asked. "You think that nice lady cop just happened to show up? I knew getting someone from the county cops would defuse the situation, so I got them there. I'd have put a bullet through Jim Doe's head if I had to, but I was hoping to avoid it. I thought you'd want me to avoid it."

"Wow, that's kind. No one's ever refrained from killing a cop for me before."

"Look, you were in a tight spot, I don't deny it. But we're already in a tight spot. You didn't choose to get into this, and I'm sorry that you're in it, but you are. You are just going to have to accept that. And when things got hairy, I got you out, didn't I? You were in trouble, and I fixed the situation. Right?" He grinned at me. "I did, didn't I?"

He did, but I didn't quite want to admit it yet, even though I was pleased, maybe even delighted, that I no longer had to believe Melford had betrayed me. The truth was, the Gambler and Jim Doe were looking at me now, and they'd be looking at me regardless of whether or not I was spending time with Melford. Going it alone just didn't make sense—not when having Melford around would actually keep me safer.

More out of frustration with myself than Melford, I kicked at the dirt and then walked around to the passenger side. "I'm not happy about this."

"What can you do? You can either watch the world come tumbling down on your ass or you can get the hell out of the way of the rubble."

"Keep the aphorisms coming. They're cheering me up."

Melford studied me, looked me up and down. "You're very cynical. On the other hand, you're also perfectly presentable. All washed up, blood off your face. I'm glad to see you're ready to go."

"Go where?"

"To play detective."

Chapter 25

*H*IGH NOON was on the TV, but B.B. didn't much feel like watching it. He could remember once liking that movie, thinking that Gary Cooper was cool and efficient, bucking up to do what he had to do, but now it seemed dull. Cooper was old compared with his earlier movies, as tired and irrelevant as his character. And as westerns went, it didn't stack up against the really good ones. Now, *Shane.* That was a movie.

Feeling good about himself, his future, his phone call, B.B. strolled over to the closet to examine himself in the full-length mirror — not out of vanity, but to make sure his linen suit wasn't too wrinkled. Always the problem with linen. "Wear it once and throw it in the trash," Desiree liked to say. He'd been keeping on his sunglasses, even inside, since calling Doe, but now he removed them. The suit looked good, and the black T-shirt, too — crisp and right around his neck. He hated a T-shirt with a sagging neck. The hair was okay. A bit long in the back and thinning in the forehead, but that was that. The leather brown color was more real than nature herself.

He did a half turn to make sure his ass didn't look big. When he moved he caught a glimpse of the phone on the nightstand. The one on which he'd placed his defining call to Doe. The one on which Desiree hadn't called him. Where in the hell was she? What was she doing?

Now that his revenge against the Gambler was in play, he needed her to keep an eye on things, make sure all went as he intended. He supposed that maybe if the kid kept moving, she might not have had a chance to check in yet, but he didn't quite buy it. Nor did he believe that something had happened to her. Not Desiree. No, she was punishing him. She was still angry with him over that business with the boy.

All he'd wanted was to help him, give him a ride, a good meal at the house, and then get him to wherever he wanted to be. How could it be that even Desiree doubted his motives, that even she saw something sinister where there was only kindness? And what would she say about his wanting to taste wines with Chuck Finn? He shook his head. No, his plan was perfect. Get rid of her by promoting her. It would be a hard transition, but he'd live with having to pick up his own dry cleaning. Hell, maybe he could give Chuck a little part-time work as a valet.

Everything was on the verge of falling apart, and everything was on the verge of being fixed. How ironic and how pleasant that it all hinged on doing to the Gambler what he ought to have done two or three years ago.

Just like that, there he was, only for a second, back in his Las Vegas apartment, falling back hard, knocking his head against the wooden frame of his futon, blood from a cut on his forehead dripping in his eyes, blood from his nose dripping into his mouth. Above him, broom handle brandished like a Homeric warrior, the Gambler squinted in joyless intensity.

For too long he'd held off on dealing with the Gambler, who now was making money, enjoying power, and oblivious to the fact that he lived by B.B.'s grace. No more of that. Doe would solve the problem, and if he dug his own grave in doing so, then B.B. could live with that.

Something—something bad—had evaporated, fled his body. It had been weeks, maybe months, since he'd felt this energetic. B.B. replaced the sunglasses, stepped outside the room, and gave his eyes a minute to adjust to the blazing sun. It was another scorcher today, close to triple digits and humid enough for fish to swim through the air. Reflected light shot off the cars in the parking lot. With one hand to his forehead, he gazed across the courtyard and at the mostly empty pool. This wasn't much of a vacation motel—the guests were people who stopped for the night out of desperate fatigue. Still, the owners, a bunch of Indians, like more and more hotel owners these days, optimistically kept the pool up, waiting for that better class of clientele that would surely arrive when Ganesha so ordained.

Right now, the only adult by the pool was an enormous woman in a lavender one-piece, a year or two on either side of forty, lying with shades over her eyes, chewing gum, smiling into the heat. B.B. gave a slight sympathetic shake of his head. The poor pathetic thing, a baking seal with a bleached blond bob, legs like condoms overfilled with curdled milk. Across the pool from her, playing loudly, were two boys he'd seen before. The two aimless, neglected boys who, if left to follow their sad course, would lead empty, disappointed lives. These were boys, he knew, in need of mentoring.

Part of him felt he ought not to be looking for new mentees. He had Chuck Finn waiting for him at home, after all. But he was here, and the boys were in need of a guiding adult presence. It would be wrong, selfish, to fail to do what he could.

B.B. crossed the parking lot and shuffled over to the woman on the chaise longue and blocked her sun. She lowered her sunglasses and squinted up. He smiled his most ingratiating smile. "Excuse the interruption," he said, "but are those your boys?" Of course they weren't, but B.B. knew the drill. Show her some respect, and she'd defer to his charitable impulses.

"They bothering you, too?" She wrinkled her nose as though she had to sneeze.

He shrugged. "I'm just wondering."

"They ain't mine," she told him. "I wouldn't let my boys act that way if I had any. I think they're with their father, and I saw him leave early this morning in his truck. Left them alone, I guess. He was kind of cute," she added thoughtfully.

This was all good news. No parent around to impose misguided values on the children. No hypocritical guardian of right and wrong to impose the pinched morals that denied boys what they needed.

"I'll go talk to them," B.B. told her brightly, as though volunteering to do the dirty work. "Ask them to quiet down."

"Kind of you."

An awkward pause. "I like your sunglasses," he told her, not able to think of anything else to say.

"Thanks."

"I'll let you get back to your sunning."

"You bet."

Though B.B. couldn't see her eyes, he felt sure they were closed now, and the gum chewing resumed with its lulling bovine rhythm. He stayed a moment longer than necessary, staring in train-wreck style at the folds of fat emerging from under her white suit. Her breasts were surprisingly small considering her magnitude. It must be hard on a woman, he thought, to be so massive and not even have the bust to show for it. Still, there were some men who found obese women attractive. It was a funny world.

B.B. strolled over to the boys, who were playing at the other end of the pool. They splashed around the deep end but seemed capable-enough swimmers. They darted back and forth, up and down, while talking about a comic book character called Daredevil. From what B.B. could tell, this Daredevil was blind and so sounded like a low-rent sort of superhero.

"How you young men doing today?" B.B. asked. He sat on a chaise across from them and smiled a new smile, the one that he knew neglected, aimless boys—boys in need of a role model—found reassuring.

"Fine," one said, and the other echoed in mumble. The older one, who was probably about twelve, was blond and tan and fit, with firm pecs, a flat stomach, and tight little arm muscles. His nose was a bit too long and too narrow for him to be truly handsome, and he had a bit of a receding chin, but he didn't look weak for it. No, with his trim, lithe physique, he wasn't the kind of young man who took crap from bullies. The other boy, much darker and covered with unsightly freckles, was probably closer to nine. He was thinner, less graceful.

B.B. cracked his knuckles and leaned forward. "You like this blind superhero, huh?"

"Yeah," said the blond kid. "Daredevil."

"It's a shame," B.B. observed. "The way they force that stuff on you. You can't turn on kids' programs anymore without seeing someone in a wheelchair or on crutches or missing an arm or doing sign language like a monkey. And now they're giving you blind superheroes? They want you to look up to some blind gimp beating up on bad guys with his cane?"

The blond kid didn't say anything. The younger one said, "I'm sorry." He said it very quietly, and he held his head so far down that the water bubbled around his lips.

"And the Hulk," B.B. said. "Half the time he's a loser egghead, and the other half he's a big green moron. What the heck is that?"

"I don't know," the little kid bubbled.

"Now Superman," B.B. said. "There's a superhero for you. He's smart and strong, and he's that way all the time. He *pretends* to be a dweeb, but that's only to put people off guard. And Batman. You know why I like Bat-man? Because he's really a regular guy. He doesn't have any superpowers. He's just a man who wants to do the right thing and uses the resources he has to help him do it. And he's got Robin to help him. He's Robin's men-tor. I like the way they work together, the way they learn from each other. That's how it is between a mentor and the boys he helps."

"They're DC," the blond kid said.

Something twisted in his gut. Something ugly and mean and judg-mental was now stomping toward him like an ogre. "What does that mean?" He felt his face grow hot. Were these kids calling him a queer?

"We don't read DC comics," the boy said. "We read Marvel. DC is, you know, stupid."

Okay, they weren't calling him a queer. Just stupid. Well, that was fine. Kids often had this notion that adults were somehow dorky or clueless. He could live with that for now. Let them spend some time with him and they'd know better.

"Yeah?" B.B. asked. "So, who else do you like?"

"I like Wolverine," the boy said defiantly. "I read mostly X-Men."

"That's great," said B.B., who lamented a world in which kids read a comic book called The Ex-Men. What was going on, exactly? Blind guys and transsexuals? "Listen, I was thinking about heading out to get some ice cream. You boys like ice cream?"

"Ice cream," said the beautiful blond kid with an unmistakable note of caution in his voice. A sort of "Who wants to know?" kind of tone.

The thing you had to remember, though, was that these were kids, and they had thoughtless, neglectful parents, the sorts of parents who instilled fear in their kids because they couldn't be bothered to teach them how to distinguish between dangerous strangers and kind people who wanted only to help. They knew adults often told them not to do things, but they also knew that adults often had their heads up their asses. The trick was to get them to see that the "Don't go off with strangers" rule didn't apply here, couldn't apply here, not when this stranger had their best interests at heart. Once you broke down those barriers, you were home free. "There's an IHOP down the road. I thought you boys might want to get an ice cream with me."

"Really?" the little kid asked. "What flavor?"

"We're not supposed to," the older boy said, looking at his brother rather than B.B. "Our dad said we had to stay here. And he says we shouldn't talk to strangers."

There it was, regular as clockwork. "I'm sure your dad means that you shouldn't talk to bad men. I can't imagine why he would have any problem with you talking to a nice man who wants to buy you ice cream. Anyhow, my name is William. Everyone calls me B.B., and I work with young men like you every day. I'm a mentor."

They didn't say anything.

"We're even staying at the same motel," he continued. "I'm over in room one twenty-one. What are your names?"

"I'm Pete and he's Carl," said the little one.

"Pete and Carl. Well, it looks like we're not strangers anymore, don't you think?"

"I want strawberry ice cream," the little one said. He nearly sang it. Too loud for B.B.'s taste. The last thing you wanted was a bunch of meddlers getting involved in what they didn't understand. "I don't like chocolate."

"Forget it." His brother shook his head. "I can ask my dad when he gets back tonight."

"Tonight?" B.B. asked, letting the judgment and incredulity seep into his voice. Caution was one thing, but they were standing in their own way. When was the next time they were going to meet someone who was willing to help them, to make them feel important and special, in control of their own destinies, if not their lives, at this moment? "You want to wait until tonight? I'm going for ice cream now. It's hot, and I want ice cream, but I can wait a few minutes if you want to run upstairs and get changed. How fast you think you can be ready?"

"Five minutes!" the younger one said.

"Wow, that's fast." B.B. grinned. "You think the Ex-Men could get ready that fast?"

"Even faster!" the little kid shouted.

It was hard to keep a little triumph from creeping into his smile. Jesus, he was on a roll.

"I don't think we should go," the older one said.

B.B. shook his head sadly. "Well, if your brother wants to go by himself, that's okay, too. You sure you want to stay alone?"

Doubt stretched its shadow across his face. His feet twirled anxiously in the water. He bit his lip. "We're not either of us going?" It was a question, not a statement.

"Just because you don't want ice cream doesn't mean your brother shouldn't enjoy it. I think it's wrong to deny things to other people because you don't want them yourself. That's what they call being selfish, Carl."

"Yeah," his brother agreed.

"I don't know," he said again, which was not exactly a yes, but certainly a retreat from "We're neither of us going." B.B. was gaining momentum; he could feel it. The thing here, he knew, was to go with the flow, to keep it outside of his head. If he thought too much about it, if he concentrated too hard, he would say the wrong thing and blow it. Stay in the zone.

"What's going on here?" the sunbathing woman asked. She now stood directly behind B.B., hands on her massive hips, sunglasses propped on her head. Her exposed brown skin glistened with suntan oil. Glimpsing her over his own sunglasses, he was struck by the prettiness of her eyes. Not that B.B. went for fat bossy cows, but still, there was no denying it—they were stunningly green, healthy-lawn green, emerald green, tropical fish green.

"My goodness," B.B. said. "Those are the prettiest green eyes I've ever seen."

"Tell me something I don't know. What's going on with you and these boys?"

"I was asking them to play quietly," B.B. said, "so they wouldn't bother you anymore."

"And ice cream," the little one said. "Don't forget the ice cream."

B.B. went pink as he looked at the woman. "I thought that if I bribed them with a little ice cream, they might leave you alone."

"You're sweet," she said. "Now why don't you get out of here before I call the cops?"

B.B. took off his sunglasses entirely and met her gaze. "Lady," he said, "I am the cops." He'd tried this one before. Always worked like a charm. Better than telling someone he ran a charity that helped young men.

She wasn't going for it, though. "Let's see some ID."

"I'm off duty. I don't have it on me."

"Well, if you go and get it now," she said, "you'll have it ready by the time your fellow officers get here."

"Fine," he said. "I'll be right back. See you in a minute, boys."

B.B. walked breezily toward his room, where he would have no choice but to hole up until the cow finished baking.

Chapter 26

MELFORD HAD BEEN DRIVING in silence, and I was paying him very little attention. Mostly I was trying to come up with ways to convince myself that my run-in with Bobby wouldn't end in disaster. It was only once we'd pulled into Meadowbrook Grove that I snapped out of my fog.

I stared at the trailers, the ragged lawns, the empty lots. "What the hell are you thinking? We need to stay away from this place, not go back to it."

"Your plan of avoidance sounds fine in theory, but the truth is that we need to figure out what is going on. And to do that, we have to learn who that third body in the trailer was. As near as I can tell, the only lead we have is going to be what the neighbors can tell us. So you're going to go into salesman mode, only instead of selling worthless encyclopedias, you're going to ask about Bastard and Karen and who might have been by to see them last night."

"Should I also ask them if they've seen anyone who looks exactly like me fleeing the scene of the crime?"

"Relax, Lemuel. No one saw you."

"If it's so relaxing, why don't you do it?"

He shook his head. "Me? I stand out too much. Dig my crazy hair. You've been in this neighborhood before. Besides, you're the salesman. This is your territory."

There was no way to fully express the degree to which I did not want to do this thing. "What if that cop drives by and notices me? Should I explain to him that it's my territory while he punches me in the stomach?"

"It won't happen. I'll be keeping a lookout. If anything goes wrong, I'll grab you and we'll take off. You'll be perfectly safe."

I then leveled my most compelling argument. At least most compelling to me. "But I don't want to do it."

"And I don't want us to get fucked, Lemuel, but we very well may if we don't take charge of the situation. Believe me, I don't like this any better than you do, but Jim Doe is now on to you. And whoever sent that woman we saw at lunch is on to you. We've got to take action instead of sitting around and waiting for everything to catch up to us."

I knew he was right. I hated it, but Melford was right. There was no getting around this. I couldn't simply recede and think that, well, maybe things might have been different if I hadn't gone to jail for multiple homicides. I had to do this.

"So what do I tell people?"

"I don't know. But if you can convince people to spend a ton of cash on books they don't need or want, how hard can it be to get them to gossip?"

He had a point.

"One more thing," he told me. "It's not going to happen, but let's just say things go totally haywire."

"Shit," I began.

"Let's say things go completely nuts," he continued, "and you end up with Doe again."

"Screw this," I said. "I'm not going."

"It'll be fine. I'm just giving you worst-case scenario advice. If you end up with him, and you're in some kind of danger, hit him in the balls."

"You think that'll hurt?"

"Trust me, smarty pants. He's had some testicular distress recently, so he's going to be extra sensitive. Give him, you know, a good smack to the nuts. It should make all the difference."

"And you know this how?"

He smiled. "Because a friend of mine recently had cause to smash him in the nuts," he told me. "Now enough with the questions. Get going."

It all felt too familiar. Hot, covered with a slick of sweat, the plankton coating of grime on my tongue, standing at a door, ready to knock, the sickly smell of pig shit wafting through the air. Only this time I wasn't trying to make money, I was trying to get information—information wanted by an assassin, not me.

I stood on the stoop of the trailer several doors down from Bastard and Karen's. I'd already had one no-answer, two suspicious doors closed hastily in my face, and one veiled threat from an exceptionally short and obese man in boxers and a sleeveless T-shirt. Then there was number five. The day before, it had been dark and empty when I'd passed by. This afternoon, I could see lights on in the living room and hear the hum of the window-unit air conditioners. A woman in her sixties opened the front door but refused to open the screen, as though that would somehow protect her. Her hair, dyed to the color of yellow grapefruit, was cut short and permed into a dense jungle of cheerlessly fisted loops. She wore thin sea green sweatpants and a University of Florida T-shirt on which a saucily agitated gator charged forward.

"Hi. I'd like to ask you a couple of questions about your neighbor over there, Karen."

"I don't want to buy nothing," the woman told me.

"I'm not selling anything, ma'am." I said, noting how odd it felt to mean it this time. "I was hoping you could answer a couple of questions for me. You'd be willing to do that, wouldn't you?"

"I told you, I ain't buying," she said, and began to shut the door.

Part of me was content. I might go back to Melford and say that no one would talk to me, then we'd get into the Datsun and cruise out of Meadowbrook Grove forever. But that other part of me, that niggling part, knew that Melford would send me right back out, to another part of the trailer park, this one maybe closer to where Doe kept his police station.

So I said, "Hold on." A clever little lie occurred to me, and I figured I had nothing to lose. "Ma'am, I'm really not selling anything. I'm a private detective." Private detectives were on the brain, after all, following my conversation with Chris Denton. So why not?

She looked at me, this time more kindly. "Really?" Her eyes were wide with wonder.

"Yes, ma'am." It was incredible to me. This being assertive business actually paid off.

"Like Cannon?" she asked.

I nodded solemnly. "Exactly like Cannon."

"Not exactly. We'll have to fatten you up first." She opened wide the screen door.

Her name was Vivian, and she sat me at a padded card table in her kitchen and served me a can of Tab and supermarket-brand frosted oatmeal cookies that she daintily placed on a layer of paper towels.

There were pictures of poodles everywhere—on the walls, in frames on the counter. I counted at least a dozen. But there didn't seem to be a dog around, though the place had the wet smell of dog hair.

"Oh, that girl was always a slut," Vivian said thoughtfully. "Just like her mother. Whores, the two of them. And into drugs, too."

"What sort of drugs?" I asked.

"I wouldn't know *that*," she said with a cluck of her tongue. "I hardly even know what people today take. In my day, we just drank, you know. The other things, like reefer and such, were for coons."

"Raccoons, ma'am?" I asked.

She giggled and waved a hand at me as if we were old joking pals. "Oh, you stop."

"What about the man she was seeing?" I ventured. I liked the way it came out, all TV and professional sounding. "Are you familiar with him?"

"You mean that Bastard fellow? Oh, yes. I didn't much care for him. Not a nice man. You could tell by his name. Not a proper nickname, I don't think."

"That's right," I agreed. "Nice people have nicknames like Scooter or Chip."

"That's right. I heard he was into drugs, too. And I heard he was selling them with—"

And then she stopped. She stopped, she looked around the trailer, and she flipped at the metal ring on the top of her can of Tab.

"Go on," I urged.

"It don't matter. But she and her boyfriend were into drugs all right. And that's why her husband took her kids away, because she was hooked on something, and they say she was letting that Bastard fellow have his way with one of the girls."

"Ma'am," I said evenly, "tell me more about the business with the drugs. Does this have anything at all to do with the police chief, Jim Doe?"

Vivian looked down. "Oh, no. Not that I heard nothing of. I got nothing bad to say about Jim Doe. He's always been nice to all of us. Except for the smell that comes over from his pigs there, he's done nothing but good here. I'll tell anyone that."

"I don't want to make you uncomfortable. Just one more question." I was beginning to feel my audience straining, and I wanted to get out before I frightened her too much.

She shook her head. "I don't think so," she said. "I think we done enough questions today. I think maybe it's time for you to go."

"Just one more," I urged.

"No," she said. Her face had grown pale and her skin slack.

"All right." I stood up. "Thanks for your time. I really appreciate it. I'm sorry if you feel like talking to me might get you in trouble with that policeman."

The woman said nothing.

"I can promise you," I continued, "I would never do or say anything to let him know you'd helped me. But the thing is, if he knew you spoke to me, he wouldn't have to know what you said, would he? I mean, you might tell him that all you did was give me cookies and a drink and smile at my questions, right?"

"That's right," she said slowly.

"That's all he would get from me, if it came down to that, though I'm sure it wouldn't. So, since I'm here, and he's not going to find out anything about what was said, there isn't anything wrong with answering just one more question, is there?"

"I guess not," she said.

"You're absolutely right," I told her, as though this argument had been hers all along. "Do you know if there was a woman in her forties or early fifties who might be a regular visitor at Karen's trailer?"

Vivian nodded. "Probably her mother," she said. "If it were anyone, it would be her mother, the whore. She sometimes comes for a visit. Karen says she comes without calling, just pops in without knocking, like she's trying to catch her daughter at something. That would probably be it. They're both whores," she added thoughtfully.

"Okay," I said. "Thanks so much. You're really going to help me crack my case." It sounded pathetic, but it seemed to soothe her.

"Well, you can come back anytime if you just want to talk, a polite young man like you. I'm happy for the company. Ever since my Rita went missing, I've been so lonely."

My first thought was that there was another dead person in Meadowbrook Grove, but something told me I was wrong. "Your poodle?" I asked.

Her eyes brightened. "Do you know her?"

She sounded as though we were at a party and she mentioned someone who might run in the same circle I did.

"No, I just noticed all the poodle pictures."

"Oh, yes. She disappeared a few months ago. I'm just so broken up about it. She was so beautiful. Not one of those tiny toy poodles, either, but a proper standard poodle. Black with a white patch on her head so she looked like she was wearing a hat. Such a sweet girl, my Rita. She always loved to play with the little children around here. And she loved fruit. You know, strawberries and grapes and bananas. All the kids knew it and would bring her fruit to eat. She was so happy and fat. I just wish I knew what happened to her, where she is now."

Her eyes were watering, and I turned away. "I'm very sorry she's disappeared," I offered.

She sniffled. "You're very kind." And she surprised me by giving me a kiss on the cheek.

Melford had agreed to hang back two or three trailers down, but when I came out of Vivian's house, I saw no sign of him. My stomach churned, only a little at first, but as I walked closer to where we'd started and still couldn't find him, the idea of being trapped in that trailer park alone, where Jim Doe might easily find me at any moment . . . well, none of that sat well.

I went back almost precisely to Karen's trailer, but I realized that was a terrible idea, so I moved again toward Vivian. Still no Melford. The sweat now came streaming off me, and the hog lot smell began to give me a headache.

I began to walk the dusty streets back toward the Kwick Stop. Once I was there, I would at least be out of Doe territory. It was like walking through a minefield, and I expected some kind of boom with each step. Every time I heard the rumble of a car behind me, an invisible fist squeezed my heart. Every grasshopper disturbing the weeds, every lizard darting to safety. It was all terror.

But I made it to the convenience store without incident, and as I approached I noticed a familiar-looking car in the parking lot. It was Melford's Datsun. The car pointed away from me, so I could see only the back of his head—and the back of the person in the passenger seat.

It took an instant to see that it was the mysterious woman who worked for our unknown enemy. It was Desiree.

Chapter 27

A T THAT MOMENT, I believed my best option would be to run away. Away from Melford, away from Jacksonville — away from all of it. At least I told myself it was the smart thing, since I found it easy to ignore all of the difficulties bound up with fleeing. It didn't matter, anyhow. I was beyond smart. Way beyond smart. I was well into pissed off.

I went over to the car and rapped on the driver's side. Melford rolled down the window. "How'd it go?"

"You fucking shit," I said.

His eyes widened. "That bad?"

"You were supposed to wait for me."

"And I did. Right here."

"No, you were supposed to wait for me in the trailer park."

Melford's face crinkled in puzzlement. "Why would I do that? I would just be drawing attention to myself. We agreed to meet here."

That wasn't how I remembered it at all, but Melford recalled the conversation with such conviction that I began to wonder if I'd made a mistake. He, after all, was the one used to formulating covert plans, cooking up schemes. Maybe I'd heard what I'd wanted to hear since I didn't like the idea of him leaving me all alone.

"What's this?" I asked, gesturing with my head toward Desiree, who had been smiling agreeably at me the whole time.

"You remember Desiree," Melford said.

"Of course I remember her. What's she doing here? What are the two of you doing sitting so cozily together?"

"Excuse us," Melford said to her. He got out and led me about fifteen feet away, over toward a pair of newspaper vending machines. "So, what did you learn?"

I figured I would hold off for the moment with the Desiree issue, since arguing with Melford probably wouldn't get me anywhere. I told him what Vivian had said, that the older woman was likely Karen's mother.

"It looks like she went over there at the wrong time," Melford said. "Doe clearly had his reasons for wanting to keep the deaths secret, so he killed her as well."

"What reasons are that?"

"Drugs." Melford shrugged, as though the topic bored him. "Doe's got some sort of scheme going on, and he's more afraid of an investigation that will unearth his operation than he is of linking himself to homicides. And that, my friend, is good news."

"Tell me how a crazy cop who deals drugs is good news."

"Look, Doe and his friends hid those bodies. They don't seem so bright, and I'm sure they left an evidence trail a mile long. If the bodies do show up, the evidence will lead back to them, not to us. At that point they can't very well say that no, they didn't kill Karen and Bastard, it was prob- ably a salesman who did that—they only buried them. Doe and his friends have plenty to lose. And what that means, Lemuel, is you are in the clear."

"What are you saying? That I can just walk away from this?"

"That's what I'm saying. I'm going to give you a ride back to wherever you want, and as far as I'm concerned, you can go back to your life. You keep quiet about everything you saw, stay away from that cop, and all will be fine."

"But what about this money they're all looking for?" I asked. "They're not going to forget about it, and as long as they think I have something to do with it, aren't they going to keep after me?"

"Forget the money," he said, not for the first time. "It doesn't matter. They sent Desiree to follow you, but she's going to tell them you have nothing to do with the money. Trust me. She's on our side, and even if she weren't, she'd have no reason to tell them you ripped them off when you didn't. They'll have to look somewhere else."

I sucked in air through my teeth. Could it really be true? Had these assholes, for stupid and ill-advised reasons of their own, protected us from scrutiny, all to conceal their sordid little drug deals? I could hardly be- lieve it.

If I were honest with myself, I would have admitted that my relief was marbled with disappointment. I hadn't liked the terror of being arrested, I hadn't liked being slapped around by Doe, but I liked the feeling of being a part of something, and Melford had made me feel it was something important, something more than murder. In a couple of days I would be home, I would quit selling encyclopedias, and everything would be back to where it was. And I would still need $30,000 to get to Columbia next year.

Desiree stepped out from the passenger side of the car. She was wearing the same jeans as before, but instead of the see-through shirt and dark bra, she wore a butter yellow bikini top.

She had a nice body, there was no denying it, voluptuous and trim all at once, and under normal circumstances my biggest problem would be how to avoid staring at her breasts. But right now I had to figure out how to avoid staring at her scar. It was huge, unlike anything I'd ever seen before, running from her shoulder, down her side, and disappearing into her pants. It covered most of her side under her arm and nearly half her back.

It wasn't just that it was unusual. I remembered what Bobby had told me: The Gambler's boss, Gunn, had a woman with an enormous scar working for him. Desiree worked for B. B. Gunn. Melford had been sitting companionably in his car with a woman who worked for the enemy—the big enemy.

Not looking at the scar was incredibly difficult. It was as though it had its own gravity, pulling in my eyes. I decided to conceal my discomfort by asking about it.

"Can you tell me about your scar?" I said.

I regretted the words the minute they came out. This was life and death, here. She wasn't just an attractive woman with large breasts, a butter yellow bikini, and a scar the size of a hand towel. She was some sort of agent of evil. Wasn't she?

She looked over at me and smiled. "Thank you for asking." Her voice was sweet and vaguely vulnerable. "Most people think it's polite to ignore it, pretend they don't see it. This is where my sister was before they separated us." She ran her left hand along the scar, grazing it with the tips of her unpolished fingernails. "She died."

"I'm sorry." I felt stupid saying it.

Desiree smiled sweetly again. "Thanks. You're very kind. You and Melford are both very kind."

"So," I said, rubbing my hands together, "what can we do for you this time?"

"Mostly," she said, "I came to see Melford. I want to hear more about helping animals."

I sat in the backseat, sidekick status withdrawn, instantly converted to third wheel. I felt sullen and rejected—and cramped, shoved back there as I was into the too small space designed for Japanese children, not American teens and a library load of tattered paperback books. When I asked where we were going, he explained, not very helpfully, that we were driving around. He wanted to keep me busy and away from Doe until my pickup time.

It was hard to hear everything from the back, but I could see that Melford had Desiree enthralled. She sat up front beaming at Melford as if he were a rock star, as though she had a crush on him. I didn't like her fawning all over him, and I didn't like that I didn't like it. I recognized that churning, uneasy feeling working its way through my chest as jealousy, but jealous of what? Did I want the sexy half Siamese twin, or did I hate having to share Melford?

Once again, I felt I was missing something, maybe everything. Why didn't Melford want to know more about her before inviting her into the car? It seemed to me that the superassassin might be less detail oriented in his work than it had at first seemed.

After about twenty-five minutes on the highway, Melford pulled off and stopped at a 7-Eleven, saying he was thirsty and had to wash up. When he walked away, I felt a sickening panic set in. I didn't want to be left alone with Desiree. I had no idea who Desiree really was, other than an employee of B. B. Gunn. I didn't know what she wanted.

But Desiree showed no signs of finding the situation awkward. She turned around and grinned at me conspiratorially. "I think he's so sexy."

I fidgeted with an empty plastic cassette holder I'd found on the floor. "I'm not sure you're his type. Being female and all."

"You don't think he's gay, do you?"

"Well, I did kind of assume it. But look, that's not important. Who are you, anyhow?"

"Why do you think he's gay? Because he's a vegetarian?"

"Of course not," I said. "I don't care if he's gay or he isn't. I was just letting you know that you may not be his type. But we can discuss that once you tell me why you're following us around. Melford might not care, but I do."

"It's so wrong," Desiree said, "to just assume things about people, to label them based on appearances. I've worked so hard at trying to understand my real self. I've been reading about auras and reincarnation and using the I Ching. And you? Boom. You decide he's gay."

"Look, it's not a big deal to me. I was just saying."

"Have you even asked him?"

"No, I haven't asked him, because I don't care." My tone was growing increasingly shrill. "I haven't asked him what his favorite color is, either."

"Why are you getting so worked up about this?" Desiree asked.

Melford came out of the store, a bottle of water in one hand, his keys in the other.

"Lem thinks you're gay," she told him when he opened the door.

Melford settled behind the wheel and pivoted around to me. He grinned broadly. "A lot of people think that, Lemuel. I wouldn't sweat it. But you don't have anything against gay people, do you?"

"No," I blurted. "That's not the point. I want to know who Desiree is and what she's doing following us around."

"What does that have to do with my sexual orientation?" Melford asked. "I don't get it."

"Neither do I." My voice came out high-pitched.

Melford glanced over at Desiree. "Lem has a valid question. Who are you, and why are you following us around?"

"Me?" she said. "Some very bad people asked me to keep an eye on you, Lem, find out if you were up to anything improper."

"And is he?" Melford asked.

"Not as near as I can tell. But I'll have to keep following him to be sure. Unless"—she glanced at Melford—"someone distracts me."

Information came out slowly over a leisurely drive up and down the highway. Desiree worked, as I'd already suspected, for B. B. Gunn, who was centered near Miami and who used both the hog trade and the encyclopedia business as some sort of front for selling drugs. Desiree seemed eager to avoid getting too specific. She made it clear that she wanted to leave B.B., but while she didn't want to betray him, she'd reached the conclusion—thanks, in part, to the *I Ching* and in part to Melford—that she needed to make amends for her involvement in such an enterprise. For some time now she'd been looking for something, she said, some kind of meaning, and at the Chinese restaurant she'd become increasingly convinced that Melford's interest in kindness to animals might be what she sought. I had no idea if her conviction would strengthen or waver when she discovered the project involved killing people.

"So, what do animal rights people do?" she asked. "Blow up slaughterhouses and things?"

Melford shook his head. "For the most part, no. The principal arm of the movement is a loose affiliation of activists collectively known as the Animal Liberation Front. The thing that makes it work so well is that to be a member of this group, all you have to do is espouse its values, take action, and attribute that action to the ALF. No training camp, no indoctrination, no oath of loyalty. On a small scale, they generally vandalize fast-food restaurants or hunting shops, anything to throw a monkey wrench, even a tiny one, into the machinery of animal misery. But more sophisticated operations involve things like rescuing lab animals or breaking into research or farming facilities to take pictures and expose their cruelty."

"I don't know," Desiree said. "It sounds sort of weak. Do you really want to dedicate your life to pestering people to stop doing what they're never going to stop doing anyway? Maybe you should take stronger action. Beat up some fast-food executives or something."

"The ALF believes that its people must never harm anyone, not even the cruelest of animal tormentors, since their core belief is that human beings can live their lives without harming any creatures."

I tried not to react when I heard this.

"They can't take down someone really nasty?" Desiree asked.

Melford shook his head. "Anyone who would do that, who would even be suspected of thinking about that sort of thing, would be shunned by the organization and the entire animal rights movement. They're all about saving lives, even human lives. Though property is always a legitimate target."

"I respect that," she said.

"There are those, however," Melford went on, "who take action when the ALF won't, who believe that violence is, under extreme circumstances, a necessary evil. The core of the animal rights movement never condone this sort of thing, not even in private, I suspect."

"That sounds about right to me," Desiree said. "It doesn't make any sense to support the idea of protecting the rights of all beings if you then start picking and choosing. Otherwise, we're all like people in a restaurant, picking from the tank which fish we want to eat."

Melford smiled. "That's right."

Desiree smiled at this lie, as if she were so happy to have Melford's approval. The crazy thing was, I knew how she felt. And I knew he was lying to her. So what did that say about the ease with which I'd come to value his opinion? If I didn't know from personal experience, the personal experience of seeing him kill two people, I would never suspect he was lying. I suddenly felt distinctly uneasy, like I wanted to get out of the car. Like I wanted to get away.

"Can I ask a question?" Desiree said.

"Of course."

"What about medical research? I mean, it may be unpleasant to use animals as test subjects, but we get results. And isn't it important to find cures for diseases?"

"Absolutely it's important to find cures for diseases," Melford agreed, "but using animals to do so is another matter. Look, there are two aspects to the answer—one ethical and the other practical. The ethical issue is that it may be expedient to torment and kill animals for our needs, but is it the right thing to do? If we could get better results by using prisoners or unwanted children or unlucky bastards picked by lottery, would that be okay? In other words, do the ends justify the means? Either the lives of animals are to be valued or they're not, and if they are, then making exceptions because something is really, really important doesn't make sense."

"I'm not sure I buy it," she said. "They're animals, not people. Shouldn't we have the right to take advantage of our position on the food chain? We don't judge lions for eating zebras."

"Lions can't choose not to eat zebras," Melford said. "It's not ethics for them. It's what they're designed to do. We can choose whether or not to harm animals, so we can be judged by that choice."

"Okay, I accept that," she told him. "But I don't know that I accept that we should die of diseases rather than use animals to help us overcome them."

"That's a tough one. It may be the toughest one for people to get past. The ethical person can sacrifice hot dogs and hamburgers, but the question of animal testing seems to provide a real dilemma. So here's something to keep in mind: Most animal testing is utterly worthless."

"Come on," I chimed in. "Why would they do it if it was worthless?"

"Don't fool yourself. Medical labs may be full of well-meaning researchers, but they need funding to do their work. Researchers have to apply for grants, and grant proposals have to be written so that they are successful. And to get grants, researchers have to use animal research—it's just that simple. Grant providers have come to believe in the efficacy of animal research, and no amount of scientific fact is going to sway them."

"Maybe they believe in it because it works," Desiree suggested.

"Most of the animals they use for research are mammals and are closely related to us, but that doesn't mean they respond to diseases or to drugs the same way we do. Chimps are our closest relatives. They're more closely related to us than they are to gorillas, but you know what happens if you give a chimp PCP—angel dust? It goes to sleep. PCP makes a great chimp tranquilizer. Think about that. A drug that turns us into monsters makes them sleepy, and they're the nearest thing to humans out there. So if a drug works or doesn't work on a chimp or a rat or a dog, what does that tell us about how it will go on humans? Ultimately, it tells us nothing."

"Haven't there been lots of breakthroughs that have come through animal research?"

"And there will probably be many more. That doesn't mean it's the best way to go. Advocates of medical research ask if we'd rather live without the polio vaccine, since the polio vaccine would never have come about if there had been no animal research. It's a false argument. Sure, we're better off with a polio vaccine than without one, but human beings are clever and resourceful. There are alternatives, including using volunteers and lab tests. Some scientists are even beginning to work with models built entirely from computer software. To say that we would never be where we are without animal research is to assume that research would close down without animals. Of course it wouldn't. We'd find new ways. Necessity is the mother of invention, so if we outlawed animal testing, we

might have more advanced computers now because we'd need more sophisticated computer models to save lives. And because animal research is
so unreliable, the better question to ask would be what we might have discovered if we didn't rely on it. The defenders of vivisection like to suggest
that it's a choice between animals and disease or testing and cures, but
what if just the opposite is true, and using unreliable biological models has
set back medical science? Maybe without animal testing we'd have a cure
for cancer by now."

"I don't know," Desiree said absently. "You make a good case, but if
I'm sick, I want them to do everything possible to cure me."

"You want them to do everything possible, but not anything conceiv-
able, whether it benefits you or not."

"True."

"And, as an ethical person, even if you want to allow for animal testing, don't you think there should be some sort of standard of need? Maybe
a tester should have to make a case for why it is necessary to sacrifice a
monkey or a dog or a rat for a particular cause. Right now they are free to
slaughter and torture however many thousands they like without oversight.

"And you know there's a whole lot of animal testing that has nothing
to do with health. Cosmetic companies subject millions of animals a year
to torture to see if this new and improved nail polish remover does as
much damage to a rabbit's eyes as the old version. You'd think it would be
enough to know that putting corrosive material in your eyes is a bad move,
but these guys need to test it out."

"Why?" I asked.

"Who knows why? Insurance liability or some nonsense like that.
They just do it."

"Come on," Desiree said. "You're telling me that big corporations pay
who knows how much just to torture animals unnecessarily? I don't believe it."

"Really?" A strange sort of smile came over Melford's face. "You don't
believe it? Lemuel, you don't have to be at the pickup until what? Ten-
thirty or eleven, right?"

"Right," I said slowly.

"And you have nowhere you need to be before then?"

"Well," I ventured, "it would be nice to go to a movie."

"Nice try."

"I don't know what you're thinking," I told him, "but I really don't like it."

"No," he said, "you won't like it. You won't like anything about it."

I guess we were already heading in the right direction because Melford hit the gas harder.

"Where are we going?" Desiree asked.

"Well, I wasn't planning on doing this so soon, but I've already done the logistical work, so why not." He grinned at her. "We're going to visit a research lab."

Chapter 28

W E DROVE FOR ABOUT AN HOUR, farther away from Jacksonville, until Melford pulled off and took us through a bleak landscape of fast-food restaurants, topless bars, and pawnshops. Finally, he turned again and we went about another ten miles through wooded roads until he stopped and parked in a little strip mall with a jewelry store and a dry cleaner. We got out and he walked to the back, where he proceeded to take out a black garbage bag full of black sweat clothes.

"Dig around," he said. "Find something that fits, but don't put it on yet, or you'll be hot as hell." He picked up a black gym bag and slung it over his shoulder, and then he reached into a cardboard box and handed us each a lump of cloth. "You'll need these, too."

They were ski masks.

I already had as many legal problems as I needed, so I had no desire to break into an animal-testing facility, but I knew better than to bring that up or to suggest that maybe I should wait in the car. I was in, and I wasn't getting out.

Melford opened up his gym bag and passed around a bottle of bug spray, and once we'd applied that we began the trek through a fairly thick copse of pines. It was still light out, but the mosquitoes were buzzing around my ear, moderately deterred by the repellent. The cluster of trees smelled of rotted leaves and the sourness of an occasional decomposing opossum.

Desiree didn't say anything. She had a look of amused determination

THE ETHICAL ASSASSIN ··· 249

on her face. But why should she care? She clearly did illegal things all the time. One more wasn't going to bother her.

Finally we began to emerge and Melford held up his hand, the platoon commander ordering us to stop.

"This is as far as we go for now," he said. "It's Saturday, and there won't be anyone there, but we're going to wait for dark all the same. Shouldn't be more than an hour and a half or so. In the meantime, I'll go over with you the reconnaissance I've already done." He reached into his pocket and pulled out several pieces of paper, which he proceeded to unfold on the ground. They were hand-drawn maps of the interior of a building.

"What exactly are you planning?" Desiree asked.

"Nothing fancy," he said. "This is a simple hit-and-run. You wanted to know what animal rights activists do—well, this is it. We're going in, we're going to take pictures and collect evidence, and we're going to get out. Simple as that. Then I'm going to pass along the swag to an animal rights organization, and they'll make the images public and try to stir up controversy. Pretty basic, yes?"

"Sure," Desiree said. "Piece of cake."

Piece of cake. I looked through the woods at the building beyond. About a hundred feet of well-manicured grass spread out between the edge of the woods and a squat white building without windows. A thin layer of shrubs outlined the structure, but that was all as far as gardening went. It looked bland, harmless, except for its menacing blankness. At the far end, just before an oceanic expanse of parking lot, I saw a concrete slab sticking out of the grass with the company's name chiseled deep.

Oldham Health Services.

Like the coffee mugs and boxes in Karen and Bastard's trailer. Melford had claimed to have no idea what it was. And now we were about to break in.

It wasn't nearly dark enough to move until almost nine o'clock. Melford smiled at me. "Don't worry," he said. "We'll get you back in time to keep you from getting fired."

The three of us sat there, listening to the chirping cicadas and frogs and night birds, watching the poorly lit grounds of Oldham Health Services grow dark. "These guys are so behind the times," Melford explained. "Up north, they'd never leave a lab like this so vulnerable. But animal rights activists haven't really made themselves known in Florida, so the bad guys feel safe." He took a look around. "Okay, put on your sweats."

Desiree began to unbutton her jeans, but Melford shook his head. "Over your clothes, my dear," he said. "We want to be invisible going in, but we want to look normal once we're inside." He glanced at her bikini top. "You'll want to leave the sweatshirt on, I think."

Once we were clad in black and had our masks on, he gave the forward gesture, and we charged onto the lawn like a trio of commandos, heads down, bulleting into the unknown.

I was already starting to sweat, but I felt the rush. For an instant I understood why Melford was Melford, I understood the thrill of doing something illegal, of breaking boundaries, rejecting the mundane and the stable. And it wasn't as if we were burglars, motivated by base greed. We were defying authority for a moral cause. Whether it was my cause, whether I believed in the cause, seemed irrelevant. Just being there made me feel alive.

The yard was poorly lit, and Melford led us around the side and up a set of concrete steps that led to a metal side door. He opened his bag and removed his pick gun, the one he had used on Karen's trailer, and within two minutes the door had clicked open. We slipped inside.

It was pitch black in there, no lights on and no windows. Melford took out a flashlight and instructed us to remove our masks and sweats—all but Desiree's top.

"Security is light," he said in a whisper. "Some guards, almost no cameras. If guards do show up, leave the talking to me."

Once we'd stuffed the clothes into his bag, he hoisted it up and we began to talk again. We were in some sort of storeroom—metal shelves full of boxes, most marked MEDICAL SUPPLIES. There were glass jars of dangerous-looking liquids, bags of dog food, cat food, rabbit, rat, and monkey food. All of these emitted their own pet store smell, but from farther beyond I smelled odors far more clinical, things chemical and antiseptic.

Melford found the doors out of the storeroom and we came out into a long corridor of plain cinder-block walls, adorned only with an inexplicable teal racing stripe, and dingy beige linoleum floors. The main lights were off, but enough fluorescent bulbs were illuminated that Melford could turn off his flashlight. The place looked like a hospital after hours.

We made a right, and then another right, and then we went up a set of stairs to a floor that looked remarkably like the one from which we'd come. We followed Melford down a corridor to a door marked "Lab Six," which was locked, so the pick gun came out again. Desiree stood nervous watch while I tried to peer inside through the dark glass square and Melford worked the lock. In less than a minute we were inside.

When the door came open, I knew I had crossed something more metaphorical, but also more tangible, than a door's threshold. Yes, I'd seen the hog farm, seen how terrible it was, the misery and—if such a term can be applied to hogs—the degradation, but this was different. The hog farm was, after all, owned by a crooked cop, and it was a place whose purpose was the raising of hogs so they could die. It was a way station between nothingness and death, and it wasn't meant to be anything more. The pigs were pre-bacon, pre-pork, pre-ham, their slaughter was ordained and inevitable. It was a place of horror and misery, perhaps unnecessary horror and misery, but that it should be miserable and horrible made a sort of functional sense.

This was something else. Three of the walls were lined with small cages, each of which contained some kind of brownish gray monkey about the size of a child's doll, thin, with expressive faces. The room stank, not like the hog lot—which was the smell of fear and feces—but of living putrefaction. It smelled of fresh shit and of vomit and piss and rot. At first I thought the monkeys were asleep, but when Melford turned on the light, I saw that their eyes were opened. They lay on their sides, most of them panting, their eyes wide, following our movements with unmistakable terror. Many of them were letting out whimpering noises. One bit its lip and gripped the wires of its cage in its fingers with a repeating, desperate pulse.

Across the room, one of the animals rose, dragged itself upright, and hissed at us—a weak but defiant hiss. It bared its teeth. Then its legs appeared to buckle under its weight, and the monkey fell back into a brown pile that might have been its own feces or maybe monkey chow.

Melford reached into his bag and found a camera, which he handed to Desiree. "Start taking pictures," he told her. He, meanwhile, began to search the lab and quickly found a clipboard, which he held up to us.

"Okay, here it is. You know what these monkeys are being tested for? Cure for cancer? Brain regeneration for stroke victims? Heart surgery to help babies with birth defects? Guess again. They're part of an LD50—that's 'lethal dose fifty percent.' These are routine studies done on standard household products to find out what quantity causes death in fifty percent of the test subjects. They do it with drain cleaner, dish soap, motor oil, you name it. You know what's being tested here? Photocopier paper. How much paper these monkeys can be force-fed before fifty percent of them die."

Desiree stopped taking pictures. Her gaze fell on one monkey, lying on its side, one arm straight back, the other resting limply on its face. Its chest heaved up and down in pained respiration. "But why? What does that tell them?"

"Exactly what you think—how much copier paper will kill fifty percent of the test subjects," Melford said. "Look, you have to understand that these experiments aren't goal directed anymore. Maybe there was a time when LD50 tests were designed to discover something useful. It didn't make it right, but it made it practical, at least. Now it's just something that's done. It's a standard test because insurance companies want data to help them determine liability and flesh out their actuarial tables. They do it because not doing it might help some lawyer down the road argue that the company didn't perform all necessary safety tests. They do it because it is what they do. Millions upon millions of animals are tortured and killed each year just because."

"I don't believe it," she said.

I'd said the same thing that afternoon. Looking at the hogs, listening to Melford explain how they were housed, why they were housed that way, and what it did to them and the people who ate them, I hadn't believed it. Looking right at it, I hadn't believed it.

"Believe it," Melford said. "Lemuel, over here. We're in luck. We've found some videotapes."

So while Desiree finished snapping pictures, he and I shoved videotapes into his bag. We then shut out the light and left the lab. Melford looked at his watch. "We shouldn't push our luck, and we don't want Lemuel here to turn into a pumpkin if he doesn't get to his pickup, but why don't we do one more lab. I kind of want to see Lab Two for myself. I've heard things."

We followed him around a corner, where he opened another door. Here we were met by the sounds of subdued whimpering. The smells weren't much different from those of the monkey lab, but when he turned on the light we were met by a room stacked with dog cages, two or three on top of one another. Thin wooden boards separated them, but they did a poor job, and the feces from the animals above dripped onto the animals below.

A few let out tentative barks, but mostly they watched us. They rested, heads on paws, eyes wide and brown, watching. Off in the distance I heard one let out a whimper.

Melford handed Desiree the camera, and she began to snap photos again. He looked around until he found the clipboard he wanted. "Oh, no," he breathed. "They're scheduled for an LD50 test for pesticide to start in two days. This is what sucks about this kind of operation. There's nothing wrong with these dogs. Those monkeys were the living dead, but these guys are savable. Unfortunately, we can't do anything. If we try to get them out of here, we'll get caught, they'll get brought back. The best we can do is document this and get the evidence into the right hands and wait for a better day."

"Where do they get these dogs?" Desiree asked.

"A lot of shelters have deals with places like this. They send over unclaimed strays. But the truth is, labs have backdoor deals with animal abductors. People will steal pets and sell them to a place like this for fifty bucks a pop. You can make decent cash if you don't have scruples."

Desiree put down the camera. "Melford, we can't leave them here. They would at least have a chance if we could let them out in the woods."

"We can't do it," he said. "How are we going to herd twenty or thirty dogs out of here without alerting the guards?"

"I'm not leaving them," she said.

"You are," he told her. "If we all go to jail, we won't do any good. You want to walk this path, you have to harden yourself. You can't blow up every Burger King you drive past. You can't liberate all tortured animals from all the factory farms. You want to, but you can't, and it drives you crazy sometimes because everything you do is just a drop in the bucket. This isn't a fight for the moment or a year or even a decade. This is a battle that will be resolved over generations. And right now we have to make choices. We do what we can and we stay free and keep going and chip away at the edifice. Our getting arrested and those dogs being sent back to their cages isn't going to accomplish anything."

"Doesn't choosing who lives and who dies make us as morally suspect as the people who put these animals here?"

"No," Melford said. "They put the animals here, not us. And we're doing the best we can—which right now is to bear witness."

"We're taking one," I said. "We can take one, can't we?"

"How do you choose which one?" he asked.

I pointed. It was a black poodle. It wasn't Rita, Vivian's black poodle, but it was a black poodle, and I knew that Vivian would take care of it. I knew that she would regard it as some sort of divine compensatory gesture. Maybe the idea was silly, but I believed it. I believed that dog could have a home and someone to love it. This was no longer abstract, no longer theoretical.

"We're taking this dog," I said. "If you don't like it, you can leave without me."

Melford swore but didn't say anything else. Desiree, however, nodded at me. "If Lem knows someone who'll take the dog, we can't leave it here to feast on Black Flag."

"She's a poodle," Melford said. "She'll bark."

"I don't believe this." I could feel myself getting agitated. "Melford Kean, with ice water in his veins, is afraid to do the right thing?"

"It's a matter of being practical. I don't want to fight a battle that will lose the war."

"It's one dog," Desiree said, her voice hard. "We'll keep her quiet. And I'm with Lem. We're taking the dog whether you help or not."

Maybe it was that he didn't think he could dissuade her, but I had the sense that it was because he liked the fact that she felt so adamant. "Boogers," he said. "Let's do it."

He went over to the cage and began to open it very carefully. I suspected he knew enough to suspect that a dog that had been mistreated the way this one had might well turn on him, but she came out docilely and licked his hand. I figured that was a good sign.

"Okay," he said. "Let's try to pull this off."

But when we turned around, we saw the guard standing at the door.

Melford didn't see it, but I did. Desiree reached into her back pocket and removed a switchblade. She didn't open it, but she balanced it in her palm.

She might believe that Melford was committed to nonviolence, but she clearly had not yet signed off on that part of the Animal Liberation Front manifesto. Maybe the two of them belonged together.

"Can I help you?" Melford asked. He had found a leash and was in the process of attaching it to Rita's collar. He hardly even bothered to look at the guard.

"Who are you?" he asked. He was in his forties, overweight to the point that he had trouble walking. He stared at us with dark and heavily bagged eyes.

"I'm Dr. Rogers," he said. "And these are my two students, Trudy and André."

The guard stared at us. "What are you doing here?"

"I'm running a 504-J," Melford said.

From the puzzled look on the guard's face, it seemed pretty clear to me that Melford had just made up the 504-J.

"How come I didn't get any word that anyone was going to be here?"

"Do you really think I would know the answer to that?" Melford asked.

"You have your ID card?"

"I'll show it to you on my way out," Melford said. "In the meantime, you can see I'm doing something. Are you new here? Because you're supposed to know that you must never disturb the staff when they're handling animals."

The guard stopped to think for a minute. "I've been here all day. How come I didn't see you come in?"

This question must have stumped Melford, because he paused.

"Right," the guard said. "I'm calling Dr. Trainer, and if he doesn't know what you're doing here, I'm calling the cops. Now put the dog back in the cage and come with me."

"No, wait," Melford said. "Let me show you something first." He handed the poodle's leash to me and walked over to his black bag. I stood frozen with fear. Desiree had her knife out, and now Melford was going to take a gun and kill this guard, just for doing his job. This wasn't some nefarious force of evil, like he claimed Karen and Bastard were. This was some poor working asshole.

I tensed, ready to dart forward, but when Melford took his hand out of the bag, he didn't have a gun. He had a stack of money. They were twenties, and I couldn't tell how many, but there was easily $500 there.

"I don't know what they pay you to keep guard over this house of horrors," Melford said, "but you have to know what goes on here is wrong. So I'll make you a deal. You take this cash and let us walk out with this dog. It's one dog. No one will miss her. No one will know we were here. Anyone asks, you say you have no idea. Simple as that."

The guard looked at the money and then around the room. Sure, there was no sign anyone had been here. We hadn't vandalized the place. Many of the cages were empty anyhow, so no one would notice one more empty one. He didn't know about the missing videotapes, so it seemed like a good deal.

The guard snatched the money. "I'll make my rounds again in half an hour," he said. "If you're still here, I'm calling the cops and I'll deny you gave me anything."

"Fair enough," Melford said. He turned around to grin at Desiree, who already had the knife back in her pocket.

Most of the ride back went silently. We made a stop at a 7-Eleven and bought some doggie treats and water for the poodle, and she happily ate and drank in the backseat with me. She hardly made a noise. It was just one dog, I thought. One dog rescued from being forced to eat insecticide. We'd made some small difference.

I told Melford where Vivian lived, and we stopped outside her trailer; he tied the dog to the door, rang the doorbell, and we drove off. We were halfway down the street when her door opened and we heard her muffled shriek of joy. What we didn't hear was the subsequent disappointment. It wasn't her dog. Her dog was gone, maybe dead. But it was a dog, and I had to think it would be some comfort.

We were tired from what we had done and what we had seen, but I was lost in another thought. Why had Melford said he had no idea what Oldham Health Services was if he'd been keeping his eye on the place for who knew how long? And what was its connection to Bastard?

It was just shy of eleven when Melford dropped me off outside the Kwick Stop. It was only after I was out of the car and it had driven away that I recalled that Melford had said I was done with him, that our business was over. Did that mean I would never see him again? Was he hurt that I hadn't said good-bye? And did I really care if I hurt the assassin's feelings?

Not that it mattered. Maybe it was because of everything that had happened in the last day, but I didn't believe I was done with Melford, and I found it even harder to believe I was done with the Gambler, Jim Doe, and the rest. When I was back home, away from Jacksonville and book-men, I'd believe it.

I walked over to the pay phone just outside the Kwick Stop's door. It was late to be making the call, but, surprisingly, Chris Denton picked up on the first ring.

"Yeah," he told me. "I've got your guy."

"And?"

"And not much. He's a Miami businessman, deals in livestock, and also deals with some door-to-door encyclopedia outfit. He also runs a charity. That's about it. No record, no arrests, no stories in the media other than the usual business crap."

"That's all you've got?" I asked.

"What do you want me to do—tell you he's a mass murderer? He's just an asshole, like everyone else. Like you."

"I was hoping to get more for my money."

"Too bad," he said. And he hung up.

I stood there by the phone, letting disappointment wash over me. I don't know what I had expected. Maybe some missing piece, something to help put it all in perspective. Maybe I wanted something that would have helped me feel safer.

And I didn't buy it. If B. B. Gunn was the head of some kind of drug and hog operation, whatever that would look like, he must have had some dealings with the law. An arrest that never went anywhere, unfounded allegations that made their way into the newspaper, something like that. Why had Denton come up empty?

As it turned out, it was my fault. I never noticed that Chris Denton's number was in the same exchange as the one Karen had put on her application. It was a Meadowbrook Grove exchange. And Chris Denton, I would later learn, knew Jim Doe.

When I hung up the phone, I had the feeling someone was watching me. I looked up. There was Chitra, her eyes narrow and, I thought, judgmental.

"Hi," I said. "This is your pickup too?"

"Yeah," she told me. "You weren't selling today, were you."

"Not selling?"

"I've been here a while. I saw you get out of that car your friend was driving. Did you go swimming?"

"What?"

"That woman in the front was wearing a bikini."

That was about as far as our conversation got before Bobby pulled up in his Cordoba and she melted back into the store.

Ronny Neil and Scott were already in the car, Ronny Neil in front, whispering conspiratorially to Scott in the back. Did that mean something? Bobby had been picking me up first for weeks.

Why should I care who got to sit in which seats? I was planning on leaving and never coming back. I had bigger and more important things to worry about than whether or not Bobby considered me the best bookman in his crew. I was more interested in making certain I didn't go to jail for murder or get killed by drug dealers.

The Cordoba came to a stop in front of the store, and Bobby pushed himself out. The engine was still running, and from inside Billy Idol crooned about eyes without a face, whatever the hell that meant. Bobby grinned and came around to the back, flipping open the trunk with a flair of his wrist, as if he were a magician performing a trick. His blue oxford shirt was partially untucked, and he'd spilled something sodalike on his pants.

"So, besides running errands for the Gambler, did you have any time to make money?"

I shook my head. "I blanked."

Bobby sucked on his lower lip. "That was a pretty primo spot I gave you. Might have helped if you'd been there."

"I was out there most of the day. It just didn't work out."

"Yeah, right."

"It's not like I blanked on purpose," I said, even though that's exactly what I did.

"So, what happened?"

I shrugged. "I don't know. Bad luck."

"No such thing as bad luck, Lemmy. You make your own luck." Bobby looked at me with a kind of seriousness I had never seen before, and I knew he didn't want to hear my bullshit excuses. He gave his head a little sad shake and then shut the trunk. "You guys want to go behind my back, fuck me up, that's your business. Get in the car."

I had to climb in the back with large, smelly Scott. When they picked up Kevin, there was no way Scott would scoot over to the middle, which meant I would be squished between them, breathing in the stink of Scott's unwashed body all the way back to the motel.

But, I told myself, it would all be over soon. Tomorrow would be the last day in town. Monday morning Bobby would head for home. We would stop on the road to sell, and I'd be back by two or three A.M. early Tuesday, and I would never have to sell books again. Just two more book-selling sessions and then freedom.

A tinny Genesis tune was coming through the radio now, and I tried to concentrate on it. I'd read once that if you had a really bad headache, you could make it go away by thinking about some other part of your body instead. That's what I was trying out. I figured if I listened to Genesis, if I concentrated on Phil Collins's voice, I might not smell Scott quite so much.

"I bet you blanked today," Ronny Neil said from up front. "I didn't. I got me a double."

This was where Bobby would tell him to be quiet, that they didn't talk about how it went in the car. But Bobby didn't say anything. He just stared ahead as he drove.

"You ain't gonna answer me?" Ronny Neil said.

Scott shoved an elbow into my ribs. "I heard someone say something to you," he told me. He scratched at a zit on his nose.

I still didn't say anything. I decided instead to nurse my indignation.

"Well, did you blank or didn't you?" Ronny Neil asked. "I thought you understood English so great."

"You know we're not supposed to talk about it."

"I don't hear Bobby complaining."

I paused to let Bobby chime in, but he didn't say anything

"We're not supposed to talk about it," I said again.

"Shit, boy, you worry too much about what you're supposed to do and what you're not supposed to do. Me, I'm gonna celebrate in style. A double. With that bonus I got me six hundred dollars today, and I get me some pussy."

"Yeah," said Scott.

"Yeah what?" Ronny Neil asked his friend. "Yeah, your buddy is going to get some pussy? You know you ain't. Who would get with a fat, lisping fuck like you?"

Scott laughed.

"How much money you think that Chitra will want for her to give me some of that pussy she got?" Ronny Neil asked. "How much you think?"

"I think she's giving it away," Scott told him. "Those Indian girls are horny as shit. The dots they got on their heads make them horny. She don't have a dot, but it's the same thing."

"Shut the fuck up," Ronny Neil said. Then, on second thought, he added, "Horny as shit. I heard that, too."

Back at the motel, after everyone had piled out of the car, Bobby put a hand on my shoulder to hold me back. We watched as Scott and Ronny Neil walked off, with Kevin lagging behind good-naturedly, trying to stay in the conversation, not seeming to notice or mind that Ronny Neil and Scott didn't give a damn about him.

"Wait a minute," Bobby said. "I want to talk to you."

I sighed. "I'll do better tomorrow," I said, though I knew I wouldn't. I'd blank again tomorrow because I wouldn't try again tomorrow. It was that simple.

"It's not that," Bobby said. "I want to know what's going on with you and the Gambler."

If it weren't for the darkness, Bobby would have seen the cloud of fear pass over me. "It's nothing," I said, reaching for words that would comfort him and in no way encourage him to bring the conversation to the Gambler himself.

"Don't tell me it's nothing. This morning the Gambler seemed ready to string you up. Now the two of you are best buddies and he's sending you on errands. Plus, he's leaning on me to do whatever those two baboons, Ronny Neil and Scott, want. He told me to give them whatever spots they ask for, Lem. He told me to treat them like kings. I'm going to do what I'm told, but I want to know why."

"I don't know why."

"Come on, Lem. I know your story. You want to go to college. A little more than a year from now you'll be studying for midterms and trying to talk sorority girls into coming back to your dorm room. I'm still going to be here. This is my job, and I want to keep doing it. I like that I make money doing it. I'm good at it."

"I know you are."

"Yeah, then why are you screwing this up for me?"

"Because I blanked?"

"You know that isn't it. The Gambler is angry with me, and I can't figure out what his deal with you is. You've got to tell me what's going on, because I don't want to burn out here. I've put too many years into this. It took me two years to be a crew boss. I can move up in this organization, but not if the Gambler is angry at me. So, you've got to tell me what's going on."

I shook my head. "I don't know."

"Is it about the reporter? Have you talked to that reporter he mentioned?"

I shook my head again.

"Because you were asking those questions this morning."

"I was curious is all."

He waited a moment to see if there would be more coming. There wouldn't be. "You won't tell me?" he asked, his voice gone quiet now.

"There's nothing to tell, Bobby."

"Fuck!" He slapped his hand down on the back of the car. "I've been your friend. I've looked out for you, and I've helped you make a lot of money. And this is how you treat me?"

"If I could tell you something, I would," I said, almost whined.

"Get the fuck out of here," Bobby said.

I started back to the hotel, and I thought that the next two days were going to be the most miserable of my life. And that was saying a lot.

Chapter 29

I WASN'T SURE I WANTED TO GO to the pool that night. What I wanted was to keep a low profile, to slink through the rest of the weekend without making anyone else hate me, without having any more conflicts with Ronny Neil and Scott. Or the Gambler. Or Bobby. On the other hand, if I was never going to come back, then I was never going to see Chitra again, not unless I arranged to see her. So maybe that was what I needed to concentrate on.

I looked out the window to the pool area. People were beginning to congregate. No sign of Chitra, though. I could go out there, have a couple of beers, and see if she showed up.

I left the room and went down the stairs, this time unhindered, and began to make my way across the path. I walked quickly, with my head down, the way I did when I was lost in concentration, and the noise was almost drowned out by the sound of my own footsteps. That is, it would have been drowned out by the sound of my own footsteps if there hadn't been a voice my whole nervous system had been wired to hear. I had become like a radar dish, tuned to one signal, and when that signal was anywhere in the air, my dish rotated toward it.

It was Chitra's voice, musical and lilting. But this time it was not so soft. It was strident.

"Ronny Neil, please."

A couple of vending machines stood behind the building with the check-in desk. More than once I'd heard couples making out in there when I came back to my room late at night. Only now it was Chitra back there. With Ronny Neil.

Were they having a fight? Could she have lied to me so brazenly about her connection with Ronny Neil? Was she so foolish, and was I so foolish as to have believed her?

"I got me a double today," I heard Ronny Neil say.

I took a step closer.

"Yes, that's nice, but you brought me here under false pretenses. I don't want to stay."

"Sure you do, baby."

"No, Ronny Neil. Take your hand off of me. I don't want to stay."

"Give me one kiss. Come on. It ain't so hard."

I knew this was a gift. I could walk right up to that vending machine and be the hero. If I rescued Chitra, there would be no going back. The only problem was, I didn't know how to rescue her. I wished Melford were here, with his gun and his bravado and his cool disposition. Melford would know exactly what to do.

I looked around, as though the answer might be somewhere nearby. I heard voices from the pool, laughter, the grating sound of patio furniture sliding against the rough chattahoochee. And there was the throbbing in my head, the veins or arteries or whatever they were in my temples thumping, thumping like the pulsating gong of cowardice. I felt sure I was going to walk away. Chitra could take care of herself, for a few more minutes, anyhow. I would get a couple of guys, and we would all come back. My role would be diminished, but Chitra would be safe and the risk would be spread more comfortably.

I felt sure I was going to walk away, but that wasn't how it happened. I pushed my way through the bushes and found Chitra pinned to the Coke machine. Her head was flush against the bright red façade of it, her ponytail squished, her face in a glowing mask of fear and contempt. Ronny Neil stood right before her, bent over slightly, holding hard to her wrist.

I wanted to shout something melodramatic and absurd, but I choked down the words, because the thing was, Melford might be crazy, he might be a homicidal freak, but he still knew a thing or two about the world and about human nature.

"Hey, guys," I said. "What's going on?" I walked past Chitra and toward the soda machine, then fished into my pocket for some change. My hands were shaking badly, but I was certain I could keep everything under control. I turned to Chitra. "Excuse me for a sec," I said.

She stepped forward, and I slid the coins into the slot and pushed the button for a Sprite.

Not that which soda I picked made a difference. I could have pressed the button for goat piss if it were on there, for all it mattered. But the Sprite landed at the bottom with a hollow and metallic thud, and I took it out, popped the top, and turned back to the two of them.

"What's up with you two?" I asked. I kept the wavering in my voice to a minimum.

"Why don't you fuck off?" Ronny Neil said.

I shrugged, as though I'd been asked if I had plans for the weekend. "I don't know," I said. "Never really thought about it."

"What?" Ronny Neil sneered.

"I don't know why I don't fuck off," I explained. "I'm not in the mood to fuck off right now, I guess." I looked over at Chitra. "You want to take a walk or something?"

The thinnest of smiles appeared on her lips, as though she suddenly understood the game. "Yes," she said. The smile was growing. "I think I'd like that very much."

I looked over at Ronny Neil. "See you back at the room."

Easy as that, we walked away.

We crossed through the registration area, where Sameen gave me a curious glance, and then out to the pool area. We figured, without discussing it, that Ronny Neil wouldn't follow us that way. I stopped to toss out the Sprite and pick up a couple of tall boys from the cooler, because, holy hell, I needed a beer. I handed one to Chitra and then opened my own. It didn't taste all that much different from the Sprite when you came down to it, but it was good. I needed a drink. I'd never needed a drink in that manly way before, but I needed one now.

I was calmer than I would have thought, maybe even than I should have been. My heart pounded and my hands still trembled, but I didn't care. The grateful heat emanating from Chitra, her appreciative silence, her relieved and amused smile, were all like the pendulous watch of a hypnotist.

We walked past the pool and back to the cloister of the motel. I had no idea where we were going, and I could tell Chitra had no idea, either. None of the book people were staying in this part of the building. We went up the stairs and walked along the second-story balcony, looking out over the railing, painted white but with rust showing through. We stopped where the floor turned, filling out the boomerang shape of the wing. Here was another pair of vending machines—food and beverage—and a groaning ice machine as well.

Now Chitra was leaning up against a vending machine again, and there I was, just like Ronny Neil, slouching in front of her. Only this time she was smiling. She took my hands.

"You're very clever," she said.

"That makes one of us. What were you doing behind the bushes with that idiot?"

She laughed, and her caramel-colored skin darkened with a blush. "He told me that the vending machine had some sort of Indian soft drinks in it. I can't believe I fell for it."

"Me either. Wow."

She laughed. "I know it sounds foolish, but this motel *is* owned by Indians, you know. It was possible."

"True enough," I agreed. "They have that chutney-o-matic in the lobby."

She was still laughing. "You can stop making fun of me now."

"Okay," I agreed. "Maybe I will."

We said nothing for a long time. She held my eyes and we grinned. I knew I ought to kiss her. I knew it. But she was from India. How did they do things there? I might offend her. Maybe kissing was the last thing on her mind, and she was involved in some mysterious Hindu gratitude ritual, and if I tried anything, she'd hate me. I'd be as bad as Ronny Neil.

But then she was no longer holding my hands. She had her hands on my arms, and she was rubbing them back and forth. I took a step forward, and Chitra reached out and put her hands behind my neck and pulled me in for a kiss.

Her lips were soft and warm, and I could feel her breath swirling around in my mouth in little eddies. And then she pulled away again. And smiled.

I had sort of been hoping for something more passionate, more bodice ripping. On the other hand, I liked the slow sweetness of it.

"I'm glad you were the one who rescued me," she said. "I would have hated to have to kiss Scott that way."

"I'd have hated that, too. Listen, Chitra. You look really beautiful by the light of that Coke machine. Don't get me wrong. But I'm wondering if we might go somewhere else a little more, you know, private."

"Are you trying to get me to go back to your room?" she asked.

I let out a nervous laugh that even I thought sounded dorky. "So we can see Ronny Neil again? It wasn't really what I had in mind. Frankly, I was thinking of anyplace with chairs. We could call a cab, get a drink or something. Just so long as we get away from here."

"Do you want to go get a hamburger?"

"No," I said. "I really don't."

"Me either. I'll stop teasing you. You know, it's amazing how you don't notice the things all around you. You don't imagine possibilities, even when those possibilities are right in front of your face."

I stared at her. It sounded too damn much like something Melford would say. "Chitra, I really like you, but I have no idea what you are talking about."

Her big eyes, dark and wide, locked on mine. "What I'm talking about is that rooms at this motel only cost thirty-nine dollars per night."

I felt as though I'd been kicked in the stomach by the most pleasant foot on earth. I was scared, even terrified. I wanted to say no, to put on the brakes, but that was another form of cowardice, and I knew it.

"Really?" I said.

"I'm quite sure. There's a big sign out front with the price."

"That's not what I meant."

"I know what you meant. I'd like to get a room with you. I don't know what will happen in it, but I think I can trust you. I just want to get away from everyone and everything for a while, to talk in private, to have our own space. I know a motel room is suggestive, but I can trust that nothing will happen that I am not ready for. Can't I?"

"Of course you can," I told her, strangely relieved that I might not have to lose my virginity just yet. "You know," I said, "if they find out, they'll fire you."

"I don't want to come back. Not if you're not going to be here anymore."

This time the foot in the stomach was not quite so pleasant. I hadn't told anyone about not planning on coming back, not even Melford. "How did you know that?"

"Come on. I saw you getting out of your friend Melford's car tonight. It's clear you're not even trying to sell anymore."

"That's pretty complicated," I said.

"You don't have to explain anything to me."

"I want to, but I can't right now."

"Is everything okay? I mean, he's not getting you involved in anything dangerous or reckless, is he?"

I didn't want to lie to her directly, so I approached it obliquely. "Melford's a complicated guy."

"I notice you haven't answered me. I still think there's something strange about him."

"There's nothing that's not strange about him. But my not selling isn't really his doing. It's mine. I don't want to do this anymore. The money is good, but it's not worth it."

"I know what you mean. I made so much money last weekend that I hardly even noticed how miserable I was. But this weekend it feels more like a forced march. I was looking forward to seeing you again this weekend, and if you're not going to be here, I think I would be miserable."

I couldn't believe I was hearing these sweet words. I felt unworthy. "I feel the same way," I said. Stupidly, I thought.

She laughed a little. "My father will be happy to hear about this. We need the money, but he hates me doing door-to-door sales."

"You think he'll like me better than Teddy?"

"His name is Todd. And as long as you are neither Todd nor Pakistani, everything is negotiable."

"Well, there's two things going for me. So, let's get a room," I told her. "It's on me."

"A woman loves a big spender."

We turned to head back to the stairs, and we both stopped in our tracks. Bobby was standing there, arms folded, eyes little slits of judgment.

"They told me you came this way." Bobby was glaring at us. At me, really. His round face was red. His eyes were red, too, as though he'd been crying.

I opened my mouth to make some lame excuse, like we were just getting an orange soda. I decided to save it.

"The Gambler wants you in his room right now," Bobby said.

There was something dark in his voice. It took me a moment to put my finger on it, but once I found it there was no mistake. It was more than anger. Rage.

"What for?"

"Just come along."

I looked at Chitra. "I don't know. I don't want to leave Chitra alone. Ronny Neil sort of attacked her before, and he might still be hanging around, looking for trouble. It's not safe."

"No one likes a tattler," Bobby told me.

"A tattler? You can't tattle on attempted rape."

Bobby seemed unmoved. But Chitra put a hand on my shoulder. "It's okay. I'll go down to the pool, make sure I stay with other people."

"Don't go anywhere alone."

She smiled. "I won't."

Bobby sensed that our farewell had run its course, so he pushed me forward.

I watched Chitra descend the stairs, and only when I saw her get to the pool safely did I turn my attention back to Bobby.

"So what's this all about?"

"Like you don't know," Bobby said.

"No, I don't know. Tell me." But it could only be about one thing, I figured. Bobby had said something to the Gambler about seeing me in his room, and the chain reaction led to my being dragged off there. My leg muscles stiffened, and I was within seconds of darting off, but then Bobby said something else.

He said: "Christ, you don't deserve it, but I didn't say anything to him about your being in his room. You fucked me over, but not enough for me to want to see you get your ass seriously messed up. He'd kill you if he found out."

Okay, so this wasn't about my being in his room. "I appreciate your not saying anything, but if the Gambler doesn't know about that, then what is this about?"

"Come off it, Lem. You lied to me and you made me look bad. Maybe so bad that I won't be able to keep my job."

"What are you talking about? How did I lie to you?"

"Give it up. Isn't it obvious that you've been found out?"

"Bobby, I have no idea what you mean."

Bobby let out a sigh. "The reporter," he said. He then looked at me with a kind of "I dropped the bomb on you, baby" smile.

"The reporter? What about the reporter?"

"The guy from *The Miami Herald*. He's in the Gambler's room."

That sounded like bad news. Hick cop Jim Doe might be too stupid and too invested in his own crimes to figure out what the hell had happened with Bastard and Karen, but a reporter from *The Miami Herald* was something else entirely. But if I had reason to be afraid, I didn't know why Bobby had reason to be angry.

"What does this have to do with me?"

"I thought you were too smart to stab me in the back. Especially after everything I did for you. And if you're not going to be too smart to stab me in the back, I'd hope you'd at least be smart enough to cover your own ass. Did you even tell the guy you weren't supposed to help him out? If you had, he might not have come knocking on the Gambler's door."

"Bobby, this is all a big mistake, and when I meet this guy he's going to tell you it was all a big mistake. Believe me, I have no interest in talking to any reporters."

"Sure," Bobby said.

We were now outside the Gambler's door. Bobby gave it a curt, irritated knock, and in an instant the Gambler opened up. He flashed a murderous glance and mouthed something that I couldn't quite get.

Sitting near a glass table by the far window sat a man in a white linen suit with a black T-shirt. His eyes were hidden behind his glasses, but I had the feeling he wasn't looking at me. Not really. I thought that odd, and I thought that he didn't look like any reporter I had ever seen. Not that I'd ever seen any in real life, but this guy was way more *Miami Vice* than *Lou Grant*.

When the door opened wider I saw another man, sitting on the opposite side of the glass table. A steno pad rested against one folded knee, and he twirled a felt-tip pen, fingers twitching with desire to write. This clearly was the reporter.

It was Melford.

Chapter 30

···

I STARED AND STARTED TO SPEAK, but I checked myself. I'd never asked what Melford did for a living, and he might as well be a reporter as anything else. He might as well sell me down the river as anything else, too. But the thing was, Melford wasn't going to screw me over lightly, not when we knew each other's secrets the way we did. At least that's what I had to assume.

So the best thing to do was to sit tight and follow Melford's lead and hope to hell this thing didn't turn out to be the total disaster it looked like.

Bobby took a seat on the dresser, the Gambler on the bed. I eyed the older man with the linen suit, to whom I hadn't been introduced. I had the sense that this guy was important, that he was maybe beyond names or something scary like that. Like maybe this was B. B. Gunn.

"So, you're Lem," Melford said, standing up. "Melford Kean. It's finally nice to meet you in person." He held out a hand. His hair had been combed back. He looked almost like a regular person, though a tall and pale one.

We shook. "Um, we've never met before in any form. In person or out of person."

"Lem," Melford said with a grave voice. He shook his head as he sat back down. "It's clear to me now that you weren't supposed to talk to me. If during our phone conversations you had told me that, I wouldn't have betrayed your confidence. But you didn't tell me, did you?"

"I haven't told you anything about anything," I said. "We've never spoken."

"Let's be honest," Melford said. "There's no point in lying."

I had no idea what I was supposed to do. Should I go along with him or not, though not going along with him would have involved exposing my connection to the murders. But there was something encouraging in Melford's eye, and I was almost certain he wanted me to keep going the way I had been.

"Look, I'm sure you're very good at your job," I said, "but there's some fundamental mistake here. I've never spoken to you about my work. I've never spoken to you about selling encyclopedias. And I've never spoken to you on the phone."

Melford shook his head. "I'm sorry I got you in trouble, but denying it isn't going to help. I think maybe you should tell us why you called me in the first place. Maybe we can hash out some of your complaints in front of these guys. In any case," he offered with a self-satisfied smile, "I'd like to hear how they respond to what you have to say."

I was floundering. I didn't know what Melford expected of me. Should I keep denying the charges? Would that be enough? And why the hell would he do this to me without giving me a heads-up?

"You need to listen to me," I said. "There's been a mistake."

"Jesus fucking dick," the Gambler snapped. "B.B., what do you want to do with this asshole?"

The man in the linen suit looked up. "I don't really know. I'm waiting for Desiree to call me back. I want to talk to her before I make any decisions."

The Gambler snorted at me. "I'm getting sick of hearing you deny it. You've spoken to him, and we know it. Now, say whatever it is you want to say so we can tell him what bullshit it is."

"Well, I think maybe we should go a little more gently with Mr. Altick," Melford suggested. "The fact is, he was shy enough about talking to me in the first place that he disguised his voice on the phone."

I suddenly felt like I was being prompted. "Disguised my voice?" I asked.

"Yeah, it was a pretty good job. You sounded totally different with your southern accent and all. It was very convincing. And your lisp."

And that's when I almost got it. I hadn't realized that Melford had overheard enough of my encounter with Ronny Neil and Scott to have picked up on it, but clearly he had. I still had no idea *why* he was doing this, but at least the *what* was clear. "I don't have a lisp."

"I can see that now."

"Hold on one second," Bobby said. "The guy who called you had a lisp."

"That's right."

"Did he have kind of a high-pitched voice?"

Melford nodded. "Now that you mention it."

"Fuck," Bobby said.

"Scott Garland, that piece of shit," the Gambler said.

"I don't get it." Melford looked at them blankly.

"You fucking asshole." The Gambler slammed his palm down hard on the table and then jabbed a finger in my direction. "Did you have to piss him off so much that he'd do something like this to get back at you?"

"I think," Bobby proposed, "that you may be taking this out on the wrong person." He looked at me. "I owe you an apology, Lemmy. I should have known you wouldn't do something like this."

"Give me a fucking break," the Gambler groaned. "Get out of here," he told me.

"Wait," B.B. said. "I don't get it."

"If I could suggest something else about Scott and Ronny Neil—," I began, but I didn't get any further.

"Get the fuck out of here!" the Gambler shouted again. And I did.

From the railings I could see Chitra down at the pool, drinking a tall boy and laughing at something that Yvette from Jacksonville was saying. No sign of Ronny Neil or Scott, and I had a feeling that the two of them would be disappearing pretty soon. The Gambler wasn't going to take this lightly.

Melford's ruse had been brilliant. He'd taken the heat off me while putting it onto my enemy. Granted, this would have been a lot better if he had warned me. But maybe not. Maybe Melford could tell that I wasn't built for this kind of deception and that preparation would only have made things seem false.

None of that explained why he would bother to show up at all. To help me exact petty revenge against Ronny Neil and Scott because he'd seen them picking on me? It didn't ring true.

I glanced down at Chitra once more. I wanted to get that room with her, more than ever. But first I needed to make a call.

Back in my room, I dialed the number and a weary-sounding *Miami Herald* operator picked up. I asked if there was such a thing as a night desk editor. I hadn't known that I was aware of any such position, but there clearly was, because without responding the operator put me through to a ringing line.

In a second, a woman picked up the phone and mumbled her name with a fatigued slur. Something McSomething.

"I don't know if you can answer this," I said, "but I'm calling from outside of Jacksonville, and I'm wondering if you have a reporter named Melford Kean on staff."

The woman laughed. "Kean, huh? What's the trouble?"

My stomach did little loops. I was on to something. "No trouble. I'm just wondering is all."

"Kean," she said again. "Is he bothering you? Please tell me he's bothering you."

"He's not bothering me. Just confusing me a little."

"Yeah, he's good at that."

I thought for a second. What exactly did I hope to learn? "What story is he working on?"

She laughed again. "What is he working on, or what is he supposed to be working on? Anything is possible with that guy."

"But he is a reporter at your paper?"

"Yes, like it or not, he is."

"And you don't like it?"

"Nah," she said, moderating her tone. "The kid's great. Just a little weird. But that doesn't mean he doesn't do a decent job, when he puts his mind to it. Or goes after the story he's assigned. Or makes deadline."

"That bad?" I tried to sound sympathetic, like the kind of person to whom she would want to open up. "How does he keep his job?"

"This is where being a pampered, overeducated rich kid comes in handy for him. He's the son of Houston Kean, a big shot in the business community here. The guy owns about a million car dealerships and he advertises a ton with us. A ton. So if the publisher wants this big advertiser's son to remain employed . . ." She paused for a few seconds. "It's late and I'm cranky. Forget I said any of that."

"Sure. No problem. But can you tell me what story he's working on?"

"I guess so. I mean, why not, right? There are two things. One I can't tell you about except that we got a tip from another reporter, one who didn't want to take the story herself. A woman who works for one of the local TV stations, but her beat is supermarket openings and celebrity visits, so she passed it along. There's some funny business going on in a trailer park near Jacksonville. But that happened after Kean already left for Jacksonville, and it's about as much as I can tell you."

"And the other story?"

"Get this," she said, as though we were old friends. "Pets. There's been a string of dog and cat disappearances in the area, and he went down to investigate. Pets. A hot piece of investigative journalism. He's been working on the story for three weeks, and he's yet to file a single paragraph. It's like he wants to get fired. I don't get this guy."

I got him. I got him with no trouble, because suddenly everything started to make sense. Well, not everything. But some things, and that was an improvement.

I was not about to waste any time. I ran down the stairs and found Chitra still in midchatter with a small cluster of friends. She looked happy and radiant, as though the business with Ronny Neil had never happened. That was bad. I wanted her to be afraid.

I took her hand. "Come on," I said as I yanked her up. "We have to go." I pulled her by the hand into the little building with the registration desk. "I need a room," I told Sameen, who appeared very disturbed that I was still holding on to Chitra.

"Yes, certainly," he mumbled.

"Sameen, I need it to be on the far side, by the parking lot. As far away from the Educational Advantage Media group as possible." I took out my wallet and put three twenties on the desk. It was half the money I had on me, and I hoped I wouldn't need it later. "This is a secret. You understand, sir? There's a man in our group who tried to hurt this young lady tonight. I'm trying to put her somewhere she'll be safe."

The look on his face changed considerably. He slid the money back toward me. "I do not need to be bribed to do the right thing," he said softly. "You are a good boy to help her."

I blushed, since I didn't feel like an especially good boy. "Thanks."

I grabbed the key and, still holding her hand, half jogged around to the back of the motel, where we found the room. I opened the room, led Chitra inside, and shut the door softly, as though afraid to alert anyone.

"That's some story," Chitra said. She turned on the light and began to look around, as though the room might somehow be different from the one she was already staying in. The one with all her clothes, I thought.

I took her hand again and kissed her swiftly on the lips. "Listen, Chitra, there's a lot going on and more than I have time to tell you. I need to go somewhere, and it is a little dangerous. I don't want you to open the door for anyone but me. And if I'm not back by meeting time tomorrow morning, don't wait for them to come looking for you. Call a cab and get out of here. Go to the bus station. Just go home."

"What is this about? Ronny Neil can't be that dangerous, can he?"

I shook my head. "It's not about Ronny Neil. Not the way you mean. I think this whole operation, Educational Advantage Media—all of it—is a front for something else. I don't know what, exactly, but it involves drugs, and there are some pretty high-powered guys involved, and people have already been hurt. Don't trust any of the bookmen, especially not the Gambler. Bobby might be okay, but I'm not sure enough to tell you to trust him."

"Are you serious about all of this?"

I nodded. "I wish I weren't."

"Let me come with you," she said.

I laughed, a stupid guffaw of air. "It's not a movie, Chitra. I don't know what I'm doing, and I don't want to take you along for the fun of watching me try to figure it out. I just want you to be safe, that's all. That's how you can help, by being safe."

She nodded. "All right."

"Remember, don't let them come looking for you. If I'm not back by nine tomorrow morning, call a cab and go."

"Okay."

"And give me your home phone number," I said. "In case I'm not dead, I want to call you."

Chapter 31

T HE REPORTER WAS GONE, convinced that the story was all a hoax. He'd seemed reluctant at first, but a few hundred dollars had set him straight. The Gambler knew those guys liked to act all high and mighty, but they were no better than anyone else.

Now it was just him and B.B. He dumped some Seagram's vodka into a plastic bathroom cup and then pulled the wet carton of orange juice from the ice bucket. Little disks of ice scattered over the brown carpet, and he idly kicked them under the dresser while he mixed the drink.

"You want?" he asked B.B., bracing himself for rejection, since B.B. generally wouldn't drink anything but his fancy bullshit wine. Screwdrivers were beneath contempt.

B.B. shook his head. "Nah."

"We've got things to discuss," the Gambler said. "Big, strategic things that always work better with drinks. You want to get some wine and then sit down to hash it out?"

"Nah, I'm okay."

Jesus, what was wrong with this guy? Another bombshell dropped, and he sat there looking like a retard. The screwdriver was too vodka heavy, but he drank it down because . . . why the hell not. He then sat at the foot of the bed and looked at B.B.

"Well, let's do it. What do you think about the kid?"

"The kid?" B.B. asked. "Which one? The older one?"

Holy hell. He was still thinking about those boys outside. His little empire was falling down around him, and he was still thinking about sticking it to those boys outside.

"Altick." The Gambler tried to rein in his impatience. "You think he's probably okay?"

"Yeah, I think so."

"What did Desiree say about him?"

"She didn't see anything weird with him," he said, and then turned to look at the window, even though the heavy cloth curtains had been drawn closed. "She said he seemed okay."

The Gambler got the distinct impression that B.B. hadn't even talked to Desiree. Not that it mattered. Altick was clearly a red herring in all this, a poor asshole who'd been in the wrong place at the wrong time. Not that it meant his troubles were over. The way the Gambler saw it, Doe was beyond corrupt, they had a reporter snooping around, the boss was coming undone by boy buggery, and they had three dead bodies floating in a pit of pig shit. And Scott, one of his own boys, had been the one to tip off the reporter. Scott was going to have to go down for this.

Why would Scott do it? The Gambler had always taken care of him and Ronny Neil. A sellout for big money he could understand, but talking to a reporter? Out of some sort of resentment toward Altick, no doubt. It was a bonehead move, there could be no denying it, but maybe the problem was that he hadn't given those boys enough to do. Maybe he needed to give them more responsibility in order to motivate them, find a way to channel Scott's rage.

"So, what's your next move?" he asked.

B.B. appeared suddenly to come awake. "I need to get my money, Gamb. I can't have money like this just falling off the face of the earth."

"We've got to face the real possibility that Doe is bent, and if he took the money, we're not getting it back without some serious violence. You want to risk that?"

"I got the DevilDogs in Gainesville," B.B. said. "We know for a fact that it was Doe, we have them ride down here and beat it out of him."

The Gambler shook his head. B.B. was supposed to be the mastermind, but he'd become like a body without a head when his freaky bitch wasn't around. "The county has made life hell for motorcycle gangs here. You know that. The DevilDogs come riding in, the sheriff's department is going to be all over them. If a mayor and police chief get worked over and killed, even a bullshit one like Doe, it's going to mean a big investigation. And we're fucked if one of those numbnuts gets nailed by the cops. You think they're going to keep their traps shut? Next thing you know, we've got the DEA involved, which means they'll find something or someone who will tell them about the lab, and that's going to ultimately lead them back to us."

"Okay," B.B. said quietly. "What do we do, then? How do we get the money?"

"I guess we have to figure out a way to get Doe to 'find' it, to make him realize that it doesn't make any sense to rip us off."

"How do we do that?"

The Gambler said nothing.

B.B. took this as a sign that the Gambler, too, was out of ideas. He stood up and walked to the door, rested one hand on the knob. "Let's wait until Desiree gets back. She'll figure something out."

"So, that's it?" the Gambler asked.

"For now, yeah. That's it for now." Then, all at once, his face grew bright with a private joke. "There'll be more later, though." And he was gone.

Two drinks later, his head filled with muted vodka clarity, the Gambler answered a knock at his door. It was Doe, leaning against the doorjamb, dressed in uniform, bottle of Yoo-hoo dangling in one hand.

"I got a noise complaint," he said. "Neighbors say there's a sound of vibrating bullshit coming from your room."

The Gambler stood aside to let him in and then quickly shut the door. "You want a drink?" he asked, holding up his cloudy plastic cup.

Doe held up his bottle. "I don't leave home without it."

The Gambler sat in his chair by the window. "So, what do you want?"

"I got a noise complaint," he said. "Neighbors say there's a sound of vibrating bullshit."

"It wasn't funny the first time."

"How about the second?"

"Doe, this isn't the tryouts for *MAD* magazine, so how about you tell me why you're taking up my time."

Doe took a swig and flashed his crooked teeth. "I hate to bother you when you're sitting in a cheap motel drinking vodka by yourself, and normally I wouldn't, but hell, Gamb, I think you'll want to hear what I have to say."

"Then say it."

"First of all, let's cut the bull-fucking-shit, okay?" He walked over to the dresser and slammed the bottle down hard. A crack appeared in the particleboard. "I know that you and B.B. are full of little ideas about how I ripped you off, is that right? That maybe I killed Bastard and took the money, and now I'm trying to pin it on this fucking hapless kid to get myself off the hook. Does that about cover it?"

The Gambler tried hard to look impassive. This, he knew, was a showdown. Doe was there either to get himself off the hook for what he'd done or to set the record straight. Fine. Either way, it didn't much matter in the end, since there were more important things than the $40,000. The continuity of the operation, for example. And power. When this little duel was over, the Gambler needed Doe to think of him as tough, decisive, and in charge. Everything else, even that chunk of cash, was secondary.

He took a sip of his drink. "That pretty much covers it."

"And you want me to come up with cash or face consequences, I suppose."

"I've had thoughts along those lines, yes."

"Maybe you want to shut those thoughts the fuck up. Did you ever think of that?"

"No, I never thought of that. But since you did, maybe you should tell me why."

Doe shook his head in sad disbelief. "First of all, I didn't kill Bastard. And that means someone did, and that someone is still out there and has the money. You can believe me or not, but we've been doing this thing long enough that you know if I'd killed him, I'd admit it. Hell, if I stole the money and killed him, I'd still admit to killing him. I'd say he tried to rip us off and got caught and tried to kill me."

"Now that we've established how you would be lying if you were lying, let's hear number two."

"Number fucking two," Doe said, "is why the fuck would I rip you off? You cut me out or try to find the balls to take me out, I'm worse off than if we keep going on like we've been. I'm earning way too much from this shit to dick it up, so think with your fucking head for a second instead of B.B.'s.

Snoop into my shit, if you want. I don't got any debts, I got a pile in the Caymans. I want more, and I'm not going to fuck with the system."

It was all true. Doe had relatively little to gain in the short term and nothing to gain in the long term by ripping them off. In fact, the only thing that made the Gambler still doubt Doe was the Altick kid, who said he'd seen the chief snooping around Bastard's trailer. But that could have had something to do with the girl, he supposed.

He sat still, looking thoughtful for a few more minutes. "And those are your two points?"

"No, I got one more point. Point number three," he said, "is that B.B. called the station today, disguised his voice, and said that you killed Bastard and took the cash. Now, I don't know who has the money, but maybe that doesn't matter so much right now, because B.B. has decided to fuck you up, and I think you want me on your side."

"How do you know it was B.B. if the voice was disguised?"

"Because he's an asshole, and I recognized him. Besides, who knows that Bastard is dead besides you, me, B.B., and his whore?"

Doe gave a half nod. "And how do I know you aren't setting him up?"

"I guess you don't. But you maybe want to decide what you believe, because if B.B. figures out I'm not going to deal with you, he might have a backup plan that takes you by surprise."

The Gambler finished his drink and set down the plastic cup. "Okay," he said after a minute or so, a minute he needed mostly to keep Doe waiting. "I'll keep this information in mind. But let's be clear about something. I don't care if you stole the money or not. This is your house and your mess, and you need to clean it up. I'll look into what you say about B.B., and I'd better not find out that you're fucking with me, or I'm going to be pissed off. But if you're not, then we're going to be under new management, and new management says you clean up your fucking mess." He stood up. "Because if you can't get your act together, then you're fucking worthless to me. So by Monday morning I want that money or I want to know what happened to it. And if you go with choice number two, you'd better make me believe you're telling the truth. Now get the fuck out of here."

Doe finished his bottle and dropped it on the floor. "I like that," he said. "I like that forceful shit. We need more of that around here." He walked to the door and then turned around. "You want me to take care of B.B.?"

"Why?" the Gambler asked. "Because things on your end are running so smoothly that you have lots of extra time?"

"No," Doe said, "because I figured you might want to keep your hands clean. But have it your way, boss."

When Doe was gone, the Gambler rose to fix himself another drink. Fucking B.B. trying to screw him over. Why? And his efforts were so inept, it hardly mattered. An anonymous phone call. He'd lost it completely, and even if he hadn't been conspiring against the Gambler, he'd have to go, just for safety's sake.

So maybe there was some order in the universe, he thought. Maybe there was a way to turn liabilities into assets. And maybe, he thought, there was a way to turn Scott's inappropriate rage into something more useful.

After his unsatisfying meeting with the Gambler, B.B. had gone out to a local McDonald's for a strawberry milk shake and to take in the local scene. He liked to go to McDonald's. There were always lots of happy kids getting the crappy food they loved. In his work with the Young Men's Foundation, he saw only the unhappy boys. He liked the happy ones, too.

B.B. brought a newspaper with him but couldn't be bothered to read it. He looked into nothingness and tried to avoid the stare of the big-eyed black kid behind the counter who acted as though he'd never seen a man drink a milk shake before. He ought to have seen it. It probably happened pretty often in here.

After nearly an hour with no one interesting to look at, B.B. went back to the hotel. He figured he ought to be thinking about the money, but that was Desiree's job. And where was Desiree? He hadn't heard from her all day except for one hasty phone call in which she'd said that the kid appeared to be hapless and clean, but she was going to keep tailing him. It wasn't like her not to check in more often.

Approaching his room from the parking lot, he could see there was a piece of paper taped to his door. It was yellow, wide-lined notebook paper with torn perforation. When he pulled it free, it took a good chunk of the door's aqua blue paint along with the tape.

It would be from the Gambler, or maybe Doe, possibly even Desiree. Instead, a clumsy, childish hand had written in scrawling letters, "Mister my Dad called and said he wont be back before Late and my little brother gone off with his aunt. Can I have that Ice Cream now, and mabey talk about some stuff that's going on with my dad? Carl. Room 232."

B.B. folded up the note and held it in his hands. Then he unfolded it and read it once more. He held the paper in one hand and then the other, as though he could gauge its import from its flimsy weight.

Could it be a joke? Who would play such a joke? And what would be the point? On the other hand, how would that kid know his room number? Maybe he'd asked the Indian behind the counter. The guy wasn't supposed to give out that sort of information, but he probably didn't know any better, since who knew what sorts of ideas about privacy they had in India, where cattle wandered in and out of people's houses? Besides, Carl was nothing but a little kid who surely didn't mean any harm. Carl, he thought. Carl.

B.B. went into his room and washed his face, combed his hair, and put on a little bit of aftershave. Not too much, since kids didn't like too much, but enough so that he'd smell mature and sophisticated. That's what boys Carl's age wanted in a mentor. They liked to be in the presence of a grown man who knew how to talk to a boy.

Not that Carl was worth all this fuss. No reason to think he was. Back at home was Chuck Finn, and Chuck Finn would be worth the fuss. Even so, spending a little time with Carl might be productive. It would certainly be helpful to the young man, and that was why he did this work, after all. He did it for the young men, and for himself, if he was going to be honest. He liked the feeling of being helpful. And there was something else, too, something on the edge of his vision, just outside his range of hearing, a smell too vague to identify but strong enough to notice. But this wasn't the time. Maybe next week, maybe with Chuck, but not just now.

B.B. felt as though something from the highway had soiled his suit, so he dusted himself and headed out the door, up the stairs, and around back, where he found the room. Somewhere in the distance, he heard electronic pop from someone's room. Assholes needed to learn to keep it down. But Carl's room was mostly quiet. The curtains were drawn, but he could see a light on inside and vaguely hear a television droning. Before knocking, he took out the note and read it once more, making sure he had the room right and that he hadn't misunderstood the boy's intentions. No, there could be no misunderstanding. He'd been invited.

B.B. knocked firmly yet kindly. At least he hoped it sounded firm but kind. In the distance he heard a voice say that he should come in. He tried the handle and found it unlocked, so he pushed it open.

On the bed he saw a yellow toy tractor, so he knew he was in the right place. But no sign of Carl and, inexplicably, sheets of translucent plastic were covering the carpet. "Hello," he called out.

"I'll be right there," came the voice, high and childish. B.B. felt himself smiling for just an instant. He took another step inside and looked around. It was like every other motel room, but strangely neat for a place where two boys had been alone all day. The bed was made, no clothes around, no toys but the tractor. Most of the lights were off, and the TV, which was tuned to a sitcom, flashed blue into the gloom. The laugh track erupted as someone did something, and B.B. took a step closer to see what was so funny.

Then it struck him. The voice that called to him, it didn't sound like the boy from the pool. That boy hadn't sounded quite so young, quite so childish. In fact, the more he thought about it, the less that voice had sounded like a child's. It sounded like someone imitating a child.

Then he heard the door close behind him.

B.B. spun around and saw one of the Gambler's assholes sitting there. The fat one. A rank odor like piss wafted up. The kid's piggy eyes were wide with excitement, and he had a kind of openmouthed grin, as though he'd just issued the coup de grâce to a piñata. And B.B. knew, he fundamentally knew, that this grinning asshole was the least of his worries.

He turned and saw the other one, Ronny Neil. Ronny Neil also had a good-size grin going on. In addition, he had a wooden baseball bat with a fair number of dents in it, dents that suggested it had been used for something other than drives to left field.

"You sick fucking pervert," Ronny Neil said.

The baseball bat arced high over his head, and B.B. raised his hands to protect himself, knowing even as he did it that his hands weren't going to do him one bit of good.

Chapter 32

THE WALK TO THE KWICK STOP took a little over fifteen minutes at a brisk pace. I was certain I'd seen an OPEN 24 HOURS sign out front, and when I got there I bought a flashlight, batteries, and a large coffee to go.

I sat out front and loaded up the flashlight. The coffee was lukewarm, burned, and too thick, but I drank it quickly, and within five minutes I was ready to go again.

I didn't much like the idea of wandering around Meadowbrook Grove after dark. I would be in Jim Doe country, and if the cop found me, I had no doubt that I'd be in trouble. Serious trouble. The kind of trouble from which you don't ever return.

But I was close to that kind of trouble now. Wasn't that what I'd learned from Melford, what I'd learned to put into practice that night with Ronny Neil? It wasn't really a matter of how much trouble you were in, but how you tried to get out of it. I had to do something other than sit in the motel room. I might have done that last week, but not any longer.

I stayed off the roads. I tried to stick to backyards, ignoring the itch of insects and the various crawling, hopping, scurrying, and slithering noises of the animals I startled from either sleep or their rounds. I had to be careful of domestic animals, too. Frantic barking would draw attention. I knew from my late night rambles selling books, those long hours after dark when I was trying desperately to bag one more shot at a sale before it was time to go home, that dogs barked and owners ignored them. At least they did at nine-thirty. But at close to two in the morning, they might pay a bit more attention to furious barking.

When I turned onto Bastard and Karen's street, I stuck close to the trailers, trying to keep out of the light. It had been there all along: the box of files in the trailer with "Oldham Health Services" written along the side. It held the key to everything — to why Melford had killed them and what he was hiding from me.

I felt a strange, almost giddy excitement. Once I read through those files, I would finally know. I would finally know who Melford really was, what he was after. And I would know if he really intended to let me out of all this unharmed.

I looked around the back of the trailer and saw that the door leading to the kitchen was open. No sign of a car or of flashlight beams inside. I went up to the door to listen. No sound.

It was stupid. Idiotic. I knew it, but I went inside anyhow, because I had to see.

I turned on the flashlight for a quick scan. It was cheaply built, and the light slouched out anemically, but I still caught a glimpse of something on the kitchen floor.

I supposed I ought to be getting used to death, but the sight of the body hit me like a punch in the gut. I took a staggered step back and hit the kitchen counter.

I turned the feeble light on the figure again to be sure. But there was no mistaking it. In the distorting yellow of the flashlight beam, I saw the face of the man who'd been in the Gambler's room, the one in the linen suit, the one who'd looked as though he hadn't been paying much attention. The one I believed to be B. B. Gunn.

His face was well bloodied, but I couldn't tell how he had been killed. In fact, I was largely past concerning myself. I turned to rush out the door, but a flashlight, much brighter than my own, hit my eyes. I couldn't say I was particularly surprised. In a way, it seemed inevitable.

I stopped in my tracks. The light was too bright for me to see who held it, but I knew. It could be only one person.

"Well, well, if it ain't the hirer of private detectives," Jim Doe said.

I stared at him. How could he have known that?

"You stupid fucking shit," he said with a slight cackle. "You go to find out a thing or two about B.B., and you hire a buddy of mine to do it. Didn't you think for a minute that a guy who lives in Meadowbrook Grove might know me? But I guess it don't matter, because it seems to me like you are under arrest for murder."

There was a second, maybe two seconds, before I acted, but I thought of lots of things in those couple of seconds. I thought about how unlikely it was that Doe would shoot me, an unarmed encyclopedia salesman. Doe wanted to keep attention away from himself, not draw attention closer. Considering that our earlier encounter had been observed by Aimee Toms, the county cop — the county cop who had warned Doe to stay away from me — a shooting now would only draw the kind of scrutiny Doe could not afford. On the other hand, Doe might easily shoot me and make me disappear. And if that happened, I would never see Chitra again.

So I ran.

Chapter 33

T HE PUNK RAN. Well, what had Doe expected? That he would sit there and say, "I guess I got no choice but to come with you and probably get killed"? He was a fast runner, too. Doe wasn't about to chase after him. Christ, with the pain in his nuts he could barely walk, let alone run. He tried to pursue, made it maybe a hundred feet before he had to stop. As it was, he felt like he might faint. Or puke.

Well, let him go. It wasn't like Doe *needed* to arrest someone for B.B.'s murder. He could just toss the body in the waste lagoon. Probably better that way, anyhow.

Now, bent over, breathing in hard, painful bursts, hands on his knees, Doe spent a minute just trying to clear his head, get the swirling black things out of his vision. The problem now was going to be getting rid of B.B., and it was pretty much Doe's problem alone. Earlier that night his phone had rung, and on the other end a disguised voice, his second of the day—but Doe had known without a doubt that it was the Gambler's punk asshole Ronny Neil—had told him he'd better get over to Karen's trailer. There was a surprise waiting there.

He couldn't fault the little shit for being dishonest. B.B.'s dead body was a surprise all right. He'd been worked over good, too—beaten so that his legs were like jelly and his head half caved in. One of his eyes, bulging wide open, was half out of its socket. They'd killed him good and proper.

No message, no instruction, but Doe didn't need to be told what it meant or what he needed to do. The Gambler had taken B.B. out, which was only right. If anything, Doe was relieved that the Gambler had stepped up to the plate. Like he'd said before, there were bigger things in-

volved here, certainly bigger than his ego. There was money, and even if
B.B. hadn't been fucking with the Gambler, he'd been slipping up right
good. Still, this body presented some real problems, the first being that the
freaky cunt would think that Doe had done it. They'd dumped the body
on Doe's turf just to make trouble for him, to make sure he knew this was
the Gambler's show.

Doe didn't care. Doe didn't care who called the shots as long as the
shots got called and as long as the money came with it. The Gambler
thought he had some tough-guy shit to prove, that was just fine. He
thought he needed to put the pressure on Doe, say come up with the
money or an explanation, that was fine, too. Doe didn't get to where he
was by not being able to deal with the pressure.

He'd do what the Gambler wanted as a show of good faith, so he'd get
the message that things were working and there was no point in messing
up an orderly system. The Gambler would have to understand that this operation worked because it was under the radar. It worked because no one
was paying attention to them. That had always meant small crews, limited
exposure, and no bloodbaths. Four people had died this weekend, and that
was plenty. No way the Gambler was going to take him out. Even so, he
might get cut out or cut back or slighted. Begging to remain in good graces
might be beneath his dignity, but if it meant cash, then Doe would deal
with it for now.

All of which meant getting to the bottom of this shit. And that was
fine, too, because Doe knew what was what now. He knew why the kid had
squealed on him to the Gambler, and he knew where the money was. It
was now that simple. Find the kid, find the money.

Chapter 34

I HAD NEVER BEEN, by track team standards, an especially fast runner. I did better in longer races, but even in those I'd win only rarely. Still, I would do well once in a while with the five-hundred-meter. With half marathons the point wasn't to win, but to finish. But if I hadn't been the fastest runner in the county, or even at my own school, I was a hell of a lot faster than an aging, out-of-shape, crooked cop with a bad haircut.

I cranked my legs into the darkness, spinning them wildly until I felt like a cartoon character whose lower half was just a blurry wheel beneath the torso. Sometimes at the end of long runs I liked to push it, and I marveled that my legs could do such things, that I could move so fast and with such force without paying attention to how my feet hit the ground.

I'd never punched it like this in near total darkness with a cop on my trail. It didn't matter. I ran, and I kept running until I was sure I'd gone two miles, maybe more. I was used to pacing myself, attuning my speed to my natural rhythms, but not now. Now there was only speed. Fast as I could go, and nothing else mattered.

I was now out of the trailer park and into an area of small, older homes. It was the sort of place where half-rebuilt, half-rusting cars sat in backyards, where lawns were crisscrossed with missing grass, where broken swing sets creaked in the wind.

And it was familiar. I was sure I'd been here before. I walked for a moment to catch my breath. Two miles wasn't much, but I'd gone about as fast as I ever had. Then, while walking bent over, panting, I realized I had indeed been there before, I had sold books there.

I was just down the street from Galen Edwine, at whose barbecue I'd sold four sets of books—the fabled grand slam that had never paid off.

But Galen Edwine had taken a shine to me, the way customers sometimes did with bookmen. He'd told me to come back anytime. He'd said, Let me know if you ever need anything. I needed something now. I needed shelter and a place to rest where Jim Doe would never look for me.

It took about five minutes to find the house. I was sure it was the right place because of the garden gnomes that had so encouraged me that day. It was well after two in the morning now, and the house was entirely quiet and dark.

I rang the doorbell.

I rang it a couple of times to suggest urgency and to make certain that the unexpected chime didn't simply fade into a dream. I saw a light go on in the bedroom, and I heard a scrape just outside the door.

"Who is that?" asked a panicked voice.

"Galen, it's Lem Altick. Do you remember I tried to sell you some encyclopedias a couple of months ago? You told me if I ever needed anything . . ." I let it hang.

The door opened slowly, and Galen, wearing boxers and a T-shirt, stared at me with sleepy eyes that hung beneath a glossy slope of balding scalp. "I didn't expect you to take me up on it," he said, but there was nothing harsh in his voice. If anything, he seemed amused.

"I have kind of an emergency," I told him. "I need a place to stay. Just for a few hours."

Galen scratched his head with one hand and opened the door the rest of the way with the other. "Come on in, then."

Lisa, Galen's wife, came out in her robe, yawned a hello, and went back to sleep. If she found something unusual in a door-to-door salesman returning to their home in the middle of the night, she didn't say anything about it. Galen and I went to the kitchen, where he put on some coffee and took out a box of chocolate-covered doughnuts. I looked at the ingredients, which included butter and milk and eggs. I passed.

"You want to tell me what's going on?"

I told him. Not all of it. Not even most of it. Just enough. I told him that I'd run afoul of Jim Doe from Meadowbrook Grove and that Doe wanted to frame me for a murder that he had likely committed himself.

Galen shook his head. "Yeah, I know that guy. We all do around here. He's bad news, Lem. But I'll tell you, I know the sheriff's people have their eye on him, and I wouldn't be surprised if the FBI did, too. He won't get away with it. Go to the county and tell them everything. Believe me, they'll treat you like a hero."

I nodded and tried to look relieved, but his suggestion didn't help me. I didn't want to have to survive some long-term investigation that would eventually shift the blame from me to Doe. I just wanted to get out of there alive.

"Well," Galen said after a few minutes, "maybe you can look up something useful in those encyclopedias I bought from you."

I looked at him. "What do you mean?"

"What do you mean, what do I mean?"

"I mean," I said, "you never got those encyclopedias."

"Sure I did."

"But the credit application never went through."

"Sure it did. There's nothing wrong with my credit." Galen took me to the living room, where the entire set rested in the place of honor, on the bookshelves next to the television. The rest of the shelves were filled with knickknacks and photographs of his son and older people I assumed were his parents and in-laws. Not another book in sight.

"But they told me the credit app didn't go through. I don't get it." But I did. I got it just fine. "What about your friends? Did they get theirs?"

"Of course."

It was Bobby. Good-guy Bobby was skimming from his own sales force. Telling us sales didn't go through when they did, so he could take the commission for himself.

"They stole from you, didn't they," Galen said with unexpected gravity.

"Yeah," I told him. "They did."

"I can't say I'm surprised. Those operations aren't always as honest as you want, and maybe yours is less honest than most. You know, the same weekend you were in town, a couple of boys came by my younger brother's house, twelve miles or so from here, and they were selling books, using a lot of the same language that you used. My brother isn't married, doesn't have kids, so when he told them he didn't want anything, they tried to sell him speed. One of them seemed kind of pissed off that the other one had brought it up, but my brother looks the part. He's real skinny, long hair, tats. They must have thought he was a kindred spirit and decided to take a chance. You believe that?"

I nodded. I could believe it. Because that's what all of this had been about. This whole thing was an excuse to distribute speed. That's why Ronny Neil had said that Bobby didn't know what was going on, why it was better to be with the Gambler than with Bobby.

Bastard had worked over at the hog lot. I got the impression he'd been in on the speed deal, but when he'd been shot, Jim Doe and the Gambler must have thought it was drug related. That's why they got rid of the bodies. They didn't want the county cops or the FBI getting involved, messing up the operation.

"Do you think I could trouble you for a ride in the morning?" I asked.

"Of course."

"I need to be at my motel before nine."

"What do you plan to do?"

"I plan to get a friend of mine, get the hell out of here, and never come back."

Galen nodded. "That's a good plan," he said.

Thanks to the magic of utter exhaustion, I actually managed to get a few hours of sleep on Galen's couch before morning came. I ate a strangely cheerful breakfast—actually, I just ate some fruit—with Galen, Lisa, and their six-year-old son, Toby. Then Galen told me he'd drop me off on the way to work.

I asked him to let me out behind the motel, and I thanked him profusely. Then I knocked on Chitra's door.

She didn't look as though she'd slept much, if at all. Her eyes were sunken and red, and she might even have been crying.

"Lem," she gasped. She pulled me into the room and then pressed her whole body against mine and squeezed hard. Under the circumstances, it was just what I needed.

The downside was that it seemed to me an inopportune time for an erection, and there was no way she didn't notice, but if she found it distasteful, she was kind enough to keep it to herself. "Tell me what is going on."

I told her as much as I could in a rambling fashion. I told her about Jim Doe and the drugs and the pigs and murders, though I left Melford out of it. It seemed to me too much to explain how it was that I knew Melford was a killer and hadn't turned him in, how I'd become friends with him. It made no sense, so it was best not spoken of, particularly since she didn't much trust Melford.

"We need to go," I told her. "The Gambler's not going to be happy to see me, and neither is this guy Doe. Let's just call a cab and get out of here. It doesn't matter where. They don't want me around, will probably hurt me if they see me, but they won't come after us. They just want me gone, and I mean to give them what they want."

"Do you want to come with me? To my house for a few days, just to make sure they don't come looking for you at yours?"

"Yeah," I whispered. "I want to go with you."

We called the cab, and in ten minutes we went outside, determined to abandon whatever personal belongings—selling clothes and toiletries, mostly—were still in our rooms. Too bad for us. There was no way I was going back for that stuff.

Idling in front of the motel was a yellow Checker, but as we walked toward it, I caught the flashing lights out of the corner of my eye.

I saw in an instant, because I was getting good at that sort of thing, that it was a brown county car, not a blue Meadowbrook Grove car. And that was something. But it wasn't much. I felt that jarring electric zap in my stomach. Not a loose wire zap, but a strapped to the electric chair with a black hood over your head sort of jolt. And for an instant I felt that I would start running, commanded by my feet and a base animal instinct; I would simply take off and be gone. But that never happened.

The woman from the day before, Aimee Toms, got out of the car. Her face was blank, impassive, strangely appealing in its authority. "I need to talk to you," she said to me. "I want you to come with me."

"Am I under arrest?"

"I just want to ask you some questions."

I turned to Chitra. "You go," I said. "Go to the bus station and go home. I'll call you. I'll come see you."

"I'm not going without you," she said.

"You have to. Believe me, I'm in way over my head, but you're not in any real danger if I'm not around, and I'll be better off if I don't have to worry about you."

She nodded. Then she kissed me. I couldn't say exactly what the meaning was, but I can tell you that I liked it a whole hell of a lot.

And then Officer Toms led me into the back of the police car and drove me away.

Chapter 35

A IMEE TOMS STARED STRAIGHT AHEAD—or I thought she did, but I couldn't be sure with her eyes hidden behind her mirrored sunglasses. Even when she talked to me, she didn't move her head. Sitting behind the passenger seat, I watched her firm lower jaw work its way over a piece of gum that I knew, without asking her or seeing it, would be sugarless.

"So, what's your story, kid?" she asked after we'd pulled out of the motel.

I didn't kill them. I was there, but I didn't do it, and I couldn't have stopped it. The words sat there, drew me in with their gravity well, tried to shape my answer the way tracks shape the path of a train. But I wasn't going to give in. I was going to try to tough it out. And if things became too frightening, I could always break down later.

"I'm just trying to make some money to go to college," I told her. "I got into Columbia, but I can't afford it."

"South Carolina?"

"New York."

"Never heard of it. The school, not the city. You look kind of collegey," she observed. "Which is why I don't understand why you're getting involved in all of this."

"All of what?" My voice cracked like her gum.

"You tell me."

"I'm really sorry I trespassed yesterday," I said, "but you didn't seem to think it was a big deal then. Why is it a big deal now?"

"Trespassing isn't such a big deal," Officer Toms agreed. "On the other hand, drugs and murder—now, that's a big deal."

"I don't understand," I said. It didn't sound convincing because the fear wafted out of my mouth, the hot vapor of fear in the cold air-conditioning of the car.

"Listen, Lemuel. Lem?"

"Lem," I confirmed.

"Listen, Lem. I'm a pretty good judge of character. I look at you, I talk to you, I see you're not a bad guy. Believe me, I've been doing this long enough—and it doesn't take that long, I'm sorry to say—to know that good people get mixed up in bad things. Sometimes they don't understand what they're doing. Sometimes they're just in the wrong place at the wrong time. But instead of coming forward, they hide and lie and break more laws to cover things up."

All of this came uncomfortably close to the truth, and I knew there was nothing I could say that wouldn't reveal that closeness. I looked out the window instead.

"All I'm saying," she continued, "is that if you tell me everything that's going on, I'll do all I can to help you out, to see that you're not punished for being a victim of circumstance. Even if you think it's too late to talk, it isn't."

"I don't know what you mean," I said. "All I did was wander a little too close to a farm. I don't see why it's a big deal."

"We can do it that way if you want," she told me. She didn't say anything else until we arrived at the station.

It looked like an old office building, and except for their uniforms, the cops inside might have been just generic weary civic employees. The air conditioner gurgled mightily but produced little cold air, and overhead electric fans turned slowly enough that documents would not dislodge from desks.

Toms had a hand on my upper arm and squeezed with a kind of firm sympathy. My arms were behind my back. She hadn't cuffed me, but it seemed like a good idea to keep them back there out of respect or to acknowledge that I knew she *could* cuff me so there was no point in flaunting my freedom. As we walked down a pale green cinder-block-lined hallway, which looked like a forgotten annex of my high school, we passed a uniformed officer walking a handcuffed black guy in the opposite direction. He was just a teenager, really, tall and lanky with a shaved head and the ghost of a mustache. He might have been my age, but he had the hard look of a criminal in his eyes, violent and seething and apathetic. I cast him a glance as we passed, as though to say that we were both victims of an oppressive system, but the kid looked back with rage, as if he would kill me if he ever had the chance.

Toms shook her head. "George Kingsley. You get a good look at him?"

"Enough to tell he'd slit my throat just for the fun of it."

"Yeah, he's like that. The thing is, Lem, I knew him when he was this smart little twelve-year-old. His father had all kinds of problems with the law, which was why I knew him, but his mother's a good lady who saw he got to school and stayed out of trouble. But this kid did more than just follow the rules. He was always reading and talking about stuff. The ideas, the *political* ideas, you'd hear from him, a kid of twelve or thirteen. He was going to fix all the problems in the world. He was going to be a politician and help the black people. And he knew which laws he would repeal, which he would pass. It was incredible."

"I guess it didn't do him much good."

"As near as I can figure it, he was hanging with some of the wrong kids one day when one of them decided it was time to stick up a convenience store. Kingsley thought they were there for candy. This other kid, he pulled out a gun. Stupidest thing. I don't think the others knew he was planning anything, but they wouldn't lay it all on their friend. So Kingsley goes to juvie for deciding to buy a Snickers with the wrong people. He was only in for eighteen months, but when he came out he was different. It was like they'd beaten all the heart out of him. He went in this lively, engaged little spitfire, someone on track to maybe really change the world for the better, and he came out just another thug from the thug machine."

"That's a real tragedy," I said, doing my best to sound as though I meant it. I was having a hard time focusing on George Kingsley's problems when I had some doozies of my own.

"Yeah, it is a real tragedy. You want that to happen to you? You plan to head off to Columbus University, don't you? How about the university of getting raped every night?"

She was trying to unnerve me, but what was the point? I was already plenty unnerved. I wasn't some tough kid who needed to be scared straight. But I was a bit of a smart-ass. "If everyone knows that weaker prisoners are getting raped by more vicious prisoners," I said, "how come no one does anything about it?"

"I don't know," she said. "Maybe you can raise that with the warden once you're inside."

I didn't want to think about Melford's prison riddle, but that was all I could think about, because I now knew the answer. I understood what Melford had been getting at. I understood why we had prisons if they didn't work. I understood why we put lawbreakers in criminal academies to turn them into more dangerous, more bloodthirsty, more alienated criminals. I knew why Kingsley had gone in a victim and come out a victimizer. Prisons were set up that way because they *did* work, they just worked at something more sinister than I'd ever realized.

We sat in a small interrogation room around a flimsy metal table that had been bolted to the floor. I guess the cops thought some thief might try to make off with it if they weren't careful. The surrounding walls were all the same pale green cinder block as the hallways—except for the billowy mirror facing me. I had no doubt that someone *could* be watching from the other side, though I thought it unlikely that anyone would be bothered.

Toms sat across from me and leaned forward on her elbows. "Okay," she said. "You know why you're here."

"No, I don't," I told her. "I have no idea why I'm here." Only partially true. I had no idea what they knew and what they didn't know. What struck me, however, was how calm I felt. Maybe it was because I believed Aimee Toms to be basically friendly and maybe because I'd faced scarier moments than this—a whole bunch of them—in the past couple of days. I felt okay. I felt like if I played it cool, the way Melford did, I'd be all right.

"Let's talk about Lionel Semmes," she said.

I felt myself suck in a breath. Not out of recognition, but out of exasperation. Lionel Semmes? There was yet another player in all this? How deep did all this go? "Who is *that?*"

Toms sighed. "You might know him as Bastard."

"Oh, Bastard. Right. What about him?"

"Tell me about him."

"Well," I said thoughtfully, "I tried to sell him some encyclopedias, but he and his wife didn't want to buy. I remember him because I don't usually spend so much time with a family without making a sale. Plus he was kind of intense and creepy."

"And?"

I shrugged. "That's all. I don't know anything else. Why?"

"Bastard wasn't married, but he and his girlfriend are missing. No one has seen them since Friday night. As best we can tell, you are the last person to see them alive. That might or might not on its own make you a suspect. But then I find you at Bastard's place of work being hassled by Jim Doe, Bastard's employer. And then you were going around to Bastard's neighbors asking questions about him. You can see how my mind is working here, can't you?"

I suddenly felt dizzy. At the time, I had suspected the canvass of the neighbors to be a colossal mistake. Now I knew it. Why had Melford insisted I do it? I couldn't help but hear the echoes of Chitra's doubt in my head. Had he wanted me to be seen?

"I never did that," I lied.

"We have neighbors who say they saw you yesterday, asking questions about Bastard and Karen. At least they say they saw someone who fits your description. We can do a lineup if that's what you want, but I think we both know what the lineup will show."

"Do a lineup," I said with a shrug. I could think of nothing to do but bear down, act tough. I had to choke back a little smile because I could feel it happening to me the way it happened to the others. Here I was, nothing more than a suspect, but the system was already turning me into something else, something more badly socialized. If I stayed in prison long enough, I might even turn into something dangerous.

"We searched his trailer," Aimee said. "We found blood samples."

I studied her. She did not mention having found a dead guy with a comb-over, so I could only assume that Doe had removed him.

"We found lots of fingerprints, too. I suspect that some will be yours."

"I already told you that I tried to sell them books. Of course some will be mine."

She shrugged. "And what about the blood? Any thoughts?"

"Not really. No one was bleeding while I was there."

"It could be theirs. Could be you killed them and cleaned up, but made mistakes."

"That's crazy. Why would I kill them? I don't know them. How would I have gotten rid of the bodies? I don't even have a car."

"My guess is that you had help. I'm also guessing that whoever did it might have dumped the bodies in the waste lagoon, and as soon as we have enough evidence for a warrant, we'll find out. It would explain what you were doing there."

"Officer, you saw me. Did I look like I'd just hauled two bodies into a seething pile of pig crap? I was a little beaten up and a little bloodied, but I wasn't covered with sweat."

"Whatever," she conceded. "The truth is, we don't know. We're working on theories. That blood might have been from Bastard and Karen. It might not. Karen's mother hasn't been seen for a couple of days, so she might have killed them."

Karen's mother, I thought. The third body.

"There are other possibilities," she said. "Bastard was into stealing pets. The blood might be animal blood."

"He was into stealing pets?" I tried to sound both surprised and disgusted. "What for?"

"Hell if I know. We had a bunch of complaints about it, but we couldn't really prove anything. I talked to him myself, but . . ." She shrugged. "A lot of people were sure it was Bastard, but without evidence there wasn't anything we could do. And if he was keeping any evidence he might have at his girlfriend's trailer, in Doe's jurisdiction, we were pretty well blocked since Bastard worked for Doe."

"So you let him get away with it?" I asked. "He was taking people's dogs and cats, and you just let him do it?"

"Like I said, there wasn't much we could do legally—not without proof."

"That sounds pretty lame to me."

"Can we stick to the point here?"

"I guess so. It just seems kind of odd to me is all."

"The problem is not that dogs and cats are missing. It's that people are missing and might be dead. And I think you know something about it."

"I don't know anything about it. Should I have a lawyer?"

"You're not under arrest," she said.

"Then can I go?"

She appeared to be pondering this question when there was a knock at the door.

She excused herself and came back a minute later, shaking her head. "We just got a call that Bastard, Karen, and Karen's mother checked in. They're visiting relatives in Tennessee. I guess Karen called a neighbor who told her that everyone thought she was dead, and so she called into the police station."

Melford strikes again, I thought. I tried not to smile. "So if they're not dead, there's no murder, and you no longer have to protect me from being wrongfully prosecuted."

She winced. "Sure sounds that way, doesn't it. But I have to tell you, I'm not convinced you've been honest with me. I don't know what you're up to, but take it somewhere else. I don't want it going on around here."

I didn't say anything. There was no percentage in denying it again, and I didn't want to nod as though she were right. "I guess I'll go, then. But maybe you should take that pet business more seriously." Why was I getting into this instead of getting the hell out of there?

"Look, we've got robbery and drugs and murder and rape aplenty to keep us busy. Missing doggies and kitties are pretty low on the list of priorities."

"So a guy like Bastard can do what he wants so long as he denies it?" I applauded myself on the clever use of the present tense.

"Basically, yeah. Besides, next time you wander over to the hog lot, take a look inside. When you see how those pigs are treated, maybe you'll get a new perspective. I mean, how different are they from dogs and cats, except they're not cute and cuddly, right? So if it's no big deal to kill one, why not the other?"

It was a good question, but I suspected Melford would say she was answering it the wrong way.

Only once I got outside did I wonder how I was going to get back to the motel. I went back in and told the cop at the front desk that I needed a ride.

"This isn't a taxi service," he said.

"Well, I didn't ask to be picked up and taken here on charges of killing people who aren't dead, so maybe someone can give me a lift back."

"This isn't a taxi service," the cop said.

I conceded the point, told him I understood it was a police station, and asked if I could be put in contact with an actual taxi service.

"I'm not a phone book," the cop said.

"Can you please tell me how I can get a cab?"

The guy shrugged, reached behind his desk, and handed me a yellow pages and then pointed to a pay phone. At least I had some coins so I didn't have to hear how the cop was not a change machine.

With the cab on its way, I returned the phone book and went to wait outside. Five minutes later, the cab showed up. I told him to take me to the bus station, where I hoped I might still be able to catch Chitra. I slunk into the backseat and leaned against the torn leather, closing my eyes, almost ready for sleep.

When I felt the car slow down, I opened my eyes again, but we weren't near the bus station yet. Instead we were on the grassy roadside—a ten- or fifteen-foot patch of crabgrass and weeds that separated the road from the algae green canal. I saw flashing blue and red lights as the cab pulled over. The car behind us was navy and white, and I recognized the stretch of road. We were in Meadowbrook Grove, and I watched Doe get out of his car and swagger over toward me.

Chapter 36

$\cdots\cdots\cdots\cdots\cdots\cdots\cdots\cdots\cdots\cdots\cdots\cdots\cdots\cdots\cdots\cdots\cdots\cdots\cdots\cdots$

D OE SAUNTERED OVER TO THE CAR, licking his lips. He was enjoying this. He peered at the cabbie for a minute. "You know you were speeding?"

"No sir, I wasn't. I know this is a forty-five zone, and I was going forty-five."

"You were going forty-seven," Doe said.

The cabbie laughed. "Two miles an hour. You're gonna write me up for that?"

"Don't matter," said Doe. "That's the limit. The limit ain't a rough estimate. It's the *limit*. It's the speed over which you don't ever go, not a speed you try to stick to."

"That ain't right," the cabbie said.

"Take it to court." He grinned at the driver.

He went back to his car and wrote up the ticket. He returned and handed it over. "I'll advise you not to speed anymore in my town."

The cabbie said nothing.

"Oh, and by the way," Doe said, "you know you got a wanted criminal in the backseat?" He rapped on the window with his knuckles. "Hey there, friend. You're under arrest."

This time, at least, he didn't bother with the handcuffs. He just put me in the back of the car. The whole thing had been a disaster. I kept telling the cabbie to call the police, and the cabbie kept saying that this guy was the police. "The county," I said. "Call Officer Toms at the sheriff's department and tell her that this guy arrested me."

"Look, I don't know what you want," the cabbie said while Doe led me away.

"I just told you what I want," I shouted, but after Doe locked me away he went back for a few more words to the cabbie, and I somehow didn't think the message would get through.

Now, in the back of Doe's police car, which smelled of stale French fries, Yoo-hoo, and sweat, I glanced out the window, watching the bleak scrub brush on the empty lots pass by. I could hardly feel the air-conditioning in the back, and the sweat was rolling down my sides.

Not that my comfort much mattered, since I might very well be dead soon. I considered this idea with a measured calm, though calm might be putting it too strongly. Resignation, maybe. I ran over all the possibilities I could think of—Doe would arrest me, question me, hand me over to the Gambler, torture me, let me go, all of it—but I kept coming back to one inevitable conclusion: It seemed pretty likely that Doe would kill me. Sure, there were reasons why it would be ill-advised. Aimee Toms had her eye on the situation and all that sort of thing. But if Doe killed me and hid the body, it would look like I'd just taken off. It was what I'd been planning on doing anyhow. As long as they never found a body, Doe would be off the hook.

So, it wasn't as though I were trying to convince myself that everything would be all right. I didn't believe everything would be all right. I thought it extremely unlikely that everything would be all right. But there was a calm nevertheless, like I imagined what a soldier must feel before he went into a hopeless battle, or a fighter pilot on realizing that he'd been critically hit and that he was going down with the plane. So, here I was. Crashing.

Doe drove to the hog lot. No surprise there. He parked the car around the back, where it would be invisible to any but the most diligent search party, and then he shoved me, still unhandcuffed, toward the pig warehouse.

Maybe I should make a break for it, I thought. I'd already outrun Doe once, and he walked like a man who had trouble moving—legs wide apart, ambling, slow. But there was too much open space, and we were too far from anyone who might see or hear my efforts to escape. Doe would have an easy shot at me if he wanted. A more heroic man might have tried to overpower the cop, but I knew that would only end badly, if not laughably. So I allowed myself to be pushed forward, and I waited for an opportunity and hoped for a lucky break, or at least the ability to comport myself in a respectable way.

Doe took out a set of keys and shoved one into the padlock on the door. It opened, blasting us in the face with heat and stench. I winced but watched as Doe didn't. He was used to it, I thought. Or he just didn't care.

Doe pushed me inside the building and through the narrow corridors separating the pens. I had seen it before, of course, but now, in the dim light of the pig warehouse, with the low and despairing grunts of the animals around me, I felt a new and sharper sense of pity. Maybe it was identification. The pigs backed away from us, and the slow movement of the exhaust fans strobed their movements.

Toward the middle of the room, one of the pens contained a wooden chair, the sort of thing you might see in an old schoolhouse, the kind that had been standing since the fifties or longer. I had seen such things at my own high school, weird aberrations among the metal-and-plastic hybrids that dominated, alone and out of place like a Neanderthal among Cro-Magnons.

Doe opened the gate and shoved me inside, then latched it closed again with me inside. There was something comical in this. The gate wasn't four feet high, and it wouldn't have taken much of an effort to get out, but then it was latched for the pigs. Somehow I was troubled by the indignity of his thinking I required no more safeguards than the pigs.

"All right, then," he said. "Looks like you ain't going anywhere for a while, so I figure we can have ourselves a little talk."

"Sounds like a plan," I agreed. My voice wavered, but under the circumstances I thought I did the tough-guy thing pretty well. There was even a kind of pleasure, a satisfaction, in acting tough, in projecting swagger even while still. I understood now why people did it.

Doe studied me for a moment. "What you probably know, what you probably don't need me to say, is that I want to know where my money is."

"I figured that out," I said.

"I bet you did. So, where is it?"

"I don't know." I shook my head.

"The thing about pigs," Doe said, "is that they'll eat anything. And they love the taste of blood. They just love it. And these here pigs haven't been fed so good lately, so they're mighty hungry. If I tied your leg to that there chair and cut it open, those pigs are gonna be on you like a bunch of sharks. They're gonna be sticking their snouts in the wound, pushing it open, lapping it up. Next thing you know, that whole leg is gone, but they're gonna keep eating. They're like piranhas on land. You ever wonder if you'd even be able to feel pigs eating your nuts if you'd already had to live through them eating your leg?"

"I never wondered that," I said.

"I have—wondered what it would be like to watch it happen. I might just find out, too, if I don't get my money."

I took a deep breath. "Listen, I don't really know what's going on here. I know you had something going on with the Gambler and probably Bastard and the guy in the linen suit—"

"Sounds to me like you know a whole hell of a lot."

"But that's about it. And, look. I know that Bastard is dead and the *Miami Vice* guy is dead. I'm guessing your money is lost or there's only one person who might have it: the Gambler."

Doe thought about that for a minute. "It crossed my mind, but he says you told him I was hanging around before Bastard got killed. I think you wanted him to figure I took the money, and that means you've been running some sort of scam on us."

"Listen to me. I don't have anything to do with this. I'm just trying to make it through this weekend. I have no interest in turning you in or anything like that. Just let me go."

Doe laughed. "Ain't no chance of that until I find out what happened to the money. So, tell me this. What was going on with you and Bastard?"

"Me? Nothing. I never met him before I knocked on his door the other night."

Doe shook his head. "I don't buy it. There was something with the two of you. And you been asking about him. Even those morons at County think you had something to do with him. You'd still be there if I hadn't convinced one of Karen's neighbors to call in and say they were still alive."

Doe had called. At the time, I had thought it was Melford who'd rescued me, but it was Doe. "Well, gosh. Thanks."

"As far as I'm concerned, you knew him and had something going with him. Something to do with that missing money. Now, you want to tell me the rest?"

And that was when I realized that all of this was because of Melford. Melford had planned it all along. The fingerprints on the gun, which he claimed he would never use. Sending me to ask questions about Bastard in Meadowbrook Grove, so witnesses would report that I'd been hanging around, asking questions about a guy the cops suspected had been killed. Had he even somehow arranged for me to sell encyclopedias at Karen's house? I couldn't see how such a thing would be possible, but Melford was a mastermind. Anything was possible.

I'd thought he was my friend for trying to help me get the checkbook back, but Melford was so meticulous, he would have gotten rid of the checkbook after he'd killed his victims. The budding friendship with Desiree now struck me as implausible, too. They'd hit it off immediately, despite the fact that she worked for B. B. Gunn. Now I realized it wasn't despite the fact, it was because of it. He kept telling me to forget about the money, and now I knew why—because he had it himself. I had been an idiot. All the talk of prison riddles and animal rights and ideology had been a smoke screen. Why hadn't I listened to Chitra? She'd seen it, and I hadn't.

Something shifted inside of me. I was willing to be dignified in the face of adversity when I was the victim of a psycho cop, but not when I was the victim of a double cross. There was no way I was going to let Melford get away with it. Doe might have been disgusting, but Melford, I now saw, was diabolical.

"All right," I said. "I think I have it figured out. I think I finally understand. There's this guy, a strange-looking tall guy with white hair named Melford Kean. He set this whole thing up. He killed Bastard and Karen and then took the money, and for the past two days he's been making it look like I did it. But it was him. The whole time, it had to have been him. Look, I don't like you, and I don't want to help you, but this guy has screwed me over, and I'll help you get him and your money. All you have to do is let me go."

"So, this guy Melford Kean has the money," Doe said.

"That's right."

"And you'll help me find him."

"I will."

"And when I find him, I'll get my money?"

"Yes," I said. "I don't think it's that hard to understand."

"It ain't hard to understand your words," Doe said. "Just why I should be expected to believe such a bullshit story."

"Why can't you believe it?" I asked, almost pleaded. I was sure I would be able to save myself with this, or at the very least buy some time in which Aimee Toms might save me or I might think of something.

"Mostly," Doe explained, "because Kean's been working with me."

And there he was, walking out of the shadows, grinning at me.

"Do you really think I'm strange looking?" Melford asked. "First you tell people I'm gay, and then you tell them I'm funny looking. That's hurtful."

And in the dimness of the pig barn, under the flashing vents, he looked more than strange: He looked vampiric. His hair stood out, his face was long and pale, and his eyes were wide—not childlike wide, but insane wide. How had I not noticed it before?

"How could you do this to me?" I cried out. I felt the urge, almost unbearable, to leap up and rush him, but Doe's gun kept me in place.

"You want me to explain myself to you when you were just about to sell me out? That's pretty hypocritical, don't you think? Look, I went to Jim when I realized there was money missing, and he and I have been tracking it since yesterday. And our efforts led us to you. I thought you were clean at first, but then all the evidence pointed to your outsmarting me and getting the money out of the trailer. I think you'd better start talking."

Melford somehow believed, truly believed, that I had the money. Maybe he thought the encyclopedia business was all bullshit, or maybe he found out that I hadn't told him about the Gambler. Maybe because he played and manipulated and lied, he thought everyone else did as well, and that my complaints and fears and hesitation had all been in the service of tricking him. And maybe he'd killed Bastard and Karen for no more complicated reason than he wanted money, and now he was willing to kill me to get it, too.

I hadn't wanted to see it before, but there it was. It was ideology. The one thing about which Melford hadn't lied. We see what we think is there, not the truth. Never the truth.

"This is bullshit," I said with a kind of indignation I didn't know I

could summon. But it was bullshit. That was the thing. It was unadulter-
ated, cosmic bullshit.

Doe studied me for a moment and then turned to Melford. "You
come to me. You tell me you can hook me up. Now I better not find out
that you've been fucking with me."

"I'd never fuck with you, Jim."

"Don't sweet-talk me, asshole."

"Then how about this? I want my cut, so I've got no reason to fuck
with you."

"You sure he's got it?"

"Can't be sure of anything in this crazy world. Some people think the
lunar landing was a hoax. Of course, that wasn't really in *this* world." He
paused and observed Doe's expression. "I'm pretty sure he's got it."

"Okay," Doe said. "Let's take it outside."

"What happened to feeding him to the pigs?" Melford asked.

"I have a better idea."

With the glare of the sun in my eyes, they marched me toward the waste lagoon. I could barely breathe for the fear and the stench, and I thought that
I did not want to die with the smell of shit in my nostrils. I didn't want to die
at all, but I knew that as options tightened, goals grew more meager.

I knew Doe and the gun were maybe ten feet behind me, I could hear
him walking with his wide, awkward gait. Melford was between the two of
us, I suspect because whatever deal he and Doe had struck, there was no
trust there.

Doe told me to stop at the lagoon's edge, where the stakes in the dry
earth marked the perimeter and the flies buzzed a greedy, manic hum. A
single black mangrove tree, its roots gnarling into the pond, provided a
modicum of shade.

Doe told me to turn around. The two men stood next to each other,
but only for an instant. Doe gestured at Melford with his gun. "Go stand
over there a little ways. I want to be able to keep my eye on you."

"You don't trust me?"

"Fucking shit, no. I'll trust you when I got my money and I never hear
from you again. Until then, I figure you're about to double-cross me.
That's how you survive in this game."

"Does that mean I should figure you're about to double-cross me as well?" he asked.

"Just stand on over there and stop pissing me off."

"Always good advice when talking to an armed man at the shore of a waste lagoon," Melford said. He took a few long strides over toward where Doe had been gesturing, so now he was the third point of an equilateral triangle. Doe probably figured he could keep an eye on Melford from there, but not shoot him accidentally if he needed to fire at me. Something like that.

I tried to resist making eye contact with Melford. The powerless rage I felt at that moment was so great that I couldn't endure looking at the source of those feelings. I had broken into a criminal's hotel room, I had gone snooping around Jim Doe's backyard, I'd been in a raid on an animal test facility, I'd faced Ronny Neil Cramer, and I'd gotten the girl. I had, in short, faced down powerless Lem and replaced him with a new Lem, one who took charge of his own life. And now I was being held at gunpoint on the shore of a sea of shit, betrayed by a man I should never have trusted in the first place.

Despite my wishes, I made eye contact anyhow. A flash of something impish crossed his face. And he winked at me and with one finger pointed toward the ground.

I felt the thrill of exaltation. A sign, though an unclear one. The wink I understood—a universal sign, after all. But what did the ground mean? What did any of it mean? Had Melford screwed me over or not? If he hadn't, what was I doing here? What was he planning on doing about Doe? No, I could not assume this was anything but a trick, a ruse to put me off my guard. But to what end?

"How you like that shithole?" Doe asked me.

"Compared to other shitholes, or compared to, I don't know, an orange grove?"

"You think you're mighty tough, don't you?"

I had to stifle the urge to laugh. Doe was buying the tough thing. That was something. Not much, but something. "I'm trying to make the best of a difficult situation," I said.

Melford cocked his head slightly. The impish look, the winking companion, was gone. He looked like a bird studying human commotion from a distance, studying it with an amalgamation of curiosity and obliviousness. In the sunlight, he looked slightly less hellish than he'd appeared in the pig shed, but only slightly. Now he was only cadaverous and mean.

"I always wanted to see someone drown in a pool of shit," Doe said. "Ever since I was a little kid."

"You also wanted to see someone get eaten by pigs. I guess life is all about making choices."

"It looks to me like I'm going to get at least one wish. Now, before we even start negotiating, I want you to step on in there. Wade in until you're about waist deep. Waist deep in the waste." He laughed at that.

I looked at the lagoon. I wanted to stay alive, unpunctured by bullets, but there was no way I was going in there. No way. Besides, once I did, I was nothing more than the walking dead. I'd never be able to escape. I had to get away, but if I did that now, I'd be dead in seconds. The determination to die on the run faded like a drop of food coloring in a still lake. I would go along with what they asked. I would stall for what time I could get, and each second I would hope for something, some miracle, maybe in the form of a county police car or a helicopter or an explosion or something.

"Come on," Doe said. "Move."

"Wait a second," Melford interjected. "Let's give him a chance to answer some questions first."

Doe whipped around to look at Melford. For an instant, I thought fists would fly. "You getting soft on me?" He narrowed his eyes, daring Melford to piss him off.

"It's not my softness you want to worry about," Melford explained, "it's the bottom of the lagoon. It's all settled shit in there, and there's not going to be a solid bottom. It could suck him in before we know what happens, and then we get no answers. No answers, no money."

"I guess we'll find out, won't we?" He gestured toward me with the gun. "Now get the fuck in there. I wanna see him sink into that shit."

"But that's exactly why I shouldn't go in there," I said, making a lame stab at deploying my sales technique. Doe only looked back at me with disgust.

I looked at the waste lagoon, seething and clotted, as devoid of life and light as a black hole. I needed to go to Columbia, I needed to have sex with Chitra, I needed to live outside of Florida. I couldn't die in a pool of pig excrement; it was too pathetic. Yet the only way I could think of was a tactic from the book of a third-grade prankster. It was absurdly stupid, but it was all I had, so I took a crack at it.

"Thank God," I said, pointing to behind Doe. "It's the county cops."

Doe spun his neck around, studied the emptiness. I didn't have time to turn to see what Melford was doing because I was already charging Doe. I had no idea what I was going to do even if my charge was successful. If I managed to knock Doe down and took his gun, I'd still have Melford to deal with. I would face Melford, I decided, when I had to face Melford. I'd have to get that far.

I guessed I was ten long strides from Doe, and I had covered two of them before Doe realized how idiotically he'd been duped. He turned and looked at me. He began to draw his pistol.

At three steps he was raising it. I was going to be shot. I wouldn't even be halfway toward tackling him before I was gunned down. It had been a foolish plan, but at least I wasn't going to die in the waste lagoon. At least I would die with dignity.

Stride four, and the gun was aimed. But it wasn't aimed at me. I managed a quick glance over my shoulder and saw Melford looking at Doe and raising his own pistol.

The wink had been real. The rest had been a masquerade. Melford hadn't betrayed me. Not really. I still had no idea what all of this was about, why everything had happened, but I knew that Melford was not my enemy and that he was going to save me.

Then I heard the crack of gunfire, and the explosion came not from Melford's weapon, but from Doe's. I had come to believe so strongly in Melford's magic that it hadn't occurred to me that Doe might win the draw. Once Melford entered the battle, I had never doubted he would win.

Six steps in, and I dared another look behind me. I saw a flash of blood spraying up toward the burning rage of the sun in a cloudless sky. Melford, arms up in the air, falling back, staggering against the mangrove tree root, falling into the waste lagoon.

Doe flared his nostrils with rage. "I fucking knew—"

But that was as far as he got, because, I think for the first time, he saw me coming at him, now only three long paces away.

In his irritation at Melford and his complacency toward me, Doe skipped a beat before he began to level his gun at me. Then he moved it toward me, but it was off center. I knew, I had seen, that Doe was a good shot and a fast shot, but I would force him to become a desperate shot, and hopefully that would be enough.

Two steps now stood between us. I stretched out with an aching, hip-stretching stride, and I saw Doe squint his right eye. I saw the twitch in his wrist.

I shifted to my left. Doe hadn't fired, so I hadn't dodged a bullet. But now I was off my balance and the advantage was his. I lurched forward now. One more long step, and then I was in the air. I had never played football in my life other than the brutal touch football games I'd been drafted into during PE class, and I knew nothing, absolutely nothing, about tackle theory. I didn't know how to hit or where, but I knew what to do now. Melford hadn't been pointing at the ground when he'd winked. He'd been pointing toward his crotch, and it wasn't his crotch he wanted me to think of, it was Doe's.

I aimed myself with instinct and impulse and a paucity of physics. I landed with my shoulder, and I landed low and hard, jamming my weight into his testicles.

We collapsed together onto the hard ground. I let out a loud groan, but Doe let out a howl so warbly that it sounded almost like tribal music. I hadn't thought I'd hit him nearly hard enough. I could feel the power of the blow diffuse, go to waste, as though something had been left behind, but Doe curled into the fetal position. His hands, including the one holding his gun, folded over his crotch.

Melford had been right. My tackle should have hurt Doe, but not floored him. I recovered my own balance, squatting and tense, ready to spring. Next to me, powerless to do harm, Doe rocked back and forth, his mouth open, though he made no noise. Tears streamed from his eyes. I reeled my arm back and with all the force of rage and anger and frustration I could muster, I rammed my fist into the space directly between his legs.

I pulled back to do it again, then stopped. Doe had opened his mouth to let out another yelp, but he hadn't made it. The color drained from his face, his eyes rolled up, and he was still.

I found it very hard to believe I'd killed him from a blow to the balls, so I could only assume that he'd passed out. I took the gun, heavy and sickening, from his slack hands and rose. I gave him a couple of hard taps with my foot to make sure he was out, and then, remembering Melford, I spun around.

I was just in time to see his form sink under the greasy skin of the waste lagoon.

I didn't know if he was dead before he hit the surface. I didn't know if he was already drowned. All I knew was that he hadn't betrayed me, and he had saved my life. I had to try to save his.

I darted to the shore of the lagoon, by the mangrove, only half-aware of what I had in mind. On the surface, above where he'd sunk, there was a slight indentation, as though he were dragging down the mass of the pool with him. I looked right and left—for what, I didn't know. Maybe some hope, some option that would save me from doing what I did not want to do. But I had to do it.

I set down the gun by the shore, took a deep breath, and tensed my muscles. Then I froze. I couldn't do it, I just couldn't. Everything about me—my mind, my heart, my stomach, the cells that composed my body— screamed that I could not, under any conditions, do what I was proposing. The core of my being rebelled against it. The very stuff of life, millions of years of primate genetic memory, rebelled against it.

I did it anyhow. I jumped in.

The first thing I thought was that it felt more like jumping on a mattress, a hot, horribly rotten mattress, than jumping in water. The next thing I thought was that I was dead. Ghastly, congealed blackness rose up all around me, sucking me down, pulling as though weights were tied to my feet. It was up to my waist and then, in an instant, my chest. Panic stormed the gates of my consciousness, and I knew I had one chance before I lost myself in death and despair.

I struggled, straining my muscles, to reach up with one hand. I gritted my teeth and finally forced the arm out of the muck and felt it break the surface—I felt the relative cool of the air against it. Somehow I found one of the outstretched roots of the mangrove tree. I clutched it tight, feeling its sharp bark bite into my slick skin. With the other hand, still under the surface, I began to probe, moving around in a circular motion and then downward. It was shallow and deep in the lagoon all at once. I waved my hand as best I could, as far as it would go. I stretched as far as I could go, afraid of losing my grip, because if I did, I would fly into the lagoon and I would be lost.

The heavy, slow-moving waves smacked against my face. I could taste the filth in my mouth, smell its already drying crust in my nose. Mosquitoes, like tiny buzzards, had begun to buzz around me. The strength of the sludge pulled against me with a grotesque sucking sensation, and then, all at once, my mouth was under the surface. Then my nose.

Everything in my being cried for me to pull myself out, but I stretched farther, went deeper under. Then I felt something hard—the rubber and canvas of a Chuck Taylor. I leaned forward to make sure I grabbed shin instead of shoe, and I began to pull with my other hand at the mangrove root.

I broke the surface and gasped for air. It turned out to be a horrible move, since the waste slid into my mouth, and my stomach lurched violently. I wasn't going to vomit. Not yet. I needed to stay in control.

With my free hand, I clawed at the earth and gained purchase on the root. Another few inches, and then another few, and then it became easier. My whole upper body was out, and after that I had one knee up on the ground, then the other. I was out. Somehow I was out, and I was pulling Melford along after me onto the shore, where I let go and sat next to him.

He looked much the way I must have, like a man made of wet chocolate—I kept telling myself chocolate, hoping it would keep the nausea at bay. I couldn't see the details of his form well enough to see how injured he was. I couldn't see if he was alive. I couldn't see blood. And then there was the flicker of something.

His eyes opened wide, spheres of brightness against the darkness of his feces-covered form. His eyes lurched this way and that, and there was a moment of stillness in the air. Then, in an instant, he grabbed the gun and fired off a shot, and once more I heard Doe scream.

"Holy shit!" I shouted. "Stop shooting people."

The smell of gunpowder danced in the air, only to be instantly subsumed by the foul, head-throbbing stench of my lagoon-covered body. Fifteen feet away from us, Doe lay on the ground once more, this time clutching his knee, from which blood flowed copiously.

"He was coming right at us," Melford said. He was now standing—dark and wet and gelatinous as a swamp creature. I supposed I was too. "And don't you want to ask if I'm okay?"

I was still staring at Doe, listening to his whimpers. "Yeah," I said. "But I'm kind of getting the feeling you are."

"I think so," he said. Slow moving avalanches of pig waste rolled off his body and pooled around his feet. "The bullet just nicked my shoulder. I don't even think it's bleeding very much, but the surprise of it made me trip, and once I hit the lagoon, I got sucked in. Right now, I figure we have to worry more about things like dysentery and cholera."

Cheerful thoughts. Doe, meanwhile, was trying to pull himself up into a one-kneed crawl, trying hard to pull himself away from us. "Jesus fuck," he said. "Jesus fuck, Jesus fuck, Jesus fuck."

"Remember when I told you being shot in the knee would hurt?" Melford asked me. "I wasn't kidding, was I? I mean, look at that guy. Ouch." He shook off his hands. "I could really use a shower."

It would be wrong to say that I enjoyed seeing Doe laid low or that I was even used to this sort of thing by now. But he'd had it coming. There was no doubt about it, and my being covered in pig shit and piss because of his crimes tended to diminish whatever sympathy I might have had. Still, it was hard to say if what I felt was satisfaction or relief. I was as disgusting as a healthy human being could possibly hope to be, but I was alive and Melford was alive, and he had never betrayed me.

"You couldn't have shot him in the hog lot?" I asked him. "You had to scare the shit out of me like that?"

"I was hoping to avoid shooting him at all," Melford said. He inspected his wound with a probing finger. "Out of consideration for you, I was hoping to not have to shoot him because I know you frown on that sort of thing. Anyhow, I wanted to get him out of the lot since rescuing you is only part of what we're doing here." He looked over toward the hog warehouse. "I was planning—*Crap!*"

I didn't even have time to look before Melford grabbed my arm and yanked me into a run. Enough had happened over the past couple of days that I had my feet moving and was following Melford's lead before I glanced over toward the lot. And when I did, what I saw made me gasp.

Pigs. Dozens and dozens of pigs running toward us. No, running not toward us—toward Doe. Their hooves galloping, their mouths open and bloody, their eyes wide with rage. The ground shook against their pent-up anger, their fear, the mad porcine lust of their freedom. They were demons, red-tumored, ungainly, slack-mouthed, plump demons, the pigs of the damned, running toward Doe, who lay on the ground, screaming, trying to pull himself away. He grabbed at the dry earth, at the weeds, at white fossilized shells, trying to pull himself crazily, pointlessly, like an ill-timed desert wanderer trying to escape the blast of a nuclear test.

His fingers dug deep into the soil as he tried to raise himself onto his one good leg, but the pain outmatched the fear, and he went down again. He turned to look at the waste lagoon, and for an instant I saw it in his eyes—he was thinking about crawling in there. He would try to swim through the pig shit to escape the pigs. And if he could do it, I thought, there would be some sort of redemption in that, surely.

Then he was gone from our sight. The pigs blocked our view before they descended on him, and for an eerie instant there was only galloping and grunting. And then there was Doe's shrill scream, more surprised than afraid. The sound of his screams was nearly drowned out by the stampede sound of galloping pigs trying to make their way to Doe's body. They oinked furiously. An oink oink here and an oink oink there.

Melford led me around in a wide loop, and we came back toward the lot in time to see the pigs clustered around the scream. The ones in the back were now still and disoriented, as though they'd just awoken. Then, after a minute, there was quiet. The pigs remained motionless, perhaps confused, and then began to wander away from the shores of the waste lagoon. As if waking up from a sleepwalk, they made their way from the lot and toward the trees.

Melford and I turned around to see Desiree coming out of the lot. She wore pink jeans and a green bikini top. Her body was slick with sweat, and her scar looked like a wound, raw and fresh. "Sorry," she called. "I didn't really mean for that to happen. They got away from me. Hey, what happened to you two?"

"We had an accident," Melford shouted back to her.

"Okay. Look, I need a few more minutes. There's a garden hose around the other side, near the car. Maybe you two could wash off?"

The various changes of clothes Melford kept in the back of his car now came in handy. It was too hot for sweats, but that was all he had that fit me, and once I was washed off and out of my waste-ruined clothes, I was willing to take the heat until I could get back to my room and have a proper shower with soap.

Melford rinsed himself off carefully. The bullet wound on his shoulder was about two inches long but hardly deep at all. Ideally he would have gone to the hospital, but he had antibiotic ointment in his car's first-aid kit. He applied it liberally and then had me use duct tape to strap down a heavy dose of gauze. After that, he collected our clothes in a plastic garbage bag, grabbing them from the inside out so he wouldn't have to touch them. He tied it tightly and then placed that in a second bag. To contain the smell, I assumed.

With all that done, there was nothing to do but wait for Desiree to finish up whatever she was doing. The two of us leaned against the car, me in the sweats, he in a spare set of black jeans, white button-down, and navy Chuck Taylors. If his hair hadn't been wet, there would have been no way to know he'd just been through a staggeringly disgusting ordeal.

"They ate him?" I whispered at last, breaking what had been silence other than necessary procedural discussion.

He shrugged. "We didn't plan it that way. If anything, we planned, somewhat humanely, to do this without hurting anyone. We wanted to free the pigs, free you, and let B.B., the Gambler, and Doe work out their own problems. With a little help from the law, maybe."

I didn't know why, but I thought it best to keep quiet about B.B. being dead. Maybe Melford knew and maybe he didn't. "So was freeing the pigs part of the plan from the beginning?" I asked. "You told me Bastard and Karen didn't have anything to do with the pigs."

Melford smiled. "You've been through a lot, but you're still not ready to know. You're not ready to hear it all."

I bit my lip, half-full of pride and half-full of resentment that I had to present this information like an English schoolboy conjugating Latin verbs. "We have prisons," I announced, "not despite the fact that they turn criminals into more skillful criminals, but because of it."

Melford looked at me. "I think I underestimated you. Go on."

I thought of George Kingsley, the bright young teen Toms had shown me, the good kid who had turned into a hardened criminal. A promising mind once set on turning his energy to reform and change, now stripped of its promise and ambition, turned to a felon's life.

"Criminals are people who, for the most part, come from the fringes of society, those who have the least to gain from our culture as it is. They have the most to gain from changing society or even destroying it and replacing it with a new order that favors them. Maybe a better order, maybe not. It doesn't matter. So, because they are on the fringes they end up hanging out with those who break laws, who teach them to break laws. Maybe they go to prisons and learn how to break even more important laws. The next thing you know, these potential revolutionaries are now criminals. Society can absorb criminals fairly easily, revolutionaries less so. Criminals have a place in the system, revolutionaries do not. That's why we have prisons. To turn misfits into murderers. It may harm society, make it less pleasant, but it doesn't destroy it."

"Wow." Melford studied me with wonder. "You got it exactly right."

"How do you know?"

Melford looked at him. "What do you mean?"

"I mean, you are enveloped by ideology, too, right? So how come you're right and everyone else is wrong? How can you know it?"

He nodded. "I can't. Which makes you doubly right. But I have confidence in me. You too, now. So you get to hear everything."

With Desiree still somewhere in the barn, Melford started up the car and turned on some raucous music, which he played at low volume. He stared at the warehouse, and I could see he worried about Desiree the way I worried about Chitra, and that made me like him more, feel I understood him better. Whatever insane things he'd done, whatever unspeakable principles by which he ran his life, he seemed to me just then gentle and familiar.

He had done terrible things, things I could never condone—yet despite the moral gulf that lay between us, we were linked by this emotion, this love we felt for someone special and bold. In that, we were not so different: bookman and assassin. Maybe, he would argue, it linked us as clearly as I'd been linked with those pigs who had been in the warehouse, who had known torment and imprisonment and terror and then known freedom and revenge.

"It was the dogs and cats," I said by way of getting him started. "You came here to investigate a story about missing pets. You found out Bastard and Karen were abducting them and selling them to Oldham Health Services for medical research."

"That's right," Melford said. "Very good. You know, I grew up with a cat—a big tabby named Bruce. My best friend then, maybe the best friend I'd ever had. When I was sixteen, he was in a neighbor's yard, and this guy, who was a big, drunk ex–high school football player, beat him to death with a football helmet—just for the hell of it. He didn't like me, thought I was weird, so he killed my cat. Bruce was as much of a person as anyone. If there's such a thing as a soul, he had one. He had desires and preferences and people he loved and disliked and things he liked to do and things that bored him. He might not have been able to balance a checkbook or understand how electric lights work, but he was still a sentient being."

"That's awful," I said, not sure what else to say.

"I was about as devastated as I've ever been. My relatives and friends kept saying, 'It was just a cat,' as though somehow his being a cat diminished how I should feel about this living, feeling creature being murdered. I went to the cops and I got a lot of 'It's terrible, but it's your word against his; his parents will swear the cat leapt at him, tried to claw his eyes out.' That sort of thing. I kept pushing, but people started getting angry. The parents of the kid who killed my cat complained to my parents about my being a pest, and my parents never pushed back. Instead, they scolded me and then finally offered to buy me a new cat, like he was a typewriter—one works just as well as another. Maybe a new one works even better."

"Is that when you became interested in being a vegetarian?"

"No, I'd been one for years. I'd made the connection long before that. If Bruce was like a person, then so was the animal that my steak came from—it's just that I'd never met that person. But when Bruce was killed it made me determined to stop being quiet about it. My mother always told me that I shouldn't tell people not to eat meat. That it was rude. But how is it rude to ask people to stop their immoral behavior? It's like saying that the police are rude for arresting criminals."

"So, when you found out about Bastard and Karen, you went after them?"

"More complicated than that. I've been engaged in guerrilla actions for years now."

"The drunk football player?"

Melford shook his head. "Died tragically, actually. Had too much to drink one night and fell into a pond and drowned. Very sad business."

"So you go around killing people who kill animals? That's crazy."

"It's justice, Lem. I don't hurt people who raise animals for food. They don't believe they're doing anything wrong. I agree with the movement that our job is to reeducate. But sometimes people hurt animals when they *know* they are doing something wrong. So, when I got the story over the wire, just a throwaway paragraph, about all the missing animals here, I came to look into it. Not really thinking about resolving the problem myself, but thinking to expose it. Then I got the same problems here that I had with Bruce. The cops didn't want to know about it. They gave me a lot of bullshit about no proof. You know what they didn't tell me—that Oldham Health Services buys stray animals, no questions asked. You show up with an animal, say it's a stray, you get fifty bucks. And Oldham is a big employer for this area. A lot of jobs and a lot of revenue are tied up in its well-being. So, maybe they don't have evidence that pets are being abducted for animal research, but maybe they don't want to have that evidence, either."

"So you decided to kill Bastard and Karen."

"There was no other way, Lem. Just like today with Doe. It was him or you. With Bastard and Karen—I tried to do the right thing, but if I had left without acting and even more animals had been tortured and killed, how could I have lived with that?"

I paused for a minute. "The thing is, Melford, we're talking about animals, not people. You may have a bond with an animal, but that doesn't make it the same as a person."

"We've been at this long enough for me to get the sense that you're coming over to my side," Melford said. "So, do you think it's wrong for them to take animals away from the people who love them, to visit torture and death on the pets and sadness and pain on their owners? You think that doing that simply to make money is acceptable?"

"Of course I don't, but—"

"No buts. It's wrong to abduct animals and ship them off to be the subject of unnecessary torture. We've established that. Okay, so if I knew they were killing cats and I went to the authorities and the authorities weren't interested, what should I do then?"

"I don't know. You're a reporter. You could have written a story."

"That's true, I could have. I even did, but my editor didn't want to run it. Said I hadn't proved anything. I even got my father to lean on them, but no deal. So, ultimately what we're talking about is the choice between stopping them or simply shrugging it off with a feeling that I gave it my best."

"But this can't be the right way to do things. There has to be a better way than assassinating the people who don't share your values."

"A lot of people would agree with you, even virtually everyone involved in the underground animal rights movement. They won't so much as consider my methods even though their enemies perpetrate cruelties on a scale never before imagined in human history. I respect the principles of the pacifists. I even envy them. But someone has to pick up the sword, and that someone is me. And it's not as though what I'm doing is wrong—it is simply outside the margins of what ideology will allow. Look at the great heroes of the Civil War for the South. Robert E. Lee. There's a guy who led thousands upon thousands of men to their deaths, led them to kill thousands upon thousands of men, for what? So that people whose ancestors came from Africa could remain slaves. And they name high schools after this guy."

"It's not the same thing. I understand, Melford. I really do. I just can't get past the idea that it is wrong to kill a person for the sake of an animal. It doesn't ring true to me."

"Because you're not trying to get out of the system. Your mind is trying to pull away, but you get too far and the tendrils of ideology reach up and pull you back. You're not struggling hard enough. Remember the hog lot? Remember how you looked at it, and while you were looking at it you told me that it couldn't be true? Your mind rebelled against your senses because your senses gave you information that didn't mesh with what you are supposed to believe."

"Because I hadn't yet broken free of ideology?"

"You'll never break free. Maybe none of us ever will. But I'm not going to stop trying. I will do what I believe to be right for as long as I can, and if I go down for it, I'm willing to face the consequences. Bastard and Karen had to be stopped, and no one was willing to do it, so I did it. That's what I do."

I shook my head. "But you don't have to do it."

"Of course not." Melford nodded. "Just tell yourself that, and the rip in the fabric of reality will mend itself. Soon you'll even doubt you ever met me. Everything in your experience will tell you that I must have been a figment of your imagination, and reality will swallow up poor Melford into the oblivion of bills and TV commercials and a weekly paycheck."

"I'll miss you," I said, "but I'm kind of looking forward to it, too."

When I looked up I saw Desiree running toward us. Her scantily covered breasts swung wildly, and she was gesturing with her hands. I didn't know what it meant, but it looked significant.

She threw open the back door and jumped in. "Drive fast," she said to Melford.

He put the car into gear and slammed down on the gas. It was an old car and didn't respond exceptionally well, but it still responded, and we were off the farm and on the dirt road, heading toward the highway, before Melford even had a chance to ask.

"It's the lab," she said. "I rigged it to blow, but I'm not sure how much time we have. I figured it would be best to make sure we were away from the explosions and toxic fumes."

There's no arguing with good logic, I thought. Still, her panic proved unnecessary, and we were a good three or four miles away before the thick cloud of black smoke rose behind us. We never heard the blast, just the long serenade of police sirens.

Chapter 37

B Y THE TIME WE GOT BACK to the motel, there were half a dozen or more county sheriff's cars parked outside, their lights flashing silently against the black cloud we'd left behind us. All the guests stood outside their rooms, some fully dressed, some in bathrobes or pajamas or boxer shorts. A little girl in a pink nightgown clutched a stuffed giraffe in one hand and her distracted mother's sweatshirt in the other.

We got out of Melford's car just in time to see the cops leading the Gambler away. He was in handcuffs and bent over, doing what I would later hear called "the perp walk." Just behind him, a pair of cops were leading away Ronny Neil and Scott. Officer Toms was taking statements from some of the people from the Gambler's crew. Bobby stood by, looking stunned. Maybe before I'd learned about his little trick I'd have felt bad, even guilty, about ruining his career. I figured unemployment was the least he deserved.

"This is unexpected," I said softly.

"To you, perhaps. Didn't you wonder why I showed up at the motel room to tell them you were my source? In part it was to get your enemies in trouble, sure. But there was more."

"And what was that more?"

"I planted a few choice items from Bastard's trailer in the room and then made an anonymous call. It won't take that much digging for them to connect the Gambler to the drug trade he had going with Jim Doe and the rest of them. It will all make perfect sense."

I shook my head. "The Gambler's a bad guy, don't get me wrong, but he didn't kill all those people. He's going to be charged with multiple murders."

"Yeah," Melford said. "All he really did was use his encyclopedia salesmen to peddle speed to teenagers, many of whom are no doubt dead. Of those who live, virtually all will lead lives only a shadow of their former potential. Boy, how unjust his punishment will be."

"But don't you think that . . ."

"That what? That I should take the blame myself so the Gambler can walk free? Forget it. I'm a post-Marxist vigilante, and I have a job to do. I make the world a better place. And that world will do very nicely without the Gambler on the streets."

"Is the world better off without B. B. Gunn, too? He's dead, you know."

"Yeah, I know. Either the Gambler or Doe killed him, so either way, justice is served."

"Your justice."

"Who is fit to judge all mankind if not me?" He went around to the back of the car and opened up the hatchback. He lifted up the carpeted floor and revealed a briefcase. "That's yours. Not right now when there are cops everywhere, but before we part ways."

"What is it?"

Melford laughed. "Don't play dumb with me, boy. You know what it is. It's the forty thousand dollars they've been looking for. You take it and go to college. Who knows, you might even still be able to secure a place for the coming year."

"Holy shit." What else do you say at a time like that? "Why do you want to give it to me?"

Melford shrugged and slammed shut the hatch. "Because if I take money for what I do, I become corrupted. I can't ever think, not for a second, that I'm engaging in an action for the money or I'll lose my way. You've felt the tendrils of ideology, and I have to do all I can to resist them. I think I've set you on the right path over the past few days. You go off, get a good humanities education. Study literature and philosophy, get your fill of the social sciences, and try to do something useful with your life."

"I'm supposed to refuse to take it," I said. "Call it dirty money, tell you I want no part of it."

"I'll be very disappointed if you do that. Don't be another automaton, Lemuel, who embraces a false morality while ignoring the real evil all around you. Take the money and escape from Florida."

I nodded. "Okay. I will."

Melford laughed. "I think we're getting somewhere with you."

Then I felt someone grab me. I almost lashed out with an elbow to the assailant's head, but something in my reptile brain recognized a scent, and I froze. It wasn't a grab, it was a hug. I turned and saw Chitra smiling at me. Her eyes were wide, her lips red and slightly parted.

"I thought I told you to leave town," I said.

"I didn't listen. I'm so glad you are all right. But why are you dressed like that?"

I looked down at my sweats. "Long story." I kissed her, comfortably, as though we'd been together for so long that we didn't have to think about kissing.

"I'll give you two kids a minute," Melford said. He walked over to the car and got inside. I heard him put on some music, and watched while he nodded his head to the beat.

Chitra pulled away, but not unkindly. "I think that probably ends things for the encyclopedia business."

"Looks that way." I thought about her father needing money, and I thought about the suitcase in Melford's hatchback. All I needed for college was thirty thousand, several thousand of which I'd already saved. That meant I had a comfortable surplus. "How squeamish are you about matters of ethics when it comes to money?" I asked her.

"Not very," she said.

"Good." I put my arm around her shoulder and pulled her close, breathing in the wonderful musty scent of her hair.

"Are you hungry?" she asked.

I performed a robotic search of my systems. It took a moment, but I realized I was hungry. "Very," I said.

"Then maybe it's time we got that hamburger."

"Does your offer still stand?"

She smiled at me. "Maybe yes, maybe no. You eat the hamburger, and then I'll tell you."

Her grin was so delightfully devilish, it made my knees weak. I had been so much, seen so much. I'd almost died in the worst way humanly imaginable. I'd seen a man eaten alive by pigs. Never had I felt more alive.

"It's very tempting," I said. "It's hard to say whether or not you'll abandon your principles until you are tested by temptation."

"You're being tested by temptation now," she said. "And I am very curious to see what happens."

I thought about it for a minute. Maybe two. And then I gave her my answer.

Acknowledgments

· ·

More so than with my previous novels, I've relied on the advice of smart and attentive readers to help me figure out what worked and didn't. I owe a great deal to Sophia Hollander, Jim Jopling, Mark Haskell Smith, Tammar Stein, and Billy Taylor for their time, attention, patience, encouragement, and excellent suggestions.

Many people assisted me in my research for this novel, so I am truly grateful to everyone who gave of their time and energy: Jim Leljedal of the Broward County Sheriff's Department; Joe Haptas and Ingrid Newkirk at the People for the Ethical Treatment of Animals; animal rights activist extraordinaire Don Barnes; Jimmy the SHAC guy, last name unknown; and the animal liberators with whom I corresponded, currently serving time in prison, whose names I withhold upon their request. While animal rights issues were always at the core of this project, the novel began with a very different story, and I must thank those who helped me research the material for the earlier incarnation, even though I didn't end up using it: Michael L. Wiederhold of the University of Texas Health Science Center; and Jon Ronson, author of the absolutely terrific *Them: Adventures with Extremists*. I'll write a book about the Bilderberg Group one of these days.

Once again, I must thank the incomparable Liz Darhansoff for her tireless efforts and support. I'd hate to think where I'd be without her, but it would surely be someplace dingy. Likewise super-editor Jonathan Karp, whose advice, guidance, friendship, and open-mindedness helped make this book possible. And since I am lucky enough to live in a parallel universe in which an author gets to keep the same terrific publicist for all his books, let me put a long overdue thanks in print to Sally "the Marvinator" Marvin.

ABOUT THE TYPE

This book was set in Electra, a typeface designed for Linotype by W. A. Dwiggins, the renowned type designer (1880–1956). Electra is a fluid typeface, avoiding the contrasts of thick and thin strokes that are prevalent in most modern typefaces.